MEMOIRS OF A DEATH ROW INMATE

DANIEL DONOVAN

Printed in the United States of America

First Printing, 2023

ISBN (print) 979-8-218-22688-6

ISBN (ebook) 979-8-218-22689-3

For more information, visit:

www.danieldonovanauthor.com

CHAPTER ONE

"Please state your full name."

"James Christopher Bryant." I replied.

"And what is the purpose for your visit?" He asked.

"Suspect interview with Richard Allen Fenton."

"Identification please," requested the guard. I handed him my wallet with my police credentials and badge, and broke off my staring contest with the ground long enough to see the name on his uniform was 'A. Foster.' Foster was a short, forty-something, scrawny, almost sickly looking man with faded tattoos partially hidden by his long-sleeve, leaden guard uniform. Foster scanned my credentials, looking over a hawk-like beak of a nose with dark eyes as if the whole process was a waste of his time. Foster handed me back my wallet as two other guards stepped out from a large brownish red door behind me to assist in the process.

The security check was little more than a desk and metal detector at the end of the hallway. The desk sat across the hall from the office, which was visible through a large, reinforced glass window. The long white halls gave the impression that they hadn't painted for over a decade, resulting in a drab, faded, almost tan appearance. The hallway started with large, double doors, secured by an electronic lock. All the administrative offices, employee break rooms, locker rooms and showers were side by side, in a lazy fashion, obviously dreamed up a long time ago when architecture and creativity were a last priority when designing the building.

I waited patiently while the other guards waived wands across my arms and down my back. The guard in front of me held his hand out as the wand passed my right hip. The loud squelching sound from the wand set off my throbbing headache, and indicated its passing over the Glock 17 on my hip. I unbuckled my belt and handed the gun over, holster and all. Before they could ask, I pulled the knife from my right pocket and handed it over. The guards were getting annoyed with me as they unstrapped the Glock 26 from my left ankle. Without blinking I handed them the pen from my shirt pocket. The guard in front of me held it up.

"...The fuck are you handing me this for?" Foster inquired.

I twisted the cap off in the middle of the pen and displayed the one inch blade on the tactical pen my wife had given me for my twenty-fifth birthday. The tactical pen held more than just the blade, but their only concern was the knife.

"What are you a Swiss-army cop?" asked Foster.

I rolled my eyes and said nothing. The pounding in my head made it easier not to speak, especially since rolling my eyes exacerbated the condition. I wasn't there to see the corrections officers, and I had no interest in making small talk with them. I had nothing against them. They had a job to do, and I respected the role they played in law enforcement. My job meant nothing if they weren't there to keep the shit bags under lock and key. They didn't care about me either, and they were less happy to see me than the normal guests they screened. They knew why I was there, and they thought it was sick. So did I; so did everyone; I was in my own personal hell while fighting off what was clearly one of my shittiest hangovers ever. The thought of this visit had my stomach turning. It had for months. I was under orders, so it didn't matter what I thought. My superiors had made the decision and I wasn't about to disagree with them with ten years left until retirement. I couldn't afford to start at the bottom again. I had ten years in-service already and that was a pay cut I couldn't risk.

I didn't work for the biggest police agency in the state, but it was a respected one, and I had risen comfortably in my ten years of service. I had spent six years on patrol and the last four in investigations. I was promotion eligible, but not all that interested in advancement. That wasn't surprising for a guy like me who barely graduated college.

It's all about what you want, and I wanted to be a cop. Voted "most likely to go unnoticed," college had almost been a waste of my time. The degree helped in advancement opportunities, but if I could get those years of my life back, I would.

College sucked. The girls were obnoxious and the guys were douchebags. It was a broad analysis of the environment at a state college, but it proved to be highly accurate. I didn't fit the douchebag, frat-guy stereotype, and wasn't in college to put notches on my headboard. College was the polar opposite of my upbringing. A lot of college girls lacked reservation with their bodies in the pursuit of feminist enlightened bull-shit. Show me a woman who respects herself and earns the respect of others through hard work and perseverance, and I'll show you a woman worth knowing. The guys weren't much different, except their poor deci-sion-making was credited to their egos and lack of security.

It had been no surprise to anyone who knew me that I didn't date much until I met my wife. She didn't fall into the sorority girl stereotype. She wasn't like anyone else I had ever met. The entitled attitude of the average college student didn't sit well with her either. She never had a handout her entire life. She worked her ass off and got through college collecting degrees as she went until the wall in her office looked like a fucking art gallery; three degrees, three schools and never a shortcut taken. Someone once told me there are no shortcuts to any place worth going, and they were right. I had cut a few corners in my day, and each time it amounted to circling the block to find the fucking car keys you dropped along the way. You didn't accomplish anything; you just retraced your steps with the intention of accomplishing something which should already be done. Fuck that noise; keep moving forward with your eyes on the prize. That's what I was trying to do here.

Unfortunately life does not hand you an easy path just because you put your shoulder to the wheel. Sometimes, you still have to shovel shit to keep the lights on; that's just life. That's all I could think about as I handed over my belt, keys and miscellaneous other items from my pockets in order to step through the metal detector. You can't predict where life is going to take you, which is kind of the whole point. Life is what brought me to El Dorado Correctional Facility. My job was to put people here, not swing by once a week for the next six months like some obsessed girl-friend of a violent offender looking for some convict cock to suck.

The last place I wanted to be today was here; a close second was the feminist rally in downtown Kansas City. If you want to overcome some-thing, you build yourself up and make yourself a force to be reckoned with. Being the person who bitches loudest simply makes you the loudest bitch. The internet taught me that, and it's so fucking true.

They say the squeaky wheel gets the grease, but it's also the first evalu-ated for replacement. No one ever thinks about that when they take on the squeaky wheel lifestyle. The greatest country on earth had turned into a melting pot of entitled people aspiring to a new level of victimhood. There were real victims out there; I met them every day as a police officer. No one is throwing a parade for victims of identity theft and fraud; there's nothing to be gained from it. Claiming victim status without truly being a victim is like claiming you've been mugged as you look around for the best place to get mugged, hoping to turn yourself into an actual victim. I was here to help real people with real problems. It didn't seem like it, knowing the task at hand. I never expected this to be part of my job.

The heartache I had gone through to have everything in my life turned upside down, for this worthless fuck I was about to meet, had been too much. Now I have to hold his hand and tell him how he's not so bad, and that all those people had it coming; what a crock of shit. I thought so, my department thought so, but there was more to be gained by being here than not.

This wasn't why I got into law enforcement. I worked hard, I wrote good reports and I chased every lead I had, pointless or not. I had no intention of pandering to some sick minded fuck that had spent his time destroying the lives of others. As much as I wanted it to be, it wasn't a waste of time. There was an end game, a purpose, a deeper reason to waste every Saturday for the next six months talking with the sickest man I had ever met. He had answers, hundreds of people had questions; I had been tasked with attaining them. I couldn't miss a day for any reason. I didn't have a choice and he knew it. It's why he had chosen me. I had put him here; now he monopolized my weekends like some soul sucking school awards ceremony.

If you've never been to one, don't go; especially not as the significant other of a student. If you're a student, eat that shit up. They serve good food, but if you have no interest in the topic the Nobel Award winning speaker is about to pontificate upon, stay the fuck at home. Don't pay money to listen to someone speak on soil erosion; life is too short for that shit. Take your wife to dinner, wait for the award to arrive in the mail and then frame it; trust me, it's worth it. You have nothing to gain by going. Wait until your wife is in graduate school; she should at least be making professional contacts if you have to drink your way through a boring dinner party. Have a drink and then four more, and call a damn cab; you'll thank me later.

The guards finally finished feeling me up for weapons after which I stepped through the large metal detector twice, returning to deposit a loose coin, before I collected my shoes, belt and briefcase on the other side. My pants were too big making it difficult to hold my hands up as requested while walking through the scanner. I had lost sixty pounds in the last four months and spent zero dollars on my wardrobe. I had a mortgage to pay so clothes were a second priority. Knowing this would be a regular occurrence, it was clear to me I needed to spend the money on pants that fit. I turned everything I didn't need over to the guards who locked it into a locker, and handed me the key. My weapons were stored separately, locked away in the guard's office until I completed my three hour sentence.

Twenty minutes; that's how long it took to get from the front door, through security and down to maximum lock-up. They had a special interview room set up for me to use. I was glad they did, because I didn't want to walk down the hall past Dennis Rader, the Carr brothers, and a long line of other sick individuals just to talk with the sickest of them all. The hallway leading to the room was even more depressing than the entryway. It was meant to contain hardened criminals who were so fucked up they kept the lights as dim as possible to hide the glow of insanity radiating from their eyes. This was no place for any decent human being to spend their time. The lights only got dimmer the further I walked down the hallway. The lights flickered, creating an ominous atmosphere punctuated only by the soft voices of the incarcerated, carrying from their various cells. Ahead of me, a three inch thick metal door complete with a six by six inch impenetrable glass window at head height waited for me. My heart started racing, and my throat tightened.

I could see, through the small shatterproof glass window leading into the interview room that the source of my pain was waiting for me inside. A chill ran down my spine as the electronic lock popped allowing the door to slide open. The man chained to the table didn't turn to acknowledge me as I stepped into the room.

"I'll be right outside in case he tries anything," the guard cautioned. I nodded to him and stepped along the left wall. I circled the room until I was on the opposite side of the table from the man in the brown prison jump suit. I leaned back against the wall and set the briefcase down beside me.

I finally raised my eyes to meet those of my cell-mate. Behind black and gray, bushy eyebrows shone the dark brown eyes of malice, radiating from the face of pure evil. The large figure was partially hidden by long, unkempt salt and pepper hair, hanging along either side of his face and obscuring his hulking shoulders. The face, if clean shaven, would have caused most people to flinch and look away; the beard, fortunately, hid some of the menacing lines of his permanent smirk. He sat with his hands cuffed together and the handcuff chains run through a ring on the table, keeping his hands together. He laced his fingers from one hand through the fingers of the other and stared as if he was contemplating his next ten moves.

"Have a seat," he said, gesturing to the open chair across from him. "We might as well be comfortable. Did you bring everything you need?" The menace in his voice was natural; his calm tone, a sign that he felt in control, despite being chained to the table and floor.

"I did," I replied staying where I was. The cold, concrete walls sending chills down my spine. "Do you have the answers you promised?"

"All of them," he said; "As long as you do exactly as we agreed upon."

I stepped forward and set the briefcase down on the table. One at a time I removed the items I had been instructed to bring and sat them on the table. Side by side I placed a stop-watch, a tape recorder, a pack of Marlboro Reds, a black Bic lighter with a naked lady on it, a yellow legal pad and a small golf pencil. Across the table from me watch the bearded man with more gray hair on his face than black, almost expecting him to rip his hands free and attack. He was easily six feet tall and two hundred forty pounds, but the menace he exuded didn't come from his size, but his demeanor.

He leered at me from across the table with a face not even a mother could love. He was too content to just stare at me as he tried to use the same intimidation tactics he'd been using for nearly a decade. From the moment I first met him, he had been a master of mind games and double talk. He could make you feel both worthless and subservient with the simplest of comments. Knowing I was on a timetable gave me the intestinal fortitude to speak first.

"Let me make this clear, if at any point you fail to deliver on your end of the bargain; this is over. No more cigarettes, no more visits; you rot in here just like you deserve until your last appeal falls through, and they put you to death," I whispered.

"Let ME be clear; if you don't play my little game by my rules, you will have cost yourself the answers you seek, and the answers sought by hundreds of people. Those peasants are counting on you. Your kind already failed them by letting a guy like me walk free for so long. The police failed them; I simply did what was in my nature. Don't let them down again."

"Shall we begin then?" I asked.

"Start the stopwatch. I have you for three hours. If for any reason you decide to leave early or fail to have my memoir published and made public, you will pay dearly for it."

"Go fuck yourself," I said as I leaned in and started the stopwatch and the tape recorder. "March 11th, 2017; session one with Richard Allan Fenton." I sat down, leaned back in my chair, and looked at him. The hulking bearded man across the table stared at me with a look of loathing arrogance. I held his gaze; he was chained to the table which was mounted to the floor. I tried not to appear worried even though my heart was racing. The shackles on his wrists gave me just enough confidence that he couldn't hurt me, encouraging me to sit up to the table.

"I've been doing what I do since before you were born, kid. You think because you put me here that you're somehow better than me?" He snarled through clenched teeth.

"I've never said it, but that sounds about right," I agreed, trying to appear nonchalant.

"Well you're wrong. I might be pushing sixty, but what I've done, the impact I've made on this world; nobody will ever forget me. You're just another fucking pig collecting your taxpayer funded paycheck. There have been a million fuckers just like you, and there will be millions more like you after you're gone." He sat back and resumed his smug arrogance for a moment. "You make your living because of people like me. Without me, you wouldn't be shit. After all, I made you the success you are today. Don't I at least get a thank you?"

"I'll thank you in six months when this nightmare is over," I said.

"Your nightmare is someone else's answered prayers." He said, leaning forward with feigned sincerity. "Your nightmare is something others would die to hear, and pay money to print. Don't dismiss it so carelessly; remember I can end this at any time; so watch your fucking mouth."

"I'll try to be more respectful," I offered, trying to control my temper.

"I'm still a human being. Try to remember that and this whole thing will be a lot easier." He advised, attempting to regain control.

He was right; police work was all about treating people like people, and making sure we protected the rights of the people while we were catching the people infringing on the rights of others. We didn't put people away; we put people in front of a judge and jury and let them decide what will happen. We reported what happened and left the decision to someone else. We weren't the judge, jury and executioner like everyone thought. We were reporters in a way; we were just the first ones on the scene and if we did it right, bad people faced justice. If we did it wrong, bad people went free or good people paid the price. We didn't get to mess up and then publish a redacted version of the story; we aren't the media after all. If we messed up, we could lose our jobs or get put behind bars with people who hated our very existence. We couldn't afford to mess up, and we couldn't afford to be wrong. Sometimes we got lucky, but that was no way to approach police work.

"Let's try this again." I said, trying to get back to the purpose of my visit. "You said you had answers to a lot of questions; maybe you could indulge me with the details."

"Let me put it this way; I have stories and you're here to write them. Each story has a happy ending for both of us. I get to tell you all the fucked up shit I did, and you get to take that information to someone who might want answers. I've been dying to tell someone all the things I've done. It's hard to take credit for shit the world frowns upon. I can't exactly thrill people at a bar with a story about choking some fat housewife while her husband is in the next room watching television; can I?"

"No you can't; so why don't you tell me the story?" I suggested, hoping I could get out of the interview without becoming a murderer myself.

"I'll get to it eventually, but this first story is one of my favorites."

I adjusted the tape recorder so it was closer to him. "When did this happen?"

"Kid, like I said; you weren't even born yet. The year was 1975; people were losing their minds and the world had gone to shit around me. I watched my parents go from a happy couple to a pair of fat fucking slobs. My mom ate too much and nagged non-stop. My dad drank too much and listened too little. My parents both got fat and felt like I wasn't worth keeping around. Half the time they didn't know where I was; the other half they spent screaming at each other and beating on me. It got to where I couldn't stand to be at home anymore. My dad worked a decent job and made a decent paycheck, when he didn't drink it all away. My mom watched television and snacked all day. She didn't clean, she didn't take care of me and she yelled a lot. After seventeen years of growing up like that, you can imagine I wasn't faring well."

"I can imagine," I said as he paused for a moment. "So you're telling me all the fucked up shit you did was because of bad parenting? It's quite the cliché, if you ask me."

"Of course it is; it would be easy to blame them and try to pass myself off as the victim of poor parenting like every other fuckup who can't come to grips with the shit they did, but not me. I did what I wanted and I made my own choices, and I loved every minute of it. Even this; I love it. Who else gets to capture the time and attention of one of America's finest for the next six months. People are only prisoners if they choose to be. Even in here; I'm as free as I've ever been. You; HA! You're a fucking prisoner here. We're both locked in this room, but only one of us is truly in prison. I've captured a law man and put him behind bars with the rest of the victims of this fucked up judicial system."

I took a second to scribble a few notes in my book to keep from rolling my eyes.

"You think you're a victim? Not the unfathomable number of people you've raped, killed, and tortured?"

"People are only victims if they choose to be. You refused to be a victim and so I had to take your options away. I had to make you a player in my fantastically fucked up little game just so I could make you a victim against your will. That's the best kind of victim; the kind that doesn't want to be one. It's why I do what I do; taking people's options away is a fantastic way to go through life."

"How do you figure that? Because a lot of people would say it's in direct opposition to the way a decent society works." I insisted.

"Don't talk to me about a decent society," he ordered. "This world has never known a decent society. This world couldn't handle a decent society. A decent society is one that doesn't need rules or laws to keep it together; people just exist together without issue, but that's not the world we live in; is it? This world; this country is so consumed with regulating and restricting the people that it takes people like me to challenge the rules nobody asked for. Without rules, people are free; that's the truth nobody wants to believe; that's the truth I bring to the world."

"All you've brought to this world is pain and misery. You can pass it off as truth all you want, but it's just you trying to spin your fucked up existence into some kind of meaning." I argued.

"Aren't we all?" he asked with a laugh. "Aren't we all just trying to explain our existence to the world? In my world, you don't make any sense. People like you have no place in a rule free society. We don't need you."

"You don't need me because I stand in the way of your rampage over the decent people of this world. You may think I have no place in this world, but people like you create the need for people like me. I am a direct response to the actions of a lawless, fucked up, psycho like you. You may not like rules or laws, but this is a society with laws. If you live in direct opposition to those laws you create a need, you create an outcry from the people who can't defend themselves. Those people need me because you took away their freedom to choose a life without oppression." I insisted, my brow turning inwards slightly into a frown.

"Now that's the first honest thing you've said. Finally we can talk; just the two of us; about all my exploits and endeavors. It's why you're here after all." He shrugged, as if he was casually making a point.

"We were talking about your exploits until you went off on a self-righteous tangent." My frown became more pronounced, exacerbating my headache.

"Keep it up pig; you're about one stupid comment from blowing this for everyone." He spat.

"Have it your way; I'm here and the clock is ticking; so why don't you tell me the story you started telling me earlier."

"That's right; my way." He said pointing at his chest. "I dictate how this goes and you sit and listen."

"I'm ready when you are." I offered, surrendering to the inevitable vulgarity about to come.

"1975- What a great fucking year to be alive; and dammit if I didn't live it up that year." He sat back and smiled as if the thoughts in his head were so truly pleasing to him that he just needed a moment to enjoy them. He puffed on his cigarette as he reminisced, staring over my head at the wall behind me.

"Do you remember the first set of tits you felt? Of course you do; who could ever forget? Mine were nothing exceptional, but I remember the way they felt like it was five minutes ago. I'm walking down the street of my old neighborhood when I see the pretties little thing out at her mailbox. I'd seen her before; blonde, long legs and an ass that could have prevented the cold war. I tell you, if the government spent less time trying to develop the biggest nuclear arsenal and started looking at ass and tits then we would have stopped a couple wars short in history. Anyways; this girl...I had seen her before, and I couldn't help but stare at her every chance I got. She never seemed to notice until that day. I can remember the look on my face when she asked if I was retarded or perverted. I didn't know what to say; I didn't know not to stare. Daddy never had a talk with me on how to charm the ladies. Truth is I don't think he knew how. Momma was just looking for a steady paycheck to leech off of so she went down on daddy the first date and never looked back. My uncle told me that story when I was like, nine years old. I didn't believe him for years until I could see the indifference in her eyes and the cold resentment in his. It was obvious she had what she wanted and he couldn't cut her loose without alimony. They were stuck together, and just pretended like they didn't hate every minute of it; Catholics, right? Anyways, I didn't know what to say to her. She kept bitching at me about being a pervert until I looked down at the ground. I didn't feel ashamed for staring; I just knew it would get her to stop yelling at me. It was how I got momma to stop screaming at me when I broke something in the house. Shame is a shitty way to raise a kid, but it can be mimicked to get what you want. I pretended to be ashamed and the pretty girl stopped screaming at me. She finally went back in the house, but I couldn't get her out of my head. I hated her, but I loved what I saw. She wore this low cut dress that showed off just the right amount of skin. I knew I wanted to touch them; I just had to figure out how."

He flicked the cigarette butt into the corner behind me and leaned forward, took out another cigarette, lit it, and sat back before blowing the smoke in my face. All I could do was glare at him. I expected nothing less from him. He had this one special privilege during our face to face time. No other prisoner was allowed tobacco products of any kind. This was a stipulation of the deal, and I knew he planned to smoke all twenty cigarettes in the course of the next two and a half hours. All I could picture was putting the cigarette out in one of his eyes. The sounds of his imaginary screams resounded in my head; it felt good to hate him that much. He was a particular kind of evil, and all I wanted him to do was feel nonstop pain for the rest of his worthless life. It seemed unlikely, but the idea of him getting lung cancer and rotting away brought warmth to my mind I couldn't explain and didn't particularly care for. He had purposefully stopped right before he gave out any specifics in the story. He liked to control the pace, and I could tell he had about twenty minutes worth of story to tell and three hours to tell it in; fucking asshole. He continued to blow the smoke in my face and smile as he did so. He was enjoying keeping me in suspense as he made me wait for him to continue.

"So what did you do?" I finally asked, hoping to move the conversation forward.

"I kept watching her. She was home from college for the summer. She didn't have a job and only had friends over on a few occasions. Otherwise she kept to herself while her parents went to work each day. The mailman delivered to that street at around 11:30 in the morning. She came out to get the mail as soon as he reached the end of the block. I guess she didn't like bumping into strange men when her parents weren't around. I didn't do anything to change that either. I found a good hiding spot in the bushes across the street and watched her for a few weeks."

He sat back smoking for a minute.

"Did your daddy teach you how to talk to women?" He asked. "Mine didn't; neither did anyone else back then. Teenage boys were terrible then, just as I'm certain they are shitty little piss-ant fuckers now. I didn't bother with friends; you can't count on anyone these days and '75 was no different. I hated boys my age. They just walked around high and mighty pretending they weren't gonna turn out exactly like their weak-ass pussified fathers. I knew who my dad was, and he was just like every other dad back then. No spine, no guts, and no fucking clue. I watched him waste his life away in front of the television and I swore I'd be nothing like him a single day in my life. He thought it was weird I never watched any TV with him. He didn't know I despised his very existence. The only reason I listened to him is because he could swing a belt. Seventeen years old, I hadn't had my growth spurt yet. That happened the next summer. 1975 I was just a fat little fuck who wanted to see his first pair of boobies."

He lit up another cigarette, and continued his story, "I finally figured out how I was gonna do it. Each day I waited in a different spot. I figured out the layout of her house and found the best way to approach it without being seen. When she went to the mailbox, I used my grandpa's old hand drill and started working away at a little peephole in her bedroom wall. It took a couple days to get through but I finally did it. It wasn't big, but it was just right. It looked into her bedroom, right over her end table and towards the mirror where she did her makeup and brushed her hair before bed. I can remember the first time she brushed her hair with no clothes on. It was the last week of June and it was hot as hell outside. I had to be careful cause her daddy was a big man, and would have broken me in two had he caught me spying on his whore daughter. Her breasts were so firm and perky it made me want to die being stuck on the outside looking in. Have you ever had a boner that just wouldn't go away? I did, the first time I saw her topless. I didn't even know what to do at the time I just freaked out and walked home hoping no one had noticed. It felt weird, but I knew that I wanted to have that feeling again but with her there with me. I knew what I wanted and I went for it. That's the difference between kids back then and kids now; back then when we wanted something we figured out how to get it and we got it. We didn't sit around waiting for someone to hand things to us. When we saw a pretty girl we had to have, we made sure we got to have her. Boys don't do that now; that's why they're all growing up to be queer. If they could get a girl they would, but maybe I'm just old fashioned like that."

I sat back a little in utter shock at how vulgar he could be. I knew he was vulgar and crude; I had interviewed him before and then sat through months of trials with him. Had a police officer said a fraction of what he had said, their badge would be on the Chief's desk in less than an hour. While being politically correct wasn't exactly my thing, I knew how not to offend someone no matter whom they were or what they believed. Still reeling from the last line of bullshit he had spewed, I snapped back to attention as he continued.

"You can imagine my disappointment when she brought some guy over to the house while her parents were away. I couldn't see much from my peephole, but I could hear them. I watched them undress each other, kissing each other and all that shit before they moved over to her bed where I couldn't see them anymore. I was so angry; how could she do that to me? How could she bring some other guy over and fuck him right in front of me?"

He stared at me for a moment as if he expected me to explain how this "injustice" had happened to him. I couldn't believe the level of self-obsessed insanity I was hearing. How the hell would any of that have been her fault?

"It didn't matter; they didn't fuck for very long before he got dressed and left. I didn't see her get up from her bed when he left. I also didn't hear him lock the door. I thought, 'Well hell this is as good a time as any to step inside and say hello.' Boy was it my lucky day; he sped off in some overblown piece of overcompensating American muscle and didn't bother to lock the front door for his little fuck-buddy. I can still remember the way my heart was pounding when I slipped in the front door and locked it behind me. Look at me, I'm getting goosebumps all over again," he said holding up his arm as far as the handcuffs allowed him. He seemed genuinely thrilled with his rendering of the story.

"She was asleep when I got to her bedroom door. It was still open a few inches and I could see her sleeping, nothing but a sheet covering her sweet little body. I stared at her through the open door; I don't know if it was ten seconds or ten minutes; I just couldn't look away. I started opening the door nice and slow like. I didn't want her to wake up so I stepped into the room real quiet and kept the door open. It felt like my feet weighed a thousand pounds. Each step felt like it was the hardest step I'd taken in my entire life. It felt like I was never going to get all the way across the room to her bed, but finally I was right there; standing over her. My first love; right there within arms-reach."

He sat back and ground out his cigarette on the table top and sighed, flicking it to his right. I could feel my rage boiling under the surface. All I wanted to do was wrap a belt around his neck and pull it until his head popped off his shoulders. Between the anger and the hatred, I began to get nauseous. He hadn't even started in on the gory, horrific details about to follow, and I already didn't want to hear them. He smiled at me as he sensed my emotional turmoil. He was enjoying himself, and he liked the reaction he was getting from me.

"What's the matter detective? Is something bothering you? I haven't even gotten to the good stuff yet." He added, lifting his chin to stare down his nose at me.

"Please proceed." I begged him, trying to remain calm and collected.

"Am I making you uncomfortable? We can stop and never do this again if you'd like. All you have to do is say so, and all the pain and discomfort you are experiencing can be washed away and replaced with the guilt of failing hundreds of people expecting answers from you. Is that what you want; A lifetime of guilt instead of a few hours of uncomfortable conversation with little old me?

"I am not leaving; please continue." I said, barely above a whisper.

"I put one hand over her mouth and ripped the sheets back with the other. She was all-mine; lying there naked; waiting for me. She was a little surprised to see me though based on the look on her face. 'Shush', I whispered to her; 'I won't hurt you if you don't scream.' She tried to get her face away from my hand, but I leaned down over her forcing all my weight onto my one hand. That got her attention; she tried to grab my hand and pull it away, but it was too late for her. I took my other hand and pinned it across her throat. She started to panic then; she knew what she had done, so she started to calm down and listen to me. I slowly eased my arm off her throat and started working my way down towards her breasts. She was crying then; she knew she shouldn't have been a bitch to me. She was finally getting what she deserved and she wasn't ready for it. I squeezed both of those perky breasts; oh man, she had the body of a goddess. I couldn't stay away from her anymore. I climbed up on the bed and straddled her. She tried to struggle again, but when I started choking her again she stopped fighting; she started cooperating. I told her it was all gonna be ok and that she should just sit back and enjoy herself. I started touching those perfect breasts again. I had never felt breasts before, and it was the most invigorating moment of my young life. This sensation started shooting through my groin and up to my head and before I knew what had happened, I blew my load in my pants. I didn't even know what had happened. It had never happened to me before and I'll admit; I wasn't ready for it. I wasn't done with her though. I ran my hands up and down her perfect body while I reassured her everything was gonna be ok. She shut her eyes then. I don't know what she thought was gonna happen, but she apparently didn't wanna see it. It pissed me off; why wouldn't she FUCKING LOOK AT ME? WHY DID SHE THINK SHE COULD JUST CLOSE HER EYES AND MAKE ME DISAPPEAR? I HADN'T BEEN INVISIBLE THE DAY SHE CALLED ME A RETARD, WHY WAS SHE CLOSING HER FUCKING EYES?" He roared, yelling at the top of his voice.

I looked over his left shoulder at the door to see the guards staring in at me through the window. I heard a key in the lock and seconds later two burly officers rushed in towards us.

"STOP; EVERYTHING IS OK." I shouted as they got close. "Please leave; there is no reason for you to be in here." I pleaded with them. They looked reluctant and a little pissed off, but I didn't care. To find out what had happened, I needed to tap into his anger, his animalistic rage, and lack of impulse control. It didn't happen often, and I didn't want to waste the opportunity to get the raw, unfiltered truth from him before he reverted back to his twisted mind games. "Please, leave us alone," I begged them again.

The guards were not happy with my request, but chose to take the easy way out and left the cell, locking it loudly behind them.

"She just wouldn't look me in the eye." He continued as if nothing had happened. "And that made me mad. Back in those days I never got mad, but she just dismissed me like I was nothing but a worthless piece of SHIT! She didn't have to die that day. I didn't want to kill her, but she was rude to me. She wouldn't even acknowledge my existence, even with me sitting on top of her. What kind of a bitch does that to a kid? I just wanted to love her and show her how much I cared. She couldn't even look me in the eye, and that didn't sit well with me. I hit her; right in the fucking eye, I punched her as hard as I could."

He clenched both hand s into a fist as if he was reliving the entire moment, right in front of me. His face trembled slightly as the replay of those horrific events played in his mind. His eyes had lost their intense stare, and no longer pierced to most hidden parts of my soul. Now they stared out into oblivion as if I didn't exist. I held my silence, waiting for him to continue.

"She started to fight me, but she couldn't move me." He insisted. "I just started swinging with my right hand into her nose and eye. If I didn't get to look at her and enjoy her beauty, no one could. I don't know when she went unconscious, but it took a while. She was tougher than she looked, but I was pissed enough that it didn't matter. My fist hurt from punching her. At the time I thought the bitch broke my hand with her stupid fucking face, but it just turns out I had just bruised my knuckles so bad it felt broken. I was tired then, all that struggling and punching had worn me out. It was nice to just get to sit back for a few minutes and touch her body without having to control her."

He went from a thousand yard stare to an almost trance-like state. The memories, as he relayed them, seemed vivid, and painted with gruesome details. He started to breath normally, the cigarette in his hand burning down to nothing with an inch of ash hanging on way too long as it remained un-flicked.

"I touched every inch of her skin over the next half hour or so. I wanted to touch her face, but it was all swollen and bloody from the ass kicking I'd just put on her. I didn't even know what to do with a naked woman that day. I just touched her and tried to figure out the best ways to slip my fingers inside her. Everything was so new to me I just didn't know what to do with myself. I just sat there on her stomach, touching her breasts and loving the massive erection I had. I only wish now I had known what to do with all that enthusiasm. After a while, I began to get bored with her. She was out like a light, and I didn't want to wait around for her to wake up again. I leaned forward with both my hands on her throat and just pushed with all my weight and strength. I couldn't hear her breathing, but I could feel her heart pounding against my hands on her neck. After a little while it stopped. I couldn't believe what she had just made me do. I wanted her forever, not just the few minutes I had; or so I thought. Looking at her, lying there with her bitch face and her eyes closed so tight I never got to see the life draining from them. I felt robbed, but I felt so alive like never before. I came, saw and conquered her all in a matter of minutes; it made me feel better than I ever had in my miserable life. I became a man that day and I knew it wasn't by way of turning eighteen or smoking my first cigarette. It was because I had just conquered a woman, and I loved the way it felt. I was alive and suddenly I knew what I wanted in life. I wanted anything I could get my hands on. I wanted it all, and if anyone stood in my way they were gonna die."

He had snapped out of the trance and fixed his gaze on me again. His twisted grin returned, and he flicked the cigarette at me, just missing my right ear as it went by. He shrugged slightly as if he hadn't a care in the world.

"She was my first in many ways," he continued, "but I had just got started. I got up and walked to the kitchen. Her parents weren't due home for several hours, but that wouldn't be soon enough for me. I wanted to see all the activity, all the hustle, all the concerned people standing around wondering how something like this could happen in their quaint little town. I wanted to see the hysteria it would cause. I washed my hands in the kitchen sink with soap and water. I knew I would have to find a way to clean my clothes before my parents saw me, but that wasn't much of a concern either. Mom would be watching her stories and dad wasn't home from work yet. I could sneak in the back and wash my clothes before anyone noticed. I picked up the phone in their kitchen and wound up the dialer to call the police. It was a Wednesday, so the three cops on duty in that town were probably at the diner for lunch already. That would give me plenty of time to get out of the house and get home. I called the police and told them someone had been hurt and I had just seen someone leave in a pretty blue muscle car. That was another first that day. My first kill, my first ejaculation, my first time touching a girls boob, and the first time I framed someone else for one of my kills. Everything about that first kill was perfect except who died. I would have liked to keep her around, but life isn't always what you want it to be. I walked home, washed my clothes, cleaned up and put on a shirt with sleeves long enough to cover up my swollen knuckles. A half hour after I called, I walked back over to the house. There was so much activity; it was fascinating, police officers scratching their heads while the citizens of that fine town looked on in shock and horror when they wheeled the covered body out on the stretcher. It was all too perfect. Three days later, they arrested her little fuckbuddy and he's doing life in prison somewhere. I almost laughed when I saw the news. It freaked my dad out cause I sat down and watched the news with him that night after they announced the results of the trial. He was glad; he said we didn't need pieces of shit like that in our town anyways. It was the funniest thing my dad ever said to me. He had no idea what had happened; he was just glad someone went to jail for it. What a fucking idiot! That was when I realized what was wrong with our justice system. They aren't looking to catch the person responsible; they're looking to vindicate themselves by making someone pay when something bad happens. They don't care who it is, as long as they get to say they put someone behind bars for killing some whore who had it coming. What a shitty system; congratulations; you're part of the problem." He insisted.

I looked at the stopwatch in front of me. Somehow, there was still another hour and change to go to complete this ordeal. The smoke in the air was so thick by this time I might as well have been smoking the cigarettes myself. I felt completely drained. How could someone like this even exist? It was only the first meeting and already I thought him to be the most evil man in known history. I still had 25 more meetings with him after this one and somehow he had promised to fill them with horrifying stories of his exploits for which he had yet to receive credit.

"You look a little downtrodden, detective; have I upset you in some way? This is exactly what you signed up for when you agreed to meet with me. I know someone like me doesn't make any sense to someone of your high moral fiber, but I can promise you, these stories won't get any easier for you. This was my first time; I didn't even know what I was doing when I went into that house. I get better with time; I'm like a fine wine that way. My stories will continue to get better and better until our time is up. Then you will have all the answers, I will have my story told so no one else will get credit for my work when I'm gone."

"So none of this is about clearing your conscience before you die?" I inquired, in disbelief.

"Have you not been listening to a fucking thing I've said? I want all the credit. I can't get the credit if someone else is in jail for something I did or if you never knew I was the man you were looking for. I want the list of my victims carved into my big ass headstone. I'm going down in history as the baddest motherfucker to walk the face of the earth. People will study my cases, teach new wet nosed cops about me so they can pretend they understand someone who has accomplished as much as me. If you still couldn't tell; I don't give a fuck about all the people I killed. I did all that for me, and I loved every second of it."

He sat back and lit up yet another cigarette, "You should be thanking me too, ya know? I made you who you are. Do you really think anyone would have given you a second look if you hadn't caught me? Now you're a big shot detective who's about to have a best-selling novel to add to your resume. I put you on the map kid; you should be thanking me on bended knee."

"I caught you, I put you here; I'll write your story, but I'm here on my own fruition. You were just the stepping stone to launch my career." I argued.

"I know; not bad for your first week on patrol was it? You just happen to catch the most notorious serial killer in the Midwest because you just happened to be in the right place at the right time? I don't think so; I think there is more to your side of the story and you just haven't told anyone what really happened that night."

"You're delusional; I caught you because I was right where I needed to be. You can pretend to be upset that the rookie cop who caught you is so successful now, but in all reality, if it wasn't you, it would have been someone else. I'm good at my job, that's why you're in here. You were convicted and sentenced to death for the crimes we already proved you did; now you're just icing the lethal injection cake."

"What have I got to lose? I'm already going to die, why shouldn't I get full credit for the things I did? You got lucky kid; that's all there is to it." He said.

"My luck started with you, yours ended with me. Funny how that works isn't it?" I prodded back.

"That's exactly my point; luck is all you can hope for in life. I was lucky for thirty plus years. You got lucky on one night of patrol. Do you really think your luck is better than mine?"

"My luck propelled me ahead in life; yours barely kept you out of prison," I replied.

"Life is all about perspective; here's mine. I was lucky for thirty years; you were lucky one time on one night ten years ago. Your luck may have made you successful, but mine made me infamous. I hope you enjoy your life as a pencil pushing government drone."

"Every goddamn minute of it," I told him.

"Keep telling yourself that, pig. You're a tool of the government machine. You can't shake your dick without permission. If they tell you to jump, you ask what minority you should jump on. You have to make a press announcement every time you make a public arrest because you have to justify every time you beat the shit out of some black guy trying to put food on his family's table pushing a little weed on the side."

"You can try to simplify everything that happens to race and government control all you want, but why don't you face the fact that nothing you ever did was to put food on the table for anyone. All you have ever done was take from people and spread misery everywhere you go. If you weren't in solitary confinement, you could find a way to make prison more miserable for everyone else in here. I have purpose; I give people answers and bring a sense of balance to this world. Without me, people like you would have this entire world turned on its head forcing people to live like animals, eating each other just to stay alive. We already covered this; YOU create the need for people like me."

He sat back and stared at me for a minute. His stare made me uncomfortable, but I managed to display all the loathing I felt for him on my face showing him that he couldn't figure me out by staring me down.

"It must be nice to pretend you have all the answers." He said quietly. "You don't; you and I both know that. You're here because I have answers. You're here because I hold all the cards. It's not just me. You've never had all the answers. That's why eighty percent of reports filed with police go unsolved. You don't have answers, you have questions; sometimes you ask the right questions and sometimes you're full of shit. Eighty percent of the time," he said jabbing his finger towards me, "Full of shit."

"You're right about the questions. I have many of them which only you can answer, such as; what was the name of the girl you killed in your hometown?"

"How should I know?" He shrugged, demonstrating his ongoing level of indifference to the suffering he had caused.

"You said you watched the news when they announced the conviction in the case; that means they said the name of the girl you killed. You're a narcissist, you know her name because you like to score-keep. You would have a trophy case somewhere if you hadn't been so paranoid you'd get caught."

"What makes you think I don't?" He inquired.

"I don't know, why don't you tell me about it?" I offered.

"All in due time, young man; all in due time," He jeered at me.

"Well then tell me about her."

"I just did, dumbass." He snapped.

"No, I mean tell me something that would help us identify who she is so we can add her to your list of accomplishments."

"Ah! Flattery; what a novel approach; I thought these were all people to you? Now you're telling me they're just a name on a list for you? What would your wife think about that?" He jabbed, knowing where to find my vulnerabilities.

"You can leave me wife out of this. I'm here for a specific reason, if that reason does not prove to be worth my time, I leave, you get the needle, and I sleep like a baby tonight." I said, dismissively.

"Do you really think you're going to get to sleep for the next six months? We haven't even got started here. I know you've been appointed to the FBI task force to follow up on these cases and resolve them as they come in. That gives you, six days to attempt to track down a victim, on occasion dig them up, and then attempt to undo thirty years of shitty police work and false convictions to figure out who they are and what else went wrong on that case. You'll be flying in the morning of our next meeting just because you won't have enough time to go home and so much as wash your clothes before it's time for us to come together and discuss all my, how did you put it, accomplishments?"

I tried not to let my face display the fact that he shouldn't have known about the FBI task force. I tried to remain stoic and indifferent towards him so I picked up the stop watch and gave it a casual glance.

"Less than three minutes left in our session," I advised him, "If you don't provide us with vital information that helps in an ongoing or past investigation, this deal we have is null and void. Care to spit out something useful or am I going home for dinner tonight?"

He smiled at me and said nothing. I turned the stopwatch in his direction so he could clearly see I was not bluffing about the time. He leaned forward briefly, checked the time and sat back; all without changing his arrogant expression.

"I guess I'll be on my way," I said standing up. I casually started packing up the items on the table. The cigarette pack was empty as I knew it would be, but the other items went away quickly and efficiently. "Last chance," I advised him as I stepped away from the table. He said nothing; just continued smiling at me like it was still a big game to him.

"There are twenty seconds left on this timer, in twenty-one, I will be out that door; never to see you again until you get the needle. And then maybe one more time when I stop by to piss on your grave."

His smile got bigger as he crossed his arms in front of his chest as far as the chains would allow, "There's a body under the playground at the southeast corner of your City Park."

I glared at him for a second before knocking on the door. The sound of the key in the lock was the most refreshing sound I had ever heard.

CHAPTER TWO

The worst reports to write have no conclusion, no point, and produce more questions than answers. My first report, after meeting with Richard Fenton for the first time, was just that. Unfortunately I knew the possibility existed for some of these questions to be answered at a later date, but for now, they were just pesky questions.

I was stuck behind a desk while the CSI team scanned the playground at the park. My investigations Lieutenant was contacting the Arkansas Bureau of Investigation to see if they had records of the murder case Fenton had described to me. It was vague in details, but provided enough that the case could be reviewed to see if there had been a miscarriage of justice. The idea that at seventeen years old, he had already managed to have someone take the fall for his first murder was appalling. From the very beginning he had been on a power trip of self-entitlement and destruction which put innocent people in the crosshairs.

Police work had come a long way over the past thirty years. To hear that they brought the obvious suspect in and no doubt harassed and pounded on him emotionally, and quite possibly physically, until they had enough to force a conviction didn't sound outside of the norm for a small town jurisdiction in the 70's. The way files were kept, who knew how long it would take to uncover a "solved" case and get it into the right hands so it could be reviewed. At some point I would get to see that case, but that could take months.

A knock on my cubical wall behind me distracted me from the miserable report.

"The dogs hit on the playground, the FBI is bringing in equipment to try and pinpoint the exact location and depth of the remains."

I turned in my chair to greet my investigations lieutenant, Demetrious Carter. Lt. Carter was an impressive figure, standing six feet tall with short, neatly groomed curly hair which clung to the dark brown skin on his head. The long-sleeve button up square-patterned shirt barely contained the massive muscles underneath. A former college linebacker, his hard-hitting attitude was hard for some to handle. His good humor, mostly a thing of the past in light of the current investigation, won over lots of his supervisors, admin and rank-and-file officers. He was no stranger to friendly conversation, but his promotion to Lieutenant had made him a bit more demanding as of late.

Lt. Carter leaned on the edge of my cubicle, and waited for a second to gather his thoughts as he anticipated my follow-up question.

"Where exactly did the dog hit?" I asked him.

"Right at the concrete slab holding up the big slide; the City Manager nearly shit himself when I called. They're pretty pissed that they might have to close that part of the park and disassemble playground equipment. They said they didn't really budget for tear down and reassembly."

"Of course they don't; nobody has the budget for this. How old is that playground equipment?"

"No one is really sure; the city manager said he'd have his people pull all the construction records and permits from the build. They'll get back to us at some point."

"I know it sounds depressing, but is the dog still out?"

"He's still on scene, but they stopped looking; why?"

"Just a bad feeling; any chance they'd be willing to expand their search area and keep looking?"

"The dog is on loan to us from the FBI for about another hour or so; if we need to keep looking they can. What makes you think there will be more than one body?"

"I've been with the department for ten years now. The timing of the park construction feels off for the timeline Fenton was working on."

"I'll let them know to keep looking; I just hope you're wrong about this."

"Me too," I replied as he walked away.

"Anywhere in particular you think they should look?" He called back to me as he walked towards his office.

"Anything built or completed in the past twenty years."

"That's the whole fucking park," Carter yelled back, "Narrow it down a bit."

"Check the whole fucking park L.T."

"Whatever you say, hot shot," he said as he closed his door.

Carter was not fond of this whole operation, and he wasn't my biggest fan. I had been promoted to detective under the previous investigations lieutenant while Carter was making a name for himself as the midnight Sergeant, working the bar district. We had a lot of mutual respect for each other, but we butted heads on procedure and more often than not on the approach we would take in various cases. We were each right about half the time, though neither of us would admit it to the other.

The report didn't take long, it just lacked the conclusion I was hoping to provide. Each time I came home with an answered question or a case solved I could take some semblance of satisfaction from my time spent with the devil-incarnate. This week may have brought something new to light, but it didn't immediately solve a mystery the way I had hoped it would. I knew some of these cases would take me out of town, but I was already assigned to the FBI task force following all these leads. It was for that reason only I had been able to make a phone call from the prison exit and had dogs searching hours later. I wouldn't get this lucky every week. Sick of sitting and waiting for word from the park on what was found and where, I decided to go down and talk with the FBI agents working the scene.

I checked out one of the unmarked investigations vehicles and went out into the parking lot. The sky was gray and looked like it might rain. The wind had picked up since I left the prison three hours ago making a cold day colder. It only made sense that it would start to rain on a day like this; Mother Nature was a bitch that way. It had only been a matter of weeks since all the snow had melted and the weather became unpredictable.

"Kansas fucking weather," I muttered to myself as I climbed into the blue Honda Accord; hoping to God it was one of the vehicles with working heat. It was; making the five minute drive to the park a little easier to manage. I started on the west end of the park and circled around the north end. I could see the crime scene tape across the open fields blocking off the southeastern corner of the park. This unfortunately eliminated all the playground equipment available to the public. The weather was already preventing most people from spending time at the park; the rest were turned away by uniformed officers and several detectives at the scene. As I circled to the east side of the park and entered the parking lot off Eleventh Street, I could see the FBI agents starting to search outside the crime scene tape. I could only hope the rest of their search was pointless. Something about this whole arrangement with Fenton seemed off-putting. The US Government was ready to put dozens of agents as well as multiple local jurisdictions to work running every which way on the word of a psychopath. If the dog had already turned up one victim, it would stand to reason there might be more.

Fenton had been killing in a three-hundred mile radius of this park for at least the last five years he was free. The odds of him managing to hide one body at the park in the middle of all the construction made it all the more likely he had hidden more. Local news crews were already on scene giving the public their spin on the story. Fenton would love to know how much attention these investigations were getting. He knew in the end, he would get all the credit; at some point someone would leak the nature of the investigation's being completed and Fenton would be infamous. He already was, but he was going for a legendary level which would cement his name in serial killer history. Three books had already been written on him which he claimed did his story no justice. He wanted the truth to get out and he wanted me to write it. All the media frenzy surrounding Fenton was enough to make me long for financial and property crimes again.

I pushed my way through the growing crowd of reporters and showed my ID to the agent watching the tape. After being waived through, I stopped to survey the park, turning slowly until I was facing north towards the line of fraternity houses on the south side of the bar district.

"Bryant?"

I stopped suddenly and turned at the sound of my name.

"It's me; Terry? We met at orientation for the task force?"

A medium-built, slender man with dark brown skin wearing a top-of-the-line black suit, white shirt, and tie approached me from the direction of the playground equipment. His wide smile immediately brought his name back to mind, having met him once before when I wasn't terribly hung-over.

"Oh shit; my bad Terry, I didn't realize it was you." I offered, feeling like an ass for being rude.

"Don't worry about it Bryant, I know you've already had a long ass day." He replied shaking the hand I offered.

"That's the fucking truth; hard to believe the amount of shit I've already had to put up with today." I confessed.

"How was seeing Fenton for the first time?"

"Like someone stabbing me in my ears and soul for three hours straight."

"That sounds about right," said Terry as we started walking towards the playground. The CSI techs were already cordoning off a smaller zone which would need to be excavated. "How did the mayor take the news about tearing up the playground?"

"Like a fully conscious colonoscopy, I'm sure; between her and the city manager, I expect a full-fledged meltdown before any digging commences." I paused for a moment and surveyed the playground where the CSI techs were working. "What's the exact spot the dogs got the hit?"

"Right smack dab in the middle of that concrete pad," Terry replied.

"Shit! This is gonna take days," I exclaimed.

"He must have known that too."

"Fenton? Yeah that's right up his alley. Even his confession is a fucking pain in the ass. It's all a big mind game to him. He gets the satisfaction of knowing we're out here running every which way whenever he gives us new information." I said.

"Did you expect anything less?" Terry asked.

"I expected it, I prepared for it; there's just no way to be completely ready for everything that guy is going to put us through."

"There's the understatement of the year. My wife is still pissed I volunteered for this assignment." Terry admitted.

"You volunteered?" I inquired, in disbelief.

"For this assignment, not yours," he responded. "There isn't enough money to make me volunteer to spend three hours a week with that fucking madman."

"It must be nice to have choices in this whole thing." I admitted, begrudgingly.

"Hey you should be proud of what you accomplished. Not many rookie officers catch a serial killer their first month on the street, let alone get the chance to uncover all the other twisted shit they've done and not been tried for." Terry insisted, trying to make me feel better.

"What's his end game in all this? I know he wants infamy, but how is getting credit for eleven murders not enough for someone; especially when you've already been given the death penalty? Do you know how difficult it is to get a death sentence handed down in the state of Kansas?" I asked.

"Oh, I know what you mean, some of the other agents and I have a pool going. I think it's so he can get a stay of execution while the other trials commence; like Ted Bundy." Terry suggested.

"I could see that being a possibility."

"My boss, Supervisory Special Agent Wells on the other hand, thinks this guy wants to go down as the most notorious killer in American history. What do you think it is?"

I thought for a moment. I had already done enough guessing as to Fenton's end game. The stay of execution made sense, but given he had already signed away his right to council and agreed to speak with the authorities meant the trials would be brief.

Fenton had gone back and forth between Jury and Bench Trials. The psychopath seemed to prefer a larger audience to his trials, but had been less and less impressed by the jury's reactions after each trial had ended with a guilty verdict. The last five cases had been Bench Trials as the evidence had remained almost identical for each of them. Identical method of operation had been Fenton's downfall. Over his thirty year killing career, he settled into a pattern so exact and so precise that it led to convictions for each murder that followed the pattern. These eleven murders spanned five states; Oklahoma, Missouri, Kansas Iowa, and Nebraska. After the fourth guilty verdict, he had fired his attorney and began representing himself.

"I think he means exactly what he told me today; he wants all the credit, all the fame, all the notoriety that goes with all the horrific things he has done and is proud to have chiseled into his headstone." I surmised.

"That sounds about right." Terry agreed.

"I'm being literal; he wants his victim's names etched into his head-stone." I advised.

"Are we really going to do that?"

"He mentioned it today; it isn't a part of the agreement though. I'm just hoping they plant him somewhere in town so I can swing by once a week and piss on his grave."

Terry and I watched for a few moments as equipment was assembled to scan the area where the dog had hit. The equipment was all provided by the FBI and had been routed by plane from Chicago after I called the task force with the information Fenton had provided. It was amazing to see how quickly people were willing to work when they believed they could solve double digit cold cases. Hundreds of thousands of dollars had been allocated by the FBI to complete this investigation. From the looks of things, we were going to use every penny of it.

"Hey! Jones!" A voice called from across the park.

Terry and I turned towards the pavilion to the northeast end of the park where the bloodhound had been completing a grid search. A petite, Hispanic female agent was waving at us from just past the garden area of the park. Terry and I began walking that way as a slight mist began to fall on us. The weather had already been wearing us down, and the mist made everything even worse. We navigated around the wire fence that separated the Hayley Marten Memorial Garden from the rest of the park, and walked the short remaining distance to the pavilion.

"Bryant, I wanna introduce you to Agent Maria Martinez and Agent Rodney Davidson. They head up our Tracking and Victim Recovery Team with the Bureau." Terry advised, gesturing to each of them in turn.

"Nice to meet you," I said shaking each of their hands, "Glad to have you on the team."

"I wish we were here under better circumstances." Davidson said, almost apologetically. Davidson was a short, grizzled man in his late forties. His high-and-tight haircut was hidden by the dark blue FBI ball cap he was wearing, but he had the demeanor of a man with military service.

"Don't we all," said Martinez as she took a small blue flag out of her bag. Martinez was almost my height with light brown skin and jet black hair pulled into a ponytail, poking out the back of her dark blue, standard issue navy-blue FBI ball cap.

The two agents were wearing jeans and matching dark blue jackets with "FBI" in large yellow letters on the back and left breast area. Davidson's was a slim fit, hugging his narrow frame all the way down to his black leather boots. Martinez's jacket hung a bit loose, slightly oversized around the torso and the sleeves pulled up to her elbows.

"I take it you found another body?" I asked, hoping they hadn't.

"I thought it was the wind and the rain making things complicated for Major here," said Davidson gesturing at the bloodhound who was lying on the corner of the Pavilion concrete foundation, "But now I'm not sure."

"You aren't sure if you found another body? How does that work?" Terry asked.

"I think we have three more bodies," said Davidson.

"What do you mean, you think? Either the dog hit or it didn't." Terry insisted.

"The locations don't match the timeline for our suspect."

"What timeline?" I asked.

"Fenton has been in prison for ten years now, that garden was commissioned by the City after a donation, and opened to the public in April 2012." Davidson said.

Terry and I looked back towards the garden. Two blue flags could be seen waving in the wind nestled underneath two large bushes on either side of the sidewalk leading up into the garden.

"Where's the third body?" I asked not wanting to know the answer.

Martinez said nothing as she leaned over and pushed the blue flag into the soft mud next to the pavilion.

"Major is lying on it," Davidson said apologetically. "Does the construction of the pavilion fit Fenton's timeline a little better?"

"Completed in 2003; right in the middle of Fenton's hay-day," I whispered just loud enough for them to hear me.

"I'll get the CSI techs over here to cordon off this half of the park," said Terry walking back towards the playground.

"I know we said we'd only be here for another hour or so, but its clear there is more going on out here than we originally expected. Detective Bryant, you were right to have us keep looking; someone's been hiding bodies at this park throughout the past fifteen years."

"Not just someone," I said shaking my head. I pulled out my phone and started dialing. "L.T., you might wanna get down to City Park; we've got more than one suspect hiding bodies down here."

I turned and started walking towards my car, shaking my head.

"This day just got a hell of a lot longer," Davidson said as he began cursing and muttering under his breath.

———

Lieutenant Carter had called in two more Detectives when I got back to the Law Enforcement Center. Months of planning had gone into preparing for these investigations and it had proven effective. Sorted and categorized, files were arranged into two boxes; unsolved homicides and missing person cases. The missing person files were already being reviewed by Detective Shirley and Detective Ross.

Jeanine Shirley was the head homicide detective having spent over twenty years with the department. Fittingly her desk was in the back corner away from all the bustle of the investigations bullpen. She was a startlingly-tall six feet two inches, with long light-brown, almost blond straight hair pulled back into a tight ponytail. She was complete with her usual gray pant suit, white blouse, duty weapon on her right hip and badge hanging on a chain around her neck

Detective Robert Ross had come over late last year taking over one of the permanent Detective positions working major crimes. He was an average height, slightly balding man in his mid-thirties. He wore a yellow shirt, black tie and pants, with his badge clipped to the left side of his belt and his back-up weapon in a brown leather holster tucked down the middle of the back of his pants.

Both of them were on the far side of the bullpen from me, with the backs turned slightly towards me as they each reviewed case-files in old, tan file folders.

"What cases are you two reviewing?" I asked as I whipped my coat onto the back of my chair and snagged the top file from the box in the middle of the bullpen.

"I have the Holton-Brand file." Called Shirley, holding up her file casually as if to prove her statement, though there was no way to read any of it from across the room

"I have the Warren file. We started with cases which fit the timeline of the construction of the various locations at the park where the dogs hit. Assuming these victims aren't from out of town, these cases are the most likely to match our victims since Fenton went away. That leaves you only five files which fit the timeline for Fenton; from 2003, 2005 and 2006," Ross advised.

"Sounds good, I'll start with the 2003 file, 'Hayley Marten' since it fits with the completion of the Pavilion. Why does her name sound so familiar?" I asked.

"It's because you reviewed her file a dozen times already." Ross answered as he put headphones on to drown out the noise.

"Maybe," I muttered to myself, flipping open the file and staring at the picture in front of me. Hayley had been a pretty blonde sixteen year old High School Junior who had gone missing in January of 2003, less than a month before her seventeenth birthday. I remembered the time well because I had just started my second semester at the state college here in town, and her disappearance made national headlines. Vanished without a trace was the reoccurring theme to the statement collected from family and school faculty. Hayley had been an Honor Roll student who lived only minutes from the high school. She had walked home from school every day until after an away basketball game, when she never made it home. She was a Varsity Basketball player, avid musician, and all-around model student. The report was full of photocopies of photocopies of old hand-written reports filed away for years until they had been made into elec-tronic records by the city. The reports were hard to read and had fewer conclusions than the report I had just finished.

Still troubled by the feeling of knowing Hayley's name from another source, I did a quick internet search.

"Hayley Marten Memorial Garden dedicated in memory of missing teen opened in June of 2012" read the first headline."

"Fuck, I was just there." I muttered under my breath. I pulled out my phone and dialed a number I reference from a spreadsheet on my bulletin board.

"Hey Jones, its Bryant; where were the other three bodies located again?"

"One was found under the pavilion and two in the garden area; why do you ask?" He inquired.

"I have a victim that fits the timeline for the pavilion victim. The coincidence there has me thinking we need to look closer into that case. Do we know when the exhumation will begin?"

"We're getting a lot of pushback from the city, but as it stands, we should be started first thing in the morning." He advised.

"Ok thank you Terry, keep me posted, will you?"

"Sure thing," he replied.

I resumed review of Hayley's case and started thinking through how all the pieces fit together. We had a lot of possible answers in front of us, but we needed to see the bodies before we could be sure. Her home address had been in the 600 block of Colorado Street. This area had been deemed "Historically Significant" over fifteen years ago which had left the area excluded from private or publically funded upgrades, remodeling and construction. As a result, this area of town never saw any improvements or changes. The property values had skyrocketed as a result, but it had left the homes barely livable and laughably overpriced.

According to police records, Hayley's father Greg had plead with the city for infrastructural changes to older neighborhoods in order to add additional lighting to make them safer for citizens to walk at night and harder for criminals to target people in those areas. When the city waived him off, Greg assaulted, then City Manager, Miles Thomas, resulting in a protections order which still stood today. Greg made national headlines again when he told Miles Thomas to "Go fuck himself" on national television. He had said this unashamedly in front of a crowd at City Hall with his fourteen year old son Connor standing by his side. The footage of Greg and Connor giving police officers the finger as they were removed from the steps of City Hall could still be found online.

People had rallied around the Marten family as a result, which allowed Greg to expand his concrete and landscaping business exponentially. Everything he did was privately funded, the City refused to even hear bids and proposals from Greg, which he never attempted to provide. The City had bastardized the father of a missing child, which didn't sit well with the people. City Hall was overhauled the next two elections with every single incumbent member of the City Government voted out by record numbers. Greg had campaigned hard for this and had the support of thousands of local citizens as well as national organizations. Greg had even been encouraged to run against Thomas for City Manager, but had vehemently refused to do so. He instead rallied behind the current mayor, who at the time was running for city manager, and endorsed several others for public office to great effect. Greg then relinquished himself from the public eye and ran his business quietly.

It had surprised everyone when in early spring 2012 Greg requested and offered to pay for a memorial garden at City Park as an olive branch of sorts to the city. Greg funded and completed the project himself with the help of only a few employees. He finished it in less than two weeks after working night and day to complete the project. No one had seen Greg in the public eye since then.

CHAPTER THREE

The loud pop of the electric locks always made my stomach lurch. I had been in and out of the county jail for ten years at this point, but the locks always caught me off guard. With no indication of when they would unlock, all I could do was hope the control operator didn't wait until you were bored, and started looking around. Here in El Dorado it was even worse. The past week had been a nonstop shit show of meetings, reports and standing out in the cold while the CSI Techs excavated the four bodies.

The meltdown from the mayor had been an epic, childish display of someone on a power trip. Never had I seen a public official throw a temper tantrum quite like this one. She may have only been five foot three inches tall, but she had the rage of someone twice her size. Her screams about police incompetence still rang in my ears as I walked the long concrete hallway to the meeting room with Fenton. She berated Command Staff as if they themselves had buried the bodies in City Park. Why she felt she needed to blame a group of individuals who had all been no more than Sergeant's at the time of any of these murders made no sense. It was nice to know I wouldn't be voting for her in November, but in the mean time she would be a thorn in our sides. The excavation had taken days just as we had expected.

The identities of three of the four bodies were still unknown, and making a positive identification was going to be a long process. The two most recent victims from the garden were still preserved slightly, and it was the hope of all involved in the investigation that they would be easiest to identify. Police and public records were much better maintained in 2012 than they had been in the early 2000's. Still, it could take weeks if the victims were not local residents or had not been reported missing locally. Being a college town, they could be from anywhere in the country.

I took a deep breath and tried to subdue the chill that ran down my spine as Corrections Officer Foster pushed the button, signaling the control room to open the doors. I flinched again, hating the adrenaline rush that accompanied being startled. I tried to shake it off, and stepped into the room.

"Good luck." He said.

"Thanks." I replied trying not to appear as nervous as I was. I hoped over the next 25 weeks that I would get over the nausea I experienced before each of these interviews. It seemed like a rerun of last week; Fenton sat with his back to the door, and I couldn't help but circle him along the wall as far from him as I could get.

"Come now, Detective; I thought we had a nice chat last week? Don't tell me you're still nervous about seeing an old friend, are you?" He goaded, attempting to incite me to an early bout of rage.

"I've seen and heard some pretty horrific shit in the past week; you can imagine what it would be like in my shoes if you had a soul." I said, attempting to dismiss him.

"Hurling insults before the clock starts? Once again, you're making this much more difficult than it need be. I am an untapped well of knowledge from whence answers flow like oil. After all; it's going to make you a very rich man."

"I don't want any money from this. I don't want any part of this," I said as I sat down across from him.

"My; what an ungrateful cunt you are, Detective," He leered at me. "Still can't accept the fact that I made you who you are and you owe your very career to me?"

"I accept what I must, not a bunch of lies." I snarled back at him trying to control my tone. I lined up the required items on the table and slid the lighter and cigarettes across to him.

"Ah! The reward for my participation in this little therapy session," he beamed as he ripped the plastic off the cigarettes and began tapping the pack on his palm. The cuffs around his wrists limited his mobility, but he continued as if this was any normal of occurrence.

I started the timer and tape recorder and sat back with the pencil in my hand. "What have you got for me, this week?"

"I think you mean, what do you have for me? After all, I gave you something last week." He prompted, looking for his due acknowledgement.

I tried to hide my disgust for a moment before exhaling slowly. "Thank you."

"For what?" he prodded, arrogantly.

"For helping 'us' find that body; you held up your end of the bargain last week. You had answers like you promised and for that, I say thank you." I reluctantly offered.

"It was my pleasure," he whispered as he blew a cloud of smoke in my face. My skin crawled as I resisted the urge to stab the tiny pencil into his eye. My allergies had finally settled down after the last meeting with him. Cigarette smoke played havoc on my sinuses, and I still had a long twenty-five weeks ahead of me.

"So tell me about the victim; how did you know him?" I asked.

"Don't play stupid with me; you know I didn't know my last fifteen or twenty victims by anything more than a fond memory." He swept his hand backwards as if dismissing the very notion of attachment to his victims.

"Well then tell me what you remember."

"I don't remember anything about that particular victim." He replied, shrugging indifferently.

I paused and looked at him for a moment. The mental game of chess we were playing was beginning to get interesting as we each made moves to see what the other would reveal.

"I know; which leads me to wonder; why you would know where to find the body?"

"Oh, bravo Detective; you can do basic math. Ten years in prison with a victim from nine years ago; your mother must be so proud of her big detective."

"Exactly; how did you know there was a body at that exact location?" I insisted.

"I'm in prison, not dead. If you knew anything about real homicide investigations you would know that a perfect alibi is frequently constructed to fit the situation. I have the perfect alibi, I was in prison. Someone else has a perfect alibi for their time spent killing people in your precious city. I figured it out from behind bars; you couldn't figure it out from the crime scenes."

"These murders took place before I was in investigations; I'm not a homicide detective now, and I certainly wasn't then."

"But you found the bodies; you know the time period in which they were buried." He pried.

"But we only found one body."

"No you didn't; you found four."

There was a long pause as we stared each other down. The sheer volume of information he knew, which he should never have been privy to hearing, was startling.

"You told me about one body." I continued.

"But I never said it was one of mine."

I stared at him for a moment. He could not have been less specific about the body when we met last week; the location yes, the body no.

"What is my victim type? I know you know it, you testified about it in court in eleven different trials."

"High school and college age females, blonde or brunette, ages 16 to 26 standing no more than 5'6" tall and weighing less than 140 pounds." I said, reciting it from memory.

"And how many girls did you find this week?" He prodded, trying to pull the information out of me.

I didn't answer him; he was babbling now because he thought himself to be clever. I didn't want to slow him down while he was on a roll.

"You found one, which means you can bet your bottom dollar the other three were planted there by someone else." Fenton put too much emphasis on the word planted. He knew more about the investigation than the police did, and he had learned it all while behind bars.

"Who were these people?" I asked.

"Again; I was in prison; you know, that place you put me?" He said, spitefully.

"But how would you know the other bodies were all male?" I inquired.

"I have a special gift, but I'm not the only person in this world, or for that matter this state, who possesses such a gift."

"And you know this person?"

"No, they were after my time by a few years. I just recognize when someone like me is at work. It's nice to know someone else is fighting the same fight I fought for over three decades."

"But how can you recognize when someone like you is at work?" I wondered.

"I know you're not a real homicide detective, but I'm sure you're familiar with the term victimology," he taunted.

"Studying the victims to understand why they were victims of the crime in the first place. This helps establish the motives, background, and personality of the suspect which, when done correctly, can lead to the apprehension of the suspect."

"Very good detective; do you see the flaw in that process?" He said, pressing me.

"To study victimology you have to have victims, which would indicate people are already getting hurt or killed." I admitted.

"Ah, circle gets the square; not exactly a technique used in proactive policing, wouldn't you say?"

"But we have victims; it shouldn't take long to figure out what the victimology was behind their murder." I insisted.

"What do you need to establish that a crime occurred?"

"A victim, evidence and/or witness testimony," I replied.

"How many classifications of victims are there?" He asked rapid-fire style, as if he was quizzing me for an exam at the academy.

"Multiple; individuals, businesses, society and several others I can't name off the top of my head." I answered.

"What type of victims are these?"

"Individuals," I stated. "More specifically, they are murder victims."

"Well they are now," he said menacingly as he fired up yet another cigarette.

"What do you mean?"

Fenton sat back and smoked for a minute as if he hadn't heard me. These pauses were becoming routine already as he attempted to keep me in suspense for a while.

"Did you know I barely graduated high school?" He asked, as if the last few minutes of conversation had never happened.

"What did you mean, they are now?" I asked, again.

"That's for you to figure out, Detective. Now answer my question."

I sat back frustrated. He was alluding to something I had overlooked in the course of investigating the bodies found at the park, but he was hanging me out to dry on what it was. What a dick!

"No, I was unaware you barely graduated." I finally responded. "According to public records, while you were born in 1960, no other record of you exists until 1985 in Oklahoma which leads us to believe your entire identity is a fake."

"Our identities are what we make them. You are correct there though, I made my own identity. This world is made up of those willing to do what is necessary and those willing to be victims. I did what was necessary and made a name for myself. Our parents name us, but it's up to us to make that name work. If you get the name of someone weak, it is an obligation to find and take a name that commands respect and gives us every chance to succeed."

"So you didn't like the name your parents gave you?"

"I did not; it was a weak name given to weak people by people who had no creativity or energy invested in its origin or meaning. If I wanted the name of a miserable piss-ant, I would have been a miserable piss-ant. I was not weak like others were who had that name; I was strong. I made a name for myself in two ways. No one with a weak ass name ever went down in history for anything worthwhile."

I made a mental note of this statement before interjecting. "So you changed your name; when did that occur?"

"Back when it was easy to do so. I was never very computer savvy; besides computers are a great way to get caught. For a one man army such as myself, I didn't need to communicate with anyone. I hunted the old fashioned way; a vehicle and patience. All good things come to those who wait."

"And in your case, young girls came to you?"

"Why do you think I set up in college towns? An abundance of the right demographic of young women is all you need; because college age girls are foolish and careless. They are easily distracted, and even easier to catch. In my experience all you need is the right ploy and the right location. Poor lighting helps; old college towns don't update their infrastructure. Everything is historically significant bullshit, which means they won't update the brick roads in town, they won't expand the roads for fear of cutting down a few trees, and they won't add lighting to an area which is known for its rustic appeal. They almost beg people like me to take advantage of their city and their people."

"So you already know about the four victims we located. One of them does fit your criteria; care to tell me about her?"

"Oh I hardly remember every detail about someone who died over a decade ago; you may need to refresh my memory."

I had been expecting this from him. He loved reliving his accomplishments, but had been smart enough to properly hide, or not collect all of his trophies. I knew I would have to give him a jumping off point so he would begin to unravel. He had a habit of talking too much, and it seemed only right to open up the dam and let him spill everything he could. I reached into my jacket pocket and pulled out a picture. Sitting back a little I held it up for him to see.

His eyes lit up. It was as if he was coming alive for the first time in years. He was visibly breathing harder and he made an effort to reach for his groin, but the chains held his hands above the table. Then he reached for the picture.

"I don't think so," I said stowing the picture away back in my pocket. "Clearly the photo of that young girl triggered a response from you; why don't you tell me about her?"

"Her name was Hayley, and she was one of my favorites." He grinned.

"I thought you said you didn't know the names of your victims?"

"That's what I said; she was different though. After all, not every girl I met had a student identification card and a driver's license on them. A televised candlelight vigil made it all the more memorable for me. It's hard to believe they were holding vigils for her before she ever died. I took a lot of girls in my career, but none of them had quite the publicity that she did. I guess that's what pretty white girls get in the 2000's."

"So you remember her? My real question is, how did you know there were three other bodies buried in that park close enough to her that we would find her if we located the others?"

"That's my favorite part of our little game here; I know so much that you think I shouldn't. You didn't think I'd make this little arrangement if I wasn't going to have fun, did you?"

"I thought you wanted full credit for your, accomplishments, I believe you called them?"

"That's exactly what I want from all this. However, I find it to be beneficial to have just as much ammunition against you as you have against me. I can promise you, this is only the beginning; beside, shouldn't you be thanking me? I helped you find three missing people you would have otherwise never located. I've accomplished more from behind bars than your entire department could accomplish in nine years."

"The real question is still, how did you know?"

"I know people who know people who know things." Fenton said, smugly.

"Well it seems like it would be difficult for anyone to reach you here; according to jail records you haven't received a single piece of mail or a phone call in the past decade." I said, poking for a nerve.

"That's hardly going to stop someone, like me." He replied without noticing my attempt to get under his skin. "I read people, I know things about people they don't know about themselves. I use that to my advantage very effectively."

"But for that to be the case, you would have to have some level of contact with people. That's pretty minimal in here. To top it all off, they would have to have something to gain from you. You have nothing to give anyone, but yourself. Let's face it, you're no prize." I slighted.

"That's where you're wrong. I'm retired; which means it's time to pass my skills on to the next generation."

"So you've been teaching a psycho's: 101 course in your free time?"

"Nothing quite as elegant as that; I call it mentoring capable young minds." He sneered.

"So there's more than one?" I asked, trying to hide the concerning possibilities this notion created.

"Of course there are; you cops always think people like me are a one in a million. The truth is there are more of us than anyone wants to admit. All we need is the right influence, the right push, in just the right direction, and you can turn someone like me into a legend."

"So who pushed you?"

"I did." He sneered. "Only I can push someone to this level of greatness. I just hate the idea of being the last one. I may want to be the greatest there ever was, but I'd hate to be the last of my breed."

I sat there for a moment staring at him. He appeared more smug than usual, and that gave me reason for pause. He never said anything he didn't mean, and that was the disturbing part. I mulled the information he had provided over and over again in my mind. The issue with most police investigations was asking the right questions. He had provided a lot of questions which needed to be asked of the right people. It was bothering me, and I knew he could tell. He smirked at me across the table as he lit up yet another cigarette.

"I'm here for a reason, you have information I need and we've been here a while talking about the last time I was here." I said, frustrated by the entire process.

"We learned so much from your last visit. I survived for years on my skill and tenacity; you succeed based on luck and a corrupt legal and political system."

"We also learned where four missing people had been hidden after they were murdered. We also learned that only one of them had been killed by you." I inserted, trying to move the conversation forward.

"That is correct; as usual my information comes with a price." He warned.

"You already have me here for the second Saturday of twenty-six, what else do we have to give you?" I wondered.

"I have nothing in my cell; nothing to keep my memories alive, nothing to keep me going. All I ask is that before I give you any additional information, you show me that picture again; this time hold it there for thirty seconds so I can burn it in my mind for future use."

"You're disgusting." I said under my breath.

"And I'm ok with that," he said with a big smile. "You know the rules, I get what I want or you get nothing." He said in a sing-song voice. "If you get nothing, this whole arrangement goes to shit and the precious flow of information you need, stops right here and now."

Once again this man had the ability to disgust me to the core of my being. I hadn't brought the photo for his sexual gratification; I had brought it for a positive identification of the body. Nothing about the remains located had been easy to identify. It had taken until Tuesday morning to get the body recovered and another full day to get the dental records confirmed. Dentals were all that was left to get a positive identification of Hayley's body. The family would not even get a chance to view the body; it was far too painful after all these years to see a loved one as nothing but bones. A casket made no sense for a body as decayed as

Hayley's. It had been the most difficult autopsy I had ever sat through. I continued to relive that autopsy in my head as I held up the picture for Fenton to memorize for his sick fantasies.

The autopsy had confirmed what I already believed. Hayley had been killed just like Fenton's other eleven victims. The only things missing were the usual signs of rape and disfigurement which were only evident in the soft tissue. The cause of death was just like the others; one deep, single puncture to the jugular vein and evidence of the victim being hung upside down, tied around the wrists and ankles. This was an effective way to kill someone, just not as fast as actually severing the artery and/or the vein in the neck. The puncture was narrow, but deep, caused by a surgical scalpel being stabbed directly into the neck far enough to hit the vertebrae. The death it caused was slow, allowing Fenton to enjoy every last minute of it. The other details of the killing were only known to law enforcement agencies involved in the cases. All of the tell-tale signs, that Fenton was responsible, had been there.

I quietly stowed the picture away in my jacket pocket. Fenton closed his eyes and sat back in his seat. I didn't mind giving him a minute to fantasize. I was holding back the rage building in my chest, and I was almost positive I would start strangling him if he said anything before I could calm down. The image of the dirty skeleton of Hayley Marten displayed on the autopsy table was still burned in my mind. I could still hear the voice of the Medical Examiner ringing in my ears.

"The remains on initial examination are female, age fifteen to seventeen, blonde hair, fractures to the top of the feet and ankle area. Cause of death appears to be a single stab wound to the throat. Located in the oral cavity of the victim was a red in color rag. The rag appeared to be glued together with a currently unidentified substance. Rag was sent to the FBI for DNA and further analysis."

I had sat for over two hours reading the coroner's report as well as listening to the Medical Examiner from Kansas City provide his finding by audio recording. The notes had been extensive, but still seemed to be a carbon copy of the past cases. Everything was the same besides the name and the body on the table.

The pain must have been showing in my eyes because Fenton opened his eyes and ceased his sick fantasy long enough to sneer at me.

"Ah, detective; are you having a feeling? What a terrible thing to experience. Feelings are for the weak of mind. Feelings interfere with a rational person's ability to understand reason. They stand between the average and the exceptional. Why do you think so many sociopaths succeed in business or politics? No feelings, no obstacles; that is how I have always lived. That is why I am the most accomplished man of my kind."

I knew better than to show an ounce of remorse, empathy or compassion while I was here. These were the feelings Fenton thrived upon. He used them against his victims when he killed them.

"Detective; I feel so...nothing for you at this moment. I feel as if I don't care what you're going through at all. Your pain is my pleasure; that's my thing, you know? I sit here watching you hold back tears for a girl you never met. What if everyone stopped and had good cry for all the people who died that they never knew? This world would fall into pieces. Society as a whole would grind to a halt; industry would cease, the economy would crash, our governments would fall, our living conditions would be horrific, our world as we know it would cease to exist. But here you sit, holding back your tears as if the pain you pretend to feel will somehow give you purpose as you move forward with your life as if nothing else is happening. Your tears are a lie, and you know it. Weak people trick themselves into believing they care about others; they don't. Nothing you do now or later can change the past; so why bother to pretend."

The pencil snapped in my hand as I gripped it tighter and tighter. My fist was shaking as a whole new emotion began to overtake me. I started to sweat involuntarily as tremors began working their way up my arm and into my torso. I had never felt such hatred in my life. I knew I hated him already. I knew nothing would give me greater pleasure than to kill Fenton right there. Fenton leaned forward and taunted me, he voice going back and forth between yelling and quiet incitement to violence.

"Well maybe I had you all wrong detective; you seem to be showing an emotion I can get behind." He leaned forward as he began to laugh at me again. "HAHAHA RAGE; I fucking love it. Doesn't it feel good to lose control, go on, MOTHERFUCKER, HIT ME; gouge out my eyes, it's the most visceral thing in the world to experience. Let it out, just let it out. You'll feel like a man for the first time in your life; YES!" He screamed as I stood abruptly to my feet both fists planted firmly on the table. Fenton leaned forward in his seat and turned his chin slightly to the right.

"HIT ME, DETECTIVE! Take all your anger out on me. Make it all better; it just might work."

"You have no idea the amount of self-control it's taking me not to strangle you right now." I insisted, hoping my threats paired with my restraint wouldn't come across as contradictory.

"I don't know anything about self-control, detective; only patience."

"Oh, I'm fresh out of fucking patience Fenton. I've had enough of your bullshit. You sit here acting like you have the answers for everything all while keeping a stash of all the fucked up shit you've done. Now I have to sit here for three hours a week and listen to you ramble on about what's wrong with the world when the real problem with this world is wrapped up in that fucked up mind of yours and comes pouring out of your mouth without an end in sight. You are EVERYTHING that is wrong with this world, and we will all be better off when you're dead."

Fenton shrugged with his hands as far apart as he could spread them given his handcuffs. "Kill me then, and make all your worries go away. As you say, the world would be better off without me."

I thought about it for a moment. Was Fenton worth the years in prison I would serve? He was awaiting his death sentence already; there was no reason to snuff him out just yet. I had a wife to think about and a career to finish out. I'd book a front row seat to the lethal injection and take every bit of satisfaction out of it I could. I took a deep breath and sat back down in my chair. It was at that moment I became aware of the two guards standing just inside the doorway. In my blind rage I hadn't seen them open the door, or the shocked looks on their faces as I stood over the table, plotting Fenton's demise.

"Bryant, are you going to be okay?" One of them asked.

"Everything is fine now gentlemen, thank you for your prompt response." I said casually as I leaned back and took another deep breath. The two guards locked the door again on their way out, shaking their heads at what they had just witnessed.

"I am so disappointed in you, detective. Here I thought you had just a little bit of that primal instinct left inside you. I thought, 'maybe he does have the balls to kill me right here;' but I was wrong. You're just as weak as the day I met you."

"And you're just as sick as the day I met you. So are we going to sit around complimenting each other or are we going to get around to what you have for me today?" I demanded.

"Well; while we're on the subject, we might as well discuss the young blonde you brought in for show and tell." He said with a grin.

"Have it your way; I'd love to give the family a few answers to go with their grief." I replied.

"What would you like to know?"

"Start at the beginning, like any other fucking story you tell." I said, trying to cut through the bullshit.

"Well, it was a cold day in January. Not everything is so vivid anymore, but I remember the cold. She was bundled up tight and loaded down with a couple bags. It must have been about 11:30 that night, and she was walking home like she did after every practice and every game. I had been watching her for a couple weeks, so I knew the routine pretty well. I had her route mapped out perfectly. I knew how long it took her to get home; approximately eleven minutes; I knew how long she would walk through the dimly lit section of the city; about three minutes. I let her walk past me two nights in a row. It gets dark pretty early in January so it worked out really well. I parked my vehicle in the area for over a week so it wouldn't seem suspicious to anyone in the neighborhood."

"Smart thinking on your part; what kind of vehicle did you drive?" I asked, trying to get a piece of helpful information during the torrent of nonsense Fenton spewed.

"One story at a time, pig; the time will come for the vehicle story, but it's not today. People have a bad habit of falling into patterns, and it makes them susceptible to victimization; she was no exception. She walked the same route home, crossed at the same intersections, and walked on the same side of the street each and every day, just like most of my victims. She was too weighed down to struggle, and too scared to fight. I don't recall exactly, but I think she may have been one of the youngest I ever had." He admitted.

"Here's what we're gonna do from now on. Before you start indulging in explicit details, maybe keep some of the gory details of your actions to yourself. Just tell me if you followed your usual pattern of torture and abuse and then continue after that."

"Detective, have you gone squeamish on me? That hardly seems like the efficient way for you to write a report. Don't you need the details to make all this stick in court?" He jabbed, knowing I did not.

"You know the details of the deal. You tell us everything, I write it into a book and publish it, and you still get the death penalty. That's why I'm not reading you your rights before each meeting. You are already getting the death penalty. Additional convictions are just a formality. People want answers and to see the remains of their loved ones returned for a proper burial. That's what we're doing here. You want the infamy, I want the answers; everybody gets what they want. Unfortunately for you, that means you will never set foot out of this prison for the rest of your life."

"If I wanted it to be part of the deal it would have been. I want to go down in history as the most prolific serial killer of all time." He advised, continuing his subtle, fucked up way of boasting.

"Well you have a long way to go on that one. You're still about thirty-five short of the U.S. record of confirmed kills." I advised.

"So far; that's the important detail you're leaving out. So far, I'm thirty-four short of Gary Ridgeway. The key detail with that statement is, so far. It's only the second time we've met. I have to give you information each week which will lead to a minimum of twenty-five more victims. I'm only getting started; we have so much to discuss over the coming months. Besides, I know exactly where I stand overall and officially; I meticulously ponder my spot on the list and look forward to moving up that list a little bit every week. I look forward to usurping Jake Bird and Belle Gunness on the list this week. After them, it's on up the list past Arthur Shawcross and Carl Watts."

"You seem to be up to date on serial killers here in America. Did you not aspire to go for the world record?" I wondered.

"Well it's a lot easier to kill people in Mexico and South America. I could have easily topped the world record if I lived somewhere like that. I was born here, so I went for the record here. National pride and what have you. If only they had a medal ceremony for people like me; what a grand occasion that would have been. I prefer the thrill of the hunt, that's why I spent two weeks researching and following Miss Hayley around. I love the chase; I love finding my next target and rubbing one out just to the idea of having them. After a couple days of that, I start my recon work, my research, and within two weeks I have them. Hayley was no different. The only reason it took two weeks was because teen girls have such an affinity for going out with friends and talking on the phone while they walk. The night I took her she was incapable of fighting back. She was tired, daddy hadn't been at the away game to drive her home, and she had to carry all her dirty basketball clothes home with her. She was a fighter though, I remember that much. She was the reason I stopped taking teen girls. I was getting older and my desire to fight someone into submission was gone. I wanted it to be easy, and she did not make it so. That was why I kept her as long as I did. One of my greatest achievements was having my way with her while we watched her daddy and little brother plead for her 'safe return' on the evening news. It was pathetic to watch, but what an accomplishment it was for me to know I had that much power; not just over her, but her whole family."

He sat back finishing out another cigarette as he watched me growing hot under the collar again. My willpower was being put to the test more so than it ever had before.

"It was almost a shame to let her go. In fact, I'd have kept her longer if I hadn't discovered her daddy's company was breaking ground on the pavilion at the park. It was the shallowest grave I ever had to dig. Her dad was nice enough to pour a great big concrete pad right over the top of her. He didn't even know he was my greatest accomplice at the time. What did his face look like when you told him he buried his only daughter?"

He was bating me with this question, and I didn't want to respond. The whole situation was fraught with unfortunate coincidences, which made the entire case a disgusting mess to sort out. I made a note in my note book as if I hadn't been listening to him. When I glanced up at him, he was leaning forward, gawking at me with his stupid fucking face.

"You haven't told him yet, have you?" He laughed suddenly causing my insides to crawl, "Oh isn't this delicious? Poor old daddy dearest still doesn't know his little girl has been dug up from where he left her, and here I am unable to watch his reaction on the evening news. I'm sure it would have been just like last time I saw him." He held his hands up together and looked at the ceiling as he mocked real emotions, "Bitter tears, heartfelt pleas and regret for being the neglectful father he is, I could die happy now."

"How would you expect someone in his position to react? He lost a child." I said, somehow still in complete disbelief at his arrogance.

"That's the point, just like that; that's how I want families to respond." He said.

He began his mocking voice again as he swung his head from side to side, "Oh no, I'm a shitty parent who didn't make time for my kids or teach them about the uglier side of life, pity me, pity me, I just need your thoughts and prayers to get through this; pity me, pity me I'm a useless sack of shit who lost a pretty blonde white daughter to the forces of evil, no one has ever been in my position before; pity me, pity me."

The watch was counting down on the table between us leading me closer to my escape from this hell hole with its lunatic occupant. I took shallow breathes as I attempted to remain calm.

"Twenty minutes," I said to myself as Fenton ceased his tirade.

"So how long did you keep her?" I asked dreading the answer.

"Almost two weeks; it was the best time I ever had with one of my victims. It was almost too good to be true. Two weeks, I even thought about settling down with her after the first week. She was exactly the kind of girl I wanted to have around. She reminded me so much of that first girl I had, I felt like I was seventeen again."

"How did you manage to keep a girl around for two weeks?" I asked.

"Ah, even though it is one of my greatest accomplishments, some things are best kept secret. It's a professional secret passed down from accomplished artists such as myself to the next generation of aspiring predators. I was good at what I did for a reason, no one knew my secrets. If I told you how and where I kept each of my victims it would ruin it for those just like me. I had everything I needed and never left the girl alone. People with jobs and families get caught because they need to commute between home and work and home and victims. I made all of that go away by clever planning and a higher intellect than those looking for me. Part of a higher intellect is; knowing what to share and what to keep close to the chest. That's the difference between me and all the perverts out there jerking off to the teen girls getting dressed in front of their open window; my intellect." He boasted.

"If you say so," I said, dismissively. I continued to watch time dwindle away on the watch in front of me. "It looks like we're running low on time today. I'd love to sit around and hear about your great intellect, but you have to hold up your end of the bargain or else you get stuck with your official number at twelve, which isn't even honorable mention on the worlds list of sick fuckers. Care to tell me about your next victim or can I make plans for a barbeque next weekend?"

"Detective, I'm disappointed in you. You still think you have the high ground? You're wrong, I was all set to give you an easy find right here in the Flint Hills, but then you had to go and get all high and mighty on me. That's too fucking bad, I was hoping to save you some travel, but it appears you are going out of state for this one."

I was kicking myself for this one, but I knew it was only a matter of time before this agreement took me to other states. Fenton was believed to have killed in six states, five of which had been confirmed; Iowa, Missouri, Nebraska, Oklahoma and Kansas. We were still waiting on something official out of Arkansas. He had claimed an Arkansas murder last week, but the details had been so vague I hadn't made the trip.

"In Lincoln Nebraska is a neighborhood called Irvingdale which is located around the Irvingdale Park. There is a white house built in the 1920's in the 1900 block of Van Dorn Street. In the backyard of that house are two bodies buried beneath a shed. Those two bodies are hidden approximately twenty years or more, but I expect you'll have a fun time digging them up. The city of Lincoln bought up a bunch of properties in the early ninety's around the park area so they could dictate who bought them and how they were maintained. Even though the properties were sold to individuals over time, the area is still considered City Property, and you can't do any kind of remodeling, construction, or digging without the expressed written consent of the City of Lincoln. The bodies in the yard are those of two twenty something bimbos I picked up back in 1992 while I had my feet up in Lincoln for a little while. The names of the women, who knows;" he said shrugging carelessly. "Where they came from, that's for you to figure out. I will say this; I expect this little excursion to be an absolute bitch for you. That's what you get for being a condescending little prick."

I scratched a few notes down as he finished his last cigarette and sat back in his chair glaring at me.

"Well, I'd love to stay and chat, but I hate your fucking face." I said as I began gathering the items on the table saving the watch for last. "Anything else you'd like to talk about during our last couple minutes?"

"Nope, you can go now," he said dismissively.

I sat there and stared him down. I knew every detail of the deal with

Fenton, three hours, not a second less or the deal was nullified on his end. I ran the clock out picturing myself putting my gun in his mouth and blowing the back of his head out. I enjoyed this briefly as I pictured the various blood splatter patterns on the wall behind him. I couldn't help myself; I smiled, trying to confuse him. He always had the right things to say to me to make me hate my very existence. It was my turn to play mind games with him.

Fenton's expression never changed. His loathing became more evident as I watched him fight to control his temper. He was not an emotional person, but he was human, and somewhere underneath his arrogant exterior was a nerve, and I intended to find it. The three hour mark went by on the watch as I stowed it away again, showed him my tall finger, and walked out the door.

CHAPTER FOUR

It was a long drive back to the department from El Dorado. Lt. Carter was pissed to hear where the next bodies were located. He already hated this entire process. He was only going along with it because of the pressure the Justice Department was applying. They had leaned hard on the department and FBI to resolve these cases without the cost of charging them at a Federal level. The Feds were happy to know Fenton was already getting the death penalty, and jumped at the opportunity to resolve dozens of missing persons and unsolved homicide cases without having to prosecute them. Lt. Carter's displeased tone still rang in my ears as I continued north towards home. Unfortunately, I wasn't going home. I was going to my desk in the bullpen to write yet another conclusion less report. All this, while trying to coordinate with the FBI and Lincoln Police Department to begin locating, exhuming, and identifying the bodies Fenton had mentioned. I pictured twenty plus more of these out of town trip.

"How I was supposed to get the ball rolling on each of these cases, follow through on them, and then get back to the prison for the next therapy session with Fenton." I wondered.

My phone vibrated in the cup holder next to me. Using the car Bluetooth to answer, I silently prayed it was someone other than Lt. Carter calling to give me shit about the next assignment.

"Hey, it's Detective Bryant." I said after the car stereo beeped to acknowledge the call being answered.

"Hey, Bryant, it's Terry." A friendly voice greeted me over the speakers.

I let out a deep sigh. "Oh, thank God, I thought it was another supervisor calling to take a verbal shit on me."

Special Agent Jones laughed briefly as he reassured me. "No it's just another LEO down in the shit with you looking for shovel. Hey, I've got good news and bad news, which one do you want first?"

"It's been a shitty day; why not start with the bad news?" I offered, shaking my head in dismay.

"Irvingdale City Counsel told us to kindly go fuck ourselves for requesting to dig up one of the yards in their pristine, white picket fence neighborhood." Terry advised.

"It's nice to know local politicians are assholes the world over, so I'm not surprised there. I just hope they don't stall as long as the last group of taxpayer-funded ass clowns we dealt with this last week." I grumbled.

"That's where the good news comes in," said Jones with another short laugh. "We have an FBI field office in Lincoln. I called them the second I heard about the new victim locations, and they fired out search warrants for the locations you described."

"I was only given one location, why do we need multiple warrants?" I asked.

"Well the Lincoln office did some fast research on that block Fenton listed. Two of those houses were painted white back in the 1990's and two of them are white now. Given Fenton's sophisticated level of intelligence, for someone without internet privileges, they thought it best to have warrants for each of those four possibilities. That's why Irvingdale is pushing back so hard; property values along that three block stretch by the park are at an all-time high, the last thing they want is for Federal agents to start digging up bodies in the back yards and ruining an upscale neighborhood."

"I can see their point. How soon will they have the warrants ready?" I asked.

"They're on their way to the judge now to get them signed. They want to start the searching the area first thing Monday morning."

"I guess I'll be heading that way Sunday evening then." I acknowledged, begrudgingly.

"Your department already booked us on a flight leaving at 6:50 tomorrow night."

"That sounds like a plan; hopefully I can finish this report in a hurry and get home. I'm beginning to forget what my wife looks like after all this time."

"I'm right there with you, brother; god-speed and good luck to you."

"Thanks for the update Terry."

Finally a bit of good news; it was nice to have the FBI working with us at times like this. Usually the jurisdictional cooperation was messy, even when it was cordial. So far, the FBI and other involved departments were still on the same page. The only things I was still waiting on was follow-up on the Hayley Marten case, and locating the closed homicide case from Arkansas. We didn't have a lot to go on in Arkansas, so we were relying on multiple departments digging out files from decades ago. There were so many departments involved in that process I couldn't keep all the names straight. It was a small town thirty or so years ago which could mean any number of small towns or up-and-coming cities throughout the state.

My phone vibrated again in the cup holder causing my skin to crawl. There was no way I was getting a second friendly call in a matter of minutes. This one was definitely an ass chewing; for what, I did not know.

"Detective Bryant," I answered, cringing the moment I heard a reply.

"Bryant! WHAT THE FUCK IS GOING ON? Who have you been talking to about the Hayley Marten case?"

Before I could reply, Lt. Carter continued. "The fucking press is outside wanting an official statement on the finding of Hayley Marten's body at City Park. That information is barely privy to you at your pay rate. How the hell is this EVEN POSSIBLE?"

"L.T., I have no idea who would have given out that information. I can count, maybe, ten people who would even know the identification of those remains. They're all Law Enforcement, or the State Coroner in Kansas City. Everyone signed the non-disclosure agreement as a part of these investigations. That information hasn't even been provided to the Marten family yet."

"You can bet your ass it has now!" Lt. Carter swore.

"WHAT?" I asked, in dismay; unable to control the volume of my response.

"Greg Marten is on his way down to the L.E.C., and he's demanding to know why he was informed by the press about his daughter's remains before he's been contacted by us."

"Did he say who contacted him?" I asked, bewildered and slightly pissed.

"Some local hack at the Gazette called him and asked for his response to the news. Some fuck named Tim Lane, who turned around and called me for our official statement."

"That's insane, Carter. No one in the loop is stupid enough to ruin their careers by leaking to the press; besides this is national news. Why would someone leak sensitive information to a local newspaper? We've got a fucking fox in the henhouse."

"Easy with that accusation, Bryant," Carter growled over the car speakers.

"You're thinking it, I'm saying it Carter; otherwise you'd have waited to have this conversation with the entire team." I insisted.

"I want a list of everyone privy to this information by the time you get back to the L.E.C." He ordered. While I could have easily given him the list over the phone, I could tell he was in no mood for extending this conversation any further.

"You got it L.T.," I assured him as he hung the phone up with a crash.

I flinched as the sound echoed through my ears, leaving a slight ringing in its wake.

"Damn I hate it when he calls me on a landline just so he can slam the phone down when he's done." I mumbled to myself.

I picked up the phone, switched to private mode, and looked up a number in between glances over the dashboard. I didn't want to go back to the law enforcement center with just a list of names. I needed answers to go along with them. My frustration was justified, but I tried to hide it as the phone on the other end of the line started ringing.

"Hey, it's Detective Bryant; can you meet me behind the Home Depot in about thirty minutes? I need to talk to you."

———

The road leading up to the Law Enforcement Center was packed with SUV's and vans, all with local and national news logos on the side of them. Dozens of reporters were already in front of cameras, strategically located around the front entrance. No doubt, putting their spin on a story, with what could only be assumed were few or no details whatsoever. I drove through the crowd of leeches as fast as I could; hoping none of them would notice the department tag on the back, and start following me. By the time I parked and got out, they had already noticed me and started swarming my way. I held my bag in close and doubled my walking speed in an attempt to get in the back door before one of the talking heads could stand in the way. I almost made it. The reporters started barking questions faster than I could identify who was speaking.

"Detective; what can you say about the finding of Hayley Marten's body?"

"Sir, can you tell us what your department is doing to make sure people in the community are feeling secure at a time like this?"

"Have you spoken to the family yet?"

"Why has it taken so long to find her?"

"Were you out at the park last week when the bodies were discovered?"

"Do you have any new suspects in the case?"

I turned suddenly to the crowd now blocking my way into the building and shouted as loud as I could over the noise.

"I have no statement to provide. For an official statement, contact our Public Information Officer, Amy Collins, and route all questions through her. Thank you." I started attempting to push my way into the building, but the swarm of information hounds kept pressing me with questions and preventing me from getting to the door. Behind the crowd, I watched as Sgt. Ellis emerged from the L.E.C. along with two other patrol officers in uniform. Together they began pushing back the crowd from the sidewalk to allow me inside. I reached out and lightly poked the floating ribs of a few reporters, watching as they flinched and stepped aside as I coaxed them out of the way. They didn't realize what I, or the three uniforms, were doing as we stepped through the crowd gently moving the press out of the way. Sgt. Ellis reached me, threw an arm around my right shoulder where my bag was located and together we used our free hands to push the vultures back until we reached the door.

"Thanks buddy, I owe you one." I admitted.

"That's Sergeant to you." Ellis cracked with a grin.

"Oh, my bad, I thought since we graduated the academy together I could just call you buddy or dirty son of a bitch like I always have." I cracked, smiling as I gave him an enthusiastic hand-shake.

"Just as long as you throw Sergeant in front of it, you can call me whatever." Ellis replied.

"Either way, thanks. Do you think there's anything we can do to disperse the crowd outside? They're blocking the way, patrol can't even go 10-8 there's so many bodies in the street."

"I have a couple Swing Officers coming in to help push them back up front again."

"Are you doing another 'squawk and walk'? Did IA not bend you over a barrel the last time we used that trick?" I asked; shaking my head at the thought. When crowds gathered in the streets and parking lots after bar-close, it often took a lot of work, or creative measures to clear them out. Large crowds often lead to fights, so sending everyone home, in the most effective way possible, was a crucial element of working the midnight shift. The "squawk and walk," as we called it, involved multiple squad cars sounding their sirens and air horns at close distances to the crowd. The sheer volume was enough to scatter some people, and others would soon follow. If the crowd migrated, so did the squad cars until people took the hint and dispersed.

"They did." He replied. "I took my two days and went fishing; this one was ordered by Lt. Carter though, so I think I'm off the hook."

Behind the crowd of press personnel, two patrol Chargers rolled up and began wailing their sirens at the crowd who began covering their ears. The sirens paused briefly for a public service announcement over the car loud speaker.

"ALL MEMBERS OF THE PRESS ARE CORDIALLY INVITED TO REMAIN AT THE FRONT OF THE LAW ENFORCEMENT CENTER WHERE THEIR QUESTIONS WILL BE ANSWERED IN A TIMELY MANNER. PATROL UNITS ARE COMPLETING MANDATORY MONTHLY TESTING OF PATROL UNIT SIRENS AND UNNECESSARY PERSONS IN THE AREA MAY BE SUBJECT TO LOUD NOISES WHICH COULD BE HARMFUL TO YOUR HEARING. PLEASE VACATE THE AREA TO ALLOW FOR NORMAL POLICE ACTIVITY AND EFFICIENCY TO RESUME."

The crowd began moving up to the front of the building in a hurry. Additional sirens began wailing as the late swing shift started going 10-8.

"Ah, now that's a thing of beauty." I said as the crowd dispersed.

"Good luck, Carter's in an extra piss-y mood today." Ellis advised.

"I'll go blow some sunshine up his ass and see if he throws up a rainbow for me." I called to Ellis over my shoulder as I reached the door to the investigations wing. I swiped my key card and walked to my desk.

"My Office, NOW," Lt. Carter ordered, the second my bag hit my desk. I could see Ross and Shirley already seated in the office with their backs to the bullpen, facing the lieutenants desk. I hoped the ass chewing would be more polite than the usual one-on-one I received.

"Do you have that list I ordered?" Lt. Carter demanded.

"Yes, sir," I replied. "Ten people knew this information; four of us are in this room, Agent Jones and Supervisory Special Agent Wells, Dr. Weiss and Dr. Wesselman at the State Coroner's Office and then Captain Hamell and Chief Irwin."

"We are overlooking someone who needs to be on this list. What about family members have any of you discussed this case with family?" asked Lt. Carter.

"Just that it sucks to find four bodies in the park where we all patrolled over the past decade. Otherwise none of it was discussed in detail, definitely no names." I told them.

"What about you two?" Lt. Carter asked.

"Tara's still in the FBI training academy for another month. I don't have anyone else to talk with, and don't talk details with anyone outside of work anyways." Shirley replied.

"I leave work at the door until someone calls me in the middle of the night to assist on an investigation," stated Ross. "I'm not a fan of traitors, and don't intend to be one either."

"We're overlooking someone in this process," declared Lt. Carter.

"There's one more name we need to add to that list," said Shirley.

"I thought you said you didn't talk to anyone about it?" Carter asked, looking confused.

"I don't mean us, I mean Fenton." She replied.

"Who the fuck is he going to call from inside solitary confinement with no phone?" asked Carter, in bewilderment.

"No she's onto something; Fenton knew about the four bodies we found at the park before I told him." I advised. "He knew only one of them fit the timeline for his killings."

"How did he know about the other three bodies then?" Ross asked.

"Someone is feeding that animal information on this investigation. He is using someone with connections to the outside to run his errands and complicate this process for us." Shirley observed.

"That's a short fucking list; they limit the number of people with access to death row inmates. We're looking at maybe twenty people at most." Ross offered, with a slight shrug.

"I can confirm that." I said. "With the staffing shortage they're experiencing I'd put the number at around eighteen. They run a maximum of six per shift around the clock in that wing of the prison. Everyone is on lockdown and only allowed out of their cells one at a time which reduces the need for a large body of personnel."

"Call Agent Jones and have him send over a list of all corrections staff working maximum security at El Dorado. He can get that info faster than we can." Lt. Carter said to me as the phone on desk started ringing. He picked it up. "Carter? Thank you, have Ellis show him into the conference room."

Carter hung up the phone. "Scratch what I just told you. Ross, call Agent Jones and get the list from him. Bryant and Shirley, you are going right now to meet Greg Marten in the conference room. We need to know what he thinks he knows and then give him a formal next of kin notification. I know now, we should have done the notification two days ago before the press got wind of it."

Ross stood up and exited the office followed by Shirley.

"Bryant one more thing, close the door." Carter instructed.

I closed the door and moved closer to the desk as Carter motioned me over.

"From now on, and I know this isn't your fault, if we ID a body, we contact next of kin before anyone goes home that night. This is the procedure until we find out who's fucking us from El Dorado."

"Agreed," I said as I felt my phone vibrate. I checked it as I turned towards the door.

"Fuck!" I said turning back to Carter, "The judge in Lincoln kicked back the search warrants for the Irvingdale locations. They need my report to complete new affidavits."

"Hurry up with the interview and next of kin notification. Then knock that report out for the feds. Then I need a supplement on the Hayley

Marten case before you leave with whatever her dad gives you. Talk with Shirley; she has the original case number for the missing person report." He ordered.

"Yes sir." I replied as I left the office.

Shirley was waiting outside the office for me with her notebook in hand. She stowed her phone in her back pocket as I emerged and walked with me towards the conference room.

"Have you done many next of kin notifications?" She asked.

"Not recently. I did a few on Patrols as a rookie, but then most of the murders stopped."

"...Because you put Fenton away for life." She stated, casually

"Something like that, we haven't had many homicides since then." I said.

"Oh I'm aware, I almost got sent back to patrol when the R.A.F. killings stopped. Luckily there's a lot of other crime happening allowing me to stay in investigations." She responded.

"I wasn't aware you had been in investigations that long." I admitted. We paused outside the conference room door.

"I did a couple years here, then a few as an SRO and then got promoted to Sergeant on patrol. I didn't care for the patrol supervisory duties so I finagled my way into a training position for a couple years. I was back in investigations when you got hired and stepped down to detective from the Sergeant position. Totally worth the pay cut; but now I get to do fun stuff like this." She stated sarcastically as we reached the conference room door.

I opened the door and we stepped inside to see Greg Marten pacing back and forth on the far side of the table. He turned to face us as I closed the door. Greg was only about five feet eight inches tall, but the energy of his grief seemed to fill the conference room. His hair was prematurely gray for a man only in his mid-fifties. He was slender built with leathery skin and thick, calloused hands from working outdoors most of his life. Tears ran through the wrinkles on his face like aqueducts, carrying them down the side of his face past a thick, black and gray five o'clock shadow onto his tan Carhartt coat. It was obvious he had been in tears for some time, but the sorrow he felt was quickly being replaced by an undeniable rage.

"Where is my daughter?" He asked as he choked back a sob. "WHERE IS HAYLEY?"

I found myself at a momentary loss for words, but Shirley stepped up and allowed her experience to take control of the situation.

"Mr. Marten if you'll have a seat we can answer all of your questions," she replied compassionately.

"I DON'T WANT TO SIT DOWN; I'VE DONE NOTHING BUT WAIT FOR FOURTEEN YEARS WONDERING WHAT THE HELL HAPPENED TO MY DAUGHTER. I WANT ANSWERS, AND I'M NOT GOING TO SIT AROUND ANY LONGER WHILE HER KILLER RUNS FREE."

"Sir," I interjected softly, "Your daughter's killer is not running free."

This stopped him in his tracks. He stared at me for almost a minute as the tears began flowing again.

"Oh my God," he whispered as he covered his face with one hand.

"Greg, could you please sit down? We have a lot to tell you and we're going to tell you everything we can today. But first we need to know that everything we discuss in this room stays in this room until we can make the information public." Shirley told him.

Shirley and I sat down at the table opposite Greg and waited for him to sit. He seemed hesitant. I could only imagine how many times he had replayed this exact scenario over in his mind, knowing it could never have been as difficult as this was about to be.

"Please?" Shirley requested as she gestured towards the chair across from us. "I'm Detective Shirley and this is Detective Bryant. We will do our best to answer all your questions."

Greg looked skeptical, but finally sat down and tried to compose himself again; wiping tears and snot onto his coat sleeve.

Greg looked at me through bloodshot eyes as I started speaking. His stare seemed to bore a hole, right down to my soul. It was hard to make eye contact with him

"Greg, I know this is the hardest thing you may ever have to hear, and I apologize for the manner in which you became aware. I take full responsibility for withholding the information from you until you found out from someone else. I apologize for placing this investigation ahead of doing the right thing, and notifying you the moment we had confirmation. As you know, our department recovered the remains of several individuals in City Park this past week. I'm sorry to say, we have confirmed, one of the bodies recovered from City Park was that of your daughter, Hayley." I advised, trying with all my might to show him the compassion he deserved.

Greg exhaled sharply and began sobbing into his hands, leaning forward to rest his elbows on the table. I knew Greg was experiencing a world of pain. It wasn't long before I began to fight tears as well. I tried to stay present in the moment; to hold back the guilt I felt for putting him in this position. Intrusive thoughts began to invade my mind as we listened to Greg sob, bitter, broken-hearted tears. I heard the coroner's audio report echoing in my head with the horrors Hayley had experienced before she died. I lowered my head, still fighting my own tears, and allowed Greg a moment to grieve. Several minutes passed with no sound outside of Greg's miserable sobbing. Over time, Greg's curiosity outweighed his grief, and he attempted to compose himself again.

"Who...," he asked sniffing several times and wiping snot on his sleeve again, "Who did this to my angel?"

He stared at us, completely indifferent to the snot running from his nose down his top lip. I wanted this process to provide some kind of closure, but it wasn't. We were twisting a knife into a fourteen year old wound.

"This is the part of the process in which we need your assurance that the information we provide is held confidential for the time being." I explained softly. Shirley pulled a form out of her notebook and slid it across the table. I had not been looking forward to this. The Department of Justice wanted to resolve old cases, not have victims' families hash out their discontent in the media. This case had been played out in the media already; they had no interest in it happening again.

"What I am handing you, is a Non-Disclosure Agreement. It is a legal document which states you can be held liable for breaching to the public the information we are about to tell you," stated Shirley.

"Unfortunately, Mr. Marten, we are unable to continue discussing this case in detail with you unless you sign it." I explained.

"You mean; I won't learn anything else until I sign this document?" He demanded.

Shirley nodded to him.

"Will I be prosecuted for breaching this agreement?"

"This is a legally binding document, you can be prosecuted for breaking it," she stated.

I knew she was lying to him, but we needed his cooperation in every way possible before we spoke any further. The reality was we could do little more than pursue some kind of civil settlement. Shirley placed a pen on top of the document, and allowed Greg to think it over. Greg signed it without reading it, and then pushed it back towards us.

"Now tell me who killed my daughter." He said in an exhausted whisper.

I fidgeted in my chair a little as I contemplated the best way to wade into such a sensitive subject. I wanted to relay the information without needing to expose the ungodly details which surrounded the death of his daughter. This was no time for a careless slip-of-the-tongue.

"Sir; do you recall around the time of Hayley's disappearance a number of missing persons and homicides occurred?" I asked.

"Of course I do; it was all over the news, women were disappearing like crazy all over northeast Kansas. Everyone was running scared," he replied. He looked confused, but with growing concern.

"And if you weren't already aware, we caught the man responsible. He recently completed his appeal process, and received the death penalty." I continued.

"What was his name?" Greg asked, as if he was remembering something terrible.

As if there was some unseen power in uttering the man's name, I hesitated a few seconds before finding the stones to open my mouth again.

"His name was Richard Allen Fenton," I said.

I watched Greg's face as he took an unexpected walk down a haunted-memory lane. He paused as if he was trying to remember something he had buried deep down. His eyes began to widen, and I could tell the dismay had struck home in his heart.

"Do you mean, the South Side Sadist?" Greg asked, as the horror began dawning on him.

"That was what the media labeled him." Shirley explained.

"My baby was murdered by a serial killer?" He asked, in a dishearteningly weak tone.

"Yes; she has been confirmed as the twelfth victim of Richard Allen Fenton." I said softly.

Of all the horrible turns this conversation could take, Greg had taken the worst.

"Oh my God, how did she...I mean, how did he...?"

"I'm going to stop you right there Greg." I said, cutting him off. "You are experiencing a terrible loss, and going through something no parent should ever have to experience. We have recovered your child, and will be returning her to you early this week. That is what you should be focusing on right now. If you look into or demand to know the manner in which he destroyed lives, you are only going to find pain you should never know. Here is the important information you need to know. Fenton has been convicted on all eleven of his other murders, and has been sentenced to death for them."

"How did you know to look for her in City Park? How did you know she would be one of the four bodies you found?"

"How..." I started to ask him a question, but Shirley waved me off and interjected.

"Six months ago Fenton struck a deal with the Department of Justice in which he offered to give up the locations, of what he claims, are multiple homicide victims of his dating back around thirty years."

"Wait, what deal did he make? Reduced prison time? Getting off death row?" Greg began to panic. The thought of his daughter's killer going free sent him into frenzy. He began to wave his hands slightly, as if shrugging, trying to figure out what was happening to him now.

"None of those were requested by Fenton, nor were any of them ever an option." I insisted.

He looked slightly relieved, but not without additional questions.

"Then what deal did he make?" He wondered.

"He asked us to write his story and publish it for the world to see." Shirley explained.

"By us you mean...?" He trailed off as he pointed a finger casually back and forth between us.

"Detective Bryant was selected to meet with Fenton and write the story to be published. Fenton wanted to live on in infamy through the untold stories, of what he believes are his legacy. Because the DOJ struck this deal with Fenton demanding Bryant write the story, we are at the center of the ongoing investigations along with a task force from the FBI."

Greg sat silently, staring at the table a moment as he pondered all this. His eyes darted up to mine and turned from curiosity to a glare. "So you're just going to write the biography for a serial killer; just like that?"

"It is because of this deal that we located and recovered your daughter. We have been tasked to resolve numerous unsolved cases, and bring closure to families spanning over five states. You are just the first person to receive word of the fate of a loved one. Believe me; I did not sign up for this project, or this burden. I was ordered to by my chain of command, all the way up to the Department of Justice. My task is to sit with Fenton every Saturday for three hours while he pompously tells the stories of his sick and twisted 'accomplishments' as he calls them." I said; throwing up finger quotes to be certain Greg didn't misunderstand my use of the term.

"How long do you have to do this?"

"Today was week two, I have to meet with him twenty-four more times to complete the deal as Fenton demanded. If I miss a meeting, the deal is off; if I fail to get a publisher on board the deal is off."

"But what about a trial; what about justice for all the other victims?" Greg asked.

"There isn't going to be any more trials for Fenton." Shirley advised.

"Why? He's admitting to countless other murders; he isn't going to be held responsible for them?" His frustration was growing again, and I could not blame him.

"He is being held responsible for them. He received the death penalty for his last three capital murder convictions. The appeals process is complete; Fenton will be put to death." I said, trying to reassure him.

"But what about justice for my Hayley; Don't I get to see the son of a bitch on trial for her murder?" He implored.

"He will never live to see court proceedings for all the victims he's claimed. We will all be dead by the time thirty more murder trials have gone to court with the hope of more convictions. He's already sentenced to death for his crimes; thirty more convictions won't kill him any faster than the process that's already started. If we fail to hold up our end of the deal, the truth about all his victims, missing or otherwise, dies with him on Christmas day." I explained.

His anger was starting to come back through the tears.

"This is so fucking sick." He said, growing more and more furious.

"You are the only person I know who could believe this process to be sicker than I do." I said.

"How do you even figure into this? You can't be over thirty, maybe thirty-one at most. You weren't even a cop when Hayley died. Why did he ask you to publish his misdeeds?"

I broke eye contact with Greg for a moment to search for the words to say. I was thankful Shirley came up with an explanation so I didn't have to.

"Detective Bryant is the one who caught Fenton, and put him behind bars ten years ago as a rookie patrol officer."

"YOU did?" Greg asked, in what was obviously disbelief, "How?"

"Right place, right time," I said simply; hoping that would suffice for now.

There was a brief moment of silence before Shirley broached the last subject on our list of topics to cover.

"Greg, when did the Gazette writer contact you?" She asked.

"I'm not sure. It was maybe three hours ago; Long enough for me to call my son who drove in from Lawrence to be here with me during this whole process."

"What did Tim Lane tell you when he called?" I asked.

"He didn't tell me anything; he asked me if I would provide a comment on the discovery of my daughter's remains at City Park. I didn't say anything to him I just hung up the phone. The digging at the park was days ago, I didn't make the connection to Hayley until he mentioned her." Greg admitted.

"Greg, I am truly sorry you found out that way. We wanted confirmation from Fenton about Hayley before we made the notification. We wanted to have some kind of information to provide you to allow some type of closure. Having her back, but not knowing what had happened, seemed cruel at the time. I know now finding out this way from the media is a far crueler thing than I ever could have imagined. I am truly sorry." I apologized.

"It's done now; there is nothing we can do about any of it now." Greg whispered softly as he stood up from his chair. "If it's okay with you detectives, I'd like to begin the funeral arrangements for Hayley. Do you know when I can expect her returned to me?"

"She will be here by late Monday morning, here's my card. Call me Monday, and let me know where we can deliver her for funeral arrangements." Shirley offered.

"Thank you." He replied quietly as he walked to the door. Shirley and I accompanied him out the back door where a gray sedan pulled up to the curb for him. A young man in a white shirt with a red tie stepped out of the driver's seat and looked over the top of the sedan at Shirley and I as Greg opened the passenger side door.

"Let's go son." Greg said as the young man climbed back into the car.

"Do you recognize that kid from somewhere?" asked Shirley.

"That's Conner Marten, I haven't seen him since I arrested him for disorderly conduct and 'Minor in Consumption' nine years ago; you?" I replied.

"I haven't seen him since the press conference in 2003 where he stood next to his dad pleading for Hayley's safe return. You arrested him back in what, 2008?"

I waited until the car navigated the crowd of vultures trying to photograph them as they left.

"He was only nineteen; he picked a fight with a guy and yelled out some anti-gay slurs to a very crowded bar." I explained.

"That was disorderly in 2008? It must have been a unique situation."

"It was; he was in a gay bar at the time." I replied.

"Shit; that will do it." Shirley said as we walked back towards the door.

"Why do you ask?"

"I recognize him from somewhere else, I just can't figure out from where." She said.

"Let me know what you come up with. Also, why did you stop me from asking him about the other bodies?" I inquired.

"He knew there were a total of four bodies recovered and that is not public information." She explained, sharply. "There were three burial sites discovered, but that was all that was released. How would he know additional details like that?"

"I don't know, but Fenton knew we found four bodies too, and I'm still not sure how that's possible." I admitted.

"Whoever our inside man is, they're leaking information both ways. Someone was able to tell Fenton about three murders that happened after Fenton was incarcerated that even the police didn't know about. That same person could have very easily have told Tim Lane about Hayley being one of the recovered bodies." She said.

"Well maybe that explains why Tim failed to meet me an hour ago. I called him and set up a meet, but he never showed. I wanted his explanation about tipping off Greg and try to figure out who might be his source."

"No way does a reporter miss the chance to get a one on one interview with the lead investigator on a series of homicides. That seems out of place." She observed.

"I agree, let's see if we can locate Tim and see what's going on." I said as we walked in the back door.

"You let me handle that, you've got two reports to write before you go home tonight. I know you get precious little free time during all of this." She offered.

"Thanks, I know you know what I'm going through. How have you been holding up? I know you've been rattling around in an empty house for the past few months." I said.

"Tara wanted to go federal, this is the price we pay for her to complete the training. We don't like being separated, but I don't have to tell you what it's like, you know it better than any of us." She said, with a compassionate tone.

"Thanks again, I owe you one." I said as we reached the door, and stepped inside.

CHAPTER FIVE

The sound of my work phone ringing woke me in a panic. My sleep had been uneasy for the past two weeks, or maybe two years and it seemed impossible to fall asleep with all the haunting images in my head. The clock over the mantle said 2 A.M. as I sat up from my reclined spot on the couch. I dug my phone from in between the couch cushions, and tried not to sound delirious when I answered.

"Bryant." I mumbled into the phone.

"It's Carter; we need you to come in and help work a homicide."

"I'm not supposed to work call-ins while I'm on the task-force. I leave for Lincoln tomorrow evening; I was supposed to get some time off." I grumbled.

"Patrol just found Tim Lane's body hanging from the rafters of the pavilion at City Park."

"Fuck; ok can someone come pick me up?" I asked.

"I take it you overindulged when you got home last night?"

"Like I said, I was supposed to be off in the morning." I replied, running low on patience.

"It's ok, I figured as much. I'll be outside in five minutes to get you, so be ready."

I stumbled around until I found my shoes where I kicked them off by the fireplace, tucked in my shirt, sat back on the couch. I glanced around trying to get my bearings enough to lean over and put my shoes on. I left my tie hanging on the door to the hall closet and grabbed my phone. I winced briefly as the bright screen hit my dry, bloodshot eyes. I formulated a brief text to my wife to let her know I'd been called in to work, so she wouldn't have to wake up or be worried when she did. Throwing my jacket around my shoulders I walked out the front door and locked it behind me. I walked about ten feet down the sidewalk towards the road when I realized I should have put on a coat instead of a suit jacket. Just as I was about to turn back and get a coat, Lt. Carter pulled up in front of the house. I increased my pace towards the car and reached it before the cool breeze made me shiver.

"I got you coffee and a day old donut from the gas station." Carter said as I closed the door behind me.

"Thanks L.T.," I said as I accepted the hot to-go cup of coffee and took a sip. Satisfied it was hot enough to scald my tongue; I grabbed the donut and took a bite, speaking through it as I chewed. "I thought the crime scenes were still taped off and monitored; how the hell did he get up into the rafters?"

"Patrol had a series of vehicle burglaries in the northwest and several bar-fights; the uniform at the park got pulled to help cover the streets. In the hour the scene was unsecure, someone hung Lane from the rafters and left him there for us to find."

"Left him there for us?" I asked, confused.

"Apparently there's a message on the body. Shirley tells me you tried to arrange a meeting with Lane yesterday before you got back to the L.E.C, but it didn't happen. What was that about?" He inquired.

"I called Lane to set up a meeting to ask about the call he made to Greg Marten. He agreed to meet me behind the Home Depot, but he never showed. I waited thirty minutes for him before wading through the see of scavengers outside the PD." I explained.

"You know, back before I worked here, behind a store with no cameras is where officers invited people to meet when they needed to pound information out of them. Was that your plan?"

"As nice as it would be to get to hit a reporter in the face, no, that wasn't the plan. Lane ran a story on that series of home invasions we were having in 2015. He started to see a pattern, but no one was listening to him; not even me. He staked out a neighborhood for over two weeks before he got photographs of the burglar making entry into a house. He called us, and we were waiting for the guy when he stepped outside."

"I remember that summer; 'Raccoon Bobby' we called that guy. He was slick, quiet and burglarized homes while people were still inside without ever waking them." Carter remembered.

"Yeah, it's pretty impressive for someone who smoked as much meth as he did." I quipped.

"That was the other reason for the name. Skinny forty-something white guy with such big bags under his eyes he looked like he had a pair of black eyes. That guy slept for two straight days after they booked him. He hadn't had a pillow under his head in several months." Said Carter; shaking his head in wonder.

"Well Lane turned the pictures over to me and testified to help put him away for a dime. Lane and I kinda became friends after that; the only person in the media, I could trust. Or so I thought. I couldn't believe he called the Marten family to tell them Hayley had been located. I was so pissed I might have hit him had he showed at the meeting."

"Didn't he get nominated for some community award?" Carter inquired.

"Hell yeah he did, I nominated him for helping us out. He lost to some politician who opened the methadone clinic earlier that year."

"You mean the clinic Bobby broke into a week before his arrest? The one that closed down after the second doctor got assaulted in 2016 for withholding 'scripts from a meth-head?"

"Ironic! Huh?" I said, smiling.

"Nope; just sad," Carter replied, as he turned on Leavenworth Street into the park.

Patrol units on scene had the area lit up with their "take-down" lights when we arrived. I could plainly see the body hanging from the rafters, even from the car.

I sipped the, still scalding, coffee as I walked past the bleachers in the pavilion, and stood looking up at the body. Tim was wearing his favorite blue suit with brown shoes, all of which were covered in what appeared to be blood and mud. The rope had been slung over the railing, leading up to the stage, using a rock tied to the end. The rope had then been tied to the railing by the stage with the rock still attached.

"Is there any way we can cut this guy down?" I asked, struggling to look any longer. It wasn't often you got called in to work a homicide case where you know the victim. We were in unfamiliar territory here. Normally I would have been recused from the investigation just for being acquainted with the victim, I was probably too close the victim to see the scene clearly. I stepped aside to allow the CSI tech and a uniformed officer to spread a tarp underneath the victim's location hanging from the rafters.

"CSI just finished taking pictures of the scene; we're cutting him down now." Corporal Roberts advised. Cpl. Roberts had been the supervisor on scene up until Lt. Carter's arrival. I watched as Cpl. Roberts and one of his officers pulled on the rope to raise the body slightly to allow the rope to be untied from the railing by Lt. Carter. The body was then slowly lowered to the concrete floor where two other uniforms, wearing disposable gloves, caught Lane under each arm and gently lay him down onto the tarp.

The CSI tech handed me a pair of gloves and then began circling the body taking more pictures. Two of the uniformed officers checked out with Lt. Carter and exited the scene to return to patrol duties. The CSI tech, a thirty-something female with her hair pulled back in a single braid, attempted to get every angle of the body she could. Finally, she gave me a "thumbs up" to indicate it was okay to approach the body.

"Flashlight," I requested of the patrol officer, who was standing just behind me, watching the events unfold.. The officer pulled out a small flashlight from his belt and handed it to me. I shined the flashlight across the small cardboard sign hung around Lane's neck. It read, "Talebearers and Liars must die, FUCK TWELVE."

"Twelve?" I asked to nobody in particular.

"Its common street lingo for police," explained the CSI tech.

"What's your name?" I asked her.

"Jasmine Miner; it's nice to meet you detective Bryant." She replied as she moved in to take a better picture of the sign.

"Okay Jasmine what can you tell me?" I asked as I checked the body for a pulse.

"Not much, I just got here myself." She replied. "Although with his hands and feet bound and the rope tied off we can rule out suicide."

"Well his body isn't cold yet and it's still pretty flexible. The marks around his neck and the petechial hemorrhaging in his eyes and on his face suggest asphyxiation was the cause of death. This man was still alive when he was hoisted into the rafters." I said, stating my observations out loud.

"So this is my fault?" asked the officer whose flashlight I held.

"What's your name rookie?" I inquired.

"Preston, Dale Preston; it's my first week on solo patrol. If I hadn't left then maybe he'd still be alive or maybe I could have seen who did it..."

"Preston!" I said sharply standing up to face him. "Look at me right here. You followed orders; you did not desert your post. If it wasn't here, it would have happened elsewhere, so this is not your fault. What I need from you is this, contact dispatch and request the exact time you were sent in route to the other call. Then I need to know exactly when you got back so we know when this occurred. We need to know what resources we have around the area to help get this bastard on camera coming to and from the scene. Okay? Get me the time frame pronto and then start your narrative."

"Yes sir!" Preston said, and then jogged off towards his patrol vehicle.

I started patting down the pockets on the victims pants and jacket and started pulling items out as I found them. Miner indicated a spot next to the body, on the tarp, for me to display all the items to be photographed. I lay them out, side by side, until all the pockets were empty.

"That's odd." I said, unable to keep my confusion to myself.

"What is?" Miner asked.

"All of his items were in his left pants pocket; His pen, his notebook, his wallet, and his keys; all of them. Normal people who wear a suit five days a week keep their pen in the jacket pocket next to their notebook. Wallet and keys make sense, but not all of it together. Someone rifled through his pockets, put almost everything back, but not where it came from." I speculated; still feeling confused.

"What do you mean, almost everything?" Miner inquired, further.

"His phone is missing for one. This guy was a reporter, his phone was his lifeline. Now look at his notebook." I said, pointing to it on the tarp.

"What about it?" She asked.

"Do you make a habit of ripping each page out of your notebook as you use it? Neither do I, neither does anyone else I know, media or officers. Someone ripped every bit of paper out of the notebook that had writing on it. That means someone either found something they were looking for or possibly something we'd be looking for, and took it."

"What do you think was on it?" Preston asked as he returned to the scene and overheard the end of the conversation. I made every attempt not to roll my eyes at a question which had no reasonable answer. I prevented the sarcastic comment I'd have normally made from escaping my mind and instead provided a plausible, but still vague answer.

"Hopefully it was the smoking gun to figure out who killed him. That at least means there is one, but this is all speculation of course. What's the time frame we're looking at?" I asked him.

"Between 0045 hours and 0150 hours, sir," he replied.

"That gives us a 65 minute window to check traffic cameras and local businesses for footage of this guy near the scene."

"There isn't going to be any traffic camera footage."

I stared at Preston until he became uncomfortable and explained himself.

"During my Neighborhood Training Exercise I dealt with a lot of traffic issues. I talked with employees down at City Hall and they said the traffic camera's only have a live feed because they don't have the space to store all the data for an extended period of time. They said hundreds of cameras would require an inordinately over-sized storage facility to hold enough servers for all the footage from even a weeks' time." He explained.

"Well that leaves us with local businesses," I said trying to stay motivated for the follow up investigation about to occur.

"There are none for at least a full block of the park." Preston said. He again looked awkward for a moment before continuing, "This was the area for my NTE so I know it pretty well."

Miner completed her photographs of the items from the victim's pocket and started placing them into a brown, paper evidence bag.

I stood up and was about to take off my gloves when a thought occurred to me. "Hand me the keys from the evidence bag." I instructed Miner. I took the keys from her and held the key FOB up in the air and started pressing buttons. To my surprise, a car alarm began going off nearby.

"Whoa! How did you know?" Preston asked, appearing impressed.

"I didn't, that's the point. But that means one more detail can be added. Either Lane was attacked here or he drove here with his killer. We need to sweep that vehicle for evidence. Roberts, what are the odds of getting a positive K-9 track after having eight to ten people out here walking around the crime scene?"

"Somewhere between unlikely and impossible," he replied.

"That's what I thought; we need a second CSI team to check the vehicle while we finish up over here."

"I can stand by until we have a second team on scene." Preston offered. "I'll just work on my narrative in the car."

"Clear it with your Cpl. Roberts, but it's alright by me. Just don't get into it until CSI has someone to check for evidence." I advised.

"Yes, sir," he replied.

"And stop calling me 'sir'." I called after him.

"If we can find the victims phone number, we could have dispatch attempt to locate it through the service provider," offered Miner.

I took off my right glove and pulled out my phone, "Hey Roberts." I called out to him as he gave Preston the go-ahead to secure the victim's vehicle.

"What can I do for you?" Roberts asked.

"Write down this phone number and see if dispatch can get a location on the phone. The number is for our victim." I told him, holding up my phone to show him the number. He pulled out his notebook, and jotted it down.

"You got it, give me a minute." Roberts replied.

"If you're done with pictures can you swab all these items from his pocket for DNA? Get a buccal swab from our victim too so we can rule out his DNA. We don't have a suspect yet, but if we do we will want DNA evidence if we can get it."

Lt. Carter strolled up as Roberts walked away towards his unit. "What's the news?"

"I'm damn sure this is a murder. The question is whether or not Lane was attacked before he was supposed to meet me or after. Something prevented him from meeting with me and I'd love to know what that was." I surmised.

"Alright then, are you finished up here so we can head back to the L.E.C.?" Carter asked.

"Almost; I'd really like to have a look at Lane's vehicle. The rookie is securing it where it's parked over by the north baseball field." I replied.

"Then let's head that way; we don't need a thorough look I'm assuming, just enough to know if there's something of immediate value still inside."

"That's all I need." I advised.

"Hey Bryant, the cell phone is pinging in the 500 Block of Leavenworth Street on the north side," Roberts yelled from his over by his patrol unit.

"That's the post office." I shouted back. "Get some uniforms over there ASAP, do a grid search of the lobby and surrounding property in case the phone was ditched in the vicinity."

We left the pavilion area and started walking towards the baseball field to our east. The morning dew was starting to collect, get our shoes and the cuffs of our pants wet as we walked through the grass leading up to the road running through the middle of city park. Ahead of us we could see Preston's patrol Charger pulling up near Lane's vehicle in the parking lot. Preston put the spotlight on the vehicle as he put the car in park. He got out in a hurry and ran towards the vehicle, waving to us as he ran.

"Hey! There's a lady in the back seat of the car, I think she's hurt." Preston called to us. We started jogging towards the car as Preston reached it and whipped the back door open.

The flash of light as the car exploded nearly blinded me, but I couldn't focus on my eyes over the ringing in my ears. The heat wave hit us on the other side of the street as shattered glass peppered us in the face. I ducked my head in pain and held my ears as blood started to run down my face.

Lt. Carter too, was kneeling next to me, holding his ears. We both tried to stagger to our feet, but it was no easy task. My equilibrium was totally fucked causing me to fall onto my hands and knees twice before I gave up and started crawling towards Preston's patrol unit. The Lane's vehicle was completely involved now, lighting up the entire park in a bright orange, glow. There was no sign of Preston anywhere. The heat increased exponentially as I approached the patrol unit which was parked over thirty feet from the blazing car. I opened the Chargers door from my spot on the ground, climbed inside, and hit the unit's "officer down" button. I grabbed the handset mic and started screaming into it.

"DISPATCH WE HAVE AN OFFICER DOWN, SEND FIRE AND EMS 10-39 TO THE NORTH SIDE OF CITY PARK; REPEAT OFFICER DOWN!"

I hit the button for the trunk of the Charger and started crawling through the gravel to the rear of the unit. Reaching the trunk I fought both to stand and, for what seemed like an eternity, to release the restraints which kept the fire extinguisher tethered in place. In my panic and years out of patrol I had forgotten how to release the extinguisher. Fighting for another eternity I finally released the extinguisher and began searching for Preston. I circled to the opposite side of the patrol unit from the fire and spotted what looked like a person folded in half and on fire next to the right field fence line. I managed to get to my feet and started stumbling towards the fence. The grass around the body had caught fire so I started squeezing the handle to put it out. In my panic I forgot to pull the pin on the extinguisher and struggled to release it. Finally freeing the pin I started spraying the fire in the grass before working my way close enough to start dousing the flames on Preston. Finally putting out the fire I went in close to see if Preston was still conscious. The polyester blend patrol uniform had melted to his arms and torso in front and his face was burned beyond recognition. I searched by the light of the fire to find a spot on Preston which wasn't burned to check for a pulse. Finding none, I attempted to check for a pulse on his neck but could not find one.

"I NEED EMS RIGHT NOW, OFFICER DOWN," I screamed as loud as I could.

Everyone seemed so far away, and I had never felt as alone as at that moment. The rookie I had just been talking with five minutes prior was dying right in front of me and no one seemed to give a fuck. I started to scream again, but it was drowned out by the blast of the gas tank exploding on the already burning car. I sat there a moment, staring at Preston who hadn't moved since I reached him. I didn't know what to do. His uniform was melted to his vest, and I didn't know if CPR would make the damage to his torso worse or not. I tried anyways and pressed my hands down left over right to start CPR and immediately stabbed a piece of glass from his vest into my right hand.

"FUCK!" I screamed as I tried to ignore the pain to keep going. I switched to just my left hand and received the same results with glass stabbing into my hand.

"OFFICER DOWN, I NEED HELP," I screamed again, trying to get anyone in the vicinity to come and help. I stared at the blood coming from my hands, wondering if it was mine or Preston's.

"What the fuck am I supposed to do?" I thought.

As I contemplated my next move, I felt arms wrap under my armpits and someone started dragging me away from Preston's body.

"STOP, you need to help him, GO HELP HIM." I plead with Corporal Roberts as he pulled me further and further away. I looked down at my legs. My pants were on fire. About the time I started to panic again, LT. Carter was kneeling next to me with Roberts, slapping at the flames to put them out. I realized then the grass around me had never been fully extinguished, and I'd been kneeling in burning grass trying to resuscitate Preston. Another uniformed officer had an extinguisher going to town on the grass, while yet another jumped into Preston's unit. He backed it up down the curb into the roadway and then back up over the curb on the other side, getting it out of harm's way.

The ringing in my ears covered the sounds of the sirens from the fire department as they arrived on scene. Several started dragging hoses out while two more ran to the fence and grabbed Preston by his arms and ankles and carried him towards the road. I was in excruciating pain, but somehow, completely numb.

CHAPTER SIX

I tried my best to keep from wincing as EMS wrapped my hands. The glass had been lodged firmly into Preston's vest; so luckily, none of it had transferred into my hands. Fifty feet; that was the difference between having my hands bandaged and having my body wrapped in a bag. It felt like my ears were never going to stop ringing, but even that couldn't drown out the pounding in my head. The cuts on my head and face from the flying glass stopped bleeding with a little pressure. I could feel the scabs pulling slightly every time I turned my head or moved an eyebrow. I glanced over at Lt. Carter, sitting on the bumper of the other ambulance, having one of the cuts on his forehead bandaged. The blanket over Preston's body only added to my guilt. I thought waiting with the vehicle would prove to be a simple, risk-free task. Several firefighters examined the smoking, charred frame, frame of the vehicle with huge flashlights.

With my head throbbing even more, I slowly stood up, bracing myself on the side of the ambulance. Lt. Carter stood up, made a concerted effort not to look at Preston's body, and started walking towards me. He held an ice pack to the side of his head, attempting to get the pain to stop. I could tell his thousand-yard-stare matched that of my own

"Let's get the fuck out of here." He said, barely audible over the ringing in my ears.

"Are you good to drive?" I said; holding up my bandaged hands, "Because I can't even grip the wheel."

I stood up slowly, feeling the exhaustion set in.

"It's just my head. Early Sunday morning traffic should make it easy to get out of here. We just have to get past the media." Lt. Carter advised while we walked towards the car.

"I can't wait to see how they spin this to make us look bad." I said, sarcastically.

"That's why we're leaving; we've suffered enough casualties today without one of us getting an IA for punching a reporter. You have a plane to catch this evening, and we can't afford any delays."

"What about you?" I asked Carter.

"I'll be here overseeing the three homicide investigations, and acting as the go-between for the KBI. They're already in route to start investigating the explosion. The bomb team is standing by, but everyone's been alerted to respond at a moment's notice."

"Too bad I get to leave this shit-show for another in Nebraska." I stopped suddenly as my vision turned blurry and the world started spinning uncontrollably. Carter threw my arm over his shoulders and kept me on my feet as he assisted me towards the car.

"What did EMS tell you about your head?"

"They didn't think I had a concussion, but told me to take a few days off and rest." I explained.

"Good luck with that; maybe you can catch a nap on the plane."

"That will be a nice forty-five minute nap at best."

"It's all you're gonna get 'til late tonight, so you better make the most of it." He encouraged.

"At least I get the chance to go home first."

We walked together in silence for a moment. My vision started to clear up as we approached the car. Reality set in again as I felt all the pressure in my head rush towards my eyes. Tears welled up as guilt began to flare up. I strained hard not to let any of them escape, but it seemed to be impossible.

"L.T., did I do that? Was it my fault?" I asked trying, unsuccessfully to keep my voice from cracking.

"No; none of that was your fault"

I could hear Carter choking back tears as well. Neither of us had ever lost a coworker before. Our community had been spared the trauma of losing officers through one of the worst periods of time in law enforcement. The country had been rife with officers killed in the line of duty over the past few years; just not here.

The drive home was completely silent. What could you even talk about in a moment like this? We had been placed on a task force to solve decade's old murders with a known suspect already behind bars. The risk should have been little to none. The realization that we had completely underestimated the situation took ahold of us both. In a matter of hours the entire approach to these investigations had been turned on its head. We had an unknown player in the game who was hell bent on making a name for themselves. Three people had died within hours of each other, and we had nothing to go on to start investigating. The worst part was the realization that every available officer and detective was going to be thrown at this with a vengeance; except me. I had to keep on track with what I was already doing. I had to travel to other states and have a therapy session with a psychopath once a week. It was all connected, though none of it made any sense at the moment. The dead reporter held the key to the unknown player's identity, and I wanted desperately to suspend my investigations elsewhere to focus on solving this one.

I hated being on the outside looking in on an investigation. Active investigations had excitement, passion and a timetable making the investigation both dynamic and thrilling. Cold cases had their moments, and deserved every second spent on them. They typically lacked the urgency of an ongoing threat which could create more victims without being addressed. I was caught in the middle of both types without the liberty of choosing which one received my attention. To top it all off they each had a difficult emotional connection, which made clarity and reason, hot commodities. I leaned back in my seat and closed my eyes for a moment. I had lost two people in a matter of hours which I only knew slightly, but for each of which, I felt entirely responsible. Preston had been young, and clearly ambitious, with potential for a bright career ahead of him. Tim Lane was a newspaper man who had barely survived the career altering transition of the print to online forms of media. He'd been in the habit of planting himself in the middle of major issues facing the public, risking humiliation and his career, if the story didn't sell. The father of two, Tim hadn't been one to be tied down if it meant preventing him from publishing his next story. Both would be remembered for what they had contributed to these cases, even though the public might never know them as more than a face on the front page.

"Was there somebody in that car?" I asked.

"Yeah, they had to wait for the fire to be out and the metal to cool down before they removed it from the vehicle. There wasn't much left."

"So that's gonna take a while." I complained.

"No kidding; we have more to handle than we were expecting. Three homicides in one day; we haven't had that many in the past three years."

"All this work to do and I'm headed to fucking Nebraska."

"It could be worse." He offered.

"It could; How?" I asked.

"You could be going to Arkansas, or El Dorado?"

"Well I'm not totally out of luck; I still get to go to both of those places at some point."

"Yeah; you lucky son of a bitch," he replied.

"That's me; the lucky one." I sat back and closed my eyes; hoping the pain in my head would subside. I couldn't focus. I couldn't string together enough thoughts to even begin making sense of the situation. There was so much happening here I was already having trouble giving a shit about the situation in Irvingdale. Twenty-six years had gone by. Why was my presence required? The FBI and local authorities were already on the ground; I was just another suit in the crowd. On the upside, the only paperwork I would have to do is the documentation of the findings for the book. With all the paperwork I had been doing on the local cases, I'd hardly had any time to put together the final piece of the deal. The documentation of the investigation and the history of Fenton's misdeeds was the essential aspect of the deal. I had twenty six weeks with twenty-six meetings with Fenton, followed by sixteen weeks for completion and publishing of all three volumes of the book. This gave Fenton two days to read it prior to his execution on Christmas Day. Sixteen weeks wasn't enough time to write, edit and then complete the publishing process. The forty weeks I had was already not enough to complete this task. In light of all that, I was happy to get some out-of-jurisdiction victims to recover.

"Bryant!"

I startled awake, and the pounding in my head came roaring back. I had unexpectedly fallen asleep, but Lt. Carter's voice snapped me back to reality. I leaned the seat back up, thanked the Lieutenant for the ride, and walked inside. It was barely 0600 hours and I was exhausted. I managed to get the key into the lock allowing me access to the house, but it was way more difficult with my hands bandaged the way they were. I used one of my available fingers and texted my wife, filling her in on the situation before I lay down on my side of the bed, without ever turning on the light. This was pretty standard for us after all our years together. This way she didn't wake up before she needed, and she wouldn't wake me up after a late night on a call-out. She'd be pissed knowing I was going to bed without showering, but it wasn't like I could clean myself without the use of my hands. The smell of burned hair, sweat and tears was awful, but I was too exhausted to care. I barely had time to kick my shoes off before my fatigue took over and I fell asleep.

———

She was already gone when I woke up. This was more common than not. In all our time together she had never been one to sit around the house idly. The house always looked amazing despite the fact that I struggled to help as often as I should. She was amazing like that though. She held down a fantastic job as a medical doctor and managed to keep a slob like me in a clean house with clean clothes. I wished she was here to help me wash up after getting blown to hell by the car bomb. Unfortunately, I had to make it on my own. The only thing harder than turning the water on was trying to shower without getting the bandages on my hands wet so I eventually thought "Fuck it" and did the best I could. I managed a decent shower, or at least good enough the other people on the plane wouldn't hate me for smelling like someone demolished an ammo dump. I checked around the house to see if my wife had left a note telling me when she'd be back. She hadn't left a note or texted, but I was use to that. She'd be back whenever she needed to be. After checking the fridge, I hoped she was out shopping, because the shelves were bare. I pulled out a microwave dinner I had stashed at the back of the cupboard, and made a second rate meal for myself. It was awful, but convenient. After showering and reapplying bandages to my hands, I had only half an hour to pack and leave for the airport.

I opted to skip the button up shirt, for obvious reasons, and simply throw a blazer over a nice long sleeve shirt. I hoped my hands would be better by the next day so I could operate the buttons on my dress shirts or even handle my sidearm properly. Gripping it was difficult which made tucking it in my waistband that much harder. I opted against wearing my backup weapon. I slipped it into my luggage and hoped I would be capable of carrying a full loadout in the near future. I skipped the hanging bag for my large suitcase; there was no way I was carrying two full bags with zero functioning hands. I would hang my nice clothes when I got to the hotel later. I used one finger to bang out another short text to my wife to let her know I was headed to the airport. The ringing in my ear sounded briefly like her cell phone, but I shook it off and went out to the garage. I was glad to have traded in the small five-speed sedan I'd driven for years for something bigger and more comfortable. It was so much easier to load up an SUV than a small, fast back car. I opened the garage door from the interior door and waited as it went up, hoping to see my wife's car coming up the driveway; it wasn't. I hung my head a little, wondering how many of these weekends were going to end without seeing her. It seemed like forever, and I missed her like crazy; especially when times were difficult.

"She always knows how to make things better." I mumbled to myself as I backed out of the garage and down the driveway. I opened my favorite contacts list and clicked on my wife's icon. I put the phone on speaker mode as I started down the road.

"Hey baby, I just wanted to call and at least hear your voice again." I said as the phone went to voicemail after a few rings. "It seems like this weekend got away from me and I wasn't able to see you. I miss you and I hope you had a good week. I can't wait to hear if you got that promotion you've been wanting. I know you've worked hard for it. I'm really proud of how hard you've been working the past few months to keep things running at home while you're putting in the long hours at work. Call me when you get the chance. I miss you like crazy and I love you so much. I'll text you when I land in Nebraska, and try to call you before bed tonight."

I sudden feeling of overwhelming depression swept over me. This was already the longest few weeks of my life, and shit was only getting busier. I just wanted to see my wife.

"As soon as this is all over, I am taking her on a very long, vacation; we both need it." I mumbled to myself as I precariously navigated the vehicle along the entrance ramp to the highway. I suddenly felt the overwhelming urge to cry. Tears welled up in my eyes again as I maneuvered the steering wheel with only my fingertips. I choked back a sob which threatened to strangle me, painfully tightening my neck muscles. I wiped my eyes on my blazer sleeve and tried to shake my head to clear it. That seemed to only upset the delicate balance already there and brought the throbbing pain back with a vengeance.

"Get it together you fucking pussy." I said to myself. I managed to clear my head for a moment and decided to check in with Lt. Carter. His phone rang for what seemed like an eternity before he finally answered.

"Hey, LT., I'm just letting you know I'm about to pull into the airport; any new developments?"

"None so far; I only just woke up myself. Detective Shirley is taking lead on Lane and our John Doe; the KBI got here around ten O'clock this morning and they're taking lead on the Preston investigation. I don't have any answers for you yet. I can barely hear myself think over the pounding in my head. How are you doing?"

"About the same; the pounding in my head came back a minute ago and I'm just hoping I have no reason to use my weapon in the next forty-eight hours. I can barely grip the son of a bitch." I admitted.

"You shouldn't have any need for it. The plane is chartered by the FBI so it's only you and Federal personnel on board your flight. They've been briefed on the recent events and instructed to focus only on the situation in Irvingdale. I asked Agent Jones to take care of you so you don't have to drive yourself anywhere for the next couple of days until your hands are healed."

"Thanks LT., let me know if we learn anything."

"You got it Bryant; have a safe flight."

CHAPTER SEVEN

If she wasn't already, my wife was sure to be pissed at me when I got home. I was out like a light the second my head hit the pillow at the hotel in Irvingdale. By the time the morning rolled around, the only thing that woke me was the pounding on my door. Knowing the pounding on the door would only continue until I got up, I climbed out of bed, walking with a slight limp as I crossed the room. I observed my failure to lock the door the night before, which was out of character. Standing in the doorway, suited up and sipping coffee from a Styrofoam cup, Agent Jones could tell right away that I had slept in my clothes.

"Hey!" He greeted me, "Shitty night?"

"What other kind could I possibly have? Let's be honest, they're all bad nights."

"I heard about the rookie, how are you holding up?" He asked, changing to a somber tone.

"Like this; hungover and disheveled. It's like I'm getting to string together all the worst days of my life and live them back to back."

"How hungover are you?" Jones asked as he followed me into the room.

"Enough that the pounding in my head is because of the booze and not because of the concussion; but not so hungover that I can't drive or do my job," I replied, digging with my poorly bandaged hands into my suitcase for some pain reliever.

"I guess that's the sweet spot." He said sarcastically.

"Yeah, well I'm coping with a lot; granted, not well, but I'm coping."

"Lt. Carter kinda filled me in on the situation last night. He said you were dealing with some series shit and that anything I could do to help would go a long way."

"He's pretty generous for a supervisor." I acknowledged. "He had to drive me to and from the scene the other night. He was pretty intuitive about my state of mind that night too. I have no idea how I'm going to do another twenty-four weeks of this. There is no way I can ever explain all this to my wife." I filled a plastic cup from the bathroom sink and started chugging water, trying to prevent the hangover from making today even worse.

"Yeah, your wife," Jones said, awkwardly. "I think she will understand what you're trying to accomplish here."

"I just feel like it's been forever since I've seen her." I confessed,

"I know buddy, why don't we get some breakfast and head to the park. They have the Operations Command Center set up already, and they're ready to start around 0830."

"Sounds good, I'll just send my wife a quick text and let her know I was thinking about her."

Jones looked awkward for another moment before replying. "Do what you gotta do, buddy."

I finished sending my wife a text and slipped my other shoe on. I hadn't realized I had one off until I walked back from the bathroom. I needed to lay off the sauce a little. It seemed like I had been hitting the bottle harder than normal lately, and that wasn't like me. Or was it? The past few weeks had been stressing me out more than any other time in my career, and I had clearly not been handling it well.

"Thanks, man." I said to Jones. "Between you and Carter, you guys have really been looking out for me, and I want you to know I really appreciate it. This whole ordeal is nothing any of us wanted, but having a good team makes the whole process suck a lot less."

"That's what we do. Believe it or not, the Feds don't always come in and ruin everything. Sometimes we make a good addition to the team."

"You have at least; I'll take what I can get." I shrugged.

"Let's get breakfast." Said Jones as he helped me put on my blazer.

I had the tallest cup of coffee the café sold and chugged it as fast as the temperature would allow. I tried to blend into the background of the crowd of officers, agents, supervisors and detectives who were at the Operations Command Center. The OCC, as they called it, was nothing more than the inside of a tent with walls to help with the search warrants. There were four houses to hit and all of them had angry residents standing by to make sure none of their property was damaged. Some lucky homeowner was going to be the recipient of a new in-ground pool. Or at least they were going to have the hole in the ground to install one. We were looking for two bodies and hopefully they had been planted next to each other.

I glanced around the tent at the crowd of people decked out in uniforms and suits. The large white tent was walled in on all sides, with nothing but a doorway leading out to the parking lot. A series of lights had been hung from the canopy, ensuring the interior was well-lit for the occasion. Beneath the feet of the tent's occupants, fresh, spring grass was trampled. I had barely managed to look around the park before entering the tent. The sun was my mortal enemy, and I dared not raise my head for long under its ever-punishing glare.

I didn't realize how long I'd been spacing out until I glanced up and everyone was looking at me.

"They were wondering if you could fill the teams in on exactly what Fenton told you." Explained Jones quietly, leaning in over my left shoulder to coach my response..

I cleared my throat before I began. "Fenton described the two victims as twenty something females buried underneath a shed in the back yard of a white house built in the early 1900's. The only other information he provided was that the city of Lincoln would not appreciate one of their historic areas being dug up to recover the bodies. This is all the information he provided. We have Agent Martinez and Agent Davidson here from the FBI's victim recovery team. They are going to spell out for you how this is going to go; Agent Martinez?" I gestured to Maria as she took several steps forward with her bloodhound Major on a leash.

"Thank you, Detective Bryant. We have strict guidelines as part of the cooperation between this investigation and the City of Lincoln. Agent Davidson and I will enter each yard with Major, our bloodhound. No one else will enter until we have positive confirmation from Major of the pres ence of deceased victims buried in the yard. We will be checking every house and every yard with Major. Detective Bryant made the observation last week that sometimes the timeline we have or the events as we know them to be are not the limits of what may have happened. Utilizing Major, we recovered additional bodies from previous unsolved missing person's cases in his jurisdiction. We will be doing that again here. Fenton has proven to be a sadistic, manipulative, and informed son of a bitch. He has information the public does not, and has been wielding it as a weapon against this task force. I want to thank the local Lincoln Police Department for their assistance, and I am going to refer all questions about this operation to either Detective Bryant for big picture issues or Deputy Chief of Police William Parnell, who will be here to oversee this operation."

Deputy Chief Parnell stepped forward and took off his hat.

"The goal here ladies and gentlemen is to do this with as little impact on the local community as possible. Right now, the citizens of Irvingdale have been told this is a joint training exercise with the FBI and other participating agencies. The residents of the home or homes where bodies are located will be informed of the type of investigation being conducted, but all others will be kept in the dark beyond the scope of the search warrant until a formal media notification can be completed. All personnel not escorting a dog will remain within this enclosed tent or the immediate area around the tent. Please try and limit the number of people standing around outside. The media is already poking around and we don't need loose lips sinking ships around here. I will personally be escorting the recovery team and the dog to each house and try to placate the residents as we go. One of my officers will inform those with equipment for digging and imaging as soon as we have identified the location of the bodies. If there are no questions, we will be on our way."

I took another long swig of my coffee while the recovery team and Deputy Chief left the tent. Looking around, I was surprised to see this gathering of Feds and local LEO's different than any other of which I had been a part. Search warrants typically consisted of heavily armed people making a forced entry into a residence, which might contain dangerous or otherwise heavily armed people. Not this time around. I saw Officers with shovels and other various gardening tools. It looked like a photo op for a

Habitat for Humanity work force featuring local law enforcement. No one had a rifle or a shield; no one was checking weapons and racking rounds into their guns. People just stood around and 'shot the shit' while waiting for instructions on where to dig. So it goes with twenty-five year old cold cases.

"How you feeling now?" Terry asked, approaching with another cup of coffee, this time, from the refreshments table.

"Better, thanks for making the extra stop," I said making a 'toasting' gesture at him with my coffee cup and bandaged hand.

"I figured you needed coffee before we got here, not after."

"You would be correct; I'm starting to feel like my old self again." I lied.

"That's what I was going for; hopefully we can wrap this up in one day."

"Good, maybe we be done in a reasonable time so I can get back. I have way too much to do back home to be up here watching an exhumation."

"To me it would have made sense to bring you up after the bodies were recovered and we were piecing together the evidence and comparing it to Fenton's timeline."

"That's all part of Fenton's grand plan. I have to be wherever the action is happening. I can hardly write about this whole process if I'm back-home on the sidelines for all these out of state trips."

"Does Lincoln fit well into Fenton's timeline?" Terry asked.

"There was not a lot of missing persons cases here in the '90's so who knows. I'm hoping your office can get ahold of those files on short notice."

"They started checking into it as soon as we heard from you Saturday. It shouldn't take forever, but it will take a while. Everything from back then is still all paper. They didn't put all their old reports into digital form so we have Junior Agents combing through them for possibilities."

"We can narrow it down further when we find the bodies." I hoped.

"Any new developments on your cases back home?"

"Nothing yet, Terry; I don't suspect I'll hear much until I'm back home. The KBI is handling our rookie and the bomb investigation. The body in the car is going to take a while. It was burned beyond recognition and had to be transported to Kansas City for autopsy. We may not hear anything for a week or so."

"What about your newspaper man?"

"That one will be a little easier since we already have an educated guess on the cause of death. Now all we have to do is find the psychopath behind all this and put him on death row."

"Isn't he already there? I mean; isn't this all Fenton's doing?"

"Fenton may be the man behind the curtain, but this seems out of his method of operation. I could see him leaking information to the media and then tying up the loose end, but that certainly doesn't explain the body in the car or the bomb. Fenton did everything quietly. He took his victims quietly, he killed them in private, and he disposed of their bodies where no one would find them unless he wanted them found. The hysteria around him back home started with the Haylee Marten case. It got so much attention from the media that the fear around town became almost crippling. Two months later another girl went missing. They set curfews, the bars closed early, they had safe ride programs for students and the police department started packing the streets overnight to build reassurance throughout the community. They had to; five women went missing in the Manhattan area that year. It was one of the reasons I became a cop. They were looking to hire a bunch of cops, but they were having recruitment issues at the time. I applied in 2006 as soon as I turned 21 and finished my degree while I was at the academy and field training. It was several years after Hayley Marten disappeared, but women had started dropping off the map left and right again in our region. In September 2006 they found a mass grave with four dead women. They all fit a similar description and had been taken within the past three years from the Manhattan area. A lot of people thought it was human trafficking until the bodies were found. That was a shitty year for everyone. They streamlined the training program and shortened it by a couple weeks. Four out of five new officers went straight to the midnight shift. That's how I got there, that's how I was able to catch Fenton."

"They really sent that many people to the midnights shift?" Terry asked, bewildered.

"Yeah, for the longest time we had maybe eight or ten officers on midnights. After I applied, they bumped that number up to around fifteen or sixteen; twice as many as any other shift."

"Goddamn!" He exclaimed. "I can't believe that actually worked.

Usually throwing bodies at a problem like that helps with public opinion for the department, but rarely yields any results."

"We got lucky." I admitted. "He stayed in our jurisdiction longer than he did anywhere else. It was target rich and he enjoyed the media attention. We found four bodies back then. We had at least eight missing person cases going on though. Haylee was one of them that we never solved until now. There might be three more victims out there somewhere waiting for Fenton to disclose their locations."

"How many of them do you think we found at the park?"

"None," I replied. "The other bodies we found were buried on sites with well-publicized completion and build dates. Fenton was behind bars for all of them and they were only buried enough to allow the sites to be completed after the digging was done. Otherwise we'd have found them back then when the digging started. We have a dozen missing person cases that have gone unsolved. We're hoping the other three bodies we found will solve some of them."

"Do you think you have a possible copycat killer?"

"Doubtful, they were all men. I have no idea who we dug up last week. The autopsies are stacking up in Kansas City. We haven't brought them this many bodies since Fenton was locked away. Now he starts talking and we have a long wait list for autopsies again. It's a fucking nightmare any time he's involved."

I was interrupted by the sensation of my phone vibrating in my pocket. I excused myself from the tent and answered it outside, squinting against the bright morning sun."

"Hello?"

"Bryant its Carter; I've got a slight update for you if you have a minute."

"Sure thing L.T., I'm waiting for the recovery team to locate bodies anyways. What's up?"

"We went to make the victim notification to Lane's wife, Emma; turns out she's missing too. No one has seen or heard from her since Saturday afternoon. Their kids have been at Tim's parent's house since Saturday. We didn't know what to tell the kids so we asked the grandparents to keep it quiet for a while. That won't be easy; we didn't tell them what had happened yet either, not with the investigation ongoing like it is. We haven't been able to locate Emma Lane anywhere so far. We tried to ping her phone, but it's apparently turned off. The last record the cell phone company had, it was at her house. The last call she got, was from Tim around 1700 hours."

"That's around the time he was supposed to meet me behind the Home Depot. He never showed; maybe she would be able to tell us why. Where are they on the autopsies in Kansas City?" I asked.

"Well they put a hold on our Park victims while they push forward with the active new homicide cases from Sunday morning. Preston was killed with an improvised explosive device with some type of aerosol dispersant. Between the fire he inhaled and the blow to the head he took when he hit the ground, they don't think he felt much. Tim Lane was just as we thought; death by asphyxiation due to hanging. He was still alive when our killer hoisted him up there. We "pinged" his phone and it was moving this morning. When we tried to keep track of it, it was shut off and we lost it."

"So someone has his phone in town?"

"It looks that way; unfortunately we have no way of determining who or where, so there's a nice "fuck you" to start off this investigation," said Carter, sounding frustrated.

"That seems like its par for the course; we either have dead ends or U-turns it seems. Has Preston's family been notified?"

"Yeah; it happened first thing this morning. Ellis notified his girlfriend, and I notified his parents. They're pretty shook up. We haven't lost an officer since 1987, and this one kinda took us all by surprise."

"How did his girlfriend take the news?" I asked, knowing the answer.

"Like you'd expect; instead of seeing her boyfriend come home after the night shift she was greeted by a police Sergeant and a Chaplin. We assigned an officer from our Peer Support Team to look after her, so hopefully we can make this situation suck a little less for her."

"Nothing can possibly prepare you for that front door notification. It just crumbles your world," I said. "Now to change the subject to something less personal, where are we on the identification of the body from the car?"

"That's gonna take a while. There was nothing, but a skeleton and odd tissue remaining. They have to get DNA and dentals to be sure. The KBI have stepped in and are pushing hard to get results from this incident through the backlog of evidence at their labs. Normally this might take weeks to get, they're promising results within the next couple days."

"I'm glad we're getting some inter-agency cooperation through all this." I admitted, relieved.

"I know we have a lot of issues administratively in this state, but losing an officer in the line of duty makes everyone play nice for a while."

"Hang on a second L.T.," I said into the phone as Terry approached me from the tent.

"They just wrapped up the search at the first house; nothing so far."

"Thanks for the update, Terry; sorry about that L.T.," I apologized.

"Don't worry about it, Bryant; I know you have a lot of shit going on too. I was instructed to tell you to get back here as soon as they have bodies out of the ground. They have coroners and FBI agents ready for identification of any bodies recovered and they're going to conference call us twice a day with updates. I've been authorized to recall you as early as Wednesday morning if they have everything well in hand up there."

"I don't see any reason for me to be here past Wednesday, so that sounds good to me. I just have to fulfil the basic requirements of the deal and make sure I have all the information for the story."

"How's that coming by the way?" He asked, knowing the answer.

"It's like documenting the worst shit ever and then having to reread it over and over again for grammatical errors. Progress is slow, but I'm working to streamline the process so it doesn't read like the world's longest, most boring suicide note." I replied, realizing the dramatic approach I was taking.

"Well keep it up; do you remember the deadlines for the first volume?"

"The first eight weeks have to be completed by late May, the next ten weeks by the beginning of August and the rest is due for completion by November. The writing may not be an issue, but I can only assume the publishing aspect will be a total bitch. Have we had any luck in that realm?"

"We've had a couple of "fuck you" replies and a few that say they want to see completed manuscripts before they pretend to be even slightly interested." Carter advised.

"So they want the first manuscript in hand and then they'll think about it. That sounds about right; good thing we're not in any kind of hurry." I said, facetiously.

"We just gotta have a hardback copy of volume one before July, how hard can it be?"

"It can take as much as eighteen months to go from manuscript to published work so I foresee us having issues with these deadlines. Is no one interested in the confessions of the world's sickest fucking guy?" I asked.

"They're interested in the story, not so much how we're getting it or what we're giving up to make it happen. They all think this is pretty sick, even coming from the US Government."

"We all know it's sick; somebody just has to get on board sooner than later." I added in frustration.

"Just make sure you're writing as much as you can in your down time." He instructed.

"What down time?" I quipped.

"Exactly, make some and stay as current as you can. It will prevent us having to turn it all in at once."

"Will do," I said and hung up the phone. I glared at my phone for a minute. The sun reflecting off of it only made my head hurt worse, but I was past the point of caring. My life had become one big headache with which I was growing uncomfortably complacent. I couldn't remember the last time I had been pain free, but having a car blow up in front of me hadn't helped at all.

"The second house is clear."

"Thanks, Terry," I called back. I rubbed my head and looked around for some shade outside the tent. I hated being in the sun, but I hated being around all these people too. I didn't know ninety-nine percent of them, and wasn't one for small talk. I wished then for the clarity to have gone to the hospital Sunday instead of drinking myself to sleep again. Pain meds would have been a welcome asset to my ever dwindling level of motivation. I liked to stay busy, but not this fucking busy. Busy to me meant coming in once in a while to help with an active case and a search warrant. I spent enough time typing reports as it was without adding the memoirs of the world's shittiest person to the equation. Six months; no vacation days, no sick days and no weekends; fuck my life. Fuck this fucking story, I'm already sick of writing it. Go fuck yourself Fenton, you world class douche canoe.

Talking shit on Fenton, even in my own mind, helped brighten my spirits a little. I was out in the fresh air and sunlight while he was in a concrete cell hoping his memories of women were enough to get him off. Special chains with the sleeve ending in thick, rough leather mittens had been fashioned just so Fenton would stop jerking off to the female jurors the first three trials. It's not as if the judges well placed "Contempt of Court" ruling was going to increase Fenton's prison stay at all, but it was entertaining to watch him struggle to make his hands accessible for the remainder of his trials. After firing his defense attorney, he had given away his say in the jury selection process. A parade of young college girls, young mothers and classic grandmothers made up the majority of the juries from then on. Typically seven or more of them were women, and the young ones were placed down front. The frustration on Fenton's face had been epic. He looked like an old quarterback playing a cold weather game; hands stuck in the sleeve as if he was warming them for the next play. Only HE couldn't take them out. After that he switched to bench trials, nothing but a judge staring at him in disgust. It hadn't changed the outcome of the trials, but it was slightly less torturous for Fenton with each passing conviction.

I drained my coffee and looked around for a trash can. Across the street, a flurry of activity in the third house indicated Major had located the graves of our victims. I squinted against the sunlight, wreaking havoc on my hangover, at the residents of the third house as Deputy Chief Parnell informed them of what was about to happen in their back yard. Deputy Chief Parnell appeared to be trying to comfort them, but it was not going well.

"Oh, it's show time now." Terry said, walking up next to me.

"They look exactly as I pictured they would be. After all, finding out you have been living in a house with dead bodies in the back yard for all these years would be unsettling to me too."

"Did they not wonder about that particularly green area of grass in the yard?" Terry asked.

"I'm sure they just ignored it. Better to live in ignorance than find out the truth. I just feel bad they have to move out of their house for the next few days."

"Seriously; have you seen the hotel they're planning to put them in until the recovery is complete? They are getting all expenses paid by the

FBI until this whole process is complete. I wish I could afford to stay there even one night."

"The Holiday Inn Express not doing it for you week after week?" I joked.

"That's funny." He replied, "I miss my pillow-top at home."

"Well, that's what you get for pampering yourself, buddy." I smirked at him.

We watched for a few minutes while the Deputy Chief finished talking with the residents. A uniformed officer jogged across the street to join them before escorting the couple into their house. The Deputy Chief crossed the street towards us shaking his head.

"This shit better be worth it." He said, through his teeth.

"People are missing loved ones buried in that back yard. Whether or not it's an inconvenience to us all, and I assure you, no one is more inconvenienced then me; solving these outdated cold cases is bringing closure to people from all across the Midwest. I know for a fact this will be worth the trouble. I've been the bearer of bad news to one family already; it's one of the worst things we have to do in this profession. Keep this in mind; this is very likely one of several burial sites in this state. Fenton was only tried and convicted of one murder here in Nebraska. This shows his time here was longer than we first thought. We're in Lincoln; the other victim was found in Omaha. There's a good chance this won't be our last trip to Nebraska."

"Let's just hope it's your last trip to Irvingdale," said Parnell as he turned and walked away.

"Fine by me," I said quietly to Terry before gesturing over my shoulder. "Then we don't have to work with deputy chief douche nozzle over there."

"Don't let him get under your skin."

"It's not just him; he's just the first of many in a long line of administrative assholes that are going to hover over our heads with their condescending tone and criticism."

"Nice to hear you're to the cynical stage of your career, finally." Terry said, shaking his head.

"Been there for about ten years now," I replied. "My point is, the task force has to go around to every victim recovery all around the goddamn country and these departments want to act like we planted the bodies in their jurisdictions ourselves. Trust me; this whole situation would suck if all hundred or so victims were located in my own county. None of us want to trapes around to different states looking for decades old murder victims, so I wish they'd stop pretending any of this is our fault"

Terry stopped and looked at me for a moment, watching me locate my sunglasses in my jacket pocket and placed them mercifully over my eyes.

"How's that hangover treating you?"

"Just like before, but with more sunlight burning holes in my retinas."

"Get some more coffee and then start chugging water. It's been a while since I've recovered from a bender, but that's the way I used to do it."

"This isn't my first hangover, Terry, but I appreciate what you're trying to do."

The crew from the tent made their way across the street to the house and filed one at a time around into the back yard. We watched for a few moments until we saw the residents stumble out the front door carrying suitcases. The officer escorting them helped load their luggage into their SUV, and then followed them down the road in his patrol unit.

"Do you wanna go over and take a look?" Terry asked.

"Not yet; I'm planning to wait until they reach the bodies, otherwise we're just more people standing around watching cops dig a hole in the yard."

"Sound point; do you wanna use this time to do a little writing?"

"I left my laptop at the hotel; if I stare at that screen in my current state, my head will split in half."

"Care to help us review cold case files? We collected all the hard copy files over in the tent, and we're narrowing them down."

"Anything's better than just standing around."

————

"Detective Bryant!" called a voice from outside the tent.

I turned from the stack of missing person files and caught a glimpse of the Deputy Chief as he poked his head into the tent. He gestured for me to join him outside the tent.

"Come on Terry, I bet this will concern both of us."

We had narrowed the stack of files down to six; all of them fit the profile of Fenton's victims and all went missing within a three year time period in the early nineties.

"Let's go see which of the six missing persons they found." Said Terry as we put on our jackets, stretched, and stepped outside.

"Now Detective Bryant, you told me we were looking for two bodies is that correct?" Parnell asked. He waved me off before I could say anything, "Because for some reason, we went on a recovery mission for two people and we stumbled on what appears to be a 'Pol Pot killing field' in that back yard. We aren't even sure we're done yet."

"How many bodies do we have?" I inquired.

"Four; so far and we're positive we aren't done yet. How is it possible to be this incompetent?"

"Hey! Listen, asshole, feel free to be as fucking upset as you want, but this is hardly outside the realm of possibilities. We have six possible victims and it would not be out of the question for all six of them to be buried in that backyard. The last time Fenton told me where to find one body, I found four, those four resulted in three more fresh dead bodies, one of them a young officer from my department. So why don't you think for half a second before you open your fucking mouth to me about shit not being what it seems. I am here because I have to be. I am here to help in whatever way I can, but it had better start with an iota of respect."

"That's enough, Bryant," advised Terry, quietly.

"You insolent son of bitch," Parnell spat with contempt. "I'm calling your supervisor. You are fucking finished."

"You have no power over me; I'm working as part of the Joint Task Force with the FBI, so I am here as a courtesy and nothing more. If you have a problem with me, take it up with the Department of Justice; on everything outside of my jurisdiction, I answer to them. So blow it out your ass, I'm going over to check on the burial site."

I stormed off before the Deputy Chief could say anything else. That was sure to come back and bite me, but at this point I didn't care. I was done listening to people bitch at me about things outside of my control. Fenton was already ruining my life enough without every Chief of Police from here to Arkansas blaming me. I crossed the street slow enough to make traffic wait for me; making a scene as I did so. I ignored the honking horns until I reached the other side and ducked under the crime scene tape. I waved my badge at the officer pulling scene security duties and turned the corner into the back yard.

"How many bodies do we have?" I asked when I reached the dig site.

"Five; and that's the last of them," hollered one of the CSI techs meticulously scraping and brushing mud off a set of bones.

"No sign of a sixth missing person in that big ass hole?"

"Sorry Detective Bryant; just the five. We checked the whole yard, this spot lit up like a Christmas tree when we used the scanning equipment."

"Anything that makes these victims stand out from the usual dead bodies you've uncovered?"

"If you're talking about being wrapped in plastic, two of them were; if you're talking about red rags stuffed in their mouths, the other three all had them. I've never seen anything like this before, have you?"

"Twelve times so far, this brings us to fifteen and counting." I replied.

"So this is something specific you were looking for in this case?" The tech inquired without looking up.

"Yes it is; it is the calling card we were expecting to confirm. Now we just have to identify them."

"That will take a little time, but we have like five agencies involved so it shouldn't take as long as usual, especially when we get them to the lab."

"Let's hope not, now if you'll excuse me, I'm going to find a new way to piss off your Deputy Chief."

"He's not my chief, but it shouldn't take much; seems like he walks around with his panties about ninety-five percent bunched."

"Well, mission accomplished I guess, I already bunched them the rest of the way. I guess that means I'm leaving for dinner."

"I'll be right here in this hole if you need me." The CSI tech hollered as I walked out of the yard.

Terry met me at the crime scene tape outside the fence.

"Oh, he's pissed now; you know its way fucking early to be pissing in someone else's pool right?" He cautioned. "We have so many more pools in which to swim, so maybe tread lightly with the brass before you get shit-canned for being a smart-ass."

"I could only get so lucky; they wouldn't fire me at this point unless I paraded down Main Street with my dick in one hand, shooting my gun off indiscriminately."

"That was graphic; why can't you just put on a professional front for the next six months until you get back to your cushy desk job?" Terry asked.

"I would love to, but I'm not going back to that any time soon; after this I have to do the press for the book, book signings, lectures at police departments and criminal psychology classes all across the country. This nightmare doesn't end for me at the completion of these investigations; it just turns into a circus with more cameras. I don't think I'm going to get my life back any time soon."

"Is that why the booze?"

"Yeah that's part of it; I'm having a hard time managing to wrap my head around the fact that I'm never getting off of this shipwreck. We're up to seventeen victims recovered already and there are so many more to go. We have to notify next of kin, provide the public with some form of explanation all while trying to figure out who the fuck is still trying to kill us. This whole thing wrecked my hometown for years; now we're in another city uncovering five more bodies. It may have been twenty-five years ago, but shit like this lingers. There's no way he was as prolific a serial killer as he claims without some of these bodies being recovered already. They called him the Southside Sadist in Manhattan. Who knows what they called him in every other town he ravaged?"

"I think it all depends on if they find the bodies during the crime spree; these are all just missing person cases from the nineties, but who knows. The next town we're in might be different." Terry offered.

"I know; between the never ending bad press and the "Odyssey by Psychopath" I'm writing in my free time, I'm having a hard time mentally keeping it between the mustard and the mayo on this little journey of ours. If it doesn't give me an incurable condition, it will almost certainly be the end of my career. This is only the second week; I'm miserable twenty-four hours a day already, and I've only had to do one family notification so far. There might be a hundred more and each one of them is slowly draining my will to continue. I have no support system anymore; my parents are both dead, and I haven't talked to my wife in what seems like an eternity. How is anyone supposed to survive being in my shoes?" I demanded.

"I wish I could give you some kind of life changing advice that would put all of this into perspective, but I can't." Terry admitted. "All I can say is that if you don't find a way to see the greater good in all of this its going to kill you. I know you've been saying you don't want a penny from all of this, but let's face it; you're doing most of the work and having to deal with the 'poster child of evil' every week. By the time you get off this hellish ride you're going to be at or near the fifteen year mark and eligible for retirement benefits. Use the money from the book to keep you going until you can start drawing on your pension," he suggested.

"What would I do with all that free time?"

"Keep writing, start a business, do some consulting for the Bureau, take a daily dump on Fenton's grave, maybe learn a new language or travel the world. All I'm saying is that if you need it, sit down and talk with someone; or give me a call and we can get shitfaced together and work out our issues. I know what you're going through, and maybe while we're at it, I can talk about how my wife wants to pop out a baby, even though I spend most of the year on the road, and will be for the next few years."

I paused to think about it for a little bit. I wasn't the only one on the team dealing with these issues. These issues weren't the only ones any of us had.

"I could get drunk and work through some shit." I said with a shrug.

"I've got a bottle we can open, as long as you can pace yourself." Terry cautioned.

"I'll give it a try." I tried to reassure him.

"We're gonna try this once and see how it goes. You have to find a way to make this a therapeutic 'choir practice' so to speak. If this turns out to be a bad idea, we leave out the booze in the future."

"Deal;" I said shaking his hand. "Let's get smashed and forget about dead bodies for a little while."

We were at the park so long the sun was starting to set by the time Terry drove us back to the hotel. I listened as Terry described the twenty year old bottle of scotch we were going to be drinking when we got back. It was nice to forget about my own misery for a little while and listen while Terry described his wife's ever increasing urge to have a baby and buy a house outside of the city. Terry was only a few years younger than me, and it was nice to see his ambition and drive hadn't been dampened by his career choice. Cynicism went hand in hand with law enforcement after about the first year or so. Once you'd seen the worst of people and had them lie to your face, despite the overwhelming evidence against them, it was hard to see the good in people anymore. My cynicism had come even earlier in my career after capturing Fenton. Interviews with him and watching his demeanor as he taunted and teased every female officer or juror made seeing the good, in anyone, nearly impossible. It was in

Fenton's DNA to be this evil; the irony was that his DNA betrayed him and got him eleven murder convictions.

Terry seemed to be full of life and energy, and I could only assume it was because he took care of himself. Microwave dinners and whiskey had been the majority of my diet over the past twelve months or so leading to the slow deterioration of my physique, and unhealthy weight loss. I had been on the hefty side until recently, but I could hardly claim credit for my transformation. When I felt like eating, I didn't feel like cooking. When I felt like drinking, I didn't eat much, and lately I always felt like drinking.

"Oh that reminds me; my wife wanted me to invite you over for dinner the next time you're in Kansas City. She figured you were probably in need of a good home cooked meal given the events of the past year or so." Terry invited.

"That sound's good to me; there's bound to be more autopsies running through the regional office in KC so I should be there again real soon." I replied.

"You'll be glad you did. My wife is a world class cook. My biggest problem raising a family with her is making sure they don't get fat."

"That seems like a good problem to have." I said as we reached the hotel.

"We'll see; she's got the baby fever like I've never seen before; I may just have to knock her up."

"You'd make a hell of a dad, Terry. You're already taking care of me like some big baby with a drinking problem. How hard could it be after caring for a lush like me?"

"At least I can take the bottle away from a baby." He replied with a laugh.

"Scout's honor, I'll try to take it easy tonight." I offered.

"I'll see to that," he replied.

I took a moment to think about our conversation up to that point. Terry genuinely seemed to care about how I fared through this ordeal. I didn't seem to care at all. Up until the bomb at the park, the entire operation seemed pointless to me. We could solve cold cases, but it seemed to lack meaning, which was something I desperately missed about my job.

Day to day on patrol, you get the chance to respond to a call where you get to make an immediate impact on someone's life. CPR on a seemingly lifeless person could end up saving their life. Being first on scene to a major accident where you provide life-saving first aid, gave you something to hold onto as you came into work day after day. Investigations seemed to lack that level of response, so it took a lot more effort to see the impact, and believe you were making a difference.

Maybe that would be the key. Maybe it was time for me to hang up the suit and tie and return to uniformed patrol.

CHAPTER EIGHT

Choir practice went better than I had expected. Terry poured the Scotch at a reasonable pace, preventing me from downing the entire bottle, like the American whiskey I typically consumed. Having someone to vent to, even for an hour or two made a lot of difference. I was used to starting my evening drinking with a clear head and going to bed forgetting what issues I'd been working through. This always ensured none of them ever got solved; typically making them worse. Terry was what my dad would have called, "Good people;" kind, considerate, hard-working, and dependable. He opted for the FBI instead of law school, which made him a friend instead of an enemy.

Over my ten years in law enforcement I had dealt with plenty of lawyers, and even the good ones could be insufferable. Terry and I had extended family from the Boston area who lived within miles of each other. I had never been to Boston, but Terry ensured me we'd be going for a Red Sox game when this was all over. Terry's wife had gone to law school so we took turns throwing out our favorite lawyer jokes. We ended the night chatting briefly about the situation at hand, and attempting to find new perspectives which might prove helpful. Realizing we should have started on this topic instead of ending, we parted ways without any major epiphanies.

Scotch had a different type of effect on me than my usual booze.

Someone else controlling the pace helped a lot which gifted me with the smallest hangover I could remember having in years. A hot shower and a cup of hotel room coffee had my head clear enough to review the missing persons cases I'd spent hours reviewing the precious day. Six met the criteria for Fenton, but we'd only discovered five bodies. For anyone else I might think nothing of it, but something had been missing. Fenton's fifth victim in Manhattan, Kansas had been taken after the discovery of the graves of the first four. From all indicators, Fenton had been on his way out of town when I happened to cross his path. If he hadn't been planning to take girl number five to the old grave site, he was planning to take her with him or dump her along the way. Of Fenton's first eleven convictions, one had been found in a dumpster in Missouri in a region with two other missing women. Another had been discovered in a National Wildlife Refuge in an area of Iowa around which half a dozen other missing women were reported. I tried to piece all this together on the way to Terry's room.

It was my turn to wait on him as he nursed his hangover. I had been hitting the bottle hard for months, but Terry was not as immune to casual binge drinking as I was. He wore huge sunglasses out to the car that morning and threw me the keys. My hands, while still a bit stiff and uncomfortable, were healed enough to lose the bandages. Catching the keys was still not an easy task, but it was far better without the bandages in the way.

"If you could, take me to that same coffee house on the way to the park, I'm gonna need all the muffins and coffee they can give me." He advised.

"You got it," I told him. I drove us in silence to the coffee joint. Terry rubbed his head as we waited in the drive-thru lane to place his order. I smiled a bit as I found life on the other end of a hangover to be quite refreshing. My sunglasses were due to the sunshine, and not as a hangover necessity. I had time to eat breakfast and drink my coffee before leaving the hotel instead of having to grab them at the last minute. I was too excited about getting to work and figuring things out. Fortunately, this helped me skip the typical extra five snoozes on the alarm clock and climb out of bed on time. I hadn't felt this way about detective work since my first week in investigations.

"I think I may be on the verge of a breakthrough, I just can't put my finger on it." I told Terry as I handed him the large coffee and bag of muffins."

"Great, tell me about it while I crush these muffins." He replied in a subdued tone."

"You helped review the out-of-state cases at the start of the taskforce, right?" I asked.

"Yeah," he said, around a mouthful of blueberry muffin.

"There were two mass graves located and then three individual victims found besides them correct?"

"That sounds about right." He confirmed.

"Do you remember anything special about the other three victims?" I asked.

"The best I can remember it was, one in a dumpster, one in a shallow grave and one getting loaded into the back of a van; why?"

"What's the one thing they all have in common?" I asked, prodding him to see the connections I had made.

"Nothing; three different states, spread out over twenty plus years; what are you getting at?"

"Sloppy; they were all sloppy like they were done in a hurry," I said. "The first four bodies in Manhattan were found when a guy's dog started digging up the newest body. The fifth one was pure luck; the one in Missouri was in a dumpster with all of Fenton's signature signs. That was after the town of Maryville was in a full panic with two other girls missing over a five month period of time. They had state and Federal agencies converging on the town when the third girl went missing, and they found her body the next day after the Feds arrived. The Green Meadow girl was found by Park Rangers in the world's shallowest grave. The one thing all of these three victims have in common was they were disposed of quickly and ineffectively. Some of them were found by chance, but they all stood a better chance of being found than the mass graves at Tenkiller Lake and Tuttle Creek Reservoir."

"So you think we're only finding the one's he's too lazy to properly hide?"

"I'm thinking when shit hits the fan; he dumps the last girl on the way out of town or at his earliest convenience. Then he splits town and starts over fresh somewhere."

"How does that help us today?"

"I think they found our sixth missing person twenty years ago and don't realize it." I said.

"How do you figure? Even twenty years ago they had dental X-Rays to help identify bodies, what makes you think they made a mistake?"

"It's just a hunch, can you think of any particular groups of people who might get reported missing, but never had the luxury of modern dentistry."

"Crackheads, maybe," Terry surmised as he peeled the wrapper off another muffin.

"Or prostitutes," I said as I became more confident in my theory.

Terry ate his breakfast in silence for a moment.

"Hey, Bryant; don't take this the wrong way, but I bet if you can get off the booze, you could still be a hell of a detective."

"I'm not making any promises." I said, navigating the car into the lot at the park. "There are still some bad memories inside me I'm trying to drown."

"I just figured since you were doing all the thinking this morning, I'd give you some food for thought."

"Point taken," I said, climbing out of the car. I buttoned my coat against the wind and walked towards the tent as fast as I could.

Deputy Chief Parnell gave me a nasty look as I entered the tent. I was certain he was still pissed about yesterday, so it was time to bury the hatchet.

"Deputy Chief," I greeted him.

I approached the table where he and several local detectives were sitting around reviewing files.

"We have enough problems around here Detective Bryant, without your adding to them. Maybe you have more bodies we need to know about?"

"I don't sir, but you do."

"Excuse me?"

"I sat here with your detectives yesterday and combed through six missing person's files with them. We had five bodies in that back yard, and it's probably a safe bet they were all people we were looking for in those files. I think it's possible the sixth missing woman may have been found already. Have you had anyone comb through unsolved homicides from this time period to see if any of them match?"

"Ah, so yesterday you showed us how incompetent you are, and now you're calling us incompetent?"

"Not incompetent sir, ill equipped. DNA wasn't as widely used back in the early nineties in identifying bodies, but we have the full force of the FBI and the DOJ behind us now. It's possible a body was found months or even years after it went missing and because it wasn't easily identifiable it probably went unsolved. Especially if it was someone who you had reason to believe died of natural causes, like a junkie."

The Deputy Chief didn't say anything for a moment and I could tell he was remembering something.

"A junkie would have been overlooked if no immediate evidence of foul play was found," he said quietly.

"Or if someone gave you reason to think it was natural causes," I replied.

"Or an overdose," he said. "Not natural causes', an unattended death; It would have been completely overlooked."

"You have someone in mind already, don't you?"

"Thompson," Deputy Chief Parnell said ignoring me for a moment. "Get your ass over to the archives and evidence building; pull me a Jane Doe case from the spring of '94 found out at Holmes Lake. Get it here in the next thirty minutes or clear out your desk. Someone brief me on the six missing person's cases."

The detectives spent the next forty-five minutes presenting the details of the six cases until Thompson returned with the cold case file.

"Thompson, start spitting out the details of that case," Parnell barked, adding instructions to the team as Thomson read off each detail.

"March 12, 1994; unattended death report filed. Located at Holmes Lake Golf Course they found one unidentified female, blonde hair..."

"Put aside the missing person's with anything but blonde hair; precede Thompson...."

"Approximately five feet six inches tall...

"Does that narrow it down at all?"

"Sir, we're down to three cases meeting that description," said one of the other detectives.

"Approximately sixteen to eighteen years old..." Thompson continued.

"No help..."

"Needle with heroin residue still in the body, tourniquet still on her left arm, approximately two months pregnant..."

"Here it is sir; 'Alicia Bonner' eighteen year old reported missing in December of 1993 by a coworker," I said snatching the file off of the table.

"What was she last seen wearing?" Parnell asked.

"A red Burger King uniform with a pair of black pants," I replied, handing him the file.

"How do you know this is the one? There's nothing in this report about her being pregnant or using drugs."

"Of course not, she was eighteen working a fast food job and she was new in town. She wouldn't have confided in someone she barely knew, according to that report she had only been at that job for three weeks. Look what the reporting party gave as a statement; she often looked like she was sick or nauseous, missed work four times in three weeks and walked to work. She a: had no car, b; lived close by or c; she was homeless d; had a drug problem or e; was pregnant at the time; I passed a Burger King on the way here on 17th Street, any chance that one was there in 1994?"

"Yeah it was there in 1994," said the Deputy Chief slowly.

"And you know this for a fact don't you, because if I'm not mistaken, that's your name at the bottom of the missing person case isn't it?"

I watched as every head slowly turned towards the Deputy Chief who still had his head down, appearing to be staring at the report. He sighed in frustration.

"There was nothing to go on, not even a picture. Her coworker said the girl seemed like she was in trouble; made every indication that she needed the job and would be staying for a while. When she didn't show up for three straight days the coworker got worried and filed the report as a precaution. She couldn't even be certain if the girl was truly missing or not. I had nothing to go on so the case went inactive. There was nothing for me to do, but be on the lookout for an eighteen year old blonde girl with nausea. They found this girl month's later out at the golf course and no one made the connection. I remember that spring 'cause they were finishing up the golf course and found her in the parking lot. I wasn't there, but I heard about it. Even I didn't make that connection," he said.

"No one is blaming you for what you did at the time; nobody is perfect. We have resources available now that were just a dream back in the nineties. But its details like this that we have to be aware of when we're writing reports and especially now when we're reviewing them." I said to the entire tent. "We've all 'phoned in' a case that's going nowhere. But when we comb through these old reports, we have to be looking past the obvious and start delving into the implied. This isn't normal police work; we are hunting down the trail of bodies left by a psychopath, and every minutia of every detail could tell us who someone is, where they came from and what might have happened to them. We are playing the worlds sickest game of connect the dots. When comparing cold cases to missing person cases to long deceased bodies just located, sometimes you have to create dots based on the narrative and see if they fit. I firmly believe after speaking with Richard Allen Fenton over the past two weeks that there are upwards of fifty victims still to be identified as his. Some of these have already been found; others still need to be located and brought home to their loved ones. This girl Alicia, someone out there is missing her and wondering what the hell happened to her all those years ago. They deserve their closure, and the chance to grieve over their loss. Notifications will be handled by me and Agent Jones whenever possible. I need everyone to divide up into teams of two for assignments. I gestured at each team as I continued. "You two, I want you to scour every yearbook photo from every school in a fifty mile radius from 1992 and 1993, these are the most likely options for an eighteen year old girl to still be pictured. Work more with the first name than the second, it's possible if she was using drugs or running from somewhere that she used a different last name. If you can't find her, expand your search radius. You two; find this coworker who is listed as the reporting party, find the owner and manager of the Burger King from 1993 and 1994 and interview them. We need every bit of information they can provide as far as address and hopefully, if there is a God, a social security number for Alicia."

"I'll join that team," said Deputy Chief Parnell.

"Fine by me," I replied. "You two, get down to the City and pull me records for the past thirty years on this house across the street, I want every owner, tenant, relative, and guest that's set foot in this house in a decade around these murders. The median year is 1993; who lived here, where did they go and why did they leave? Thompson, you're with Agent Jones and I, bring us up to speed on this Jane Doe case and see to it that all evidence gathered that still exists makes it to this tent in the next half hour or else clean out your desk." Thompson gave me an odd look so I continued. "I'm just fucking with you Thompson, as fast as possible; everyone's dismissed."

The tent cleared out in a hurry, leaving Terry and I behind.

"Shit, you're a whole different person when you're sober." Terry chuckled before taking a big gulp from his coffee.

"I know; it's almost enough to get me to stop drinking." I said with a smile, "Almost."

"So what are we doing while everyone else runs around doing all the bitch work?"

"Terry, you and I are headed to the coroner's office to see if they've managed to identify any of the bodies. If no one is back after that, we're going for a tour of the house, just to see if we can figure out what the hell this place was that it could casually hide five bodies for twenty years without anything seeming out of the ordinary."

Terry and I went back to the car and headed to the coroner's office.

"When did you realize that was his missing person report?" Terry inquired.

"Yesterday when we were reviewing them; it wasn't until he got defensive about it that I decided to point it out to everyone. Parnell's from a different breed of police officer. He was an officer back before technology made it easy and efficient to be one. He acted like I had done something wrong; I thought I'd show him what it felt like to get called out."

"That's funny, 'because you know nobody in that tent including us would have done anything different at the time." Terry admitted.

"Oh I know that; he was making a scene yesterday so I took an easy jab at him. The real problem is; he is overseeing this investigative effort and clearly hadn't read his old report or any of the missing person's reports prior to today. He can't expect anything of his officers which he isn't willing to do himself. I didn't call him out on the mistake he made twenty years ago; I called him on the one he made yesterday. As soon as I deduced the connection between the two cases he made the connection and did the right thing. As far as he and I go, I consider us even. He did the right thing when the time came, I can respect that."

———————

Dr. Lydia Elmore was a widely respective coroner who had signed on to assist with any autopsies resulting from investigations in Nebraska, and anywhere else her assistance was needed. True to her word she had been standing by the moment the bodies were exhumed from the back yard and had her team transport them one at a time to the lab so she could get started on the autopsies. She had her staff work through the night to clean and examine the bodies before she went back over everything again in the morning. The stack of coffee cups on the desks and in the trash told us she and her staff had been diligent in their work, putting in long hours while the rest of us had been sleeping.

"Dr. Elmore, I'd like to introduce you to Detective James Bryant." Terry said as we entered the lab.

Dr. Elmore held up her finger as we approached and continued to stare into the microscope for another minute. Terry and I stood awkwardly by, exchanging glances with her staff that nodded and shrugged at us. The staff members quickly ducked their eyes back to their work when they saw Dr. Elmore look up from her work.

"Detective Bryant, it's an honor to meet you. I'm Lydia Elmore," she said. She slipped her gloves off one at a time and then removed her surgical mask. Dr. Elmore shook my hand and flashed a big smile at us as she waved us over to the five surgical tables with distinctly deteriorated remains on them. I was all too eager to follow Dr. Elmore over to the tables as her black skirt ended right at the knees and hugged her incredible figure as it disappeared under the back of her lab coat. Her legs were toned and tanned to the perfect degree, making it hard not to wonder how she managed to tan with the cold weather just now ending. I caught myself in need of a reply having lost myself staring longer than I should.

"The honor is mine, Dr. Elmore. I was very pleased to hear someone of your reputation signed on to help us."

"Please, call me Lydia. I get the feeling we're going to be working together quite a bit before all this is said and done." She advised.

"I'm just happy to get to know the people I'll be dealing with during my time here in Nebraska. It's already been pretty eventful." I offered.

"Five bodies in one day; that meets my standard for eventful," she said; shaking her head, causing a single lock of her long brown hair to escape the tight bun which held it in place. "Tommy, can you bring me the charts?"

"They're all set back out at the head of each set of remains, like you requested." He replied.

"Thank you, Tommy," she said, whipping out the first set of charts. "Go tell everyone to take an hour break, grab a nap and a bite to eat. I want everyone back at eleven to start trace evidence analysis and paperwork."

"Yes Doctor," said Tommy. Taking off his gloves and walking into the next room where the other staff members were already working on paperwork.

"You run a pretty good operation around here." I commented, impressed.

"It takes respect to earn respect; I treat them like family so they feel bad when they let me down. That makes them work harder and keeps the environment professional. These interns and doctoral candidates working for me know what a good review and recommendation can do for their careers. I hand pick them every year and each batch goes out with quality recommendations. They know why they're here. Now, let's move on to victim number one."

I found myself taken with Dr. Elmore as her leadership skills and natural beauty seemed to create a bold combination to compliment her enchanting personality.

"Any trouble working with remains this old?" Terry asked.

"Not even close; my specialty in my free time is remains from both World Wars as well as some from the Civil War. 1993 is a walk in the park compared to remains discovered from the 1860's. Victim number one is a twenty-four year old female with brown hair, five feet six inches tall with indicators of both drug use and various STD's. Victim one died by strangulation, was wrapped in plastic and was one of the last two bodies to be buried in the back yard. Victim one was confirmed by DNA, old dental records and medical records to be Christina Ann Richardson. Christina was treated by the local hospital for both gonorrhea and Hepatitis C. Christina has next of kin here in Lincoln which we confirmed early this morning. I have a folder for each victim with 'next of kin' information for all available."

Dr. Elmore handed us each a file as she completed her summary of the first victim and rounding the table to the second.

"Victim number two is a twenty-five year old female with brown hair, five feet five inches tall, again with identical indicators of both drug use and STD's. Victim number two died of repeated blunt force trauma of no less than four strikes to the back of the head with a flat metal object, probably a shovel. We will know more once we complete trace analysis on the metal recovered from the wounds. She was hit at least once with the edge of the shovel in the back of the head. Victim number two was also buried, wrapped in plastic and was, along with Christina, buried on top of the other victims. Victim number two is Laura Richardson, with "next of kin" here in Lincoln, Nebraska. Before you ask, yes, she is the biological half-sister to Christina and had the exact same strain of gonorrhea to go with the family connection. From what medical records could tell us, these two sisters appeared to be prostitutes. There were no signs of DNA evidence in or on either of them. Whether or not he killed them I can't say yet, but it's a safe bet Fenton wrapped them in plastic before they were buried."

"That's not exactly like him; he wasn't much for burial rituals." I commented.

"My experience says he wasn't sleeping with them, but he cared for them enough to treat them differently. I have no way of understanding why he would choose these two as the exception to his any time, any place mentality, but they were. Maybe you can find out and let us all know after your next visit to the prison." She wondered.

"You got it." I agreed, accepting the second folder from her as she continued circling the second table to the third set of remains.

"Victim number three is a sixteen year old female with blonde hair, approximately five feet four inches tall. No indicators of drug use or STD's, but she had fragments of what appeared to be a red rag in her mouth. The rag is a synthetic blend so it didn't decompose quickly as would your standard shop rag. DNA match of the rag showed that it belonged to Richard Allen Fenton."

"Nice to see he kept his method the same," commented Terry.

"He clearly didn't care about DNA evidence when he was running free," I concluded.

"From what I hear, he thought he was untouchable." She said, before shooting me a glance and a quick smile, "Until you came along that is."

I cleared my throat as I became slightly taken aback by her statement, so I tried to change the subject. "How about victim number four?"

"Well I'm not finished with victim number three. Victim number three we matched DNA to Melanie Franken; abducted not two miles from here during the summer of 1992. Her family provided clothing articles and a hair brush for tracking purposes and the police had the forethought to hold onto them as evidence."

"See Bryant; they weren't always incompetent in the '90's." Terry mused.

"I never said always," I pointed out.

"Victim number three died of exsanguination through a single stab wound in the throat. If you take a close look with the magnifying glass you can see where the blade punctured the vertebrae. Victim number three is the oldest set of remains in that grave."

"You mean they were buried at different times?" Terry asked as he took the glass from me and examined the indicated spot on the vertebrae.

"That is correct. She was buried for approximately four to five months before victim number four."

"How can you tell?" asked Terry.

"Do you want me to explain the science to you, or are you satisfied with my expertise?"

"I wouldn't understand it if you did explain it, I did not fare well in science back in school," he replied. Dr. Elmore circled to the next table.

"Victim number four is a seventeen year old female with blonde hair, five feet six inches tall with identical cause of death as victim number three. Victim four was buried around four months after victim number three, but at least six months before victim number five. Victim number four died by exsanguination and had a red rag with Fenton's DNA in her mouth. Victim number four was identified by DNA as Pamela Galloway who went missing in the fall of 1992 from here in Lincoln, Nebraska."

"I'm impressed, the Lincoln Police don't have next of kin listed with up to date contact information for these missing persons, but here you are, the coroner, and you have more than expected." I complimented.

"Thank you Detective Bryant, my staff knows to go above and beyond in every case and that's what they do. I shall pass along your compliment though so they know their work is getting the recognition it deserves."

"Victim number five is a seventeen year old female with brown hair; five feet four inches tall killed the same way as victims three and four. Identical red rag found in her mouth with Fenton's DNA on it. Victim number five was the last one buried, possibly around the same time as victims one and two. No way to tell because the other two were wrapped in plastic, but they were stacked together with victim five underneath and one and two laying over the top of five. The bodies were together when exhumed with virtually no separation. Victim five was identified by dental and medical records as Amanda Everett. She was also a local in Lincoln and I believe her father is still in the area."

"How is it that three of these girls fit Fenton's M.O., but all five were in his acceptable age range?" Terry asked.

"Again, that will be a question for Fenton," said Dr. Elmore. "All we're going to do here is speculate."

"Well I say we each throw out a theory along with say, twenty bucks, and the winner is whoever is the closest." Terry suggested.

"That is gruesomely offensive," said Dr. Elmore.

"Well you don't have to make a bet if you don't want to," he explained, apologetically

"No, no, no; I'm in, I just felt like someone needed to stand up for the sake of decency and I knew it wouldn't be the Fed or the Cop; too cynical." She replied, clearly knowing her audience well.

"A very astute observation, Doctor," I said, reaching for my wallet. "Since you assumed the high ground was yours, why don't you make the first wager?"

"I think these two women took him in when he was desperate and in return when it came time for him to run for it, he killed them, but showed them a little decency since they helped him out."

"Spoken like someone who has never met the man." I quipped. "My theory is he was a fan of unprotected sex and when he got wind of all the diseases they were carrying he decided he cared more about cheap housing and protecting his dick than he did about getting laid the lazy way."

"That was gonna be my guess, dammit Bryant. I guess that leaves me with, he preferred teens and girls who didn't see him coming over the ease of walking into the next bedroom for a little action."

"Both of you, behave yourselves while were in the lab. Some of us have to be professionals throughout our work. The bets are placed, does anyone want to up the ante?" she asked.

"Twenty dollars still sounds good to me; what do you think Bryant?"

"Agreed," I said, nodding.

"It's settled," said Terry.

We all shook hands to seal the bet and then took a step back, shifting the folders in our hands.

"Well we're all going to hell now." Terry acknowledged.

I nodded my head at Terry as I awkwardly rearranged the folders in my hands. Something about the way Dr. Elmore looked at me had me shuffling my feet, wondering what to say next. I struggled to look her in the eye and found myself staring at the floor or the victims in turn. I had a sudden realization as I got ready to thank her for her time.

"We have one more victim out there possibly, and I was wondering if we got you all the case evidence, could you provide us with any new information that might help us identify her for certain?"

"I'm happy to help in any way I can. My staff and I will be standing by the phone; just let me know what you need and we will do everything in our power to help figure this out."

"Thank you so much, Dr. Elmore, we truly cannot thank you enough for your help. We should have everything we have over to you early this afternoon." I said.

"Just give me a call, I'll do what I can," she said.

"I just realized I don't have your number," I said as I turned back from the door.

"It's in your folders; I gave you everything you need to contact me and my staff while we're on this case."

"Thank you again, Doctor Elmore."

"Once again, please call me Lydia. Oh Terry, if you could hang back a second I need to talk to you. Would you excuse us, Detective?"

I nodded and strolled out the door. It wasn't lost on me that they waited until the door closed behind me to start talking. My thoughts were wandering back and forth between Dr. Elmore, and the case files in my hands. I rearranged them once again, trying to find the most comfortable way to hold them. I felt awkward, standing outside the lab waiting for Terry to finish talking to Dr. Elmore. They were only inside for a minute or so before Terry stepped out to join me.

"You ready to see what Thompson has for us?" I asked.

"After all that in there, that's where your mind went the second you step out the door?"

"Well she's expecting the evidence so I didn't want to keep her waiting." I explained, slightly confused.

"Of course, you're all business and no pleasure." He joked.

"Well I'm married, what did you expect?"

"I'm not sure anymore; we need to talk again, though. There's a lot to discuss."

"Are you up for another round of Scotch this evening?" I asked, knowing his answer.

"Shit, no! I just now stopped feeling my pulse in my eyeballs. I think I need a day or two before I hit the bottle again."

"Understood, we can chat on the way back to the park."

"No, this isn't really work related and this isn't the time or the place to talk about it." Terry replied, attempting to downplay his previous comments.

"Whatever you need man, maybe on the plane later this week?" I offered while we walked out to the parking lot.

"That might do. I'll let you know," he replied.

"What were you and the doctor talking about in there?" I asked as we reached the car.

"You," he replied; casually climbing into the passenger seat.

"Talking behind my back now are you?" I asked him with a nervous chuckle.

"Don't worry; I only said the best things about you. She's a smart, sexy, single woman who doesn't meet a lot of guys from out of town if you know what I mean?"

"Married guys in this case, why are you so fascinated with her?" I wondered as I started the car. I backed out of the parking lot and started along the route back to the park.

"It's not her that fascinates me; it's you. You've been through a lot in the past year and a half. A lot of people who care are worried about you; that's' all. Like I said, this isn't a conversation for work."

"Just let me know, I've got nothing but time until I get back home. Hotel living is easy, and my free time is my own. As soon as I'm home though; not so much," I said.

"Cause you can go back to drinking?" He inquired, raising his eyebrows and looking at me.

"I thought you said this was a conversation for later?" I wondered, starting to get confused.

"It is; you just keep asking questions so I don't want to be rude," he replied.

"You asked me the questions, so either have the conversation or don't. Right now you're acting like my wife, and it's not a good look for you." I pointed out, shaking my head a little.

"That's fucked up Bryant, but I hear what you're saying. I'll focus on work for now and we can settle all this later."

"Sound's good, I don't think it matters though. It doesn't look like Thomson is back with the evidence anyways," I said as I parked the car near the tent in the near-empty lot.

CHAPTER NINE

The fact that we were back to Irvingdale Park before Thompson returned had me pretty annoyed. It had been almost two hours since we dismissed from the morning briefing, and there was so much still to do. Terry and I mapped out our projected path around town to notify next of kin and were preparing to leave when Thompson finally returned. He parked his car in a hurry, and grabbed a box from the back seat before double timing it to the tent.

"Ok, I did everything you asked me to, so don't be mad," he pleaded.

"I reserve the right to be pissed if the news is shit," I told him. "What do you have for us?"

"All the original evidence was preserved and available, with one exception. They cremated the body back in 1994. No next of kin came forward and after a few months of waiting they disposed of the body. The Police Department didn't have room to keep bodies around for years on end, especially if the death had been deemed accidental. This one was deemed accidental due to overdose and the whole thing was scrapped. The fact that we still have her clothes is nothing short of an oversite. After several months, they had the body cremated."

"Are there pictures of the remains?"

"Yeah, but they're old and poor quality. They had to find the original film and prints and then release them to me after they digitized everything. They wouldn't release old photos without a permanent copy being created since we're essentially reopening the case." He explained.

"Is there anything identifiable on the remains?" I asked, hoping for the best.

"Nothing but this necklace; she apparently had it gripped in her hand when they found her. They had record amounts of snow that winter and the body had been dumped in a construction area for the Holm's Lake golf course. The area was covered in snow for months until the body was discovered when they reopened the sight in the middle of March. Somehow it was pretty well preserved with only minimal signs of scavenging."

"Get pictures of the necklace and the body and go find the Deputy Chief and his team. If they find the manager, owner or reporting party from this case, they may be the only ones who can provide a positive identity for this case. Let me know what you find; if they confirm who it is, get a bulletin out over social media and do a press release with the name and details of the case. We might need her family to contact us if they're from outside the area."

"I'm on it," said Thompson as he started gathering up the evidence again.

"And get all the evidence over to Dr. Elmore's lab. They're expecting you," I instructed.

"I'll call the Deputy Chief and find out where he is and text you the information, Thompson," offered Terry.

I was immediately grateful that Thompson had the foresight to bring multiple copies of the report and photos. The body was in far better shape than it could have been. It truly spoke to how shitty the winter of 1993-1994 had been. The body had no eyes and most of the face had been chewed on by scavengers. The rest of the body had been preserved inexplicably well and that was the part I was trying to analyze. Even in heavy snowfall, scavengers are looking for easy food when they can. The idea that a body could last for an extended period of time out in the elements was out of place. I stared for a moment at the picture of the necklace. It was a heart pendant, silver in color and hanging on a silver chain.

I looked up and called out to Thompson just as he was reaching the door to the tent.

"Thompson, did the necklace make it into evidence?"

"Yeah it's there amongst the clothing and other property recovered," he said, and then turned and left.

I searched through the articles of evidence and located the necklace. It was not tightly wrapped allowing me to feel its texture through the plastic bag. I found the button on the side and pressed it gently, and felt relieved when the pendant opened to display what would have a set of small pictures inside. The photos were ruined and completely disintegrated, allowing no view of what the pictures used to be.

The photographer from 1994 didn't have a lot of training. There were no overall shots of the scene, nothing with the locket necklace opened to show the pictures inside, just close-ups of the body, the syringe in her arm, and the body once it was removed from the snow.

"Do you see this Terry? Amateur bullshit like this is why we can never get anywhere on these cases." I bitched.

Terry looked at me and pointed to the phone he was still on, "No sir," he said into the phone, "That was someone else in the tent besides Detective Bryant insulting your department's investigative capabilities. Yes sir, I'll pass along your concerns."

"Jesus Christ, Bryant," said Terry as he tucked his phone back into his jacket pocket. "Could you try, for even a second, not to piss everyone off?"

"Look at this shit! It's fucking useless," I said, slapping the photos back onto the table.

"It was an unattended death in 1994, the fact that there are pictures at all is a miracle; did you think of that?" He asked, trying to shake up my piss-pour perspective.

"The only reason anyone bothered to pull out a camera and take," I paused briefly to count the photos, "six fucking photos, is because they had to. If they thought for half a second that this chick just wandered out into the snow and overdosed, they would have barely taken the time to file a report."

"Stop bitching about what we don't have, and start using what we do have. Have you analyzed every detail of those photos? If you haven't then you're shitty attitude is probably preventing you from looking past the inadequacies' of the initial investigation and seeing the details which are right in front of you," he urged.

"That may be so, but if this is the kind of bullshit we're getting from a large police department, we are royally fucked when we start hitting jurisdictions a third of the size from a decade prior to all this." I replied, not even trying to hide my disgust.

"Take some time with the report and the photos. There has to be something in there that gives us more to go on than we have now," Terry advised.

Terry was right as usual. His role as the voice of reason was annoying, but it kept me grounded in reality. I carefully closed up my case file, set it down on one of the tables, and stepped outside the tent. For a moment I wondered why we were still doing all this business from a tent in the park. It was up to the local department's jurisdiction to determine where and how the investigations were handled. Knowing the interaction I already had with the Deputy Chief, I figured he was trying to distance the department from the whole situation. He had disguised this entire investigation as a training exercise and for that I couldn't really fault him. It kept up appearances for the department to claim to be doing joint exercises with other agencies. Unfortunately this left them with the awkward responsibilities of explaining how they stumbled headlong into a twenty year old grave with five bodies. It seemed obvious to me that Deputy Chief Parnell was doing everything he could to separate the department from this investigation. Armed with this knowledge, it had become increasingly difficult to hide my disdain for him.

The sun was starting to hide behind an ever increasing amount of large, dark clouds, indicating a storm was brewing. The limited warmth provided by the sun vanished almost immediately as the wind started gusting, blowing leaves and garbage around the park and making it difficult to see without squinting. I stepped back inside the tent and started helping clean off the tables of reports and miscellaneous trash while Terry closed the flap on the curtained, white walls of the tent.

"Hard to believe they didn't have a better place for everyone to meet," I said sardonically. I started using any object with a little weight to it to hold papers in place.

"Maybe they have a room at the Ritz-Carlton you'd find more comfortable," replied Terry, obviously running low on patience with my diminishing attitude.

"That sounds nice; can you spot me a few thousand dollars? My per diem isn't enough to cover tipping the bellhop."

"You know, you make all of this a lot more difficult than it needs to be.

There isn't a department or agency in this country that is going to complete an investigation to the standards you're expecting. We're in the business of making the best of things so stop making things worse with your shitty outlook on life." He snapped.

"That's why I drink; this is me sober. I have my good moments, and then it's just a whole lot of me bitching about everything," I spat back.

"But you're better than that! I haven't known you that long, but I've seen how you work. You're good at your job, you care about people; you want to help them. If you didn't, you wouldn't be here."

"I don't have a choice. I'm too old to start a new career, and too invested in this one to give it up. Maybe after a decade of dealing with everyone else's bullshit day in and day out, it would be nice if someone gave a shit about me. Maybe if everyone else saw what I have to go through every Saturday afternoon they'd pull their heads out of their asses and do something to help." I growled, my hands starting to gesture wildly as my anger increased.

"Look around you, Bryant; everyone else on this task force is out running down leads and doing their part to resolve this whole thing. But you can't see that; can you? Because you're not sitting in a comfy desk chair sipping whiskey, you think everyone else is trying to undermine you."

"They are; look at this fucking place. We're in a tent in the middle of a park in March in the middle of, what looks like it's gonna be, a big fucking storm. Are you telling me they don't have a fucking weather forecast in this whole fucking city? We are out here because they don't give a shit about this investigation. They're out running errands because it's the fastest way to get us out of town and out of their way. They don't care about helping us; they care about getting rid of us," I bitched.

"What makes you think any jurisdiction we go to is going throw you a fucking parade, Bryant? Did you ever think that everywhere we go; we're going places where someone failed to catch Fenton twenty years ago? Everywhere we go we're reminding people of a shortcoming in policing that failed to keep everyone safe in their community. We have six bodies here over a two year period of time. Don't you remember what it was like back when you were a rookie? Don't you remember the fear? Don't you remember the pain everyone felt whenever a new face went across the television of some poor girl who is never coming home to their family? Your community was devastated for a long time wondering what was happening and wondering why the police couldn't protect them. All of that happened right here and in other places too. Now we're back in town, digging up the past and bodies along with it. You came here with knowledge no other person involved has at their disposal. That isn't something you can hold against them. You caught him; you brought an end to his madness, but there are a lot of pieces to be picked up and you're in the driver's seat making it happen," he replied, just shy of yelling at me.

He stopped and looked at me for a moment. He was right, of course. I was bitter, and my burden wasn't there's to bare.

"Bryant, you have an incredible opportunity here. Clear your mind for a moment and think about the responsibility you have. The only person making things difficult here is you. The city isn't pleased that their white picket fence neighborhood is being dug up to uncover bodies. The department isn't pleased that twenty years ago, someone killed six people in their city and then casually left town. We are here to rip off old Band-Aids and expose a wound in this city that never healed properly. We are out here because they are distancing as much of this community and department from this process as possible; not as an inconvenience to you."

Terry stopped for a moment to breathe before reaching into his pocket and retrieving the keys I'd given him earlier.

"Take the car; go back to the hotel and pore over that case file. Clear your head for a little while and see if you can't find a new perspective on this whole thing." He tossed me the keys and then sat down at one of the tables and started reviewing one of the files.

I felt like an asshole, but wasn't quite prepared to confess as much. I had a new respect for Terry after he told me off. I resented him slightly for it, but down deep I knew I needed his honest opinion to keep my head on straight. It was way too early in this whole process for me to alienate everyone else involved. I had months of this ahead of me, and I sure as shit couldn't do all this alone. I hung my head in shame, which was disguised by my need to lower my head against the gusting wind outside. I walked to the car clutching the report under my arm to protect it from the weather.

I realized on the way back to the hotel that I hadn't done much exploring here in Lincoln since I arrived. The fact that I had noticed the Burger King on the way in that morning was nothing short of a coincidence. In all reality it was probably the only thing I retained from driving back and forth to the park the first day and a half. Obscured from view behind my perspective on life was a city moving forward. The people living in the past did so in their heads; everyone else was pushing through all the bullshit trying not to let the past bog them down. I was there to dig up the past in the literal sense. It was no wonder there hadn't been a red carpet for my arrival. I was coming into this investigation armed with answers to all the big questions. I was basically taking a confession to a crime and locating the scene. Any half-witted rookie straight out of the academy could do what I was doing. The difference, I was being unreasonable because of the manner in which I was getting the confession. The more I thought about it as I traveled north on 17th Street past the Burger King, the more I understood what Terry was trying to tell me. This task force was taking a heavy toll on me already, and we had barely started. My drinking wasn't helping me and I was going out of my way to keep everyone at arm- length. This was only my first trip out of town and I was already being an unbearable douchebag.

I sulked my way across the parking lot into the hotel lobby. The lobby turned into a huge atrium style foyer where the pool sat, void of people, in the middle. The smell of the chlorine made me wish I had the time or the energy to go for a swim. All I wanted was a drink and my reclining chair at home. I spent more nights sleeping there than in my own bed. Drinking now flew in the face of my reason for going back to the hotel. I needed clarity of mind and most of all, silence.

I took the stairs to my room and immediately scattered the photos across the bed where I could see them and begun pacing back and forth reading over the file. I brewed a cup of cheap hotel coffee in the pot and sipped it while I read. We had the police report, but it didn't include the full coroner's report. It was briefly covered in the detective's narrative, but reading through the narrative showed me how quickly officers were to gloss over the details when the cause of death was presumed. In 1994 they were still hand writing reports, so that didn't help anyone in the pursuit of vivid detail. Back when poorly written reports were torn up in front of rookie officers, they had a habit of only writing out the details deemed absolutely necessary. The longer the oration, the more likely grammatical errors were made which inclined most officers to keep it short and sweet. The only thing this report had going for it was the handwriting wasn't total shit. Half the old reports we'd been poring over had been borderline illegible due to handwriting and the quality of copy machines in the early '90's.

I tossed the manila folder on the bed by the photos and took a few minutes staring out my window. The overcast sky had crept over the hotel from the north and was bearing down hard on the park. I scanned the parking lot looking for some kind of motivation to help me go back to the report. The parking lot was almost empty, with nothing but my rental vehicle and a couple of odd work trucks pulling in to park at the back. Several bearded, muddy men climbed out of the grubby looking pearl white work trucks and ducked their heads against wind, circling around a small pile of plowed snow and ice from the last winter storm of the year. I stared into the gray and black snow pile marveling at how well it stood the test of time. I had no idea when the last snowfall had occurred here in Lincoln, but it was enough to make a huge pile of sand-filled, dirty ice.

Piles of plowed snow were precisely the kind of places my friends and I built snow forts when we were kids. Metal gardening tools cut right through the ice making impenetrable walls for a snowball fight.

Armed with a few fond childhood memories, I returned to the report and glanced back and forth between it and the photos on the bed. Something suddenly felt wrong about the pictures, and I couldn't put my finger on it. The first photo was of the girls face, or what was left of it really. It was visible out of the oddly gray snow around it revealing the faceless head and shoulders of the eighteen year old female. The photo was taken too close, without also having an overall picture taken of the body from a long ways off. I tossed the report on the bed and picked up the photo, walking to the window again as I examined it. I glanced outside to the parking lot for a second and then back to the photo. I did this several times. This body had been recovered around this time of year in 1994, and suddenly I was starting to get some clarity.

I snatched up my coat, grabbed the photos and papers off the bed and ran out the door still trying to get my coat over my other arm. I would have sprinted to the car had it not been for the wind and mist whipping against my face. I was happy to endure the rain that kicked up on the way to the park. A few moments of quiet reflection had done just what Terry said it would. I had a perspective I'd otherwise not have developed had I not taken a step away for a while. I crossed town as quickly as I could as visibility started to drop and the rain kicked up to another level. The windshield wipers were barely keeping up as the torrent of water pounded everything in sight. I reached into my jacket pocket and pulled out my phone, cursing softly as it caught on the corner of the pocket and tumbled into my lap narrowly avoiding my sensitive areas. I picked up the phone and attempted to type in my passcode in between glances over the dashboard.

"Terry? Hey I'm headed back to the park, when you see me pull up make a run for it, I need to show you something."

I whipped the car into the parking lot as close to the tent as I could get it. I placed the passenger side of the sedan towards the tent and watched for Terry to make a break for it. It was only thirty yards or so, but Terry tore out of the tent at full tilt, barely giving me time to reach across the passenger seat and unlatch the door. The wind kept me from opening it, but I held it far enough that Terry grabbed the handle and jumped inside.

"Where the fuck did this storm come from?" He swore, panting slightly as he fished the file folder out from under him where I had left it in the seat. "Thompson came back by and we cleaned out the rest of the tent. He's waiting there until the equipment truck arrives so they can load up tables and chairs. What's the emergency?"

"We're going golfing," I told him with a smile.

I drove across town headed southeast as quickly as traffic would allow. I was excited about what I hoped would be a big breakthrough, but I was getting concerned the rain was about to wash it all away.

"Where are we going?" Terry asked after he caught his breath.

"Holmes Lake Golf Course"

"You wanna see the scene where the body was discovered, don't you?"

"Not just the scene, if I'm right I'm about to answer a lot of questions that have been nagging at me since I first read this report. I was pissed because the photos didn't show the surrounding area where the body was found. There was however the most crudely drawn diagram of the parking lot with a little "x" where the body was found. I think the body was covered in snow when they cleared the parking lot of snow that winter."

"But why would they bother clearing the parking lot for a golf course in the winter? Nobody is golfing when there's six inches of snow on the ground."

"That bothered me too, but I remember researching Holmes Lake yesterday when I was reviewing that file. It's not just a golf course; it's also a country club with a reception hall. If they had a wedding or some kind of event during the winter months they would have had to clear the parking lot, probably in the dead of night or early morning to ensure it was ready for customers the next day. If you were going to dump a body on the way out of town what better place than in a pile of ice and snow where no one is going to see if for weeks or more?" I asked.

"That's a hell of a theory, but why do we need to go out to the scene?" He asked.

"Odds are they haven't changed the parking lots whatsoever. I'm hoping that little "x" on the diagram will put us right at a convenient spot for a snow pile," I explained as we turned onto Talent Plus Way and then into the parking lot.

"Ok, so it's called Holmes Park Golf Course, but every report can't be perfect. Can you make any sense of the diagram in comparison to the parking lot?" I asked.

Terry turned the diagram every which way as he glanced around the parking lot. "All they noted was the outside diameter of the lot and marked which way was north. The "x" is marked at the northeast corner," he stopped and pointed, "Right by that tree over there."

Several piles of snow surrounded a small tree just off the northeast corner of the parking lot. The spot was exactly as I thought it would be. The parking lot was a large loop, and the northeast corner was the perfect spot to pile snow accumulated along the east and north sides of the parking lot. The east side was the longest and it showed in the quantity of snow collected. Even in the middle of the rain three weeks or better after the last snow, the pile was still over three feet tall and nearly twenty feet wide.

"What are you thinking, Terry?"

"I think we should find out from management if they had an event the weekend of the 23rd through 25th of December 1993, and then see if we can get a name for the company that did the snow removal back then."

"I think you're right." I retorted as I looped around the empty parking lot again and parked in front of the clubhouse.

The rain was still pounding as we jogged the few feet from the front row parking spot into the clubhouse. I was relieved to find the door unlocked, allowing us to step inside, shaking the rain from our coats. The clubhouse was beautifully built, and I couldn't help but admire the craftsmanship as we walked from the lobby into the bar area. The ceiling was supported by large, cherry stained wood beams which beautifully accented the hardwood floors. A long stretch of red carpet reached from the front door to the back, allowing players with golf shoes to easily access the clubhouse without damaging the expensive flooring. The place was empty and most of the lights were off.

"Well, that's too bad." I said gesturing at the empty bar, "I was hoping to get a drink."

"Well you can't," a voice called out from behind us, "We're closed gentleman."

We turned to see a portly looking fellow with a double chin covered in a thin beard. The man was wearing an oversized red polo shirt with a Holmes Lake logo on it. He waddled out from one of the offices between the bathrooms and the lounge area, panting slightly as he approached.

"Thank you sir, but we're not actually here for a drink," said Terry. He pulled out his wallet and flashed his badge, "We're with the FBI, and we have a few questions for management if they are available."

"Well I'm the assistant manager, what can I do for you?" he replied.

"I'm Special Agent Terrance Jones, this is James Bryant, and we're working with a task force trying to resolve a few cold cases. We were wondering if you had records of all the events you've hosted and perhaps a list of your independent contractors for the property."

"I'm Tyler, if you gentleman would follow me, I can probably find all that information back in the office. What event are you inquiring about?"

"We're not really sure; we're hoping you hosted something back in December of 1993." I explained.

"Wow, that's a ways back; can I ask what case this is in reference too?" He inquired.

"Were you ever told about a body that was found in the parking lot back in 1994?" Terry asked.

"No, I was not, but I would have been like, six back when that happened so I doubt it would be a common topic for new hires when they get here unless the dead person used to work here."

"Well we're not sure about where the victim worked, we're just trying to do our due diligence and make sure we've run down every lead. We're trying to see if anyone who worked here or for the park might have been around the night of the incident. If you hosted an event that weekend it might make our list of potential witnesses really long," explained Terry.

"Well everything was on paper back then and we aren't in a big hurry to add old files to our system. This might be a scenario where we have to go back and find the old records in storage. Unfortunately, this might take a while to find."

"We understand," I expressed to him as I handed him a business card from my jacket pocket. "If you wouldn't mind, give me a call as soon as you come across these records."

"Yeah of course, how soon do you need this?" Tyler asked.

"I leave town within the next two days; if you could find those records as soon as possible, I would greatly appreciate it," I replied.

"I'll get to it today and call you as soon as I find it," replied Tyler as he offered his hand to each of us in turn.

I waited until I was out of the clubhouse to wipe my hand on my pants to get Tyler's palm sweat off my skin. The trip to Holmes Lake hadn't been for nothing, but it had left a few questions unanswered.

CHAPTER TEN

"Head for the hotel," said Terry, putting his phone back into his jacket. "The taskforce is reconvening in one of the conference rooms there."

"Glad to hear it," I replied. "We weren't going to get much done with this storm blowing in."

The wiper blades on the rental car were fighting hard to keep up with the torrential downpour blasting the sedan, accompanied by heavy winds and whatever debris had been kicked up already. The trees along the roadside strained hard against snapping as the tyrannical storm bowed them to its fury. Every other car seemed to be standing still in the roadway as drivers second guessed every movement in route to their destinations. Every time I started to get impatient with someone in front of me, the rain would kick up harder, making it nearly impossible to see anything but the brake lights in front of us.

Every bump in the road made Terry grip the handle beside his head. I had been in some pretty shitty situations before, but this storm was creating a visceral response in both of us that seemed to equal even the most perilous pursuits in which I'd ever been a part. The twenty minute drive turned into almost forty as we snail crawled across Lincoln, hoping every tree we passed held on long enough for us to drive under it without it collapsing.

Our hotel was nothing spectacular, but it was a welcome sight after our precarious trip. In hindsight, I probably could have done an internet search of the golf course and called the manager from the comfort of my hotel bathrobe. I preferred to do my police work in person, especially my follow up. Conversations over the phone are so impersonal. I felt like people responded better to a visit at home or on their time, in person, rather than trying to catch them when they have a minute over the phone. This was an old school form of policing I carried with me after my training nearly a decade ago, and I intended to keep it.

First contact with people especially needed to be in person. Simply calling someone to say you were a police detective always received a skeptical response. I preferred to meet people and show them they were worth more than a moment of my time over the phone. The drive back had me questioning ten years of police work with how volatile the storm had become. I parked as close to the hotel entrance as I could, apologized to Terry for how far it was from the door, and then we made a break for it.

"Whoa, shit; I miss my covered parking spot in Kansas City on days like this." Terry cursed as we reached the doors. We took a moment just inside the lobby to shake as much of the rain off our coats as possible.

"Doesn't it make you happy we won't be traveling much further north during these investigations?" I asked with absolute sincerity.

"Let's just hope the cluster-fuck stays further south until summer rolls around," he replied.

Laying the collar of my jacket back down, I caught sight of Detective Thomson, who was waving us over from the other side of the lobby.

"What do you think? 'Ya think they'll have some good news for us?" I inquired of Terry as he too caught sight of Thompson.

"As long as they have something, I'm good with it. We have six bodies and only one of them is requiring this much follow up investigation. I just want to wrap this up so we can get back to Manhattan; I've had my fill of Nebraska for the time being." He said matching my stride to cross the lobby towards the conference room.

"Detective Bryant, Agent Jones, we have everything you guys asked for and the team is set up, ready to brief you with the updates." Thompson advised.

"That is exactly how I want to be greeted for the rest of this investigation," I quipped.

"I'll make sure to tell the other jurisdictions before we get there," replied Terry with a smile.

The conference room was nothing special to see. It was complete with one large fourteen foot long by four foot wide, solid bronze color stained wood conference table with enough seating for twenty. Approximately that many people were already in the room waiting for us, sitting in identical blue cushioned rolling desk chairs surrounded by light blue, almost teal walls. Deputy Chief Parnell sat at the head of the table and the men around him seemed to be in descending order of age, leaving Terry and I as the two youngest in the room. I hadn't noticed this detail out at the park; then again, I didn't really care.

"Detective Bryant, we're ready to brief you when you're ready," Parnell stated.

"Fire away, and feel free to tell me who you are when it's your turn to speak." I prompted them. I took a second and looked around the room at each of them in turn before seating myself in one of the last available chairs.

"I'll get us started then," said the Deputy Chief as he rose out of his chair.

"My team was tasked with tracking down the general manager, managers and reporting party for the missing person's case. The managers are scattered around and none of them were available for comment. The reporting party is still living here in Lincoln, and was able to meet with us right away. We discussed your concerns about Alicia being pregnant or a drug user. The R.P., Angie, stated that Alicia had spoken to her about mood swings, nausea, sore breasts, frequent trips to the bathroom, and weight gain. Angie told us it would have made sense for Alicia to be pregnant and just not forthcoming about it since Angie did not believe Alicia had a boyfriend or husband. Angie told me the drug addict aspect didn't make much sense to her," said Parnell.

"Did she say why she thought so?" I asked.

"Angie is a former heroin addict herself. She told us back in the early nineties she was using pretty regularly and thinks she could have spotted a fellow user a mile away. Discussing the details with Angie, she seemed certain that Alicia was pregnant and trying to get on her feet before she pulled up and left town again. Angie was certain Alicia was in trouble because Alicia had told her several times she needed several months' pay to make a break for it and leave town."

"Did you get the photos of the necklace in time to show them to Angie?" I asked, butting in again.

"We got them just in time to show it to Angie. She couldn't be one hundred percent certain, but she believed Alicia had one like it when she worked at the Burger King. Angie stated Alicia was always nervously fiddling with a necklace that looked just like the one in the picture. She said it's been too long now to be absolutely certain. We contacted the former General Manager, but they stated they don't keep old employment records beyond five or six years. He told us the odds of someone attempting to be rehired after five years is almost zero so they destroy all their records around the time when they're no longer susceptible to being audited. Both Angie and the General Manager told us if we could get them a picture, they might be able to make a positive identification," said Parnell before sitting down.

"That's our cue," said a short white male standing up and gesturing to a Hispanic male across the table from him. "I'm Detective Romansky, this is Detective Luis Perez, and we were tasked with checking yearbooks and other public records for Alicia Bonner. We located a girl matching that name and description who graduated in 1993 from Waverly High School, located several miles northeast of Lincoln in Waverly, Nebraska. We did an emergency information request from the school district and we got her pictures and social security number and transferred the information to the Deputy Chief."

"We checked with the Social Security Administration and they confirmed Alicia Bonner, born in August of 1975 to parents Brad and Kristi Bonner who still live in Waverly, Nebraska," explained the Deputy Chief. "We showed the photos of Alicia to Angie and she confirmed her identity to us. We have not yet made contact with her parents."

"That's ok; Agent Jones and I will do the notification to her parents. We still have to confirm without a doubt that Alicia is the body we found. My guess is Alicia had been given that necklace by a loved one; I think her parents are the only ones who will be able to tell us for sure." I told the group.

"Due to the ongoing demands of the cases being investigated elsewhere, Detective Bryant and I will be flying out as soon as the next of kin notifications have been made," interjected Terry. "We still have a few loose ends we need someone to tie up for us if we leave before everything is done. As many of you may already know, Detective Bryant's department back in Kansas is working to complete six autopsies, three of which involve unknown victims. Your understanding and cooperation goes a long way to help resolve things here so that we can attend to new and ongoing investigations elsewhere."

"Thank you, Agent Jones," I said stepping forward slightly. "Detective Perez and Detective Romansky, I am tasking the two of you with staying in contact with the manager of the Holmes Park Golf Course, his name is Tyler, and he will be sending over event history coinciding with the disappearance of our sixth victim and also delivering contractor and employee records. Comb through them and see who might have been able to hide a body in a snow drift back in 1992 or early 1993.

I stopped for a moment and reflected on my behavior over the past two day. I realized the men in the room had done everything asked of them without complaining, which I could not say for myself.

"Folks, I want to sincerely thank each and every one of you for your assistance in this investigation," I said. "After we dismiss here, the majority of you will most likely be released back to your normal duties by the Deputy Chief. He will designate who will be in charge of relaying any additional information to the Joint Task Force. Agent Jones and I will try to complete the next of kin notifications today and early tomorrow, and like he said, we will be flying out immediately afterwards. Are there any questions?"

I looked around briefly at the group gathered around and waited for a moment to see if anyone spoke up. I gave it another few seconds just until it began to get awkward, then nodded to the group and turned to follow Terry back out into the hallway by the lobby.

"Any idea when this storm is supposed to let up?" I asked Terry, who was already pulling out his phone.

"Hmm, it says here it will take a couple hours, but we should have an opening to get to Waverly today to talk to the Bonner family." He said before stowing his phone back in his pocket.

"Perfect, I'm going to check in with my L.T. and try to dry myself out," I told him. "I'll meet you in the lobby in ninety minutes."

"We should eat something before we go," he said.

"How does pizza sound?" I offered.

"As long as it's delivery," he replied with a shake of his head.

"Oh for sure, I'm done driving in this shit," I said. "I'll order lunch and you can cover dinner later?"

"Sure thing," he said as started up the stairs towards our rooms.

———

With our bellies full of pizza and the storm having passed, Terry and I headed north. The city was an absolute wreck. The storm had taken every garbage can and loose item and thrown it from yards and driveways. Debris littered the streets of Lincoln making it slow going at first. We only had to backtrack once to get around a fallen tree, but after that we made great time. I wasn't looking forward to completing the first next of kin notification, but since there were four more families still waiting, I decided to suck it up. At least this first one could answer questions for us instead of us just showing up to ruin their lives.

"I haven't had to do these before," confided Terry. "Do they suck as much as I think they will?"

"I did one last week," I told him, "They never stop sucking. The key is to display some genuine compassion for them and never pretend you know what they're going through. Their circumstances are unique and you aren't there to be relatable, you're there to deliver a message, leave them in the good hands of the police chaplain, and then get out as soon as you can. There is no good way to excuse yourself after giving someone bad news, so just be polite and don't make an excuse to leave, just tell them we have to go and let the chaplain do his job. I already called ahead to the Waverly Police Department, and they have their chaplain meeting us at the Bonner's residence."

"And we have to do this four more times?" He asked.

"Yeah, but I talked to the Deputy Chief before lunch and he has all four of his chaplains standing by to assist us; I'm really hoping we can be done today. The sooner, the better," I explained.

I parked the car in front of the 1950's light green bungalow and took a deep breath as I put the car in park. I stared at the house with its faded white porch railing surrounding a heavily weathered porch swing.

"This is one of the worst parts of this job, you want to get used to the idea of having to deliver bad news, but not so much that you're desensitized to it. I can never shake the nausea that goes hand in hand with notifying next of kin. I really don't want to do this fifty more times over the next six months." I said, trying to shake the overwhelming urge to roll the window down and vomit in the street next to the car.

"Do you really think there will be fifty more of these?"

"I'm just doing the math. Fenton has disclosed the location of ten bodies just in our first two weeks meeting together. Three more people died during the investigation after week two." I shook my head as I reached for my door handle, "I think we've barely scratched the surface on how many lives Fenton has ended."

———

I steered Terry back down the sidewalk towards the car and managed to get him to the opposite side of the car, away from the house, before he started retching. The sound of his pepperoni pizza hitting the street made it all worse for me, and I fought the urge to join him, sweat pouring from my brow as I strained against my natural urge to hurl. Hands on my hips I paced a large circle in the middle of the street, waving apologetically to the car that slowed down and honked at me as I blocked its path. It didn't seem possible for Terry to still be vomiting a full minute later, but once the flow had started there was apparently no stopping it. The folder in my hand was one picture lighter than it had been when we had arrived. I hadn't even bothered to ask for the picture back from Kristi Bonner. The sixty-two year old woman clutched it to her chest, sobbing tears of anguish as she recognized the locket she had given Alicia for her sixteenth birthday. Her husband Brad sat dumbfounded in his reclining chair, numb with shock and unable to utter a word. I knew this process would be terrible, but nothing prepared me for the way the Bonners had responded to the news that their daughter was never going to show up with their 23 year old grandchild to meet them for the first time.

According to Kristi, Alicia had confided in them that she was pregnant while she was still living at home taking junior college classes. They had not taken the news well, and after a bitter fight, Alicia had packed her bags and left in the middle of the night in December of 1993. They never heard from her again. They were both crushed under the weight of their guilt, and immediately held themselves responsible for the way they handled the situation, knowing they had driven Alicia out of the safety of their home. That wasn't our burden to bear, so we walked out, leaving the chaplain to pick up the pieces of the broken home that had finally come unglued. We couldn't help the gnawing feeling that we had stolen all the hope the Bonners had left in them. They had held on for over twenty years to the idea that their eldest daughter was alive and well somewhere, just waiting to muster up the courage to come home.

I opened the driver's door, stepping over the pile of vomit as I climbed into the car. Terry took a few minutes to spit behind the car as he tried to rid his mouth of the nagging flavor of regurgitated pizza. He finally climbed into the passenger seat and dug around in his bag for a pack of gum. We each took a piece of gum and hoped the peppermint would be enough to wash away the feeling of disgust and the flavor of the vomit.

Terry cleared his throat aggressively and then added a second piece of gum to the other in his mouth.

"There's no way I can manage four more of these today," he panted as he wiped his brow on his sleeve.

"You've already thrown up everything you ate; we might as well get this done while you've got an empty stomach." I explained.

"Fuck me," he swore shaking his head. "Week two and I already hate this shit."

"I told you this was a shitty assignment. When this is over, we're going to a beach in the Caribbean to drink all these memories away, and pretend we were never here."

"I'm in," he said rolling his window down, watching the Bonner's house fade into the distance behind us. "I'll book that fucking flight tonight."

CHAPTER ELEVEN

I stared through the tiny window of the secure, interview room door, and could see the back of Fenton's head. He leaned back in his chair as if he was a ten year old, waiting for recess. El Dorado was exceptionally short staffed that day, so getting through security measures had taken even longer than before. I waited patiently outside the conference room for my meeting with Fenton and reflected on the past week.

Lincoln, Nebraska had been a huge undertaking. Six bodies recovered or identified, and their families notified; and that was just getting me up to Wednesday evening.

Thursday morning had brought with it the news that the victim in the car bomb at City Park was Emma Lane, wife of Tim Lane the reporter I had been trying to meet last Saturday. We had found him hanging from the rafters of the pavilion not two hundred yards from where his wife went up in a ball of flames. In the same blast we had lost a promising young officer, and confirmed the involvement of an unknown third party. Someone was running free, acting on the direction of Fenton, or at least on his behalf.

I had returned from Nebraska after making next of kin notifications to five families about six dead women. Just when I thought things couldn't get any worse, I made a notification to Tim and Emma's two daughters. Adults are hard to comfort, but ten and twelve year old girls are inconsolable. Nothing can prepare you for the anguish you will experience when telling two children they're never going to see their parents again. That had been my first task Thursday afternoon after we landed in Manhattan again. Even their grandparents couldn't bring themselves to be the bearer of bad news. They deferred to me, leaving me the sole responsibility of delivering the worst possible news. The image of their tearful faces lingered in my mind. I had seen worse, but it was hard to fathom a shittier experience.

Terry was glad to part ways at the airport when he heard what my next task was going to be. Five notifications had been too many for him; even though we were both emotionally spent, only one of us had the option of going home instead of going right back to work.

I was lost in thought, and again, startled by the locks opening to allow me in to see Fenton.

"Good luck," said the correction's officer behind me.

I turned and looked Foster in the eye. "Thanks."

He was smirking at me, but I would be too if I was walking someone else into the lion's den.

I strolled casually past Fenton, making sure to pass closer to him so he didn't think I was still nervous. I was; but that was for me to know. I whipped out the items, set them on the table and started the timer.

"So, Irvingdale is nice this time of year. It's too bad I couldn't bring you more pictures than this, but you understand there isn't much left of these women after twenty-five years." I said.

I started setting pictures of the five victims recovered from the house out in front of Fenton as he lit a cigarette, and leered at me with a smirk on his face.

"Five at a time," he said with a slight chuckle. "I bet no one expected me to stack bitches that deep. After all, I'm gifted."

"So do you recognize anyone pictured?" I asked him trying to keep him from rambling arrogantly.

"Of course I do," he replied, using one hand to slide two of the pictures towards me slightly. "How could I forget my two generous hosts after all these years. Laura and Christine, I wish they didn't have to die like they did; but so is life."

"So you lived with these two?" I asked.

"It's more like I became the operating manager for their little operation."

I looked at him for a moment hoping he would elaborate.

"Pussy; they were selling it at a prime rate, and they needed someone to kick the John's out, or occasionally collect a payment. When druggies came by for a bit of nookie, they left a little "H" behind along with their cash. When a politician came by to cheat on his wife, he paid double. We had a pretty good racket going on there for a couple years. The sister's handled the casual clients while I provided a more exotic product line."

I asked, "Heroin?"

"Underage pussy," he said with a grin, pausing to enjoy the way I cringed in response. "The only thing people pay more for is something they can't find themselves. I would find someone suitable for the business and keep them locked away upstairs. Upstanding citizens and political officials would stop by to sample the fine product I provided; and they would pay a premium. There's a reason they tried to transform that area of Irvingdale after I left; they had to cover up their own dirty little secrets."

"If you were making so much money off of these girls, why did you kill them?"

"Well now, Detective that's a foreseeable question for you to ask seeing as you're a straight laced lawman who would never dabble in darker side of sexual entertainment. Just like milk, every pussy has an expiration date. The 'best if fucked by date' comes along faster when they see as much traffic as they did. Every now and again the clients would ask for something new and fresh. So I'd do away with the sour product and go find something fresh to bring the clientele back around for another taste."

"And the sisters were okay with all of this?" I asked.

"Oh, God no," he laughed shaking his head. "Why do you think I had to kill them? They thought I was dealing the powdery goodness to some of our clients when in reality; I was dealing in something far more frowned upon. Even a couple of hookers couldn't stand the idea of me undercutting their profits by selling pussy far more inviting than their own. The system worked for a long time, until they caught on to what I was doing."

"How did they react?" I asked.

"It wasn't so much about how they reacted, but who they reacted to," he said, attempting to sound philosophical.

"Who did they react to?" I asked.

"They were unaware of what I was doing so whenever I needed to, I would just plant one of those girls in the backyard garden. Christine couldn't figure out why her garden looked so good in the summer of 1993. Little did she know I had the secret fertilizer going for her; Teenage girls really know how to sprout some rose bushes, if you catch my meaning?"

"So what set them off if they were so oblivious?"

"They took the time to go out and do a little recruiting of their own; or so I thought. They walk in the door with this fresh faced young girl, and tell me they're going to help her cause she's going through a tough time. Well I couldn't have been happier. This girl was quite the blue eyes beauty, reminded me of the first girl from back home. So naturally I let the girl get comfortable for a while before I work my magic. She wasn't like the sisters in any way. They were laced with the jungle fever and hooked on whatever blow they could get their hands on. I was just happy I didn't catch the shit from them. They were decent in the pussy department, and it was new for me not having to work for it. It was convenient at first, but I didn't really enjoy having it handed to me. I like the thrill of the hunt. Besides, once they told me they were diseased riddled cunts I stopped dipping my pen in the company ink. I started to enjoy the other product I was bringing home, and was happy to try it when they brought a new girl home as well."

"Was this the girl?" I asked, sliding a picture of Alicia across the table towards him.

"Ah, now that's impressive Detective," he sneered. "Here I was all prepared to tell you about her and then tell you where I left her, but it seems you've swooped in to steal my thunder. Tell me how you did it?"

"You know I have a propensity for good luck." I said.

"If luck is all you have, you've been gifted with a shit-ton of it," he said facetiously.

"So what was it about Alicia that ruined the delicate balance at the house?" I asked, trying to get him to stay on topic.

"She wasn't there to be a whore; she was there to get on her feet. I wasn't used to dealing with women who were willing to work hard and save up for the future. My experience was that women want it all right now and anyone standing in the way was a misogynist. I was so used to being the shit-bag around women it was odd to run into a girl who already had one foot out the door. She didn't treat me with disdain, she was just really nervous around me. She knew what the sister's and I were doing for money, but she didn't care. She worked a regular job when she actually left her room, and she wasn't willing to entertain any men. She could made far more money sucking dick than flipping burgers, let me tell you that. She seemed very perceptive of my intentions towards her. She knew I wanted a taste of her sweet nectar, but she wouldn't give me the time of day. It bothered me, but I tried to be about my business. Unfortunately, I was between girls at the time. Can I confide something to you, Detective?"

"Of course you can, if you forgot, that's kind of the whole idea here." I said sarcastically.

"There's the smartass I remember," he said before taking a long toke on his cigarette. "What I mean to say is it ain't easy hunting young tail in the winter time. Girls are bundled up and it's harder to tell if it's a bulky coat or a fatty. Given the circumstances, I thought I'd try to add Alicia to the business. The problem was she was a fighter. Normally I like that, but given I was living in a house with two other women at the time; noise wasn't really conducive to busting a nut in a pretty young thing. Low and behold, we got interrupted. Christine found me with Alicia and freaked out. Suffice it to say I did not have the privilege of tapping that sweet ass while Christine was coming at me with a kitchen knife."

He sat back for a moment and stared at his hands which he slowly balled into fists.

"Detective, have you ever hit a woman?" He asked.

I glared at him for a second knowing he was about to regale me with one of his self-righteous woman-hating tirades. "No, I have never hit a woman."

"It's far more rewarding than hitting a man. Most men can take a hit, women though," he trailed off making a short 'right hook' movement with his fist as far as he could swing it with it tethered to the table in front of him. "I can knock 'em out in one swing. They are truly the weaker sex, and I proved it my whole life. When they can't defend themselves, they do anything you ask them too, assuming if they do that you'll somehow start taking it easy on them or let them leave. It's pure stupidity; I mean have they never seen a movie? They don't portray guys like me aren't accurately in the movies, but come on. Never has a girl, doing exactly what she has been told result in anything, but her getting hurt worse. The only common sense thing to do is fight for your life, fight for your dignity, and fight for your virginity, but they don't. Women like to claim they're the smarter sex, but that's only because they lack the strength to do it another, more efficient way."

I stared at him, starting to get annoyed, and my inclination towards beating him to death started to appear in the back of my mind. The only good part about his long winded bullshit was that I didn't have to take any notes. The more of his vulgarity that went in one ear and out the other; the better, because there was never a time I would need to know any of it. I knew how he felt about women; he had been beaten down and ignored by his own mother and had spent years battling his mommy issues by subduing women to his ill-tempered perversion.

"So setting aside the fact that everything you just told me is complete horseshit, what does this have to do with Alicia?" I asked him, hoping my voice was still on an even keel, masking my growing anger.

"Strong women should be put in their place, weak women should be made to serve; it's that simple. Weak men deserve to die too because their weakness allows for women to spew venom into their minds, making them doubt who they are and compromise who they can be," he spewed.

"I disagree, strong women make their own place, and weak women are usually the product of weak men. Just like psychopaths are usually the products of weak fathers and overbearing mothers. You could lay all the blame on men in most cases. You're the spitting image of that fact, Fenton. Your father was a weak-minded, lazy, good-for-nothing drunk and look what he spawned; an arrogant woman-hating murderer who blames all of his problems on women. It must take a big man to blame everyone else for his own shortcomings." I held up my thumb and forefinger an inch or so apart, "And I really mean, short."

"You better watch your fucking mouth, kid. I'll whip it out and show you how big a man I really am," he threatened, his voice getting lower as his rage began to build.

"Spoken like a man who has two inches of unrequited fury in his pants to go along with his mommy issues," I goaded.

It was hard to get Fenton angry, but I was enjoying every second of pushing him to the limits of his normally calm demeanor.

"Get out, get the fuck out you pompous little prick. We're done here," he growled.

"Oh, Fenton; we've only just started. You already know I'll walk out of here and never come back without hesitation. Your pathetic little kill count stops at 17; I'll have to bring by your serial killer participation trophy when they stick the needle in on Christmas Day. It would be like, my little farewell gift to you. Be sure to look for me in the front row, I'll be the one with the party hat, popcorn and noisemakers leading the crowd in the chants I've been working on." I antagonized him further.

He was almost shaking with rage. Fenton hated the "everyone gets a trophy" culture that had developed over the past few decades. He wanted to be singled out as the greatest and most prolific serial killer in American history. The idea of falling short of the "honorable mention" category had him seething, near the point of explosion. He wasn't quite there yet. He was normally a master of self-control. This had added to the testimonies against him demonstrating how each of his heinous acts was thought out, premeditated, and executed with cold calculation. I knew he was about to burst, and was certain this might be my only chance to see it. I started pumping my fists at shoulder height and chanting to him.

"Fuck you Fenton, Fuck you Fenton, Fuck you Fenton," I recited over and over again.

His fists clenched and his jawline tightened. The vein in his neck started to bulge; creeping up until it appeared to reach across his forehead. I knew he was close to the breaking point; he just needed a little shove.

"N, E-E, D-L-E Needle, needle, give him the needle, needle," I chanted, acting like the worlds most fucked up cheer squad. I was really reaching now; searching fast to find his last nerve. The needle chant was just what he needed.

"FUCK YOU. YOU FUCKING LITTLE PRICK I'LL FUCKING KILL YOU. I'LL FUCKING CHOKE THE LIFE OUT OF YOUR ARROGANT FUCKING FACE YOU FUCKING ASSHOLE PIG FUCKING COP. I'LL STRANGLE YOU JUST LIKE I DID THAT GONORRHEA LACED FUCKING BITCH CHRISTINE. I'LL SQUEEZE YOUR FUCKING NECK UNTIL YOUR GODDAMN HEAD POPS OFF."

He stretched his hands out towards me as far as the chains would allow him to which still fell two feet short of my neck.

"I FUCKING HATE YOU! I WILL KILL YOU DO YOU. UNDERSTAND ME? I WILL KILL YOU. THEN I'LL BEAT YOUR BRAINS IN WITH A SHOVEL LIKE I DID WITH LAURA. THOSE

FUCKING BITCHES PUSHED ME TO IT AND I FUCKING KILLED THEM. THEN I DROVE THAT BITCH ALICIA OUT INTO THE COLD AND STRANGLED THE LIFE OUT OF HER TOO. I HAVE KILLED MORE PEOPLE THAN YOU KNOW SO DON'T FUCK WITH ME YOU PIECE OF FUCKING SHIT. AAAAUURRGGG."

His voice trailed off from the long string of threats and turned into a deep visceral scream. If anyone else at any other time made a noise at me, I would have found another place to be in a heartbeat.

The angry, out of control screaming reminded me of drug users who turned violent on a bad LSD trip or experiencing excited delirium. People in those circumstances were highly unpredictable and needed medical attention as quickly as possible. This was similar, but on a whole new level. I knew then if I didn't find a way to get him talking again I would be in a lot of trouble. The amount of time and resources already invested in the task force was enough to put me in the hot seat without being unprofessional with an inmate. I decided to wait it out and see if Fenton calmed down enough to keep talking.

It took a while, but eventually Fenton started to lower his voice enough that the second time I waved-off the corrections officers, they actually left the room. I decided a new tactic was necessary if I was going to make any headway with Fenton, and take back new information to the taskforce.

He finally paused to catch his breath, his red face indicating he was on the verge of passing out.

"You once told me that you were the most prolific serial killer in American history. You may be mad at me now, but if I leave, no one will ever know it. I will take your statement to the grave with me, and your official number won't even reflect the seven additional kills you've told me about so far. If you still want the credit for all you've done, you have to keep going." I explained slowly.

He was still breathing hard, but I knew the most casual appeal to his ego would get things back on track. He couldn't help but be proud of what he had done with his life; he was incapable of empathizing with anyone. He proved that over and over again. I didn't like stroking his ego, but it was an easy enough way to appease his rage and focus him on the information he needed to provide me.

"I didn't want to kill the sisters, ya know? I had it good there. I made easy cash money all while working another job on the side. I was stacking cash hand over fist those two years. I wanted it to continue as long as I could make it work. I was pissed when they brought that girl into the house. She didn't belong there; she ruined everything I had going for me. Most of the women I killed got a decent burial. Not her though, she got ditched in the dead of the night and covered with ice and snow. I figured a needle full of "H" in her arm would make people think less of her when they found the body. People don't care about drug users, cops especially. I learned that first hand, you know?"

"I probably understand better than most. Unfortunately cops find it hard to empathize with people who they have to watch first-hand destroy their lives, time and time again." I explained.

"But somehow have no problem with people doing it with booze?" He gave me an inquisitive look that told me he was already aware of my struggle.

"I know you're a booze hound, Detective. I could smell it on you the last two times we met. Today though, you're different; you're sober, intuitive, provocative and unbearable. I have to say, I like the hungover detective I saw the past two weeks."

"What can I say? I'm turning over a new leaf. I'm trying to prove that anyone can change, no matter what their vice of choice might be." I added.

"That's awfully noble of you, kid. The difference is substance addictions are for the weak. I've done every drug available, and I didn't let it change me or turn me into a pathetic version of myself."

"Now how did you manage that?" I asked, with all the sincerity I could find.

"I have an exceptionally strong willpower. If I want something, I go take it. Drugs are a suckers bet; that's why I sold more than I used. Drug addicts are easy money as long as you can handle them when their withdraw gets so bad they come banging on the door at three in the morning asking for a fix. They're pathetic human beings, but they always seem to have cash on hand."

"So you were a drug dealer?"

"Not always," he said shaking his head, lighting another cigarette and blowing smoke in my face. He was calm again, and trying to reclaim the upper hand.

"What else did you do?"

"Oh I did all kinds of things before we met. Hell; I was even a cop for a little while, if you don't find that too hard to believe." He said, arrogantly.

"I have a hard time believing anything you say to me. That's why the rest of my week is spent fact checking everything you've told me to try and sniff out the bullshit."

"And that's why I love our little game here," he smiled, taking a big drag on his cigarette. "I enjoy sending you all over the Midwest chasing down leads while you try and write my memoir. How's that coming by the way?"

"It is less and less about you and more about the investigation and the lives you destroyed. I think they should get something out of it, rather than just having to be victims of your sick game."

"Tread carefully as you write my stories, detective. If it's anything less than a masterpiece I'll pen a few chapters of my own, just to make sure it's a quality work of art," he threatened.

I took a moment to think that over. It wouldn't be the end of the world if he did some of the work on the book. I could use the extra time to better envelop myself in the investigations. I thought about it longer than I should have before realizing how futile it would be.

"I don't think that would be the best idea," I explained. "No publisher is going to want to stamp their name on a project written by someone in your position. You aren't the most eloquent speaker in the world, and they would have a hard time justifying their revenue to the families you destroyed."

"Well detective, I doubt it will be much different for you. A lot of people are going to be pissed when your face lands on the back cover." He said, trying to make me nervous.

"The difference; they will know by page two that I didn't have a choice in writing it. They will get the most realistic view of you, the investigation, and law enforcement possible from my writing. Your version would just be a long winded Odyssey of you sucking your own dick on paper. I wouldn't read that, and I sure as hell ain't writing it that way either." I assured him as I sat back a bit in my chair.

"I guess we'll see if I like it in a couple months," he replied with a shrug.

"So," I expressed as I continued to steer the conversation back where it was needed, "Keeping all that in mind, do you want to tell me about Irvingdale?"

"Well kid, like I said before there wasn't much else to it. I found a couple girls who were looking to go into business and didn't mind me crashing in one of the bedrooms, as long as I kept them safe."

"Do you ever hear the irony when talk?" I interrupted.

"My life is one series of ironic instances rolled into one fucked up existence. The irony that I loved having my way with women and then discarding them, but took a few years off to run a whore house with a couple local gals, is not lost on me. To do what I do you need three things, money, patience and opportunity. Some years were better than others when it came to chasing tail. I made the best of my opportunities, and took time in between to make some money. After all, money creates opportunity here in this corporate capitalist society of ours. Fuck the little man, I want a new Bentley. The real irony here is that you make a low government salary protecting people who have more money than you. If that doesn't chaff your balls just a little, than you must be on the take with somebody; at least in my experience that's what it means," he alleged.

"Well I'm guessing your experience doesn't involve a whole lot of honest day's work, otherwise you'd know it was possible for people in any line of work to make an honest living without selling out to make an extra buck." I uttered, trying once again to disguise my disdain for his inaccurate allegations.

"I've held down a few honest jobs from time to time. I didn't see the point in doing so long term. Honest jobs make good side hustles, but the real money isn't found between nine and five. I don't believe in government, and I sure as hell don't believe in cops, so why would I work a job that's guaranteed to send part of my paycheck to fund things I don't support?"

I shook my head briefly before replying, "We could sit here for hours debating the validity of taxes and how the government should spend tax revenue, but I can assure you, it won't accomplish anything."

"Exactly, cause you're a part of the problem." He insisted.

"So in Irvingdale, besides overseeing a prostitution ring and selling drugs, how did you make your money?" I asked trying to remain patient, though he intentionally kept going off topic.

"The best place to make cash money is from legitimate registered businesses and politicians who like to step outside the law to make things happen. Everyone wants to appear, 'law abiding,'" he said throwing up "air quotes," with his hands raised as far as the chains would allow, "Until they're told what the tax bill will be or that they can't do something. Those people will pay premium cash for services rendered, no matter what they are."

"So what kind of services were you rendering?" I asked him.

"I did everything from mow grass to deliver messages. If they had cash, I was available. They pay more when they know you could blackmail them for ten times the amount," he revealed.

"That makes sense; I'm guessing there was a niche market for these types of services?"

"You are correct," he divulged, "If you spend enough time in an area, you will eventually find the right people who need those services. It doesn't take as long as you'd think."

"So was that your approach everywhere you went?" I asked.

"Eventually; the real key to what I do is anonymity. I like taking young women back to my place and having my way with them. You can't do that if you're hanging out at the country club waiting for the movers and shakers to palm you some cash to get rid of a handgun they used on a former employee. That could take a while, and it gets in the way of my extracurricular activities. Everywhere I went, I found a place that needed my services." He explained.

"Where else did you render your services?"

"I spent a little time in your home town; people used my services, and I did pretty well."

"Can you tell me anything about it?" I asked, wondering who the hell would ever employ someone like him.

"That's a story for another day; we will get around to your hometown again, but for now we should talk about where you're headed next."

"That's why I'm here," I admitted. "Where am I headed to next?"

"Well you seem interested in digging into the darker side of life, so maybe I can serve you up something juicy to make this all worth the trip. This time; no tricks, no hidden bodies stacked on hidden bodies. You are going to go out and recover one body," he paused for emphasis, "But this one is special."

"Special? In what way?" I wondered, out loud.

"This one girl is the only one I was ever paid to kill. The other ones were just for fun." He said with a casual shrug, as if murder was just a way to pass the time.

"Are you going to leave me guessing who it is like the last two times or is there more to this one?" I asked, hoping against hope he would at least float me a name.

"Her name is Jessica; and you are going to want to do a full autopsy on her. She has information on her that," he paused for effect, "Might be useful when you're wading through the local political climate there."

"Was she related to someone important?"

"Related? No, not related. She was someone's mistress though, and that should make this little trip a little more fun. You're going to want to brush up on Iowa's third congressional district. Back in 1989, he was just a small time politician with a proclivity for under age women. I buried the body in the Badger Creek State Recreation Area west of Cummins, Iowa. On the west side of the lake is a deep, large cove north of G14 Highway. Approximately one hundred or so meters north of the cove, is a marked grave."

"And how is it marked?" I asked.

"You will find a tree with a pentagram carved into it. To the east of the tree, facing the lake is the grave. The rest is up to you to find. I know you'll appreciate the irony in this one."

"I appreciate you pointing us in the right direction, but why specify the quality of the autopsy? We would have performed a full one regardless of your directive," I informed him.

"Of course you would have, the difference is; I hate politicians. I may have been more than happy to take the chunk of money offered to me to knock off a sixteen year old girl, but I made sure, every bit of his misdeeds could come back to haunt him. She was the only girl I ever had properly embalmed. You'll probably want to look into the practices of the local mortician as well. Lots of dirty money to be made in rural Iowa," he said in a sing-song voice.

I casually checked the stopwatch on the table to see time had flown by faster than expected. Sobriety apparently made time go by at a normal pace. Seeing that I only had a few minutes left, I tried to make the best of it.

"Anything you'd like to add before we end our little session today?" I asked, "Anything else about Irvingdale?"

"Nothing that comes to mind," he said quietly. I took that as my cue to leave and started packing, taking the lighter and empty cigarette pack with me. I stood up to leave and showed Fenton the stopwatch running over the three hour mark. He nodded at me as I threw my bag over my shoulder and stepped towards the door.

"You didn't know Alicia was pregnant, did you?" I asked, leaning back towards him slightly.

"What difference, at this point does it make, detective," he sneered.

CHAPTER TWELVE

Iowa's third Congressional District consisted mostly of rural counties scattered with small towns in the southwest portion of Iowa. The geographical area was extensive, but Fenton had been determined to narrow down the location as well as whom his alleged associate had been. A fast phone call to Agent Jones started the ball rolling towards our trip to Iowa. Flight plans were made, local jurisdictions were made aware and Dr. Elmore's team was notified and scheduled to arrive in Des Moines, Iowa the next day to make the drive to Montgomery County Iowa on Monday morning. The only thing more difficult than chasing down thirty year old murder victims, was adding a political figure into the mix.

I wasn't super eager about this particular case, but my apprehension was well earned. Politicians cared only about getting reelected, so they were unpredictable unless you just focused on the money and the power. If you could track the money, you could predict what a politician was about to do, and how much it was going to cost the average taxpayer. It reinforced my belief that the people with enough integrity to make great leaders were always smart enough to stay out of politics. You could occasionally find someone with good intentions and motivation that was out to make a difference, but they were few and far between. People sacrificed the very framework that made the country the incredible place to live that it is now, all under the banner or change. Change is not a bad thing, but change for the sake of change rarely takes into account what is working now and what has never worked in history. This case was about to drop me right into the middle of that reality, and was destined to test my new-found sobriety.

It was hard to drive through a "hands-free while driving" community the legal way when everyone was calling me every five minutes. Agent Jones was none too pleased that our bet on Fenton's relationship to the Richardson sisters had ended in a three way tie. He agreed to pass the news along to Dr. Elmore who had been given clearance to meet us at Badger Creek State Recreation area to collect the body and transport it to her lab. Dr. Elmore would be much closer to this body location than our normal coroner out of Kansas City. It would be nice working with her again as she had proven her worth many times over with the six victims from Irvingdale.

Lt. Carter was anxious to have me back at the Police Department for an update on the victims from the park. Detective Ross and Detective Shirley were full of questions about their assignments for the case in Iowa, and were constantly texting and calling to see if there were additional details I had yet to relay to them.

I was pleased to see the media circus outside the Police Department had finally dissipated. There hadn't been much to report on since only one of the bodies from the park had been identified. The scene at the park where Lane and his wife, Emma, had died was still crawling with reporters trying to get the perfect angle to shoot their latest update on the case. This had syphoned the number of reporters waiting to ask each officer walking by if they had a comment on the first four bodies located. It was nice to be able to gas up the department vehicle in peace before heading inside as usual.

I tossed my bag and coat on the desk and headed straight for the Lieutenant's office. Carter waved me inside before I had the chance to knock.

"Hey LT., you said you've got an update for me?"

"Yes I do," he replied. "Grab a seat."

I pulled up a chair to the other side of his desk as he brought me up to date on the local investigations.

"We've positively identified one of the bodies from the park as Spencer Warren. He was a regular customer of ours back in the mid-2000's when he was facing multiple allegations for drugging and raping high school and college age males. We had multiple warrants for him when he dropped off the face of the earth back in 2008. He was one of our most wanted individuals for the past nine years after that," said Lt. Carter.

"So somebody took matters into their own hands?" I asked.

"I'm not sure about that, but he died from blunt force trauma; a lot of it. Whoever killed him knew him well enough to hate him. Most of his skull was caved in from the back. The only thing that helped us was that we had his DNA on file with the FBI and his dental records from a two year stint he did in Lancing for sexual assault back in 2000." Lt. Carter paused for a moment to take a sip out of his coffee mug. "We're getting pretty close to identifying the other two bodies from the park. We think they're on our missing person's list. Warren himself made the list after his mother reported him missing. He was a sick fuck, but he always kept in touch with his mother. I always figured it was the perfect way to drop off the radar, but I guess I was wrong."

"So we've got someone else in the area that killed, this time as a vigilante?" I asked.

"I don't know about vigilante justice. It would make sense, but without knowing who killed him, it's impossible to say for sure." Lt. Carter pondered.

A knock on the office door behind me interrupted the conversation. Lt. Carter waved again and Shirley and Ross stepped into the office. Shirley took the other available chair while Ross stood by the door, which he closed behind him. Shirley shuffled through a stack of papers in her hands and Ross addressed the room.

"So you may be in for some unpleasant surprises up in Iowa, Bryant. We checked records for missing persons across the state of Iowa. There is a huge cluster of missing person cases from the area fifty miles west of the burial site. According to Agent Jones and our other contacts with the FBI, there are at least nine women missing between the ages of 16 and 25 years of age from the area around Cass County, Iowa. Most of them are from small towns scattered around the county, but there are a few from other counties as well. They all went missing between 1986 and 1989. None of them have been recovered, and they are all missing from several jurisdictions," Ross paused as he flipped through his folder. "Six of them are missing out of various small towns in Cass County, Iowa while there are also women missing from Montgomery County, Union County and Shelby

County, which are all adjacent to Cass County. This area was believed to be a hot spot for abductions and sex crimes in the late eighties."

Ross nodded to Shirley who continued from there. "They filed over twenty-five rape cases and two additional kidnapping cases between 1985 and 1989 in Cass County alone. The method of operation is the same for all the cases in which the victim survived long enough to file a police report. The victims all woke up with large patches of short term memory loss consistent with being drugged, and all of them had been found naked in or around their homes with evidence of sexual assault. None of them had any DNA evidence on or in them as it appeared the suspect had used a condom. The victims all appeared to have been bathed and groomed when they were found. All this information was from FBI investigations in the area. They were called in once the rape cases hit double digits for the first time in recent history. We still haven't received reports from the local agencies, Agent Jones said he'd been caught up in red tape with Cass County Sheriff's office and wasn't making much headway."

"Jesus," Lt. Carter swore. "Some people know how to make life difficult."

"Is anyone else under the impression that they might have multiple suspects?" I asked. "Fenton directing us to look into a politician seems an obvious indicator Fenton wasn't the only one active in that area."

"I'd say with what we know about Fenton's methods and the details of the other cases, we have at least two suspects. Someone wasn't into killing as much as Fenton was, that's why we have all these surviving victims," Shirley articulated.

"I agree with Jeanine," I said. "From what we know so far, Fenton wasn't one to let a victim live to tell her story. Plus, he told me flat out someone paid him to kill and dispose of one of the victims. It's possible one of these girls was enough to end our second suspect's career. Anyone climbing the political ladder who indulged in such activities wouldn't hesitate to eliminate a threat to their career."

"I agree," admitted Carter. "We are going to tread lightly on this one. Bryant, call Agent Jones and let him know everything we have so far. He and his boss, S.S.A. Wells are going to take lead on anything involving this political suspect. We keep our agency out of it as much as possible. Bryant, you are there to consult, nothing more. Let the FBI do all the questioning and investigation. You are there purely to find the Fenton connection to this suspect and that is all."

"How am I supposed to write all of this into a book?" I asked with concern.

"My guess is, by the time volume one comes out, this will all be old news anyway. The press will get wind of our investigation, and they will start circling like vultures. Whatever happens will be tried through the court of public opinion long before it makes it into the book," Carter expressed.

"Then I will proceed as planned," I conceded.

Lt. Carter continued. "I am expecting case files from Agent Jones at any time. As soon as I have them, we will start going over them so you are educated on all of them before you arrive tomorrow night; any questions?"

The three of us shook our heads and the Lieutenant dismissed us from the office. I whipped out my phone as I reached my desk and called Agent Jones.

"Terry, hey man do you have anything for us?"

"Hey Bryant, I have the list of missing person cases for a hundred mile radius of Badger Creek. They all seem to be grouped to the east around Cass County though." Terry said.

"Jeanine was just filling us in on that. I would say somewhere around there is where Fenton was doing his usual business. This looks like it was just a burial site for the victim that Fenton wanted to protect. Fenton seems to think this body will be setting someone up for major political fallout," I mused.

"It makes sense; Badger Creek was a remote area back in the late eighties, so it's very likely this was just a great place to hide a body with evidence to take someone down."

"Well, Fenton is the vindictive type; I'm not even sure if this guy did something to make Fenton mad. I think he just hates politicians and saw a great opportunity to take someone down with him." I supposed.

"It's always possible. I'll send you what we have and then I'll plan on seeing you in Des Moines tomorrow night," Terry said.

"Are you bringing that good bottle of scotch with you?" I joked.

"I might be able to do a couple drinks, but after that I'm all business. No more hangovers for me." He said with a defeated tone.

"Alright then, I'll see you tomorrow, Terry." I hung up the phone and started logging into my computer to work on my report.

Behind me Ross and Shirley were gathering their coats and heading towards the door.

"You two done for the day," I asked, leaning back in my chair to look out past my cubicle wall?

"We're off to make a next-of-kin notification to Mrs. Warren. She still lives in town at the Colorado Towers," replied Ross. "We're hoping she maybe has some of his things still that we can look through. We thought he was hiding out somewhere back in 2008 until his house got repossessed and everything inside was sold at auction. We're hoping his mom still has something that will tie him to his victims or his killer."

"Good luck," I hollered after them.

"It's the least we could do after we heard you had to do five notifications yourself last week." Jeanine expressed as they made their way out the door.

"Six," I said, correcting her.

"That's right, I forgot about Lane's kids," she admitted. "Even more so, we've got this one."

"I appreciate it. I'm not sure I could stomach another one," I said, turning back to my desk.

Once again my team was looking out for me, reminding me to be grateful I wasn't doing this alone.

I let out a long sigh, and started toiling away on my report.

———

After over an hour finishing my report from the prison visit, I was finally able to start looking into all the allegations Fenton had made. It was hard to believe anyone would have trusted Fenton to help them in any way. Fenton never struck me as the kind of man to be involved in any kind of organized crime, but I had been wrong before. For the longest time I believed Fenton's only addiction was sexually driven, which resulted in the terrible things he had done. It was hard to wrap my head around the fact that he had spent a great deal of time using and dealing drugs. This involved extended amount of human contact which seemed to fly in the face of everything Fenton had ever done. It occurred to me that the only thing I truly knew about him was that he had an unquenchable thirst for young women. Everything else was still a mystery. DNA evidence had done most of the heavy lifting in the murder trials. Once you have evidence which ties victims together to one suspect its hard for anyone to overlook what Fenton had done. How Fenton went from angry teenager killing a girl who dismissed him casually, to calculated killer who piled bodies one after another into the same grave, was lost on me.

It became clear that what I really needed to do was figure out who Richard Allen Fenton really was; not just who he had become. I had spent years going through trials detailing how Fenton had meticulously tortured and killed his victims, but up until my first meeting with him for the task force, I had little to no idea how he got from here to there. He had a driver's license and social security number, all of which were found to be fraudulent. Nothing about him fit into any particular mold. The guy didn't even have a phone. The fact that someone like that could last all the way from 1975 to 2007 without being caught completely baffled me. No one was that lucky; but Fenton defied the odds for thirty-two years before I put him away. I hoped with this newest investigation that Fenton would lose the sense of anonymity he had enjoyed for all these years, and finally be exposed for who he truly was; a sick fuck with a less than ideal child-hood. Understanding how people like Fenton were born and raised helped predict the future actions and behaviors of serial killers who followed in his footsteps. The FBI had teams of people who specialized in this, but I had been tasked with unmasking Fenton, and exposing his flawed upbringing to the world.

It seemed odd to me that anyone was capable of doing what Fenton had claimed this politician had done, and get away with it. Perhaps in the Eighties there were fewer people watching, and even fewer who had the ability to share it with anyone. I was perfectly happy to be a government employee as long as it didn't revolve around constantly having to convince people to reelect me every term. The very nature of politics led good people down a dark road, and gave bad people excessive influence over others. It was too easy for someone to line their pockets through lobby-ists, PAC's and businesses who knew their money could be used to gain influence on various issues.

There was a dark history in the US surrounding law enforcement that used to be guilty of the same thing. People could hand over money and crooked cops would look the other way. It wasn't uncommon for seized drugs and money to be poured right back into the criminal organizations from whence they'd been seized, but for the most part, that was a thing of the past. Everyone had a phone with a camera and most officers had body worn cameras; it was a lot harder to be crooked when the world could see every misdeed within minutes of it happening.

It was a good thing, the evolution of law enforcement. With advancement in technology it became easier to sort through good and bad candidates, and find the one who wasn't driven by prejudice, greed, and lust for power. While a screaming protester with a phone in your face might be annoying, it was a fantastic source of accountability which prevented good cops from straying and highlighted the bad cops for early dismissal. Over time, cops were held to higher and higher standards, but it seemed to take forever to hold politicians to the same level. Politicians could still orchestrate deals in the dead of the night without anyone noticing who was enticing them to vote one way or another.

That's why I was happy to work for a police department instead of a Sheriff's Office. The idea of someone in law enforcement being elected by popular vote, and not promoted through excellence of character and superior leadership, seemed backwards and dangerous. There were, of course, good Sheriff's out there. It was just hard to tell if you were electing a politician to work in law enforcement or forcing a law enforcement officer to be a politician. Ask most L.E.O.'s and they'll give you a long list of reasons why they don't like politicians. Even the politicians we liked often supported causes we did not, or spoke in ways unbecoming of a public servant. If an officer spoke out of turn or in anger, they were disciplined, demoted or fired. When politicians do it, they called it "Political Maneuvering," which was a bullshit term used by people to excuse poor depth of character, or outright corruption.

It was with all this on my mind that I began researching political figures in the 3rd Congressional District of Iowa, both past and present. There were a lot of them, and each of them had their own reasons to be loved or hated. I truly despised all the pop-up "donate to my campaign now" ads which assaulted my vision every time I searched one of the many political figures. I had no stakes in the Iowa elections other than hoping the next candidate would be better than the one before them. This was rarely the case, whether it is Iowa or anywhere else.

Clicking out of yet another pop-up campaign ad, I wondered which of the many political do-gooders was responsible for the death of a sixteen year old girl. The FBI had Jessica Childress on file along with a picture and descriptors.

I took a moment away from sifting through politicians to review Jessica's file. The blurry picture couldn't hide the aspiration that Jessica held in her eyes. Jessica had been a high achieving scholar and athlete, who had big plans of going into public service or being a teacher someday. The file was complete with newspaper clippings from candle light vigils, loving eulogies from teachers, friends and family members, as well as report cards and a list of her many philanthropic endeavors. Jessica had championed a local group raising money for cancer research after losing a classmate to leukemia in the seventh grade. She had been an active member of the Scouts and boasted numerous accomplishments in after school clubs and teams.

Jessica had spent her free time shadowing teachers, coaches, local political figures, as well as completing multiple ride-along experiences with the local Sheriff's deputies. She interviewed the local Fire Chief for the school paper, and had her picture taken with then Governor of Iowa, Terry Brandstad and President George H. W. Bush when he campaigned in Iowa during the 1988 election. Jessica even went as far as shadowing the local school board members and political candidates for the state and local elections. I reviewed the photos and list of names Jessica had been pictured with and started seeing a familiar name and face. I flipped back and forth between the case file PDF and the most recent campaign ad to pop up on my browser. The face was the same, but it had aged considerably. Life in politics will often do that to a person.

I shook my head, hoping I was wrong as I pulled out my phone and texted a name to Agent Jones. I stared hard, pleading with myself to go home early and ask anyone who could help me to let me sit this one out. My phone vibrated on my desk and I picked it up to see Terry's reply.

"Aww FUCK," I said.

CHAPTER THIRTEEN

Feeling a little nausea after a rough landing in Des Moines, Terry and I, along with his boss, Supervisory Special Agent Wells exited the plane and headed towards the terminal, where our rental cars were standing by.

SSA William Wells was classic old school FBI. He wore his all black suit, white shirt and red tie as if it was an extension of his personality. His stride reflected his six foot three inch stature forcing Terry and I to do our best to keep up. His light brown skin showed no expression behind the classic Aviator sunglasses he wore to round out his "Fed" look. He reached the terminal a full three steps ahead of us allowing him the perfect amount of time to open and hold the door for us. Even though he was only an inch or so taller than Terry, he somehow towered over both of us, making it seem as if he was there to watch over us as we struggled through the investigation. SSA Wells was a serious man in his late forties, but time on the flight had quickly shown me he was capable of keeping the mood light, even while maintaining a serious topic of conversation. He wasn't as easy to talk to as Terry, but he had an earnest nature about him that gave me confidence he was bringing something new, and valuable to the task force.

Terry and I hopped into a black sedan identical to the one SSA Wells was driving and followed him to the hotel.

"He's all business isn't he?" I mused to Terry, as he did his best to keep up with Wells.

"He has the same mentality that you do, let's get it done and go the fuck home," divulged Terry. He navigated a tight left turn at top speed, forcing me to grab the handle located by my head.

"Perfect, we certainly don't need anyone slowing us down. I'm sure our suspect will do enough to hold us back without anyone on the team trying to do the same," I posited.

"He's tough, but he's fair. I like working with him out of the KC office. He's all business, but when the day is over he can turn it off and hit the karaoke bar with the best of them."

"Shut the fuck up," I sounded in disbelief. "There's no way that guy goes out to sing Karaoke. He looks more like the kind of guy who kicks back with a glass of whiskey and reads classic literature in the study at home."

"Actually he does that too, except it's not a study, he has a full blown library in his house," said Terry.

"No shit?" I retorted, shaking my head in disbelief.

"I'm telling you man, he's the real deal. He's probably the most well-read person I've ever met."

"Well this should be interesting then. I can't wait to see how he handles our friendly neighborhood politicians then. I hope he makes them look foolish." I said with anticipation.

"He could make a lot of people look foolish, including us." Terry advised. "We would do well to watch what we say and do while we're working with him. He doesn't take well to bullshitting and profanity, which is ironic since he always tells me to stop bullshitting when I'm wasting time. Let's just stay on topic and see if we can't make this an efficient trip."

"You got it, Terry. We swoop in, find the body, arrest the conspirators, and head for home. I'm all for making this as short a trip as possible," I admitted.

"I just wish we could find the body and arrest the suspect all in one trip. I get the feeling we won't be well received when we go to D.C. to talk to him." Terry confided.

"Do you actually think he's going to talk to anyone about this?" I asked.

"Oh hell no, he's going to be surrounded by lawyers, and they'll all be telling him to keep his mouth shut. I think the only way we get anywhere with him is if we develop probable cause in this case and get a judge to sign off on a warrant. I'd love to arrest him, but I doubt the judge will issue a bond big enough that this guy can't pay with cash."

"Really?" I asked, "Even if we go through a Federal Court?"

"You saw who this guy champions. He's all about teachers unions, big pharmaceutical companies and foreign relations. He's got campaign funds flowing in no-stop; they think he'll be the next Democratic Vice President selection. He's got support nationwide, we'll be lucky if we can even get close enough to him to put him in handcuffs." Terry replied.

"Man I fucking hate politics; when did it get so hard to hold people accountable for their actions?" I wondered.

"Alleged actions; we still have a long way to go before we have shred of proof to take in front of a judge. We might as well not think too much about how difficult it will be to get this guy to answer for his crimes, let's make sure he actually committed one first."

"You're right as always, Terry." I admitted as we parked in front of the hotel.

I grabbed my suit bag from the back seat, my suitcase from the trunk, and followed SSA Wells into the hotel. He paused just inside the door and checked the surrounding area before turning to us. "How about we check in, get a bite to eat and then a drink at the bar before we turn in tonight, gentlemen? We have an early start in the morning," suggested Wells.

"Yes, sir," Terry and I replied in unison before we made our way to the front desk.

I checked the GPS on my phone and was pleased to see the trip to Badger Creek State Recreation Area was less than an hour. Hitting minimal rush hour traffic, we could get there, exhume the body and be on our way before dinner time. Not knowing when or where we would be getting lunch, I pocketed some fruit from the continental breakfast in the lobby and made sure I had a decent breakfast. The orange juice in the drink dispenser was weak and obviously watered down, but it accompanied my toast adequately enough. I was still struggling to grow accustomed to my recently rediscovered mental clarity in the early morning hours. After months of hitting the bottle hard before bed every night, I'd forgotten it was even possible to have a drink with dinner and then just go to bed as I had done the night before. Working with SSA Wells for the first time, I was trying to follow his lead whenever feasible.

SSA Wells had perfected the work-to-home off switch, and spoke nothing of the case at hand, rather conversing casually about his wife and two kids, and discussing Terry's concerns about fatherhood. Wells completely shattered my expectations of the hard-ass FBI agent, with his easy going manner, and impeccable table grace. He spoke graciously with the wait staff, and carried on in small talk with anyone in the area who caught his eye. He was so relaxed that I almost overlooked the hawk-like gaze he cast around the room, acknowledging anyone who walked in all while sitting with his back to the elevator.

I had been surprised when he allowed me to take the seat facing the door, but it became noticeable after several minutes that he could watch the elevator door behind him using the mirror over the bar while keeping his offhand towards the door. I wondered about this until I noticed he held his left arm just perfectly positioned so that he could access his duty weapon which was slung under his left arm in classic FBI style. The gun and holster were lost to the casual glance, obscured conspicuously by his black suit jacket and black shirt. Wells had foregone the usual white shirt and red tie for dinner and had seated himself comfortably in a blazer and button up shirt.

It wasn't lost on me that he casually discussed family with Terry, but reserved his questions for me in the area of law enforcement and my career aspirations. It might have bothered me more if I had seen my wife recently. Everything I did at home seemed to be on the opposite schedule from her. It exhausted me emotionally, and made me yearn for the days I dreaded her pulling her SUV into the garage, waking me up in the middle of the day when I worked night shift. Once again I was hundreds of miles away in another state, looking for another dead body. I tried to shrug off the questions entering my mind making me wonder if SSA Wells liked or respected me, and focused on sipping my cup of coffee as fast as I could. I wanted another cup for the road; because the first one was doing just barely enough to chase away the yawns I fought to stifle.

I spotted SSA Wells and Terry exiting the elevator and thought it best to skip the second cup and just top off the first one. I located a "to go" lid and snapped it into place as Terry and Wells reached the dining area and followed my lead. They each grabbed a cup of coffee and some fruit for the road.

"Good morning detective, did you find the hotel accommodations to your liking?" Wells asked, grabbing a bagel and started towards the front door.

"Yes sir, thank you." I replied trying to match his stride. Terry jogged briefly to catch up with us until we reached the door to the parking lot out front.

"Agent Jones tells me you've been working hard lately overcoming an alcohol dependency, how is that going for you?" Wells asked, catching me completely unaware.

"I've had a few bad days, but I'm finding the results to be encouraging as it interferes less with my work." I replied. I tried to shake off the fact that I was dying for a drink, and give him the positive answer I hoped he would appreciate. Wells slowed his gait as we approached the vehicles, and turned to speak to me directly.

"I'm pleased to hear that, Detective. I'm not foreign to your affliction, for I too used to struggle with alcohol consumption. I spent a great deal of time in the Bureau's Child Crimes Unit. Some of the things I had to deal with during my late twenties and early thirties genuinely shook me to my core. I imagine you're fighting your own battle sitting down each week with Fenton. I've been impressed with your reports, but the very content of which is enough to make me reach for an extra glass of my favorite Blue Label Scotch."

Wells paused to fish the keys out of his pocket before continuing.

"Alcohol is a common coping mechanism in our line of work; unfortunately it can become a cruel taskmaster to those who allow it to control them. Please give me a call if you're struggling, I'll always do my best to be understanding. This taskforce is going to be a test to the absolute sobriety we need. Unlike a lot of others who have undergone recovery, I believe a drink to unwind at the end of the day is perfectly healthy. You can assist me with your accountability during this trip as I assure you I shall provide you with mine. This is our first of many trips together, so I believe we can benefit with the facilitation of the other."

"Thank you sir, I would appreciate the help." I replied nodding to him.

"Now to business gentlemen; we will meet Montgomery County Sheriff's Deputies and Wildlife and Park's at the scene. They will ensure security and assist with anything else we need. Dr. Elmore is already here and will be completing on scene analysis, and then accompanying the body to her lab in Lincoln. This should be a short trip providing Fenton hasn't used his unpredictable chicanery to impede the investigation with his quintessential stratagem." He orated as he unlocked the car with his key FOB.

"We can only hope." I agreed, determined to check the dictionary on my phone to figure out what he had just said.

"Are there any questions before we get under way?" asked Wells.

"No sir," Terry and I replied. Wells climbed into his car and shut the door. I went to the passenger side of the other vehicle and looked across the top at Terry.

"What the hell does chicanery mean?"

Terry shrugged at me and smiled. I shook my head and climbed into the car.

———

G14 Highway reached a dead end upon reaching into the west side of Badger Creek State Park, just as Fenton had indicated. Agent Martinez and Agent Davidson had been on scene for over an hour by the time we parked the cars and stretched our legs. There were already a handful of vehicles on scene, and a group of people could be seen walking north carrying cases of equipment with them. The sun had come out enough to require sunglasses, but the morning was still fairly cold in the early hours. Agent Martinez stepped out of the driver side door of her large, black GMC SUV and donned a hat to shield her eyes as she walked over to greet us.

"Agent Martinez, it's good to see you again." I greeted her, shaking her hand.

"You too, Detective; it's hard to believe we're doing this for the third week in a row," she replied turning to shake Terry's hand. "SSA Wells, it's good to see you again."

"Please, call me Bill," he instructed her as he shook her hand. "We've known each other long enough."

"How long do I have to work with you to call you Bill?" Asked Terry; with a grin.

"Not until we've been working together for another few years," replied Wells with a serious expression. "Same goes for you, Bryant."

"Duly noted," I offered before turning back to Agent Martinez. "Any trouble finding the body?"

"Your report could not have been more precise. We found the pentagram on the tree and the body to the east of it facing the lake. K9 confirmed it too; now Davidson is out finishing a grid search to make sure we don't have another City Park fiasco like we did in Manhattan. Have you had any luck identifying the bodies yet?" She asked.

"One of them was a victim of Fenton, another was a registered sex offender awaiting trial, and we still don't know for sure on the last two. The coroner's office in Kansas City got a little backed up that week." I explained.

"Yeah I heard about that, sorry about your rookie," she offered, shaking my hand again. "It's a hell of a thing to lose coworker; please pass our condolences along to the family."

"I'll do my best; it was pretty unexpected. I didn't know the kid more than half an hour before he died."

"I heard it was an improvised explosive that got him, is that something you can confirm?" Wells asked.

"Yeah I can confirm that, I caught some debris from it myself. Unfortunately it looks like we have an unknown player in our little game. Someone with a vested interest in the outcome of these cases," I offered.

"You keep us posted, Bryant," instructed Wells. "I'd like to assist in whatever way I can."

"Yes sir," I replied.

"If you gentlemen are interested, I can take you to the burial site," offered Martinez.

"We will start that way in just a minute, I want to meet with Montgomery County and Wildlife and Park's before we head to the scene," stated Wells.

Parked in a row, three white Ford Explorer patrol vehicles sat off the side of the road on the south side with two Deputies on foot turning people away who weren't involved in the investigation. Several Deputies were walking towards our group as we waited for further instructions. The deputies had simple, but modern uniforms; hunter green pants and outer plate carriers accompanied their tan long sleeve uniforms which shown out every side of the tactical vests containing their OC spray, extra maga-zines and various other necessities. Their uniform looked far more comfortable than the patrol uniforms I had worn in my career. Our uniforms were old and outdated, but still maintained a "classic police offi-cer" vibe the department seemed determined to maintain.

The deputy in the middle had three stripes on his sleeve indicating he was a Sergeant. He led the way and immediately recognized Wells as the one in charge on scene.

"You must be Agent Wells. We spoke on the phone yesterday, I'm Sergeant Patterson; anything we can do to help, please let us know."

"Thank you Sergeant, this is Agent's Martinez and Jones as well as Detective Bryant who is spearheading this investigation," introduced Wells, indicating each of us in turn.

"Welcome to Montgomery County," Sgt. Patterson offered tipping his wide patrol cap to the group. "Our Parks and Wildlife Officers would be here, but they caught somebody fishing without a license and now they're bogged down in paperwork."

I laughed briefly, until I noticed no one else was joining me.

"Well I'm just glad somebody enjoys a good Park Ranger joke," said Sgt. Patterson laughing uncomfortably.

"They wouldn't get it, they're feds." I offered, trying to make Sgt. Patterson feel better.

"Well I have to try," admitted Patterson as he shook my hand. "What-ever you folks need, let me know, because we're happy to help."

"Right now, we're headed out to the scene to check on the progress of the recovery team," stated Wells. "We should know shortly what addi-tional assistance will be required."

Less than a minute into the walk I became immensely grateful that Iowa had been dryer than Kansas over the past couple weeks. The hike to the wooded area surrounding the burial site would have been tricky in the tall grass of late spring and impossible after a heavy rain. Fortunately the ground was firm, making my decision to wear a suit along with Wells and Jones, a little less foolish. Wells carried on as if he was in full hiking gear, leading the group by nearly ten yards as he casually walked through the dead foliage of last fall, and navigated the budding shrubs of early spring. Thankful again that I hadn't been required to carry anything, I finally reached the burial site at the back of the group. I attempted to breathe quietly to hide the fact that I was slightly winded and circled the group who was standing around several of Dr. Elmore's grad students, who were digging carefully, nearly a foot into the ground.

Dr. Elmore stood by in a pair of Khaki's and a dark, long sleeve blue polo shirt, leaning against a shovel as she took a break with one of her interns. Her boots were muddy, indicating she'd already had a turn digging, and was perspiring slightly, wiping the sweat from her brow with the back of her sleeve. I nodded to her as she caught my eye and gave me a quick smile and a nod.

I averted my gaze from the top buttons of her shirt, which strained slightly against her breasts with each breath. I nervously went to adjust my wedding ring and realized I wasn't wearing it. It bothered me, because I couldn't remember if I had left it at home or the hotel. Even in a group of people, I felt uneasy again, just as I had when I first met her in Nebraska.

I tried to distract myself the best I could, and managed to space off long enough not to notice SSA Wells climbing into the hole to take a turn digging. It caught me off guard, but once again spoke to his leadership style. He wasn't one to allow others to do all the work simply because he was the boss. Wells dug a little more enthusiastically than Dr. Elmore's interns and grad students, but only until Dr. Elmore cautioned him on the unknown depth of the grave. I watched as Terry stood by, ready to take the shovel from Wells, who eventually handed it to him. I looked around and found the branch Terry had used to drape his jacket, and followed suit. I placed my jacket where the wind couldn't knock it down, and took my place by the hole to sub-in after Terry finished his digging stint.

Unfortunately this put me right next to Dr. Elmore which had me sweating before I climbed into the hole. The scent emanating from her sweet, fruit scented hair conditioner was a pleasant change from the smell of the lake, and sweaty people all around.

"It's good to see you again, James." She said softly, leaning in towards me so that only I could hear her.

"It's good to see you too, Dr. Elmore." I whispered back, just managing to keep my voice from cracking as I did so.

"I told you last week, call me Lydia." She replied, just as softly.

"Yes ma'am," I said as Terry handed me the shovel. Dr. Elmore and I each offered Terry a hand to help him out of the ever growing hole before I stepped none too gracefully into his place. I dug for several minutes hoping I wouldn't sweat too much through the light gray long sleeve dress shirt I had worn. Fortunately there was enough of Dr. Elmore's team that someone quickly subbed in to take my place in the hole. Dr. Elmore and Terry helped me out of the hole as it began reaching a depth just over my thigh, but not quite to my waist. I quickly retrieved a handkerchief from my jacket and sponged my face off.

The digging continued for another half hour or so. I was beginning to doubt the location when one of the shovels hit something large and metallic.

"Everyone out of hole," commanded Dr. Elmore. "We will proceed forward with only one person digging at a time. Tommy, stay in the hole and try to start clearing around the edges as best you can. Switch to the smaller tools if you keep hitting metal."

"What is it?" I wondered out loud.

"Can't you tell?" asked Dr. Elmore stepping over beside me. "It's a casket."

"Shit." I whispered, barely audible, "He wasn't kidding then."

"Kidding about what?" asked Terry.

"He said this was the only body he ever had properly embalmed. He must have put her in a casket too," I stated.

"It's definitely a casket," said Tommy from down in the hole. "I've got two separate corners already and I can feel the seal of the lid."

"Michael, climb in and give Tommy a hand, start at the far end and try not to stand directly on the casket if possible," Dr. Elmore instructed.

Another one of Dr. Elmore's interns climbed into the hole and was handed a small shovel and a bucket. Tommy and Michael spent several minutes cleaning around the edges, loading dirt into buckets and handing them up for another intern to empty and hand back. This part seemed incredibly slow, but the progress was identifiable. The lid became exposed showing a light blue tint in the sunlight and a few dent's where the shovels had been driven.

Two other interns climbed into the hole and gave Michael and Tommy a respite for the time being. The two women, one medium height and blonde, the other a young black female, each with matching hats, dug at a pace matching Tommy and Michael's. Over the next few minutes, the casket looked like it could be lifted straight out of the hole.

I couldn't figure out why my heart was racing with anticipation. I knew the girl in the casket was most likely just as Fenton had described; a 16 year old blonde girl. For some reason the tension was building as we got closer to releasing the casket from the four foot grave. The two interns began clearing down the end of the casket, revealing a handle at the end and finally the bottom edge of the casket.

I was about to ask why they were clearing around underneath one end of the casket, when I watched Dr. Elmore hand down what appeared to be a large leather looking balloon of some sort. The interns inserted the balloon, still deflated as far under the casket as possible. Then the blonde pointed to Tommy, who was standing by with what appeared to be small, portable, battery powered air compressor. The air compressor started humming and the two interns stood to either side of the casket as far as the hole would allow them. They continued clearing down the sides of the casket as the balloon became visibly inflated underneath.

It all became clear as the casket started gradually lifting out of the ground, starting at the cleared end. Tommy, Michael and Dr. Elmore laid down on the edge of the hole with shovels and attempted to cut away at the mud still clinging to the sides of the casket as it elevated gradually. I moved from side to side trying to find a way to help, but couldn't seem to find the right spot. Before I could reach down into the hole with one of the shovels, the casket was almost completely visible. Tommy cleared the sides of the casket to reveal long metal handles running all the way down each side. I watched Tommy hand the two interns in the hole, several lengths of rope which they began tying to the handles in various locations. Each length of rope was secured and the end tossed out of the hole onto the ground on either side.

"Ok everyone, out of the hole," barked Dr. Elmore. I moved around the hole and helped the interns out, then awaited my next instruction. "Everybody, grab a rope," she called out.

I seized the nearest rope to me and stood by as everyone else did the same.

"Tommy, how are we doing over there?" asked Dr. Elmore.

"We are at ninety percent pressure and leveling, it won't help us more than this." Tommy advised.

"Everyone put tension on your rope and on the count of three lift," instructed Dr. Elmore. "ONE, TWO, THREE, LIFT."

I strained hard against my rope and was pleased to see the casket rise six or seven inches. I grabbed lower on the rope and kept pulling. Dr. Elmore continued to call out instructions, keeping everyone lifting in unison. I kept pulling and watched Tommy jump into the hole next to the casket and help lift it up to ground level.

"Everyone lift and take one step away from Tommy, let's start setting this thing out on the ground," Dr. Elmore shouted from the corner opposite me. Dr. Elmore and SSA Wells teamed up on the high end of the casket and managed to set six or so inches of casket out on the grass. Two more such movements allowed them to each grab the handle and lift with their legs. All told, there were nine of us lifting the casket which felt heavy enough to require more. Slowly, but surely, we moved the casket out of the hole and laid it in the grass several feet away, where it rested while we caught our breath.

"Who'd have thought that was more work than digging up remains one bone at a time?" panted Tommy, as he leaned on the side of the grave.

"I hear you there." Terry agreed, doing his best to tuck in his shirt again.

I went the opposite way and untucked mine, hoping to catch a slight breeze to cool me down. Another minute or so passed by until everyone was done resting their hands on their hips and breathing hard. Dr. Elmore's interns began collecting the equipment and untying the ropes from the casket.

"Let's open it up," instructed Wells. "And make sure it is what we came here to find."

Dr. Elmore and Tommy began using rags and brushes to clear off the mud around the latch and release on the casket lid. This took several minutes, allowing me time to tuck in my shirt, and wipe my hands clean on a rag handed out by one of the interns. I was the last to catch my breath, but it was just in time to see Dr. Elmore unlatch the casket, and raise the lid. Wells held one end of the lid and stepped around to see inside.

Inside the casket was a shriveled body, approximately five foot four inches tall or so dressed in what appeared to be an old shirt that said "Atlantic High School" in black letters. The blonde hair was nothing but a wisp now, doing nothing to cover the shriveled skin wrapped around the skull of what appeared to be a young woman. The age or attire of the body wasn't what captivated our attention; it was the object she was holding in her hands.

"Can someone explain to me what she's holding?" I asked.

"That is a human femur bone," explained Dr. Elmore softly. "And the object at her feet is a VHS tape." She reached down towards the feet and retrieved something else. As she pulled it free I recognized it instantly. I had seen the exact same image when I was researching Jessica Childress. It was a laminated newspaper clipping from 1989 which read, "District Attorney meets with aspiring young activist."

"Is that who I think it is?" asked Wells.

"Yes it is," I replied with disgust. "That is US Congressman Simon Carroll."

SSA Wells shook his head and closed his eyes for a moment and let out a single, uncharacteristic curse. "Fuck!"

CHAPTER FOURTEEN

I sat back for a little while as Terry photographed the open casket and its contents. He took over-all photos and then photos of each item as Dr. Elmore pulled them out, one by one. SSA Wells was making notes, documenting everything as he put together the list of items being collected as evidence. The bone was examined briefly by Dr. Elmore before being placed into a bag. The VHS tape was in a clear case, wrapped in clear, plastic wrap, and appeared to have withstood the test of time.

Other than the bodies at City Park two weeks prior, there hadn't been any cases in need of a suspect. This one was instantly different. We knew it was going to be, but had become so focused on the task at hand that we lost sight of the fact that Fenton wasn't the only one involved. We didn't have a stack of bodies as Fenton had promised, but we did have a bone which didn't belong in the casket.

After several minutes, they finished the inventory on the casket and started packing up the equipment. I retrieved my jacket from the limb on which it lay and slowly put it on, ducking my left arm to slide it into the sleeve before pulling it forward by the lapel and situating it properly. My tie was already loose so I just untied it and folded it up into my interior jacket pocket.

We were up against something bigger than we were ready to face. Fenton had been very specific on the location, even knowing which congressional district Congressman Carroll represented. There was a picture of Carroll with who, we could only assume, was the victim inside the casket. This in itself was not damning evidence, but it reinforced Fenton's statement that the victim was not originally his. SSA Wells approached me with the newspaper clipping. It had been placed in a clear evidence bag and sealed with red tape at the top.

"Take a look at the note under the picture," instructed Wells, holding up the bag.

Accepting the bag from him, I pulled the plastic tight to reduce the glare and obstruction of the material, and checked the picture again.

'Pictured: Atlantic High School Student Jessica Childress and District Attorney Simon Carroll'

"That confirms my suspicions," I said shaking my head. "Carroll was surrounded by allegations of harassment and sexual impropriety when he was running for local elections. They never had anything concrete on him, and he used that as his reasoning to vote for him. He was beating rape allegations before it was the cool thing to do."

"Now he's buried those allegations deep and made it all the way to Congress. He was always the charismatic type. It's why everyone dismissed the allegations against him. All the women were just, "Trying to ruin him," or "looking for their fifteen minutes of fame," said Wells. "The problem is we still don't know if we have anything that actually proves what Fenton alleged. His testimony wouldn't account for much in court. He's on death row for killing a dozen women. How could any jury take him seriously?"

"The only way is to piece together all the evidence we have here and then try to get Fenton on the record. If we manage that, we still have to have something concrete from thirty years ago to take before a judge." I admitted, begrudgingly.

"This one isn't going to be easy," Wells admitted. "I'm going to go talk with Sgt. Patterson and see if he can help me arrange a meeting with the Montgomery County Sheriff. Hopefully with this case involving a victim from another jurisdiction, he won't be against us taking the body and assuming primary status on the case."

"What if they don't?" I asked.

"I'll make sure to ask nicely," replied Wells with a grin. Wells walked away towards the vehicles to meet with Sgt. Patterson. Montgomery County was going to have to file some basic kind of report for the recovery of the body, but if they were agreeable, it should be short and sweet. I watched Terry packaging the evidence into large paper bags. Nearby, Dr. Elmore lead her team as they packed their equipment, and one at a time, hauled things away to the vehicle.

I missed the hands-on portion of the investigation. Even as a member of the taskforce, I was not granted powers of investigation or enforcement in other jurisdictions. I was a consultant, and nothing more. The other cases in Nebraska hadn't mattered; we had the killer and there were no new investigations, just completing old ones. This one was different; we potentially had multiple suspects, only one of which was already behind bars. The other was making his voice heard on new legislation and influencing people around the country. For this case I was completely boxed into the "advisory" role and had no other power to support me.

I wondered how much participation would be allowed from me for a moment before SSA Wells returned with Sgt. Patterson and one of his deputies.

"Sgt. Patterson has graciously offered to take us to meet with the Sheriff about this case and has agreed not to interfere at this time except to gather basic information for the report and take a few photos. Jones, you stay with Dr. Elmore and the body and help them wrap up here at the scene. Detective Bryant and I will follow the Sergeant to Red Oak to meet with the Sheriff about handling the case," he instructed. "Let's go Bryant."

I stepped around the scene to follow Wells and gave Terry and Dr. Elmore a nod and a smile as I passed them. They nodded back and continued with their tasks.

I accompanied Wells and Sgt. Patterson back to the vehicles, managing to keep up with Wells pace which had been purposefully slowed so as not to exceed that of the Sergeant's. Within several minutes we reached the cars and took a few minutes to brush some of the dirt off our pants before climbing into Wells' vehicle.

"I'm sorry your involvement is going to be so limited, Detective." Wells apologized as he buckled his seatbelt. "I think this case is about to get bigger than all of us."

"I'm certain you are correct, sir. I just wish we could view that tape and see what Fenton left for us," I said as the car turned onto G14 Highway after the Sergeant's patrol unit.

"Well hopefully the Sheriff is willing to let us take this case over. If he's agreeable then we get the tape to the lab to ensure its quality before we view it. I'll have them send us digital copies when it's done. The bone is going with Dr. Elmore; she will do a full analysis on it and see if we can't gather some evidence from it. Then we just have to determine to whom it belongs, and find them. Since Fenton disposed of this victim so carefully, it's a safe bet the bone is from one of his other victims. He probably left it in the casket to connect this girl to the other victims he had."

"I was not expecting the bone when we saw it." I confessed, shaking my head a little.

"Nor was I; but then I'm never sure what to expect after reading the reports from you and Agent Jones over the past few weeks."

"Do you think the Sheriff will be agreeable?" I asked.

"I don't see any reason why not. He has everything to gain from letting us take the case now. He would find it quite difficult to conduct an investigation when the only known witness is imprisoned in Kansas, and the only other known suspect is in Washington D.C. eight or more months out of the year. He would have to turn it over to us eventually to complete the interview of the Congressman." Wells explained.

———

Nestled in the 100 Block of Coolbaugh Street, the Montgomery County Sheriff's Offices stood proudly as a light red brick building with floor to ceiling windows in the front, partially obscured by the two concrete pillars framing the entrance.

Sgt. Patterson parked in the public parking spaces in front of the building and stepped out of his vehicle to direct us in next to his driver's side. He circled the front of our vehicle towards the building and waved us over as we exited the vehicle.

"Follow me gentlemen, the sheriff is finishing in a meeting, but it's enough time to give you the short tour of the office here." He explained.

Sgt. Patterson did indeed only give us a brief tour of the building. He made small comments such as, "And there's the conference room," and "Here's the locker room," making small gestures with his arms. Sgt. Patterson circled the interior of the building quickly and ended the five minute tour by the administrative offices.

"If you gentlemen will wait here," he said pointing at several cushioned chairs in the lobby, "I'll go get the Sheriff." He then disappeared into the administrative office wing of the building.

We had only enough time to unbutton our jackets and each take a seat when Sgt. Patterson returned to get us.

"The Sheriff will see you both now, follow me; he wants to meet with you in his office."

Sgt. Patterson led us through a door, secured by an electric lock which opened when the Sergeant held his wallet over a sensor on the wall. We walked past a series of offices all with windows looking out over the parking lots and neighborhood around the building. Patterson led us past all of them to a large office at the end which contained no windows, but a large number of framed photos and certificates.

The sheriff was not an overly imposing man. Standing maybe five feet six inches tall with visibly thinning silvered hair, Sheriff Alan Browning sported a light gray suit and tie with a classic leather holster on his right hip strapping a brown handled, silver plated 1911. He stood up from behind his six foot wide mahogany desk and reached across to firmly shake our hands in turn.

"Sheriff, this is Supervisory Special Agent Wells and Detective Bryant, they're here to speak with you about the remains found at Badger Creek," explained Sgt. Patterson.

"Pleased to meet you both, I'm Alan Browning, how can I help you today?" The sheriff asked, sitting back in his chair and indicating the couch across the room from him.

"Thank you for meeting with us on such short notice. We will do our best not to take up any more of your time than necessary." Wells explained. "We are part of a task force resolving decades old murder cases. We have a suspect in custody who is revealing the locations of the bodies he buried and we are systematically closing out cases with each new body. Unfortunately, this one at Badger Creek is different."

The Sheriff looked skeptical, "In what way?"

"This case, we have been informed, there is another suspect involved; A man of power and influence," described Wells. "This case originated out of your jurisdiction and helps resolve a missing person's case which originated in Cass County."

"Cass County?" interrupted Browning, "You may have your work cut out for you."

"Can you speak further to that statement?" asked Wells.

"Well as you know Cass County isn't that far from here. We've had our fair share of issues with them. They don't cooperate on investigations and the entire system over there is overrun with nepotism. You know they've had the same sheriff for over thirty year's right? He came up around the same time as his little brother who was making his name as a local politician. They had each other's backs from the beginning and hired people who did the same. They run that county like a family business. Everything they do is about putting the family first and the community second." Browning trailed off for a second as he seemed to grasp for a second as to what he should say next.

"So they've been at the helm of power for a long time, enough for you to suspect corruption?" I asked.

"I don't want it to be said that I'm speaking ill of them. They have an enormous reach of influence and I don't want to be caught speaking out of turn," said Browning.

Wells interjected. "I can assure you everything we say here today is completely confidential. Our goal for these investigations is to have the smallest impact on the local community as possible."

"Let me tell you something; there will be no such small impact if your dealings lead you to Cass County. Especially if who you're after has anything to do with the Carroll family, which I don't want to know," hurried Browning waving his hands at us. "What I can do is this. Tell me the name of the victim if you know it and I will request the report to be faxed over from Cass County. I will also turn over this investigation to you completely if you can find a way to get in and out of Montgomery County as fast as humanly possible."

"We can do that," assured Wells standing up from the couch. "The victim's name is Jessica Childress and she went missing in 1989."

"Sgt. Patterson, call Cass County and talk to someone in records. Ask them to send over the report as quickly as possible. Gentlemen, as soon as you have it I believe that will conclude our association," said Browning.

Sgt. Patterson stepped out the door, closing it quickly behind him.

"Gentlemen, I apologize for the rapid nature of our meeting, but I hope I've made it as clear as possible to you that whatever you're involved in with Cass County is going to be met with resistance, if not outright violence.

They will protect their own without reservation, and they will do so by whatever means necessary. The Carroll family owns nearly half the property in Cass County including the towns of Atlantic, Messena and Anita. They run most of the manufacturing and farming operations, and they have people positioned everywhere to see to their business. Ryan Carroll is the most insidious man I have ever met in my twenty-five years in law enforcement, and he holds a strange sense of discretion when it comes to upholding the law." Browning trailed off as he placed his hands behind his head, clearly distraught over the business he was forced to conduct. We were interrupted by Sgt. Patterson knocking on the door and letting himself in.

"Cass County records told me they lost all records of Jessica Childress in a fire back in 1994. They did not have electronic copies available. I'm sorry gentlemen," Patterson apologized.

"If there's nothing else I can do for you gentlemen, I'll have Sgt. Patterson show you out," said Browning hastily.

"Thank you for your time sir," I offered.

"Yes, thank you," said Wells as we stood up, buttoned our jackets and exited the office.

Sgt. Patterson held the door for us, and then closed it behind him. His pace was noticeably faster compared to before the meeting, as he led us out to the lobby and to the front door again. He held it open for us and then stepped back inside.

"Good luck, gentlemen," he called after us, "You're going to need it."

"Well that seemed ominous enough." I said as we reached the car. Wells shook his head briefly, but said nothing until we were in the car.

"We may have to rethink our entire approach here. Fenton kills a girl for someone in Cass County as what I can only assume was part of a cover-up, but there's no way Fenton was in that area long enough to make powerful connections without partaking of the local women himself. My fear is that when we wrap up our investigation here, we will be forced to come back to this area before too long," warned Wells.

"I agree; how do you want to proceed on this case?" I asked.

"Let's take the body and the evidence and fly to Lincoln as a team. We will set up there again for a few days until the remains are processed and all available evidence is in front of us."

"When are we going to notify the family?" I asked. "The last time we waited more than a few days someone tipped off the family and turned the PD's parking lot into a media circus."

"I'm positive we can count on the Montgomery Sheriff's Office to keep what they know quiet for now. The only issue will be if someone in Cass County who took the Sergeant's call about Jessica tips off the Sheriff there. Ryan Carroll, brother to Simon Carroll, our suspect, tied up in a big package with a nepotism bow on it. If they get wind of our investigation they will either try to keep it quiet or tip off the family themselves. I would say everything we do in Cass County needs to be done quietly and covertly. From now on, we assume that any activities we have in or around Cass County are being monitored for the purpose of obstruction." Wells trailed off for a minute as he turned the car onto the highway heading back towards Badger Creek. "Call Agent Jones and let him know the investigation is ours. If they are done at the scene, tell him to load up and meet us at the airport in Des Moines. We need to distance ourselves for the time being."

———

Within two hours the scene had been cleared and the team was back together at the airport in Des Moines. SSA Wells seemed determined to get in the air as fast as possible, and leave the cluster-fuck of a scenario as far behind as he could manage. It wasn't uncommon for rumors to abound from one department or jurisdiction to the next about misdeeds or mishandled situations; it was another for the sheriff of another county to be completely paranoid. For someone to be that anxious they needed first-hand knowledge of the reality of their circumstances.

Sheriff Browning displayed genuine fear at just the thought of dealing with the Carroll family, and he didn't even know who the suspect was. Even without the knowledge of the suspect, he was suspicious and paranoid about us even having to conduct an investigation within the confines of Cass County. It was unsettling to say the least.

We flew on a different plane than my last few trips. Complete with Dr. Elmore and her team, the Embraer Lineage 1000 was filled to capacity. There was a minimal amount of cargo space on the jet due to the casket and containers of evidence stored below. Everyone had their personal bags crammed down next their seats; some of them still protruding into the foot space and aisle of the plane. The Lineage 1000 could hold this many people, but it was built for comfort travel, not government use and surplus storage.

The jet was ornately furnished with plush, leaden seats as well as ample couches in a lounge area completed with a spacious sleeping chamber at the back. These were not the Bureau's usual digs. Embraer had been approached by the FBI, along with Boeing, Learjet, and Cessna, for the temporary use of one of their most luxurious jets. Embraer had seen the opportunity for their jet to be seen in potentially dozens of airports during the course of our investigations, and enthusiastically met the offer made by the DOJ. Normally I wouldn't have approved of such wasteful government spending, but it was hard to complain as I sipped a mojito, and watched the college basketball tournament on the flat screen in the lounge. While I enjoyed the newfound comforts of the jet, I thought back to the cramped seats I had endured in the tiny ten-seat Cessna previously utilized for our trip to and from Lincoln last week. The Lineage 1000 had been fortuitously deployed to Des Moines as soon as the deal closed and the necessity became imminent. There was no way to fit ten people and a casket on the Cessna.

I foolishly accepted another mojito from the stewardess, knowing I shouldn't be drinking at a time like this. I kept expecting Wells to gather the troops and regale us with a motivational oration about working together to solve the case; until I saw him asleep in one of the commodious seats at the front of the plane. Fuck it! Work could wait; I was going to enjoy this.

I allowed myself to sigh quietly as I relaxed further into the cushion of the couch. I sat my glass on the table to my right and stretched my legs. Such a movement was impossible in the Cessna, and I couldn't help but soak up the comforts the Lineage provided. I pulled my feet in swiftly, slightly embarrassed to have to move them, as Dr. Elmore strolled through the lounge on the way to the latrine. I mumbled some sort of apology under my breath, but she just smiled at me as she passed. I looked up at the ceiling in annoyed frustration. Reaching back to grab my drink, I was greeted by Terry who had just been handed a fresh mojito, and looked like he was ready to burst.

"Check out this fucking jet," he said with excitement.

"This might be the happiest moment of my life," I replied, "And that included my wedding night."

"I'm about to tell Wells if we aren't flying first class on the next trip, I'm not coming," said Terry. He held out his glass to clink against mine before we each took a sip.

I had never experienced such luxury, and I was already upset with how short the trip was going to be. All told, from boarding to disembarking, the flight from Des Moines to Lincoln took less than two hours, but it was a great flight. No business was discussed between Terry, Wells and I. Wells slept while Terry and I caught most of a basketball game, and about half a buzz.

Dr. Elmore spent the flight with her team, looking over photos from the scene and assigning tasks to each member when they landed. I couldn't help noticing she managed to be about her business while sipping a mojito herself and kicking off the high heels she had changed into before the flight. Gone were her khakis and polo shirt as she had changed into a navy blue skirt with a white blouse tucked perfectly into the waistline. She somehow balanced her elegant look with her strong personality as she oversaw her group, discussing both the case as well as other aspects of their work.

I found it hard to pay attention to the basketball game as she had sat at the head of her team right where I could see her down the hallway. It dawned on me that she wasn't the only one to have changed clothes. Her team had swapped their digging clothes for slacks and button up shirts, making them look more like a team of legal experts heading to a deposition, rather than doctoral candidates heading to their lab. I was constantly finding another way Dr. Elmore impressed me as it became obvious her team waited on her every word, and worked to anticipate her next request. The team both liked and respected her as they discussed the case, and shared laughs about stories or anecdotes I couldn't hear from my seat in the lounge.

"Hey man, the games over here." Terry quipped as he caught me sneaking a glance towards the front of the plane.

"Uh huh," I replied casually as I turned back to the television.

"You're gonna give yourself whiplash if you keep turning you head back and forth," warned Terry with a sarcastic smile. He ignored the nasty look I shot him, instead taking a long drink to finish his mojito.

CHAPTER FIFTEEN

The flight was over far too soon, bringing us back to the reality that we had our hands full. I disembarked holding my bag over my shoulder and tried to carry myself as if I hadn't been drinking the whole flight. The new Jet was going to be my biggest stumbling block to my aspirations of sobriety. I said a quiet grateful prayer that I still had my sunglasses when I caught a face full of sunlight as I cleared the exit. I held the handrail on the way down the steps, and did my best to look nonchalant. I hoped to appear competent rather than on the verge of taking a headlong spill down the carpeted, beautifully illuminated stairs. There was no immediate round of applause as I reached the runway so it appeared for now I had everyone successfully convinced. Terry, on the other hand was fully aware of my state of mind as he too found the handrail a welcome addition to his stroll down the stairs.

I gave him a casual fist bump as he joined me on the runway.

"You doin' okay?" I asked, trying to suppress a smile.

"Never better, my man. You good?" he asked.

"As long as no one asks me to drive anywhere, I should be in good shape." I replied.

"Same here," he said with a nod.

I turned to make sure we were clear of the stairs just as Dr. Elmore reached the bottom. She was carrying two suitcases, as was Tommy, who followed directly behind her. Feeling like an ass, I shifted my bag into my left hand so I could offer to take one of the bags from her.

"Thank you, Detective, but I didn't get this far in life needing someone to carry my bags for me." She said with a smirk as she marched by me, high heels clicking against the pavement as she passed.

We turned a little too obviously to watch her walk away, which became even more obvious as Tommy followed right behind her.

"Thanks fellas, I've got these too; thanks for asking though." Tommy quipped with a big smile.

"Shit," I whispered to Terry. He too was looking sheepish and chided himself quietly.

"I am a married man. What the hell is wrong with me?" He asked, shaking his head.

"You're only human." I said, realizing how juvenile and stupid I sounded.

"Gentlemen," said a quiet voice behind us. We tried not to start as we turned back towards the plane as casually as possible. The intern with blonde hair and a tan skirt, bordering on too short to be professional, greeted us at the bottom or the stairs. "Dr. Elmore thought the two of you could use some coffee to go." She said reaching out her hands which held two large to-go cups with a tell-tale wisp of steam coming out the lids.

"Thank you..." I trailed off, realizing I hadn't been previously introduced.

"Call me Sam," she said with a nod. "You can watch ME walk away if you want to."

She strolled past us casually, smiling as she tossed her long blonde hair over her shoulder.

"Don't do it, dude." Terry cautioned me as he made a concerted effort to turn his back to the twenty-something grad student parading away from us. I joined Terry and acted as if something more interesting was happening back at the plane.

"Not very believable, gentlemen, but it will have to do." We turned casually to acknowledge the next grad student to exit the plane. This one was slightly taller than Sam, but sporting an almost identical skirt and blouse.

"I'm Tamara," she said offering her hand to shake each of ours. Tamara stood proudly with a posture you'd expect from an African dignitary in front of the United Nations. Tamara's deeply opaque skin seemed to both reflect and absorb the light of the setting sun as she flashed a courteous smile. Her crinkled locks were pulled back into a tight pony-tail exposing beautifully adorned earrings in each ear. She gestured with her head for us to accompany her towards the airport, and led the way by about a half step as we turned to keep pace. Behind us, another grad student reached the tarmac and jogged briefly to catch up with us.

"SSA Wells told me to tell you he is being recalled to D.C. and he needs the two of you to oversee evidence transportation with Dr. Elmore and her team. He said he would call you when he lands and that he expects an update as soon as you've reviewed the tape from the casket. This is Michael; he will be driving one of the vans back to the lab. You two are welcome to ride along." Tamara offered.

"Thank you, Tamara." I said graciously.

I was impressed once again with Dr. Elmore's team, but even more so with her. She had kept track of her team, and kept them on task all while allowing the atmosphere in the group to be relaxed and casual. To top it all off she kept an eye on Terry and I and knew we'd had enough mojitos on the plane to require a lot of coffee and a driver. I smiled a little as I sipped the coffee which was strong and black; just the ticket for a man on the edge.

———

I had been so distracted during the my disembarkation of the plane that I hadn't noticed Dr. Elmore double back from the parking lot with the third van to load all the evidence and casket for transport.

That was a hard thing to admit seeing how evidence custody was tasked to Terry during the active investigation. Dr. Elmore was more than making up for our oversight, filling out the Evidence Custody Receipt to reflect the transportation by her team to the lab.

The interns got to work immediately, reviewing the remains, collecting samples and diving headfirst into researching the victim, suspect, and region of origin. They had all seemed relaxed leaving the airport, but as soon as their feet crossed the threshold of the lab, they were all business again.

Tamara was tasked with preservation of the video, and in less than half an hour produced a DVD copy of the VHS tape for our review.

Terry and I sat back in a couple plush cushioned arm chairs in the lounge with our coffee and fired up the DVD player. I was almost too nervous to speak. We had never had something like this handed to us; a blast from the past as it was. We still sat apprehensively, waiting to see what it contained. Dr. Elmore let herself into the lounge area and surprised us both with a bowl of buttery popcorn. With a nod and a smile she sat the bowl on the table between us and turned to leave.

"You're not staying to watch?" I asked, before I could stop myself.

She turned casually at the door as she opened it, and shook her head.

"If this video contains what I assume it does, I still want to be able to sleep at night. You gentlemen have this burden to bear; I'll review applicable portions of the tape, if necessary," she said.

She was right. It occurred to me that this was, without a doubt, most likely going to be the world's sickest snuff film. The DVD started with grainy footage from the '80's which appeared to be of nothing at first. The video rolled on for several minutes with almost no distinguishable details displayed.

There was no sound at first which made Terry check the volume of the television before deciding he didn't want it to be too loud, and turned it back down a little.

Right as I was beginning to get antsy I saw the first signs of life. The video was recording inside some kind of old building, possibly a barn. I recognized what I knew unmistakably as headlights from a vehicle move past the window, partially illuminating the interior of the building, showing it to indeed be an old barn. To the right of the video camera, someone stood up from a chair and made their way towards a door next to the window. The silhouette showed something I had not expected; a duty belt

The figure appeared to be wearing an old throwback police uniform complete with a wide brimmed hat. The gun slung on the belt was hung to the right and was barely identifiable as a revolver. The man in the uniform was tall; over six feet and had to duck to exit through the doorway. The man left the door open as he stepped out to greet whoever had just arrived. In the background of the video, voices could be heard muttering softly, but indistinguishable at a distance. Several minutes passed before shadows from the headlights were cast through the open door, indicating the return of one or more individuals.

The man in uniform backed through the doorway carrying something between another individual, this one wearing a uniform and duty belt as well. The two figures turned slightly after entering the barn displaying what appeared to be an unconscious woman in their arms. The two men set her on a table, laid out like a corpse, and then stopped to stretch.

"She doesn't look that heavy, but she starts to wear on you after carrying her to and from the vehicle," said a voice in a mellow, but not overly deep, baritone.

"I'm sure you'd get used to it after a while," said a second voice.

My skin started to crawl. I recognized that voice.

"Simon say's you're the man for the job. I didn't realize I'd be meeting one of my own deputies when I got here."

"What can I say sheriff? He recognized one of my many talents, and offered a price I couldn't refuse."

"Well Deputy Dean; I hope we can count on your discretion. I don't like finding out one of my employees is working for the family without my knowledge."

"Do you discuss every hire with your dad and brothers every time you stumble onto someone with a useful set of skills?"

"Of course not, but I usually try to keep the family business separate from the public business. It prevents a disaster occurring in both worlds."

"I can understand that. Should we dispense with unnecessary formalities than, Mr. Carroll? Or should I just call you Ryan?"

"You work for the family; Mr. Carroll or Sheriff Carroll will suffice. Now here are the important details; her family will come in within the next day or two tops. I want you to be there for the missing person's report. Make the family feel like we're moving heaven and earth to find their little girl. Get a few other deputies involved and organize a big search and rescue team, and comb the entire county."

"I assume that means you want me to dispose of her outside the county?"

"Dean, I don't care where you hide the body, just make sure no one can ever find it again. Call my guy at the morgue about a cremation; that's the safest way. No one can know about this, but the three of us. My fucking brother needs me to bail him out again; but he's the high achiever. Daddy wouldn't want anything to happen to poor Simon. He can't keep his hands off the young girls and now we have to cover for him, yet again. Do your thing, dispose of the body and keep this shit to yourself."

"Just because I work for you, doesn't mean I'm a fucking idiot. I know how to do my job."

"You better make sure of it."

The second man turned to go. He reached the doorway before the first man called him back.

"Do you have what I need?"

"It's in the car."

"I'll wait with the package while you collect my payment and bring it to me."

The sheriff left the barn, but was only gone a matter of seconds. He returned with a large shipping envelope in his hands.

"Is everything there?"

"Ten thousand dollars and two brand new identities; just like you were promised," the sheriff said.

"Be sure to pass my gratitude along to Agent Sanders for me."

I leaned over towards Terry. "The guy getting paid is Fenton."

"That's what I thought," he whispered back.

I shook my head, and leaned back in my chair as I watched the sheriff exit the barn closing the door behind him. The video once again showed nothing but the illuminated window and a now visible crack of light under the door. The only audible sound was footsteps which appeared to get louder for a moment until the camera was lifted swiftly out from under the lamp shade where it was hiding, and turned towards the window. Fenton stood for a moment, not approaching the window with the camera until the headlights turned away. He then walked to the window to catch a glimpse of two Cass County Crown Victoria Cruisers on the roadway outside. One of them fading down the roadway, light bar clearly visible as they were backlit by the receding headlights. Then the video was turned off.

The video changed scenes rapidly. The camera was still in the barn, but the windows were covered with what appeared to be heavy burlap sacks, and there were several candles lit.

"That's right sweetheart; time to wake up."

A chill ran down my spine as I recognized Fenton, who was taking off his hat and removing his duty belt in the background. The girl, who we immediately recognized as Jessica Childress, was seated in a chair, hands tied behind her back and a gag in her mouth. She appeared to be coming out of a deep, possibly drug induced sleep, and was trying to shake off the confusion.

Jessica was wearing a white and yellow sun dress, her long blonde hair matted and covering part of her face.

Fenton approached from behind her and placed his hands on her shoulders.

"It's okay sweetheart; I'm with the Sheriff's Office. I'm here to help you," he said. "I need to ask you some questions, but before I take the gag out of your mouth, I need to know that you're going to be completely honest with me, especially on the sensitive subjects. I need you to tell me what happened so we can get you justice."

I was appalled. The very idea of Fenton as a Law Enforcement Officer made me want to turn in my badge and gun. He had become the very thing he claimed to hate, but it had obviously been for reasons of personal gain.

"Can you tell me what happened to you?" He asked in a falsely reassuring voice, removing the gag from her mouth.

"I went to see Simon; I had to talk to him. That's the last thing I remember," she whispered.

"Why did you need to meet with District Attorney Simon Carroll?" He asked.

She looked up at him, confused as to why he knew so much without having asked for specific details.

"I had to tell him something important, but he got really mad at me," she said, tears beginning to form in her eyes.

"What did you need to tell him?"

"I told him," she paused for a moment, looking around in despair. "I had to tell him I was pregnant."

"And that the baby was his?" He said, coercing her to continue.

"Yeah, I didn't know what to do. I found out weeks ago, I just couldn't find the courage to tell him. I knew he was an important man, that's why I fell for him. I didn't want him to marry me or anything; I just needed help to end the pregnancy. I didn't have the money for an abortion, and I was already two months along. I wasn't going to be able to hide it much longer."

"Did you go to the doctor to confirm the pregnancy?"

"Yeah, that's how I found out how far along I was," she replied.

"What doctor did you see?"

"I saw Dr. Morgan over in Messena; she was really nice and understanding. She said she would be there to help, no matter what I decided to do."

"How very nice of her; does she know who the father is?"

"No, I wouldn't tell her."

"Does anyone else know you are pregnant?"

"No, just Simon, Dr. Morgan and now you," she replied.

"That's good, that's good," he said with an ominous tone. He brushed the top of her head reassuringly for a second.

"Are you going to help me, Deputy?" She asked, pathetically.

"How long were you sleeping with the District Attorney?"

"It started back in December; I was shadowing him for one of my articles over my winter break, and it just kind of happened. I felt so bad at first; I mean he's a married man and so important around here. I didn't want to ruin his life; I just didn't want to ruin mine," she said sobbing.

"What happened next?"

"He said he would take care of everything. He was being really nice. He even got me a glass of soda to help me calm down. I must have fallen asleep, because I don't remember anything else."

"Because he drugged you," said Fenton. "He drugged you and then had his brother, the sheriff; bring you out to a remote area to dispose of you. Luckily for you, I intervened on your behalf."

"Thank you," she said, crying so hard she started shaking.

"That's right; Deputy Dean is here to help you. Now; let me get you out of those restraints."

He helped her up from the chair, turned and steered her over towards the table where she had been placed when the sheriff brought her. He brushed the hair out of her face and shushed her gently as he turned her so she was on the right side of the table from the camera.

I felt my stomach knot up.

"Here," he said casually as he leaned her forward towards the table, "I'm having trouble seeing the knot in this light."

She leaned down over the table, resting her torso on it as Fenton struggled with the knot momentarily.

"You know; you are an incredibly beautiful young woman," Fenton leered, his tone changing completely.

She turned to look back at him when he suddenly pushed her head down against the table.

"Ow, you're hurting me." She sobbed as his right hand held her head against the table, face towards the camera.

"You know you remind me of a bitch I knew once. She couldn't stand the sight of me. She closed her eyes and tried to look away because she wouldn't give me the time of day. You cunts are all the same," he said barely above a whisper.

"Please stop, I promise I won't say anything. I promise, I'll tell Simon you tried to help me," she begged.

"Who do you think sent me here?" He asked.

The audible sound of his fly going down made me sick to my stomach.

"Please don't hurt me, I'm pregnant," she pleaded with him.

He grabbed her by the hair and slammed her head against the table. He pulled up her skirt as his pants hit the floor behind her.

"You just got done telling me how you were about to have an abortion for your own selfish gain. You don't care about him, or the baby; just yourself. You make me sick, you FUCKING LITTLE BITCH."

"Please don't," she screamed as he held her down with one hand and began positioning himself behind her with the other hand.

He thrust hard, scooting the table across the floor with a dull roar, drowned out by Jessica's scream.

I dropped my head and covered my ears. The image was burned into my retinas, and I couldn't seem to shake it. I clawed at my eyes for a moment, hoping if I went blind the image would be gone, along with my sight. There was nothing I could do about my ears. Jessica's screams and the scooting of the table blackened my soul with every second. It seemed like forever, but in reality, Terry found the remote in only a few seconds. The sound of Jessica's screams still echoed in my ears, but at least the echoes weren't as loud as the video.

I looked up long enough to gag in disgust and drop my head again. Terry had muted the video, but it was still playing. I could tell Fenton had moved the table several feet across the viewing area of the television.

"FUCK! FUCK! FUCK!" I yelled, trying to shake the images out of my head again.

"FUCK THIS," yelled Terry. "This is not what I fucking signed up for."

He stood to exit the room, but I grabbed his arm and turned him away from the screen.

"Look away; just look away," I ordered.

We stood for a moment staring against the wall behind our chairs. I felt tears running down my face before I even realized I was crying. The knot in my stomach had moved up to my throat forcing me to gasp for air.

"Is it over?" Terry asked.

I hesitated and then turned my head back a forth to check the video. It wasn't.

I shook my head and snorted back the flow of mucus trying to escape the images in my brain. I looked at the floor and realized one of us had knocked the popcorn to the ground. I would never be able to eat popcorn again. I was shaking uncontrollably and checked the table between us for some kind of tissue. Of course there weren't any. I tried to stand up straight and take several short shallow breaths hoping to hyperventilate and pass out. I wasn't strapped. I knew that because I reached for my Glock, hoping I could end my suffering right then. My gun was locked up in the next room, for reasons that were now apparent.

"Is it over now?" Terry asked, covering his eyes.

"Fuck you, man. It's your turn to look." I swore, barely above a whisper.

Terry took a moment; fighting with his self and straining to find the willpower to turn his head, or leave the room. I couldn't tell what he was going to do for what seemed like forever. He would start to turn and then he would curse under his breath and look back at the wall.

The door to our right opened as someone started to enter the room.

"GET THE FUCK OUT! GET THE FUCK OUT!" Terry and I yelled in unison over and over again until we heard the door close again.

"Oh FUCK it," he yelled, and turned back swiftly towards the television before turning back.

"Is it over?" I asked.

"No; fuck no man."

"GOD DAMMIT," I yelled as I ducked my head so I couldn't even see the flicker of the television on the wall in front of us.

We waited for several minutes; neither of us willing to look, neither of us willing to ask the other to look either. We fought back tears and strained just to breathe.

We both found the courage to turn at the same time, but immediately regretted it.

"JESUS CHRIST," yelled Terry.

"HE'S FUCKING CHOKING HER NOW," I yelled hoping it would all be over soon. It wasn't. The whole thing took too long. I hated myself; I hated Terry, and most of all I hated Fenton. I thought for a moment about how I had to see him in a matter of days, and felt another part of me die a little.

"How the fuck, am I supposed to deal with him for another five months when all I want to do is shoot him in the fucking face, and light him on fire?" I asked.

"I don't fucking know man. I know if it was me I'd fucking strangle that motherfucker until his stupid fucking eyeballs popped out."

"I cannot wait to watch him get the needle this Christmas. It's the only thing I want this year," I declared.

"Save me a fucking seat, James. Save me a fucking seat," Terry agreed.

We let another moment or two pass before I snuck a look again. The worst was over. The video panned from the front seat of a patrol unit as it approached the Lonstein, Farrant and Carroll funeral home. The camera and the person holding it got out of the vehicle and proceeded around the car to the back seat.

"Terry it's over, we can look now," I said.

We turned around to watch the video for a moment as the camera panned across what was obviously a body wrapped in a bedsheet. A hand reached into view and pulled back the sheet, revealing the face underneath. It wasn't Jessica.

"Who the hell is that?" Terry asked.

"I don't know," I replied.

The video cut and then came back on. It was the middle of the night, and someone was digging by the light of a lantern. It was Fenton. The digging continued as it showed Fenton up past his chest in a hole that was about six feet by three feet wide.

After a short while, Fenton climbed out of the hole and walked over to the camera. He picked it up and panned over to a casket sitting just out of the original viewing field.

"See, I told Jessica I would take care of her. They don't know at the funeral home that they actually cremated Dr. Angela Morgan. She was a tasty piece of ass just like Jessica was. A little old for my liking, but tasty none the less," said Fenton.

The casket opened to reveal Jessica who had been dressed in the clothes we found her in earlier that day. Fenton placed the other items in one at a time. He pulled out the bone we had found, and gently wrapped Jessica's hands around it. He tucked the newspaper clipping into the foot area of the casket, and then produced a clear VHS tape.

"This tape is going to be left inside the casket for whomever it may concern someday. I hope you enjoyed my little home movie and find the contents of this tape enough to tear down a group of people who have infiltrated the already corrupt government, and made it their own personal piggy bank. May the Carroll family live to regret the things they have done, and the corruption they have shown. My name is Richard Allen Fenton, and I approved this message."

The video stopped and we slumped into our chairs.

"I don't want to do this anymore," admitted Terry.

I agreed, "Neither do I."

CHAPTER SIXTEEN

The hangover I experienced the next morning was one for the record books. The strongest whiskey in Lincoln couldn't drown out the memories of that video. The hottest water couldn't scrub away the dirty feeling that clung to me like a leech. I drank by myself that night. I couldn't even look at Terry, or he, at me. I had seen a lot of twisted shit in my career, but nothing stuck with me like that video.

Terry had snatched the DVD out of the player, placed it in an evidence bag and sealed it, trying anything to protect the world from its contents.

I spent a few minutes dry heaving over a trash can, wishing to God I had drank something sweeter than coffee before I had sat down. No amount of training could prepare me for such an ordeal.

Dr. Elmore, one step ahead of everyone as always, had Tamara standing by to drive us to the hotel. Terry sat in the front staring out the window, while I sat in the back staring at the floor. Believing myself to be more of a man than necessary, I choked back my tears, trying my best to appear stoic until I was away from the eyes of others. I had never been one to cry in front of others; I didn't want their sympathy. My eyes welled with tears no matter how hard I fought, and the snot flowed down my face.

Tamara had come prepared. She handed us each a handkerchief without a word, drove us to the hotel in silence, and checked us in. We held back a little ways while she completed the check-in for us, and then escorted us to our rooms like a couple of children. She dropped us off at our rooms and casually slipped us each a bottle of whiskey. How she knew what we needed in such detail, I'll never understand. It wasn't until the next morning, head throbbing and throat burning, that I realized how much Tamara had done to help. There's nothing you can say to people when they go through something horrible, sometimes, you just have to be there.

It was nearly noon the next day when the sunlight scorched my retinas, and woke me from my unconscious stupor. No one had called, no one had stopped by; that I knew of. There was a solid chance they had, but there was no indication. I couldn't call what I got that night, sleep. It was more like the hand of God beat me into a merciful blackout, saving me the pain of reliving my nightmare.

I hurt. I woke up on the floor, shirt still matted to my torso with nothing else on but my socks. Apparently my extensive shower had been completed at least partially dressed. My body ached like I had just lost a cage fight, and my insides hurt like I swallowed a gallon of acid. The bedsheet was half off the bed, adhered to the knuckles on my right hand, which were inexplicably bleeding. I lifted my head far enough to catch another face full of sun and lay back down.

The pounding continued so much I thought someone was at the door. I rolled over and detached the sheet from my hand, reopening the wounds on my knuckles again. I crawled slowly to the bathroom and promptly found a shattered piece of the mirror on the floor. That explained the bloody knuckles at least. I used a towel, still soaked from the night before to push the broken glass out of my way, and crawled to the toilet and sink.

The seat was down so I used it to pull myself up to my knees. I was filled with immediate regret, and a wave of memories from the night before. The toilet reeked of my vomit, a large volume of which was still floating inside. The image of me puking until I passed out by the toilet came back to haunt me for a moment. I still had the willpower to wake up and drink some more; momma didn't raise no quitter after all.

The stench brought up a new sensation, and I promptly topped off the toilet with another batch of partially digested whiskey. This time, I had the sense to flush the toilet. I pulled myself up from the white tile floor using the bathroom counter as leverage and stuck my head under the faucet. I chugged water straight from the tap for a little while, hoping it would solve at least one of my miseries.

I was wrong. Another trip to the toilet saw me summoning the porcelain demons once again, this time without having the chance to breathe beforehand. My face turned red and I nearly passed out again, slipping off the toilet seat with my right arm and bouncing my chin off the edge. The next wave of nausea ended up on the floor, though it was far less volume than previous rounds.

I swiped my hand to push away some more pieces of mirror, and fought my way to a standing position. The man in the broken mirror was a fucking wreck. I didn't even recognize him. The small cut on my chin paired nicely with the bruised cheek I had inexplicably attained. I had apparently fallen several times during my intoxicated endeavors. I splashed some cold water on my face, fought back a dry heave, and then stumbled out of the bathroom.

I found my pants, wadded up in the corner by the window; obviously thrown there without ceremony. I dug around through my pockets until I found my phone. I needed to hear a friendly, reassuring voice. I clicked the top number on my favorites list and waited for my wife to pick up the phone. It went straight to voicemail.

"Hello, you've reached Dr. Stephanie Bryant. I can't come to the phone now, but if you'll leave your name, number, and a short message, I get back to you as soon as I can. Thank you."

A robotic voice came over the phone.

"The number you have dialed has a voicemail box that is full. Please try again later."

I lay my head on the carpet and choked back tears again. My wife had always been the one I talked too when the stress of work was too much for me. Just to hear her voice over the phone for a second made me miss her. The anguish of going so long without seeing her was quickly eroding my psyche, leaving me in a constant state of inner turmoil.

I let myself cry for a moment. Why not? Nothing seemed to be going right and this was still just the beginning. I had months of this ahead of me. I knew I wouldn't be able to stomach another of Fenton's home movies, particularly the kind involving violent child pornography. I had put people away for the rest of their lives for possessing child porn. Having someone essentially gift wrap a video and place it into the middle of an investigation, requiring its review, seemed almost demonic in its nature.

As I lay on the floor, I realized my pants were still soaked with water. Apparently I had showered fully dressed; I only hoped I had the forethought to remove my leather shoes. I spotted them kicked off near the door and stumbled across the room to check them. They were dry; somehow through it all, I'd possessed that much sense.

Throwing my shirt onto the floor, I tripped my way into the bathroom and turned the shower on full blast. I let the cold water wake me up a little. It seemed like it was helping the aching muscles, but I couldn't really tell. I ran it ice cold until I began to shiver, and then cranked the hot water up enough to complete a proper shower.

I found by bag, unopened just inside the front door, and located some dry clothes. I had wasted my only suit by getting it soaked, and leaving it on the floor near my pants. I was going to be barely passable as business casual for the rest of the day. I decided it didn't matter much since we weren't investigating anything local, and all our work would be completed at the lab. I found a pair of jeans and a V-neck T-shirt, and called it good. I dug out my casual shoes from the bag, glad they were at least more fitting than my black, designer dress shoes, to accompany my ultra-casual outfit.

The day was half over already. By the time I showered and changed, it was after one o'clock in the afternoon. I found a cup near the coffee maker and filled it several times from the faucet, drinking them slowly so as not to upset my delicate stomach.

Dressed as if I couldn't decide between a trip to the mall or a round of golf, I stumbled out into the hallway. As soon as the door closed behind me I remembered my phone. I stepped back into my room, retrieved my phone and caught a whiff of my own breath as I bent over. I took a few more minutes getting ready, combing my wet, mop of a hair-do and brushing my teeth. Slightly less disgusted with my appearance, I gave my pockets a swift pat-down to ensure I had what I needed this time. Satisfied, I made my way down the hallway towards Terry's room.

I'm not sure if I stood outside his door with my hand raised for a few seconds, or a few minutes. Terry and I hadn't been able to look at each other the last hour we'd been together the night before. I was having trouble thinking about being in the same room with him again. I raised my hand a little higher, about to knock and then thought better of it. It was after one O'clock; maybe he wasn't even in his room. He may have already caught a ride to the lab. I hesitated again, and was interrupted before I could knock.

"He's downstairs, waiting for you."

I turned to see Tamara, who had walked up behind me. Without another word she handed me a bottle of water and gestured with her head for me to follow her. I did my best not to stumble as I followed her to the elevator and climbed in after her. I stood there in silence, staring straight ahead of me at the closed doors.

Tamara pushed the button for the lobby and leaned towards me a little.

"I can help you button your shirt if you forgot how, but you're on your own for zipping up you fly," she said candidly.

I rolled my eyes a little, despairing at my own ineptitude, and turned away from her slightly. I fixed my pants and shirt, having just enough time to unbutton and button my shirt which was misaligned from my initial attempt, before the doors opened.

"Is that what happens to people when they turn thirty? They can't even dress themselves after a night of drinking?" She asked.

I went to speak, but nothing came out. I shrugged it off and shook my head slightly.

"I'm not trying to be insensitive to what you went through last night." She said as the elevator doors opened to the lobby. "I just have to down-play it all so I don't think about what I almost walked into last night."

"That was you?" I asked, barely above a whisper.

"It was," she replied. "I'm just glad you both yelled at me when you did. I didn't see anything and I'm grateful to you both for having the sense to mute the television."

"Thank Terry." I told her, "He's the one who was thinking on his feet."

"Well either way, I'm just glad it was you and not me." She paused as we reached the dining area just off the lobby. Terry caught sight of us, gathered his bag and threw it over his shoulder.

"If you two have a preference for your post-hangover meal of the after-noon, please let me know. I'll pick up or order whatever you want. Dr. Elmore told me we have to watch out for you boys; seeing as you can't seem to take care of yourselves."

"And we want to say thank you," said Terry as we walked out the door.

The sun blinded me instantly making me wonder where the hell I left my sunglasses the day before. The pounding in my head made a tumultuous return, forcing me to lower my head and squint against the light.

It was going to be a long day.

———

Terry and I wolfed down a couple burgers, courtesy of Dr. Elmore and her team. We spent the first hour or so at the lab trying to remember only the important details from the video the night before. It wasn't easy; after all, the gruesome details were tattooed into my memory. The only portion of yesterday I had managed to forget was during my binge at the hotel room. What a waste of good whiskey.

I sat on a couch in the break room leaned over a notepad sitting on the glass top coffee table in front of me. I shook my head slightly to rid myself of an unwanted image and accidently set off my headache again. I grimaced slightly and reached for the bottle of Aspirin on the table. I chased a couple down with water and said a silent prayer they would kick in quickly. I scrawled on the top of my notepad, "Shit I remember," and slapped the pen down on the notepad. Frustrated, I sat back on the couch and rubbed my temples for a moment.

"Still can't shake off the bad shit to remember the important?" Terry asked. I looked up as he sat down in one of the chairs across the table from me.

"It's like I'm trying to take notes about the shittiest thing I've ever seen in my life. There may be something therapeutic about writing it down, but I'm not sure how it's going to help." I replied.

"I think we should start with the first thing we saw on the video and try to stop before we get to the bad shit." Terry suggested..

My phone started vibrating on the table in front of me, sparing me from having to make a decision.

"Hey, L.T.," I said after I answered the phone. I was hoping he had called with good news; I was wrong.

"Bryant; they set a date for Preston's funeral. It's this Saturday morning at 0900 hours. Graveside is at ten; I'm hoping that gives you enough time to make it before you head to El Dorado."

"Thanks for the update. Why did it take so long to arrange the funeral?" I asked.

"Preston's younger brother is a Submariner stationed in Hawaii. He was in the middle of a two week underway when they notified the family. They had to wait for him to get back on shore and then book a flight back to Kansas. April 1st, is the first chance they could schedule it."

"Do we have any word on the car bomb from the park?" I asked, hoping the investigation was going somewhere.

"Nothing yet; the KBI are hard at work analyzing the vehicle and what was left after the fire, but they didn't have much to work with. The fire destroyed so much after the explosion." He explained.

"Shit," I whispered. "If we can't figure out how the bomb was made it makes it really hard to trace it back to whoever built it."

"That's assuming they left some kind of trail to follow," said Lt. Carter. The disgust in his voice was obvious.

We had three homicide victims without a shred of evidence pointing towards a suspect. The investigation was still fresh, but the personal connection to the department had everyone frustrated.

The typical homicide had something of evidentiary value that could at least be tested or evaluated for additional evidence. Everything from the scene where Preston, Tim and Emma Lane had been killed was waiting in line at the KBI lab in Wichita. Evidence was processed as it came in and the KBI was behind by nearly three months. This had been the case for several years. Budget shortfalls and lack of competitive wages left the KBI lab understaffed and overworked. With any luck, our cases would get pushed ahead with some level of priority processing. This wasn't likely though. People across the state were waiting to have evidence come back to them on cases of varying priority. Homicide and rape cases, while a priority were still backed up one after another. You couldn't push one ahead of the other. Everyone deserved answers to their investigations. To push one out of the way to make room for another told victims of violent crimes that their cases weren't as important as another. My desire for instant justice would have to be placed on hold.

I hung up the phone and tossed it on the couch next to me. My frustration was building, making it hard to focus on the task at hand.

"Fenton use to be a Cass County Deputy."

I looked up at Terry who had picked up his own notepad and wrote it down as he said it.

"You're right; that seemed like a bigger deal yesterday before we watched the rest of the tape." I said. I picked up my notepad and wrote it down.

"Ryan Carroll, the Sheriff of Cass County personally delivered a drugged and kidnapped sixteen year old girl." I remembered. The important details were starting to come back to me as I wrote notes as fast as we could remember them.

"Simon Carroll; Congressman for the third district in Iowa, allegedly had an affair with an underage girl and had her killed to cover it up." Terry suggested.

"The Sheriff put Fenton in charge of the search and rescue operation, even before her disappearance had been reported."

"Someone named Agent Sander's helped them get the new identifications for Fenton," remember Terry.

We were on fire now. The details were flooding back to us one at a time making it hard to contain our excitement. Rarely was an investigation aided by such damning evidence. It was almost as if Fenton had talked things over with his victim on video for the sole purpose of taking down the Carroll family. His obvious disdain for police and politicians made it hard to understand why Fenton had been a Sheriff's Deputy, but easy to understand why he wanted to take them down after the fact.

"The Carroll family, specifically Simon Carroll, allegedly paid Fenton to kill and get rid of Jessica Childress because she was a liability to his career and to the family business," uttered Terry.

"Ten thousand dollars and two new identities was the price he demanded of them," I said. "One of them had to be Richard Allen Fenton. It explains why there is almost no record of him anywhere. He introduced himself in the video. He didn't exist before this."

"He literally handed us evidence against them for murder and conspiracy to commit murder," said Terry.

"These are capital offenses too. The murder coincided with the victim being kidnapped and raped. He is literally trying to put them on death row, just like he is." I said with surprise.

"We're only missing one thing, some kind of documented record of the transaction. If they paid with a check it would be easy, but nobodies that fucking stupid, even back then. They would have gone untraceable and paid cash," Terry revealed.

"We have to get Fenton on the record," I said, slightly disgusted at the notion.

"In a way we already do, but there are clearly details missing that we really need him to provide," Terry noted. "Do you think he would provide an official statement?"

"I don't know. It's hard to believe he would cooperate with any kind of official investigation. On the other hand, he seems hell-bent on setting the Carroll family up to take a huge fall. He might be vindictive enough to do it." I considered.

"Do you think we can play to that side of him? Play into the vindictive ass-hole that would hide evidence for twenty years for the sole purpose of burning down a sitting US Congressman," Terry wondered.

"That sounds like the Fenton I know." I acknowledged.

"That video was fucked up, but it may be the ticket to this investigation into Simon and Ryan. If they were willing to kill a sixteen year old girl to protect their lively-hood, it has to mean they're covering up something even bigger than this," Terry divulged.

"You know what," I said looking at him and nodding my head. "You may be onto something. People who do dirty shit like this are trying to wash themselves clean of something far more sinister. I think we've only scratched the surface of this investigation."

"It feels weird, but I'm really excited about the prospect of arresting a couple politicians." Terry said with a big smile.

"Crooked cops and corrupt politicians; they both need to get what's coming to them."

"You're Goddamn right," he agreed.

"Let's call SSA Wells; if this is as big as it seems; we are in way over our heads already," I suggested.

"Maybe you are; ya small town cop from Kansas. I'm a fucking federal agent; this is exactly what I wanted to do when I signed up," he proclaimed.

By the end of our four hour work day, we had assembled a family tree depicting every member of the Carroll family dating back to the early 1900's. They had been heavily engrained in the local government, commerce and education. The men owned businesses, small and large, or attained public office. The women taught in the local schools, owned businesses of their own or held seats at the table of the Carroll family law offices. They were involved in every aspect of law practices. Multiple city and district attorneys proudly sported the Carroll name as well several in private defense and business. No matter what legal aspect you were facing, there was a Carroll family attorney to represent you.

It became apparent after extensive research that if you were involved in something illegal, you were either prosecuted or defended by the Carroll family. When someone was defended by the family, other prosecutors stepped in to handle the case. If you were being prosecuted by the family, you could almost guarantee the defendant was being represented by public defense. The list of public defenders that had come and gone over the past twenty years was unbelievable. The public defender's office turned over between one and three attorneys each year. If someone signed a contract to work there, they never renewed and often paid a penalty to accept work outside of the county, often outside of the state.

From the outside looking in it was easy to see there was rampant corruption. It wasn't being conducted recklessly or publicly, but whenever the Carroll family wanted something, they got it. It took just as little time to realize who was working hand in hand with the family. Those who opposed the family were slowly and methodically driven out of town. Those who supported the family or conducted business with them were the wealthiest in the county.

Ryan Carroll had indeed been the Cass County Sheriff for over thirty years. He had run unopposed for twenty-five of them. Each local election received the attention of Simon Carroll who used his substantial national influence to guarantee ongoing success for the family, both publicly and economically. From the unwitting eye it might seem as if the family cared greatly about the local community. They built parks and hospitals, and brought manufacturing jobs to the area which received large nationwide contracts thanks to Simon's influence.

Terry and I conference-called SSA Wells and filled him in on the case.

Oddly enough, he told us to wait thirty minutes and he would call us back. When he did, it wasn't from his number.

"Boss, Fenton all but gift wrapped these guys for us. We have enough to get warrants for Simon and Ryan already. I don't think it would take long to get warrants on half a dozen other members of the family," explained Terry.

"Before we get ahead of ourselves gentlemen, we need to discuss the implications of this case. The Carroll family is protected both locally and nationally. My contacts in various federal agencies flinched when they heard who we were investigating. This is going to get ugly fast. The catch is this; once we start this investigation, we have to finish it. One person is going to lead us to another and another. This family, and the people who profit from their connections, will stop at nothing to stop us." Wells explained.

It was obvious from the noise in the background that SSA Wells was outside somewhere.

"Agent Wells, is there something we need to know?" I asked.

"This is the only thing you need to know. I am calling you on a burner phone and will be ditching it as soon as I hang up. I am outside because I don't trust the walls of my own office not to have ears. I dropped something in the mail for you, Detective Bryant. It should be there at your department by early next week. It is a list of people I want you to compare with the research you've already compiled. I will not give you information over the phone about its contents. From today forward, we speak of this case in person only; preferably in an open public area. If there was an "ultra-top-secret" classification available for this case, it would immediately receive that designation."

"Boss, is it really that serious?" Terry worried.

"Let me tell you how serious; I have arranged with a third party cyber security company to make updates to all of your computers. Bryant, I've spoken with Lt. Carter, and he has agreed to allow the organization to come in and reinforce security on all computers being used for the purposes of these investigations. Carter, Shirley and Ross will all be receiving these security measures as well as you and Terry's laptops. All online research into this case is to be suspended until those measures are in place. All aspects of this investigation are to be confined to pen and paper, and stored at a secondary location when they are not actively being utilized or reviewed. Do not store these items at Dr. Elmore's lab. It's not a security issue with her or her team, it is a safety issue. If someone gets wind of this investigation, they will try to retrieve all of it. While I have you on the phone, I want you both to print and then delete anything you have on your computers regarding the family. Then I want you to unplug them and remove the batteries. Place the computers into secure storage at the lab until they can be upgraded to the new security protocol."

"Shit!" I whispered as powered down my laptop. I struggled a moment to release the battery from underneath, but finally managed.

"Do we need to upgrade security for Dr. Elmore and her team as well? They've been doing research all day on this case," Terry disclosed.

"Affirmative," Wells replied. "I want that entire lab offline immediately."

"Yes sir," agreed Terry as he finished breaking down his laptop.

"I am hanging up; do not call back on this phone number. You will not reach me on it. I will be there in the morning to oversee the security measures for the lab and computers; any questions?"

I hesitated and looked at Terry who was clearly deep in thought. Just as he began to open his mouth, the line went dead.

"Holy shit Terry, what the hell have we stumbled into?"

"Dude, I knew it would be serious, but I think we have no idea how serious. Let's go tell the team before it's too late," he said.

We both jumped up from our seats and gathered all the paper we had been using to take notes. Fortunately, everything had been on paper rather than on the computer. We stacked it all and placed everything in Terry's satchel briefcase. Terry slung it over his should, strap across the chest and we hurried to the door.

Dr. Elmore's team jumped in unison as we barged through the large French style doors leading into their workspace next door to the lab. Looking startled, they all stared at us in shock.

"Print everything you have and shut it down," Terry instructed them.

"What?" Tommy asked.

"Print your work, then shut down and unplug your computers." I barked at them. "We have a security threat and the cyber security of the lab has to be upgraded before we do any more work on this case."

"Now, people!" Terry demanded. The team jumped again, this time hurrying to their various computers.

"Hardwire your computers to the printers. Do not use any kind of Wi-Fi connection to print. We can't risk anything being accessible through the network. If you are working on a laptop, disconnect from all browsers and internet searches and then shut off your wireless connection." I instructed them.

I marched around the room finding anything computer based, and unplugged everything I could. I found the Wi-Fi router and unplugged it from the wall, wrapped the cords around it, and set it on a desk in the middle of the room. The team was lined up at the printer with their laptops, waiting to print and not knowing what to do in the meantime.

A door behind them opened up, and Dr. Elmore walked into the room.

"Does anyone know why the internet just went out?"

"I'll tell her." I said to Terry as he caught my eye. "Dr. Elmore, would you please accompany me to your office?"

"Sure thing, Detective Bryant," she replied, with a confused look.

I lead the way and held the door for her to walk through. I closed it behind us and ran a hand through my hair nervously.

"James," she asked, looking me in the eye, "What is going on?"

I let out the breath I'd been holding and did my best to explain.

"It is entirely possible that the level of corruption we are dealing with in Iowa is more serious than we thought. We have been instructed by SSA Wells to print everything we have completed for research and evidence on this case, and then shut down the network and secure all devices."

"How is that possible? We have an incredible security system here at the lab." She explained.

"I don't know. Wells called us on a burner phone from D.C. and told us all communication on this case is to be done in person, and in private. I don't know what is going on, but it's very possible that anyone involved in this investigation is in some level of danger."

"What kind of danger?" She asked.

"I don't know; I really don't. Wells told us to shut everything down. If you have any work on your computer, you need to print it off and shut it down until we know more." I urged.

"James, you're starting to scare me." She said, looking concerned.

"I know; and I'm really sorry. I had no idea what we were getting into. I thought this was just going to be another routine investigation of a cold case, like we had here in Irvingdale." I confided.

"Are we going to be okay?" she asked.

"I will do everything in my power to ensure the safety of you and your team." I promised. "But we need to move fast. Whatever you have on your computer, print it to your desktop printer via a direct connection, not over the network, and then shut down your computer. As soon as it's shut down, we are going to disconnect everything until SSA Wells gets here tomorrow morning."

"Okay," she agreed with a nod. She spent the next few minutes printing off a stack of documents, adding paper to the printer, and then printing off some more. All in all she printed off sixty plus pages of documents and reports, before finally shutting down her desktop computer. I spared her the task of climbing under the desk, doing so myself to unplug all the wires and connections to the computer equipment in the room.

I grunted slightly as I stood up from under the desk, and brushed off my knees and hands.

For the first time since I met her, Dr. Elmore wasn't the confident woman with all the answers, simultaneously looking out for everyone around her. She looked worried, and it was a new look for her. She looked up at me from her chair and dropped her hand from her mouth to stop herself from chewing nervously on a fingernail.

"What am I supposed to tell my team?" She asked.

"Right now, we've told them all we can. All work has to stop and all connection to the outside world has to cease until we know more in the morning." I explained.

"What are we supposed to do? Are we in danger tonight? Should I go get another gun from my house?" She asked.

I smiled then. I still knew very little about Dr. Elmore, but everything I was learning made me appreciate her more and more.

I asked, "Another gun? Which one were you planning to get at home?"

"I keep a Glock 19 in a locked safe inside my desk. I have an Anderson AR-15 at home. Whenever I'm feeling nervous or insecure, I get it out of the safe and sleep with it next to the bed."

"I would not have guessed you for the type who would have a rifle at home." I said, with an ever growing smile.

"Of course not; that's the point. People don't expect me to be the type of girl to carry a gun. That's exactly why I carry one. People who appear to be easy targets have to take the most precaution. I won't be a victim; that why," she lowered her voice for a second. "I keep a Glock 42 strapped to my upper thigh. You know; just in case."

"No shit?" I asked stupidly. I realized how incredibly juvenile I sounded, but I was impressed.

She nodded and turned in her chair a little. Much to my surprise, she raised the right side of her skirt. It was more than I was expecting to see, and less than I wanted to. She showed me the holster, gun secured inside, strapped to her thigh. I stared a little too long wondering how it was secured to resist gravity, before looking away. I tried to shake it off and attempted to be coy with her.

"Dr. Elmore?" I said, unable to tell if I sounded pervy or flirtatious. I decided I sounded pervy, but it apparently hadn't come across that way. I was experiencing yet another first with Dr. Elmore, as she smiled shyly and pulled her skirt back down into place.

"I apologize." I offered, immediately. "That was really unprofessional of me."

"Don't worry about it." She said as she stood up and took a step toward me. "I've asked you a couple times now to call me Lydia. Is there a reason you still insist on calling me Dr. Elmore?"

I hesitated for a moment. The truth; I was nervous to be on a first name basis with such a beautiful woman. She had a way of both disarming me and confusing me with a single smile. How, the hell, do you even respond to that?

"I respect you. We have a professional relationship, and I don't want to sound overly familiar in a professional setting." I said with a slight stutter.

"I appreciate that." She whispered, taking another step towards me. "I've worked really hard to get this far in my early thirties. It means a lot to me to have the respect of colleagues and professional contacts. But when it's just you and me," she paused next to me and leaned up towards my right ear. "Call me Lydia."

My heart was racing like I hadn't experienced in a while. I was too nervous to speak as she casually circled me and the desk, and picked up all the documents from the printer.

It became apparent, after what seemed like an eternity, that I needed to reply so as not to be awkward.

"You got it." I paused to swallow and muster the courage, "Lydia."

I shook off the tension as best I could and circled the room, checking to ensure everything was unplugged. Nothing was plugged in, not even the desk lamp.

Dr. Elmore had gathered her documents and placed them into her briefcase. She snapped it shut and then shrugged out of her lab coat. I couldn't help steal a glance as her as she took a cardigan sweater off a hanger behind the door and draped it over her forearm.

"I'm ready if you are, James," she said quietly.

"Allow me to get the door, Lydia." I replied.

We stepped out of her office to join Terry and the rest of the team outside. I tried to avoid looking like I had just been caught doing something wrong, as Terry shot me an inquisitive look.

"Is everything shut down out here?" I asked.

"We're good to go out here, Bryant; Everything good in there?"

"All the equipment in Dr. Elmore's office is shut down and disconnected." I said, giving Terry a quick glare.

"Good; I was just informing the team that the Bureau is putting them all up in the hotel with us to ensure no one accidentally shares information before the new security protocol is put into place. We cannot have any access to the outside world until SSA Wells returns in the morning to brief us on the situation. Interns, I need your phones, tablet and anything else you could use to send messages. That includes smart watches," instructed Terry.

The interns looked at Dr. Elmore for further instructions.

"You heard the Agent, turn everything over; no exceptions," she ordered.

There was plenty of grumbling, but everyone conceded their devices to Terry, who turned each of them off, and placed them in his briefcase.

"Now if you'll follow me, we will all be riding together to the hotel," he added.

CHAPTER SEVENTEEN

The level of security being enforced on Dr. Elmore's team was more than they were prepared to handle. The four of them had been paired off into two rooms, men and women, which were side by side in between Terry's room and my own. They had nothing else to do, but watch television and raid the mini bar. The phones were unplugged and removed from the rooms meaning anything they wanted, they had to find one of us and ask for it.

This wasn't difficult since one of us was tasked with monitoring the hallway outside the rooms to ensure no one attempted to sneak away. It seemed unfair, at times, since the threat implied by SSA Wells hadn't been declared to be on Dr. Elmore's team. The security precaution was a bit over the top, but we had no idea what we were dealing with nor who, for that matter.

Dr. Elmore was in the room next to mine. Terry spoke with me about switching rooms until I described the scene of devastation from the night before. Our rooms were not being cleaned by hotel staff due to the nature of our investigation, meaning the carnage in my room was waiting for me when I got back. I took enough time to change socks and pour out the last few dribbles of whiskey from the night before, and then took up my place in the hallway.

A cushioned chair had been requisitioned from the dining area near the lobby, but I opted against it and sat on the floor. The security measures applied to Terry and me as well which meant I had to find a way to pass the time without my phone. This was a new hell for me, but fortunately the first watch was only from 1700 to 1830 when dinner arrived.

Terry had instructed hotel staff to order pizza and have it delivered at 1830. The bellhop brought up the pizza which Terry had billed to his room. I palmed the kid a five for carrying the pizza up three floors on an elevator which he seemed to think was adequate enough. I started at Terry's room and started knocking on doors, announcing the arrival of dinner. Everyone piled into the hall and decided on Tommy and Michael's room as the best place to have dinner. Everyone brought the cups from their room filled with coffee or water, and kept their complaining to a minimum; at least until I left the room.

I went back down the hall to invite Dr. Elmore to join everyone for dinner. I knocked gently and was acknowledged with a "Who is it?" from inside.

"It's James," I replied.

I heard a slight shuffling inside as if someone was moving around quickly for a second before I heard the lock turn and the door opened.

"Hello, James. I wasn't expecting any callers," she said, with what I believed to be sarcasm.

"Hey," I paused and looked both ways up and down the hallway. "Lydia."

"Would you like to step inside?" She offered, opening up the door a little further.

I felt a little out of place, but wasn't sure how to proceed. I hesitated and looked around again. It was one thing to be alone with her in her office when everyone was just outside; stepping into her hotel room seemed a little unprofessional, if not unethical.

"I, um, I just came to let you know," I paused and pointed down the hall with my thumb, "Pizza's here."

"Ah," she said as she grabbed up a hair clip off the table, "Dinner, right."

She quickly pulled her hair back into a bunch behind her and clipped it into place. I felt awkward standing there holding the door open slightly. It was quickly replaced by outright embarrassment when I tripped over my own feet stepping back to allow her room to exit into the hallway.

"Are you okay there, James?" She asked, looking a little sheepish herself.

I tried to hide my shame by ducking my head and making a mock bow. I held out my right arm as if to bid her in that direction. "Of course I am, this way my lady."

I realized how idiotic I sounded, so I kept my head bowed so she couldn't see my face as I blushed.

"How chivalrous of you," she said. She then pretended to hike up an oversized European skirt, and made her way past me down the hall. We followed the sound of voices coming from the guy's room. The door was propped open so we let ourselves in. I couldn't be sure, but I knew everyone could see right through me. My shame seemed to be on display for all to see.

After dinner I found myself pacing the hallway, trying to shake off the sense of betrayal I was feeling. I still couldn't get an answer when I called home, making my guilt all the more real. I volunteered to take the 2000 to 0200 hour watch in the hallway allowing Terry to get some sleep. In reality, it was so I could do a little thinking and try to clear my head.

I felt incredibly juvenile for the emotions I was experiencing.

"A man in my position ought to know better," I muttered to myself. I paused to check up and down the hallway to see if anyone had heard me. The more I thought about it, the more my heart fluttered in my chest. I was nervous to a point I hadn't been in years. I sat down next to the chair outside my room, and hung my head a little.

My wife and I had been friends for nearly a year before we started dating. There hadn't been this awkward phase of half flirting and uneasy interaction. I was experiencing shame for what I was feeling, and even more for my behavior. I tried convincing myself it was because I hadn't seen my wife in weeks, maybe even months. Thinking about the length of time it had been, I started to wonder what piece of information I was missing. I struggled to reach way back and remember the last time I had seen her.

She was going home to visit her family. I had to work; same old story, I had jogged to the end of the driveway as she backed out, just so I could kiss her goodbye again.

All of that seemed so vivid; but that had been around Christmas. I frowned and tried to clear things up again. I had been under the impression that I hadn't seen her since the beginning of this investigation, but it was more than that. Something wasn't right, and I couldn't wrap my head around the issue.

I thought back. I closed my eyes and concentrated as much as I could. I thought back to a moment in Dr. Ehrenberg's office. Stephanie and I had started couples counseling several years ago. I had trouble communicating; as if anyone wasn't already aware, but it had become a real issue. Stephanie and I started counseling and it seemed to help. We made more time for each other and made huge strides in our ability to communicate. The memory I was having appeared to be incomplete. I was there, but I wasn't sitting on the couch. I was in a chair by myself and kept looking from the couch to the door, as if I was expecting Stephanie to walk in late, held up by her last appointment of the afternoon.

I wasn't mad at her. Something about the memory of watching the door told me I wasn't mad, but I was in pain. I remembered crying; for several minutes. Dr. Ehrenberg handed me a box of tissues and held his peace. He appeared to know I was in pain, and wasn't forcing me to share my feelings.

I was startled as I heard a door open down the hall to my left.

I looked up quickly to see Dr. Elmore ducking back inside her room.

"Lydia?"

"Oh, hey James; I thought Terry had the first watch. I'll leave you alone," she apologized and turned to go back into her room.

"Wait," I trailed off, and she opened the door a little to look out at me. I looked up at the ceiling, hoping for some kind of encouraging sign, but found nothing. I looked back at Dr. Elmore and saw she was still looking at me, this time with concern.

"Is everything alright?" She asked, opening the door a little.

"I'm not sure; I'm having kind of a weird moment and I don't know how to handle it." I replied. I had no idea what to say, but for some reason I didn't want her to leave.

"Is it anything I might be able to help you with?" She asked. She took a hesitant step out into the hallway, watching me as I fought with myself to speak my mind.

"I don't know how to talk to you." I admitted, realizing how foolish I sounded.

"I can just go to bed," she offered, gesturing back over her shoulder.

"That's not what I mean." I revealed, fighting to say something that didn't push her away, but didn't reveal how hopeless I was feeling.

"I don't know how to talk to you because; I don't know how to feel around you." I uttered.

"What do you mean?" She turned the bar lock so that it protruded into the doorway, and held the door slightly open to her room.

"I mean." I hesitated again, "When I look at you, I feel guilty."

"But, why?" she asked. "Why do I make you feel guilty?

I put my head back against the wall and shook it slightly. "I don't know. I think it's because every time I look at you, I'm reminded of my wife."

"Is that a good thing or bad?" She asked, pensively.

"I'm not sure anymore. I look at you, I can't help but look at you, and I just start to feel guilty. I don't remember when I stopped wearing my wedding ring. It used to be a habit. Now I'm not even sure where I left it," I confided. Out of my peripheral vision I watcher as she stepped all the way out into the hall.

She was wearing a set of maroon, silk pajamas which appeared comfortable, but not extremely warm. She crossed her arms in front of her and held them to her torso. She didn't say anything which seemed to put me on the spot. Her loose, flowing pants seemed to billow around her as she moved awkwardly from side to side.

"I want the guilt to go away, but this task force just started three weeks ago. We may have to work together for months; I just don't know how to work with you when I'm feeling this way."

"Do you not want to work with me?" She pried.

"No," I replied with a little too much haste. "I enjoy working with you. I like working with competent professionals who are good at what they do. Every time I interact with your team, it reminds me that they would do anything for you. They respect you so much. Every time I'm around you and watch you work; I respect you even more."

She looked at me with what appeared to be a half hidden smile, and took another small step forward.

"I can't believe I get to work with you," I continued. "You have this energy that has been missing from my work for years now. Your attitude is contagious to everyone around you and you seem to bring out the best in everyone. I don't know how you do it. You bring out the best in me, but I feel too awkward to let it be known. I don't know how to talk to you, because I have no idea how to handle myself around a strong woman anymore." I confided.

"But why does that make you feel guilty?" She inquired, barely above a compassionate whisper.

"Because that's what my wife used to do. I haven't seen her in forever. She is an amazing woman and I hate the way I feel around you because I feel like it does a disservice to Stephanie. I feel like I'm cheating on her, and you and I haven't had more than a handshake between us."

"Why do you feel like you're cheating on her?" She asked, cautiously, as if verbally dancing around a landmine.

"I'm having a bit of a mental crisis here. I'm trying to remember what my wife looks like or how she sounds. I call her phone all the time just so I can hear her voice. I don't remember the last time we spoke. It seems like forever. I feel like I'm missing something, and I don't even know how or why. Terry keeps telling me I need to go back and talk with my therapist again."

"Did that seem to help?" She asked.

"It did back when we were doing marriage counseling, but now I seem to only remember being there by myself, and," I paused, wondering if I was saying too much. "I'm crying; and no one is saying anything."

I paused for a moment and tried to gather my thoughts. I was dumping a lot of emotional baggage on a woman I barely knew, but I couldn't seem to stop.

"Do you ever feel like a part of your memory is missing? You know it's something important but you just can't seem to grasp what it is. That's how I feel all the time now. I'm trying to remember something important; but I just can't seem to place it. Sometimes, I feel like I'm never going to see my wife again and I don't understand why I feel that way. It's a level of despair I've never experienced before, and I just want to know why."

I was fighting back tears now. I had an awful sick feeling welling up in my stomach.

"Terry talked to me, the first day I met you at the lab." She said, sitting in the chair next to me. "He told me about your wife."

"Really; Terry has never even met my wife." I interjected, staring at the wall in front of me.

"He told me that too," she said.

"Then why was he talking to you about her?"

"He said he noticed what looked like a spark between us. I had him stay behind so I could ask about you. I was curious to know more about you. You were this enigma that put away a serial killer, and after I met you, I felt a little enamored with you. Then Terry brought me up to speed on what was going on. For some reason, I still can't help the playful banter and girly flirtatious behavior I haven't tried on anyone since middle school." She confessed.

"What did Terry say that brought you up to speed?" I was digging now, a little annoyed that they had been talking about me behind my back.

"He told me not to mention it. He said it was something you were working through and he was looking for the right time to talk to you about it." She replied.

"I just wish one of you would stop speaking in circles around the subject, and just tell me what the hell is going on," I said, my voice reflecting my growing frustration.

"Terry said it was better for you to come to the realization on your own. He was afraid of what might happen if someone told you, and you weren't ready to hear it."

"I'm not a child, Lydia," I snapped.

She paused for a moment and I heard her take a long deep breath. I was looking down at the floor, ashamed of the way I had spoken to her. I wanted to apologize, but I could feel my anger boiling under the surface, and I knew I was only moments away from losing my ability to communicate effectively.

Dr. Ehrenberg had taught me to recognize when I was getting flustered, and all the signs were there. It wasn't fair to Lydia to ask her to talk with me in the hall and then act like an asshole towards her.

She moved her feet under her slightly, as if she was preparing to stand.

"I'm sorry," I confessed. I had tears fighting hard to run down my face, and I didn't know what to do. "I should have never snapped at you like that."

"I understand, James." She replied. I felt her cold hand touch my shoulder, right at the collar of my shirt. Her pinky finger seemed to stroke the side of my neck for a second as she rested her hand, trying to comfort me despite the massive asshole I had been.

"I'm afraid to go down this rabbit hole in my memory. I'm certain I won't like what I'm going to find." I confided to her.

"What do you think you're going to find?" She asked.

It felt like she wanted me to realize what I had been hiding from; like she wanted to be there when it happened.

"Did Terry tell you how it happened?"

"How what happened?" She asked.

I choked back a sob as the tears in my eyes finally made a run for it down my face. Memories were flooding back now. Vivid, painful portions of the past eighteen months I had fought, and drank to suppress, were suddenly there. It felt as if someone had stripped away part of my past and then dumped it on me as I sat there on the dingy hotel carpet.

"How Stephanie died?"

I hung my head. This was not the situation to have a major emotional breakthrough. No wonder Terry had been dancing around the subject and trying to make me go talk to someone.

It felt as if I was losing Stephanie all over again. The strain in my throat became unbearable. I had swallowed so many times to hold back the tears I had inflicted unintentional physical pain on myself. I lifted my head and took a deep breath. I turned away from Dr. Elmore slightly, still trying to preserve some level of dignity for myself. I was certain it wasn't working.

To my right, Dr. Elmore quietly cleared her throat. My shoulders started heaving from my labored breathing and bitter sobs.

It took several minutes, but I finally managed to compose myself.

It hadn't been since the beginning of the investigation, it hadn't even been since Christmas. It had been nearly fifteen months since I lost my wife. I kept looking for her SUV to pull into the garage while I was sleeping in my chair. I kept calling her phone to hear her voice. I had done it so often, I had convinced myself the next time I would see her driving up, or hear her loving greeting over the phone. I had fractured my memories with guilt, and buried the truth with alcohol. I had done it so long I had convinced myself it was all real. It wasn't. I had acted foolishly and with obvious issues that I had put on full display for everyone I worked with to see, and be concerned for me.

I slouched against the wall a bit and turned back to face the wall in front of me. I had felt silly before; now I felt foolish. I had lost my grip on reality and broadcast it for everyone to see; for how long, I didn't know.

Dr. Elmore cleared her throat again, this time she answered the question I'd posed minutes prior.

"He said it was a car accident," she whispered. "He said there was freezing rain and she got caught in the middle of a multi-car pileup. He told me you were at work when it happened, called in to work a Christmas morning domestic incident."

"What else did he tell you?"

"He told me you got into a fight with one of your coworkers; that you were inconsolable. That you've been working out of the bottom of a bottle ever since."

"Is that the kind of guy that does it for you?" I asked. I really wanted to know. The fact that she knew all this and still wanted to help and be there for me, didn't make any sense.

"Not really, but I could see your pain. I feel the anger inside you as it drives you to solve all these old murders. Terry told me that one month after your wife's funeral you started making positive strides. You were going to counseling and starting to drink less. Then the DOJ came to you with the proposition Fenton had made. They all but blackmailed you into doing this; that you had no desire to do this whatsoever because you knew the pain it would bring you." She paused a moment and gave my shoulder a slight squeeze. "And you were right."

"How would Terry know any of this? He wasn't there until the task force briefing back in January," I said, slightly miffed.

"Terry said you came in and gave a fifteen minute briefing on Fenton. Then you left the room and your department gave a thirty minute briefing on you. They said you were motivated, but still had your own demons to face."

"The two worst things I've ever had to do in my life is put my wife in the ground and sit down with Fenton again. My worst nightmares collided that year; I didn't handle it very well."

"That's understandable, you know," she offered. "No one else in the world can understand what you are going through. Some people might be able to relate to the loss of a loved one, but no one can relate to what you're going through now."

"When you say 'some people,' who do you mean?" I wondered.

"I mean me," she replied. I heard the faintest sound of a sniffle and tried to steal a glance at her. She was looking away from me slightly, using her left hand to twirl her hair absent-mindedly.

"Who did you lose?" I asked, immediately regretting it.

She took her hand off my shoulder and swiped at her cheek, attempting to hide the single tear making its way towards her chin.

"Um," she hesitated and sniffed once before continuing. "I was engaged; back in Med School. There was a guy in my class who caught my eye. You remind me of him in a lot of ways. That same spirit; troubled but still putting himself out there to help people. He spent a lot of time volunteering at local clinics. He didn't have a lot of free time, but he wanted to help when he could."

"If you don't want to talk about what happened, you don't have to." I offered.

"No it's okay; I just haven't spoken about him for almost a decade. He was working at one of the free clinics in Kansas City. This guy, this... fucking junkie came in and wanted pain pills. The doctor on staff wouldn't prescribe him any opioids. The junkie had a knife; he stabbed the doctor. Mike was just trying to help. He tried to protect the doctor and got stabbed himself. It worked though; Doctor Faulkner is still alive and practicing medicine. He's in private practice now, of course; but he never forgot what Mike did for him. He recovered, and then he came and found me a few weeks after the funeral. He thanked me, as if I had anything to do with it. Then he offered to help me pay for med-school." She wiped away another stream of tears and then smiled. "He wouldn't take no for an answer. He paid for me to go to school and double major. That's how I got this job. I was working almost full time to go to school and become a doctor. His gracious gift allowed me to quit my job and focus on my school work. I graduated; and then he wrote me the most amazing recommendation to come work for the University of Lincoln. He pulled every string and called in every favor he could to get me this gig. That's why I work so hard. That's why I make sure every med student; intern or grad student that works for me gets the best education I can give them. And then I do what he did for me; I pull strings and call in favors until I get these students the job of their dreams. They work hard; but sometimes who you know goes a long way. I still keep in touch with Dr. Faulkner. Every now and then he sends me one of his best and brightest students so they can intern with me." She sobbed, but kept smiling, "He's never sent me a shitty intern. They're always the best. He just knows how to pick them, I guess. That's actually how Tamara came to work for me."

I had been listening so intently I had stopped crying. Her story was both tragic and heartwarming. She carried on a legacy of not one, but two incredible men who had been victims of an unforeseeable event. She didn't carry herself like a woman with a chip on her shoulder. She was both impressive and driven; determined to create a legacy of her own, and help others along the way.

If I hadn't been smitten with her before, I surely was now.

She wiped the last of her tears away and placed her hand back on my shoulder.

"I'm sorry I made you talk about Stephanie. Terry said he was going to stage some kind of intervention when he got back to Manhattan with you. It seemed poorly thought out, but I didn't actually intend to intervene and steal his thunder."

"That's ok." I admitted. "I didn't realize how hard I had been repressing all this. That does explain why Terry keeps walking the fine line between enabler and advocate. He wants to help, but I doubt he or anyone in law enforcement would be in a prime position to help me the way you did."

I reached up, across my chest with my right hand and placed it over her hand where it rested on my shoulder. I lay my head to the side, resting my cheek on the backside of my hand.

"Thank you, Lydia. I can't imagine how much courage it took to talk with me about this. I am forever indebted to you."

"I didn't really plan this," she admitted. "It just sort of happened. You were having a breakdown in the hallway and I walked out at the wrong time. I was hoping Terry could give me a timeline on when he was going to talk with you. I just wanted it to be soon."

I smiled. The sound of her voice was soothing and seemed to calm the tumultuous emotional storm raging inside my head. We sat there like that for a minute. The cathartic release of pent up anguish, long held in check, was an incredible feeling. My whole body seemed to relax making it all-the-more obvious how uncomfortable the floor had become. I lifted my head slightly as a though occurred to me.

"Did you use the term, enamored, in reference to me?" I asked, suddenly very curious.

"I was hoping that went by unnoticed," she divulged as she withdrew her hand from my shoulder. She stood up suddenly and started towards her door.

"Are you really going to make me stand guard out here all by myself?" I asked.

"Yes I am," she replied. She turned back to me, and flashed a beautiful smile.

"That seems awfully inconsiderate of you." I said roguishly.

"Well, we're past the awkward stage of sharing all our past traumas and pain. If we talk much longer were going to step recklessly across the line into a date-like conversation and I'd much rather do that over dinner some time."

"Well so would I," I offered. "Would you like to..."
She cut me off.

"Don't ask me now. I'm in my pajamas with no makeup on. When you ask me out for the first time, I want to look smoking hot."

Feeling a little confused, but enjoying the witty banter I casually asked. "When will I know you're ready for me to ask?"

"I'll tell you," she replied with another big smile. She reached the door and stepped swiftly inside. The door closed with a slight bang as it hit the locking bar still blocking the door open. She opened the door and gave me a sheepish grin as she removed the bar. She paused for just a moment and looked me right in the eye.

"Good night, James."

I smiled back at her before I replied. "Good night Lydia."

She ducked her eyes and attempted to hide her blushing face behind the door as she closed it slowly behind her.

———

If I thought the hour before I talked with Dr. Elmore had been long, the two and a half hours afterwards were an eternity. Terry was out in the hall right at 0200 hours to release me, but my mind raced, unfettered, down one rabbit trail after another until he did.

I had allowed my guilt to cloud my mind and affect my judgement for almost sixteen months. The guilt I incurred for working Christmas day had left me in a state of absolute denial. I normally did the driving when we were together. Stephanie hated driving in the winter, and hated driving at night almost as much. The roads weren't my fault; the accident wasn't my fault. People had told me this over and over again, but I had piled on the blame until I had all but convinced myself that nothing had happened. I was used to working the opposite schedule from Stephanie which genuinely meant we didn't see each other for days at a time. I had turned reality into a wall of lies around me, trying to protect myself from the pain.

No wonder I had been so difficult to deal with.

I opened my bag, which I had forgotten on the floor next to me, and spent nearly an hour going over notes and passages from my rough draft about the investigation. I had referred to myself as a married man on more than one occasion. Terry, as well as Lt. Carter and Detective Shirley had casually sidestepped the topic. I realized why they had needed to brief everyone about me. I was a ticking time bomb. When I went off, it wasn't going to be pretty. They had circled gracefully around the difficult topic and managed to protect my delicate mental state in the process. I couldn't put a price on what they had done for me, but it became obvious that I needed to reach out to them and show them my gratitude.

It had been hours already, so I didn't have to hide the fact that I had been crying. Terry didn't appear to notice as he sipped from his coffee cup and started pacing the halls to stay awake.

After thanking Terry, I went to bed and crashed. My exhaustion took over, and I slept like a log.

———

Apparently Terry had been banging on my door for a while before I realized it was happening. I hadn't slept peacefully in months; doing so was an odd sensation. It was almost seven in the morning, and I realized I was an hour late relieving him to take my morning watch outside the door.

I threw on some pants and stumbled to the door, tripping over my bag on the way.

"Hey, Bryant," Terry said when I greeted him at the door. "The next shift is yours. I'm gonna get a little sleep. Can you handle taking everyone downstairs to breakfast?"

"Yeah, I should be able to handle that. Want me to bring you something to eat?"

"That would be awesome," he replied.

I spent the next few minutes knocking on doors, waking up the team and gathering them for breakfast. The only way to give Terry a break was to take everyone downstairs to the dining room all at once. It took a few minutes as some of them were still showering and getting ready. By 7:30, the group was gathered in the elevator headed down for breakfast.

It was incredibly awkward, holding the briefcase with everyone's phones. The team knew I had them, but were maintaining a professional demeanor as they managed to avoid asking when they could have them back.

Breakfast was finished in uncomfortable silence. I assumed my presence was stifling the conversation a little, but there was nothing I could do about it.

I brought Terry a couple items for breakfast along with some orange juice Dr. Elmore helped me get upstairs. My hands were full and I was right back to feeling awkward around her. The conversation in the hallway may have opened some lines of communication between us, but it didn't change the fact that we had no idea how to behave around each other in front of her team.

We exchanged casual nods, and then avoided making eye contact until she offered to help get Terry's breakfast upstairs. Everyone went back to their rooms after breakfast and I resumed my post in the hallway. I chugged my coffee as fast as the temperature would allow and prayed the waiting would be over soon.

———

I was rarely excited to see a federal agent during my career in law enforcement, but SSA Wells was a sight for sore eyes that day.

Terry and I delayed the team getting back to the lab until after nine in the morning hoping it would give Wells and his cyber security team a chance to get started at the lab.

SSA Wells came out to the parking lot to greet us as the van holding all seven of us came to a stop in back of the building. He opened the back door to the van and waved everyone out.

"Terry, you and Bryant wait right there in the front while I talk with Dr. Elmore and her team," Wells instructed. He stepped back to allow the guys to step out of the back seat and then addressed them all.

"The IT guys are inside and they are almost done upgrading your network and firewalls. You will be able to resume your research and examinations at that time. I will provide everyone here a full briefing on the matter at hand around eleven O'clock. Please make sure everyone is in the lounge area at that time; dismissed."

The team dispersed into the building and SSA Wells climbed into the back of the van. He shut the sliding door behind him, and let out a quick sigh.

I didn't say anything for a moment. SSA Wells was clearly deep in thought, and I didn't want to interrupt him. I waited for a moment, seated in the front passenger seat, wishing there was a way to have this conversation face to face.

"I may have oversold the threat yesterday." He revealed.

I glanced at Terry who was obviously confused by Wells' statement.

"So, we didn't need to worry about a security threat?" I asked.

"No, we most certainly did. The precautions I had you take may have been over the top, but not without reason. The Carroll family is wound deep into the fibers of this country. They have connections nationwide and influence internationally. Everything we do from now on has to be under the guise of covering our own asses. All research on the family is to be done on the newly secured computers and networks. If any warrants are to be sought or arrests to be made, I will be the one to handle them."

"Pardon me, sir. But isn't the point of this task force to work together to investigate these crimes?" Terry asked.

"No, this task force is to investigate unsolved murders as revealed by Fenton during Bryant's interview process. All other ensuing investigations are going to be handled on the federal level as much as possible."

"That may be an issue, sir." I interjected.

"What is the issue?" He asked.

"We reviewed the footage from the VHS tape in the casket. Most of it was nightmare inducing violence that I hope you never have to experience. But on that tape, Fenton gift wraps both Ryan and Simon Carroll," I explained.

"How is that an issue?"

"Part of Fenton's asking price to kill and dispose of Jessica Childress was two, unique, brand new identities. Ryan Carroll delivered them to him on video along with ten thousand dollars cash. Then he told Ryan to thank an 'Agent Sanders' for the new identifications. Terry and I think there may be a rat in the Bureau; someone working for the Carroll family; someone with influence and connections. New identifications aren't exactly a standard practice with the bureau. Am I right?" I asked.

"You're not wrong. New identifications are reserved for people in witness relocation and extreme circumstances like that." SSA Wells sat back and let out another frustrated sigh.

"Boss, I think for the time being we're on our own," voiced Terry.

We sat in silence for a moment. The level of frustration was building as we found ourselves slowly being boxed in with our resources being limited one by one.

"Even if we're not," replied Wells, pausing for a second, "We're going to play this like we are alone. No one else besides the three of us will be involved in this investigation. Bryant, you're still going to maintain a consultant position in all of this simply because you don't have federal jurisdiction. Terry and I will draft all of the warrants and official reports. You will advise on all things related to the Carroll family investigation and be hands on for the Fenton cases."

"What do you want us to do first?" Terry asked.

"Focus on building supporting evidence. We need everything; tax records, employment records, banking records, business licenses, marriage licenses, school records, business associations, personal associations, memberships to clubs and organizations, property records; all of it. This is going to take a while. From now on, we meet in person to discuss this matter. We will meet at least once a week when feasible to discuss developments and discoveries until we have everything we need." Wells instructed.

"Damn! That's going to take a while." I commented.

"It absolutely is," Wells replied as he leaned forward and placed his head and shoulders between the front seats, "One last thing."

"Name it," said Terry.

"Through all of this, assume someone at the federal level is watching. Your assignment is to find the best way to flush out the stoolpigeon. Once we root out the traitor in our ranks, we can bring down the whole fucking operation."

"That's going to be a tall order." I observed.

"That's why it's a team effort. When we get enough for one person, we should do everything possible to have enough to arrest everyone involved," said Wells. "We can't afford to bring in one person and allow the others to destroy or hide evidence."

"So when the time comes, we're hauling people away in buses?" Terry inquired.

"Something like that," Wells replied, "We may have to wait until all the dust settles from the task force before we start rounding up Carroll family conspirators."

"That's nine months," I interjected. "What are the odds we don't step on the Carroll family's toes in the process?"

"I would say, they're quite poor," Wells replied. "That's why we have to do everything intentionally, and efficiently."

"And if that doesn't work?" Terry wondered.

"Then we will just have to un-fuck ourselves," Wells stated, and then climbed out of the van.

CHAPTER EIGHTEEN

Funerals are never what movies make them out to be; at least not in the Midwest. Boston, New York, Philadelphia; they had a parade with bagpipes and a hundred cops in dress blues marching down the street.

My department didn't have that many people to put in uniform on the same day. Six officers dressed in their finest "blues" carried the light, maple colored wood casket bearing Preston's remains through the front doors of the local Methodist church and out to the waiting hearse. The flag draped over the casket flowed lightly in the warm spring breeze. In all reality, it would have been a beautiful day to do anything else in the world. Unfortunately we were filing two by two out of the church, trying to keep a stoic face for the family. We were all trying to hold down that bit of our humanity that beckoned us to break down in tears, stampede outside and tear the state of Kansas apart to find Preston's killer. There was nothing we could do; not today, maybe not for a while, and it ate at us.

Over a hundred officers from various agencies around the state packed the church to capacity. Nearly all of Preston's academy class was in attendance to show support for Preston's family, department, and community.

I felt slightly out of place in my uniform. I hadn't been on patrol for several years. I had dropped a lot of weight, and my uniform looked like a half empty sack. I tucked it in as far as I could manage, and struggled to maintain some level of maneuverability against the full coverage ballistic vest hidden underneath my shirt.

I scratched nervously at the red marks on my forehead left behind from the explosion. Somehow I was very aware of them, even though they had scabbed and healed over the past few weeks. Everything about that night seemed to be racing through my mind. I had no idea how much closer I needed to be to have met a similar end. It could have been a matter of steps between where I stood now and being loaded into a second hearse. I clenched my fists at my sides, almost wishing I could still feel the pain from the glass previously embedded in my skin. EMS had pulled the small shards of glass from my hands, but I could still feel it for the first week or so after the explosion. Now, all I could feel was tension; tension and rage. Unfortunately I had nowhere to channel it. I walked it off as I followed my buddy, Sgt. Jason Ellis, to his supervisor unit parked nearly two blocks away.

The neighborhood was packed for blocks with patrol units. It was an impressive sight; if not a depressing one. I climbed awkwardly into the passenger seat of the Ford Explorer and opted to ride to the cemetery in silence. No one was very talkative. A gathering of officers was usually accompanied by friendly ribbing, shit talking on various sports teams or other agencies, and tall tales of cases worked. A funeral sucked all the energy out of the group. It was just depressing.

I glanced at my watch as Jason turned on the lights and entered the massive procession heading for Sunrise Cemetery. The trip was slow going, furthering my concern that I would run late to my afternoon therapy session with Fenton. Feeling selfish; if I had been given a say in the planning, I would have scheduled the funeral on any other day of the week.

I had called the prison earlier that morning and moved the interview location to another room in the facility. I didn't trust myself alone in a room with Fenton after the past week. Between the video he left us and the officer who had died as a result of the investigation into one of Fenton's murders, I was ready to strangle him and accept the consequences.

———

The crowd at the cemetery was so large the voice of the minister was lost in the masses. I was barely at the right angle to observe the folding of the flag. An already solemn occasion became downright heartbreaking as I watched one of the honor guard take a knee and present the folded flag to Preston's mother and girlfriend. I choked back a sob and swallowed hard, fighting hard to hold back the tears. The two women grasped hands and clutched the flag between them as they wept uncontrollably. Even at a distance, I could see the tears running down Preston's father's face. He was holding it together, better than expected, as he stood stone faced behind the women, with a hand their shoulders. His face showed no expression, but the tears revealed the searing pain he was experiencing.

I swiped a hand to chase away a single tear as it escaped my left eye. I was coming down from my internal rage and starting to feel the impact of the investigation. Today started week four. Three people dead already and we had barely started.

I needed a fucking drink.

I opted not to join the massive line forming to pay respects to the family. I didn't know what to say to them anyways. I felt responsible for Preston's death, no matter who tried to convince me otherwise. If I went over there, I was certain to admit as much to his loved-ones. I stood there, waiting while the crowd thinned and people slowly filed to their cars. I took off my bus driver hat, worn only on the rarest of occasions, and tucked it under my arm. The sun stung my eyes a little, but the breeze on my scalp was a welcome relief.

**********The drive to El Dorado was even longer that week. The route was familiar and boring, giving me plenty of time to dread what I had to do. I was sick of the game and ready to hang it up. Fenton was not only pulling strings from behind bars, he was involving me in an investigation with nationwide implications.

I had spent days compiling research on the Carroll family. The level of sophistication in their organization was something out of an old gangster film. They held positive positions in the community, but people around them frequently went missing without a trace. They handled their business behind closed doors, concealing their next move until it was already complete. Fenton had been a part of the Carroll family business during its early days. He had already seen more than most people who had lived to escape the family's reach. He must have known his time was limited and made his exit when it was most opportunistic.

I wasted a few minutes wondering how someone like Fenton was able to change casually in between disguises of police, drug dealer, and sadistic psychopath without drawing any attention. In Irvingdale, he had worked some kind of blue collar job while spending his nights running a successful brothel, complete with kidnapped teenage girls. In Cass County, he had enough credibility to get into law enforcement and still make connections with the local crime family to utilize his twisted talents of rape and murder. Not only had he made it into both circles, he had done it without the knowledge of the Sheriff.

Outside the prison, I opted to lock up all my guns and knives, securing them in my vehicle. The faster I got in, the faster I got out. I was a little early, but that didn't really change much. The corrections staff didn't have to chain Fenton to a table and secure a wing for our interview this time.

Security was a breeze this time. I wasn't entering the prison and walking down the long halls of death-row inmates; I was just stepping into the visitation area. I signed in, received my obligatory pat-down, handed off the items going to Fenton to one of the guards, and stepped into the visitation room.

Fenton was already seated, still chained, but with a better range of motion without the table to hold his hands in place. He seemed to stare at me with a mixture of disdain and loathing. His expression changed when the corrections officer entered the room behind him and handed over the usual pack of cigarettes and naked lady lighter. He waited until the officer had left him alone before tearing-open the cigarettes and lighting one. He sat back and leered at me, smiling as he took a long draw and held it in, savoring it for a moment, then blowing it out slowly towards the glass.

I held the stopwatch, already running, up against the glass so he could see it when the smoke cleared. He leaned in to check the time and then sat back again. He seemed to be enjoying his mobility as he held the cigarette in his mouth and wrapped his hands behind his head. The chains on his wrist forced him to lay the chain across one shoulder to complete the motion, but he was clearly more comfortable with his hands not chained down in front of him.

I was annoyed by how much time he was taking for himself, but after checking the watch and seeing over five minutes had gone by, I stopped caring. If he wanted to sit in silence and stare for three hours that was fine by me. I let another minute go by as I set up my notepad and retrieved a pen from my jacket. My usual restrictions for what I could bring were lifted since neither Fenton nor I had access to the other. The audio recording was automatically being completed by the prison rendering my need of a small digital recorder, moot. I was in a more comfortable chair, and a more comfortable setting, but I was not in a better mood. Aside from watching Fenton have a stroke in front of me, not much was going to cheer me up.

After lighting up a second cigarette, Fenton casually picked up the phone on his side of the glass. I waited a few seconds, staring at him with a blank expression, hoping to get a rise out of him. He smiled at me, showing his indifference to my efforts and casually pressed the back of his hand against the glass, middle finger extended. I allowed myself a casual smirk and the picked up the phone on my side.

"If I'm not mistaken, Detective, this is a breach of the agreement." He drawled in his usually deep baritone.

"Not really, you might want to double check the wording on the agreement you signed." I instructed him.

"I'm pretty sure I specified for us to be in the same room together."

"No, you specified face to face with cigarettes and a lighter for your use during the interview. It doesn't say anything about sharing the same room as you." I informed him.

"Well, to say the least, this is against the spirit of the agreement."

"So is stabbing you in the eye with my pencil; I thought I'd err on the side of caution for your sake." I replied, voice dripping with sarcasm.

"Oh, you're breaking my heart, Officer Feelings." His voice changed to a predictable mocking tone. "Did someone have a bad week?"

"You already know the kind of week I had. You know where you sent me, and you know what you sent me to find. I found it; anyone, besides you, would be appalled at what I had to witness."

"Not anyone," he replied slyly.

"So yes, I can safely say it's been a bad week. That's why there's glass in between us, so I don't kill you today." I informed him.

"Wait; so you're telling me you didn't like my little home movie?" He asked.

"Of course not, if you weren't on death row already, you'd have received another hundred years in prison for rape and possession/distribution of child pornography."

He leaned forward and leered at me. "I just call it entertainment."

He sat back and smiled; watching as I grew hot under the collar again.

"Detective it must be tough for you to have this kind of moral standard. That's why nothing upsets me; no morals. Morals are for the weak and feeble who need to hold on to some kind of 'greater good' in order to dictate what they do in life. I don't; that's why I get to do whatever I want."

"Not anymore." I interjected smugly.

"Do you really think the only copy of that tape was in that casket?" He tapped his temple. "I've got all of it up here. You call it child pornography; I call it a fond memory. Morals get you killed, scruples hold you back; ethics box you in. True freedom lies in the breaking of social and religious morays and doing whatever the fuck you want, whenever you want to do it. There's no such thing as a victim. There is only the strong and the weak. If you are strong, you do what you want. If you are weak, you are subject to the whims of the strong, and will always live in subjugation of them. The only choice people have to make is whether they are among the weak or the strong."

"Don't you think that's an oversimplification just so you can justify being a monster?" I asked.

"I don't ever feel the need to justify my actions. That's a characteristic of the strong. Justification is for the government. They do whatever they want to whoever is in the way and then feed you a line about national security or public welfare, to make the weak roll over. This country; this world is full of people who roll over and beg the government for free meals, and then pretend it's all okay when they get nothing but scraps. The government likes to justify its actions by telling everyone it's for the 'greater' good." He said throwing up air quotes.

"There are people involved; of course the government has issues." I replied, "But don't you think if we spent time working for solutions we would all be better off? To be honest, most of the time government makes things worse when they try to intervene. But if there's a better way, shouldn't someone step up and offer the solution?"

"And take money away from the government? Not on your life. People who have a better way want to get paid to make it happen. Why do you think rich people start charities? I can tell you, it isn't about their public persona of philanthropy; its greed. They hide their money in charity tax shelters and host ridiculous fund raisers so other people will help keep them rich by deducting charity from their taxes. The rich are just the strong, subjecting the weak to their agendas and personal whims. The weak line up to receive their handout from the rich and the cycle continues, again and again."

I was thankful to be in the portion of the interview where Fenton had nothing to say. This gave me the opportunity to pass the time without having to write anything down. He was preaching his usual bullshit anti-government, anti-capitalism, anti-American propaganda, and I had heard it all before at one time or another. The topic changed, but the message stayed the same; fuck the system, fuck the government, do whatever you want no matter who is affected.

Fenton would have made a compelling cult leader had he seized the opportunity. Weak minded people flocked to the crazed ideology of a lunatic when it was beneficial to do so. Fenton's may not have resonated well with the masses, but it was sure to have compelled a few to fall in line. Fenton was too selfish for something like leadership. He may have appealed to a few radicals, but he wouldn't have remained in control very long before taking what he could and splitting town. Fenton raged against greed, but was not immune to it.

"So how does someone with your line of thinking find a place in someone else's organization?" I asked.

"That is the simplest aspect of my existence. Someone in power always needs a guy like me to do their dirty work. They pretend their hands are clean, but in reality, they don't have the balls to take matters into their own hands. Their strength is in their public persona. Mine is in my capabilities behind closed doors. True strength lies in doing whatever is necessary to achieve an end. I did whatever was necessary; those who couldn't payed me well to do it."

"So that's how the Carroll family fits into all of this?"

"That's right. They had plenty of people on their payroll. I happened to be one of them for a few years," he replied.

"And a Cass County Sheriff's Deputy at the same time." I said, "Quite a turn of events for me after hearing all your anti-law enforcement rhetoric over the past decade."

He held his hands out as if embarrassed to receive such a compliment, "I'm full of surprises, aren't I?"

"That's a bit of an understatement." I retorted.

"Why do you think my opinion of pigs is so low? I've been in your place; that's a cherry gig, bro."

"Not from where I'm sitting." I insisted.

"Of course not, not for you. You took down the most notorious serial killer in American history; that notoriety comes at a cost. Your problem is that you aren't willing to take the fame and fortune that goes with it. Embrace all the glory, Detective douchebag, embrace it and take it to the bank."

"I'm fine without the fame and fortune; I'll settle to watch you writhe this Christmas. That is the only compensation I want, I'd do the rest of this for free." I said.

"But you aren't," he interjected. "You aren't doing this for free. You're getting paid by your department, you will get paid when you publish my handiwork, you'll get paid by every university, department, and organization that summons you to speak about the horrors you've been witness to."

"Maybe I'll make it my retirement plan," I admitted.

"Ah, now there's the government, teat-suckling capitalist I know."

"I'm being forced to do what others would pay to do. You're handing me a story people will want to read, anyone else would be happy to write it. I'm just unlucky enough not to have a choice. When my options went out the window, I made sure I was getting paid to be here. I didn't do it out of greed, I did it because, if someone was going to get paid; it may as well be me."

"There you go, just like a government employee. Justify yourself, see if you feel better," he commented.

I was getting frustrated trying to convince Fenton I wasn't like other government employees. He would lump everyone together for his own purposes, and cared little for the differences that existed. There was no way to appease him; I just had to keep pushing forward.

"So how did you get involved with the Carroll family?"

He switched the phone from his right hand to his left and leaned forward slightly.

"Everything in life comes down to leverage. It's about seizing opportunities when they are available, and making the most out of them. The Carroll family does not include a lot of outsiders. The only way I could work my way in was to have something valuable they needed. Sometimes it's skill, sometimes it's a piece of information they need. The real key is to have something from each category. If you only have one, you are restricted to what you can do for them in that capacity. Information has an expiration date; skill does not."

"So what information did you have for them?"

"That will be a conversation for another day. Today, I want to talk about the skill I could offer them."

"But I already know your skill; killing women and hiding the bodies." I interrupted.

"That," he said, emphasizing it by pointing his finger at me, "Is an oversimplification. I have the power of persuasion. I make people do what I want them to. Sometimes that's having my way with the senator's teenage lover before hiding her body where only you can find it. Other times it's convincing someone to do something they don't want to do. Sometimes I have the privilege of making a woman do things with me she might otherwise not, but most of the time I had the power to change someone's mind on an important matter. That can be done a number of ways. You work for the government, so I don't have to explain how bribes work. Most of the time it was a matter of having something people wanted and would give anything to have."

"So you extorted things from people? That's your big secret?" I asked.

"Extortion implies I have something to gain by convincing them of my point of view. I persuaded people by giving them what they did not have; hope and confidence. "

"You don't strike me as the kind of person who provided a lot of hope for anyone." I said.

"Hope comes in many shapes and sizes. For some it's the location of a loved one, for others it's the confidence that their secrets will never reach the daylight. The Carroll family had secrets they needed to hide, the Childress family wanted hope that their little girl was still alive. The true winner in politics is the person who can ride the fence and make money from both sides."

"So that's what you did? You took information restricted to one side and used it as leverage to get information from the other side?"

"Again, you oversimplify. I took information I had to gain leverage against all parties involved. The Childress family is still in Cass County because of the leverage I provided them. I ensured the Carroll family had information against the Childress family. I then provided the Childress family with some level of hope that I had what was necessary to bring down the Carroll family. No one involved there has clean hands; that's why leverage works against all of them. Skeletons are the best leverage."

"In your case you're being both literal and figurative."

"That's right. I used my knowledge of the Carroll family's concealment of Jessica's murder and Simon's affair to get money and leverage against the Carroll family. I then used my knowledge of the Carroll family to convince the Childress family that I knew about their illegal acquisition of commercial real estate as they attempted to compete with the Carroll family. The Childress family gave up their real estate holdings under the guise they would get their daughter back. They didn't know she was already dead, of course. The Childress family made a deal with the Carroll family that transferred large portions of real estate, which over time, made both families rich. The deal was done before the search was called off for Jessica. The Childress family used their grief as a disguise for dealing with the Carroll family, and then made a small fortune leveraging their daughter's pregnancy and disappearance against the Carroll family."

Fenton sat back and smiled a bit as he lit up another cigarette.

"I hand delivered each family the leverage to destroy the other. The issue for them became, neither could use the leverage they had for fear of retribution over the leverage the other possessed. The Childress family didn't know Jessica was pregnant; I saw to it that they received copies of Jessica's medical records along with the results of the CVS procedure which contained DNA results for the baby. Mr. Childress was looking at forty years in prison for his fraudulent business activities. Simon Carroll was going to ruin his family's business when proof was discovered that he had an affair with a teenage girl."

"It sounds like you had your hands full." I admitted.

"That isn't even the half of it. I blackmailed a federal agent to provide me with additional identities the Carroll family didn't know about. The guy's brother was the local mortician. He helped me preserve Jessica's body after I had him burn Dr. Morgan in Jessica's place. I told him what he had done and what it would cost him to keep me silent. I then leveraged the agent's double dealings with me to earn his silence since he worked with the Carroll family too. No one could tell anyone anything without exposing their own treachery. God, I fucking love politics," admitted Fenton.

"I thought you hated politics?" I inquired.

"I hate politicians; politics is the art of getting what you want. Politics enabled me to operate without interruption for several years in that area. No one could tell anyone about me, they had too much to lose already."

"I have to admit, that's a smart way to play it," I said. "Didn't you worry someone would come after you to prevent you from ratting them out?"

"A little at first; the key is to know the timeframe in which you can operate and not exceed it by even a day. I had the Carroll family provide me with two new identities because I knew they would try to track me down using those names and social security numbers. I had the federal agent make me a new identity that the Carroll family would not be privy to and assumed that identity when I was captured. If one of those other two identities had popped up on the Carroll family's radar, they would have had me killed behind bars nine and a half years ago."

He paused again and pasted an arrogant look onto his face.

"My secret," he said. "Is always being the smartest person in the room. I was always good at strategy games; life is just moves and countermoves. I knew what they wanted, what they needed and what they feared. If you possess knowledge of all three things for any one person or group, you can control them; twist them into doing your bidding. I never held public office or owned a piece of property in that entire county, but I ran most of it from the shadows. They thought they were in charge; but they were simply pawns in a bigger game. Don't get me wrong, they made a fortune during the process; but they enabled me to move the pieces into place so that when the time came, I could bring down the entire organization."

If I hadn't just come from a fallen officer's funeral, I might have been a little impressed. Fenton was a master of manipulation. He had juries eating out of his hand until DNA evidence was brought in to seal his fate. After the first trial, prosecutors started leading with the heinous acts of each crime and using the DNA as the exclamation point. Fenton could manipulate people, but not the evidence against him. Fenton had finally found himself in a room where his superior intellect couldn't help him.

I sat back and made a few notes. The Cass County investigation was already more complicated than anyone would have expected, but Fenton's involvement made it even worse.

"Can you tell me anything about the bone you put in Jessica's casket?"

"Yeah," he nodded. "I could. I won't; but I could. There is going to be a time and a place for that particular story. Let's give you a few weeks to wonder about it. That's kind of the best part about being me. I have all the answers in our little game, and you have to wait week by week for me to spoon-feed you the next juicy detail."

"So you aren't going to make any comment about the bone?" Fenton shook his head and took a long drag on his cigarette. "What about the newspaper clipping?"

"If I have to explain that one to you, you don't deserve to wear a badge. I wanted you to know who you were dealing with long before you realized how fucked up your situation actually was. I told you last week before you left. I can only gift wrap shitty politicians so well, you have to do a little bit of the police work yourself."

"What other work did you do for the Carroll family?"

"I told you, I was in the persuasion business; I persuaded people." He replied vaguely.

"Were you involved in the fire that consumed police records including missing persons cases for Cass County and surrounding areas?"

"I was already on the road by the time that fire was set, but I can assure you there were other fires utilized to destroy evidence."

I was growing frustrated. My line of questioning was going nowhere.

"Are you willing to provide testimony to the crimes committed by the Carroll family?"

"Haven't I done so already?" He replied, smugly.

"Would you provide a written statement or agree to be filmed for the purpose of providing testimony against the family in court?"

"Seems like a waste of time. What's in it for me?"

"You get to take down a big time politician, and a corrupt organization."

"You're gonna have to do better than that."

"I'll get back to you," I replied, getting agitated again. "Right now; I don't know what else I can offer."

"I look forward to hearing your proposal."

"What can you tell me about the federal agent working with the Carroll family?"

"Only this; if he is still a federal agent, he is going to be pretty old; near the end of his career."

"Is there anything else?" I asked.

"You can figure out the rest on your own; earn your tax funded paycheck."

I shook my head and skipped past yet another question on my notepad without an answer.

"Then that brings us to the usual business at hand. What new victim do you have to tell me about today?"

Fenton sneered at me for a moment and put down the phone. Any time he felt like he could leave me with more questions than answers, he was pretty smug. I watched as he flicked his cigarette on the floor behind him and shook the pack to free another. He casually lit it and then picked up the phone again.

"Do you remember the first prostitute you ever fucked?" He asked.

"No, because I've never been with a prostitute." I replied, rolling my eyes.

"That's right; I keep forgetting we're speaking on the record. Of course you haven't, Detective, and I never killed anyone and stacked their body on top of the body of someone else I never killed." He leaned forward whispered into his phone, "Just nod your head if you've fucked a hooker, Detective; it'll be our little secret."

I stared back at him without moving, "I've never fucked a hooker."

He glared at me for a moment before he shrugged it off and sat back in his seat. "Of course not, you're a man of morals and ethics and other shit that keeps you from getting your dick sucked on the regular. My first prostitute was a bitch named Brenda. I assume that was her real name. Who can keep track of all these gashes and their pseudonyms?"

"You are living under an assumed name." I pointed out.

"Of course I am; I kill people. Whores just give hummers at truck stops for coke money. Why not just be honest with the clientele? I mean isn't that just business 101?"

"I could see why an assumed name would make sense for any type of criminal." I said.

"Yeah, but it makes it a hell of a lot harder to tell you about a bitch I killed in 1986 when I don't know her real name."

I shrugged slightly, as I could see his point.

"Why don't you just tell me about her?" I said, guiding him to provide more information.

"Well I was in misery, you might call it Missouri. There's this little shit town named Joplin not far from the Kansas and Oklahoma border. Nice people, shitty town; you'd like it there. Anyways; I'm passing through and this brown-eyed girl catches my eye as she walks around to different people in the parking lot of the motel, offering to blow them for a Jackson. Of course, I asked her how much for the whole package and she said she'd take it anywhere for two hundred. It might seem like I was just young and horny, but in reality I didn't want her fucked up, gap-toothed-mouth, anywhere near my dick. I told her she could shower in my room first, because she smelled like whores do. After that I took her to pound town for a little while."

He sat back and puffed on his cigarette for a second as if reminiscing about a fond memory.

"She certainly wasn't the best pussy I ever had, but she might have been the most enthusiastic."

I gave him a moment to see if he had anything else to add.

"And then what?" I asked. He had taken a long pause, and I was beginning to get annoyed.

He looked up at me as if he was just realizing I was there.

"Then I caved her skull in with a desk lamp." He said with a casual shrug.

"That's it?"

"That's it, she fell asleep; I took my money out of her purse along with the rest of her day's earnings. Hell, I was the one who got paid for sex that day. Then picked up a lamp and started beating her brains in. It wasn't as satisfying as I had hoped. Turns out, I like to kill them when they're awake enough to fight back a little. It gets my freak juices flowing. She was obnoxious though so I let her sleep, then I killed her. Didn't even bother to check out of the motel; I just dumped her body in the bathtub and left."

"Do you happen to remember which motel it was?"

"I doubt that really matters now, detective. If it's still standing it's probably going by a different name now. A gruesome murder will do that to a business. In fact, I'll let you in on a little secret. I picked up a few businesses simply by killing someone there and then waiting until the business inevitably went on sale. They are always a hell of a bargain."

"That's officially fucked up." I replied, "But I wouldn't expect anything else from you."

"Of course you wouldn't, because after a decade, you still don't understand me. I've spent hours and hours explaining why I do the things I do, but you find it hard to retain any of it because of your useless, puritanical upbringing."

"It's not useless." I interceded, "It gave me plenty of motivation to catch you."

"You got lucky, kid; that's it."

"Maybe; but it worked pretty good." I said, just trying to annoy him.

"Luck runs out, just like time." Fenton said, as if he was alluding to something.

"Yes it does," I said checking the stopwatch. The last few minutes of my time with Fenton was ticking off the clock.

I grabbed my briefcase and set it on the table in front of me. I casually opened it and began putting away my pen and paper. I smirked at him, knowing I was about to leave. This was always my favorite part of our interactions; I got to leave, and he stayed behind to watch me go.

I looked up at him as I closed the briefcase and held the stopwatch aloft to watch the final seconds tick away.

"Luck and time," repeated Fenton.

"You mentioned that, do you have anything new to add?"

"They both run out," he said again.

I rolled my eyes. He was starting to make less sense all the time, making me glad to walk away while he sat there behind the glass, unable to leave.

"Sometimes," he started, pausing for what seemed like an eternity just for dramatic effect. "Sometimes, time and luck run out in the same instance."

He stood up from his table and held the phone up so he was speaking directly into the mouthpiece in front of him.

"Sometimes, for a young rookie officer, they run out at the exact same time."

He dropped the phone and gestured with both of his hands as if to demonstrate an explosion.

"Who told you that?" I asked.

He smiled at me. His face was ripe with egotistical pleasure as he repeated the gesture again and again.

"WHO TOLD YOU THAT?" I yelled into the phone.

He looked at me and shrugged, repeating the gesture again more enthusiastically this time.

"WHO TOLD YOU?" I screamed.

I stood to my feet; face inches away from the glass as I screamed at him again.

"WHO TOLD YOU?"

He was still laughing as I smacked the glass, sending a shock wave of pain through my palm and up into my forearm. He made the gesture again, this time switching it up to include feigned eye rubbing as he jutted out his bottom lip and pretended to cry.

"WHO TOLD YOU? WHO TOLD YOU? WHO TOLD YOU?"

Each time I asked the question I pounded my fist against the glass. He had done it again. He had ended one of our meetings on his terms. He was mocking me as only he could. I had changed the setting of the meeting, and he was taking full advantage. Fenton flicked the butt of his cigarette at the glass as corrections officers entered the room and started wrestling to drag him out of sight.

"WHO TOLD YOU?" I screamed again as I watch Fenton lock his hands onto the side of the door, preventing them from removing him from the room.

Over the faint sound of the struggle, I heard him through the phone as he was removed from the room. "I hope it was a beautiful funeral."

I stood there in stunned silence for a moment, and then smashed the phone against the glass as hard as the fourteen inch cord would allow.

CHAPTER NINETEEN

April was already turning out to be a shitty month. Starting with a funeral and an interview with Fenton, it didn't look to get any better. I raged to myself the entire trip back to Manhattan, planning all the different ways I would kill Fenton, if I had the chance.

Lost in the confusion of a dozen different investigations, was the fact that Fenton still had someone feeding him up to date information. He was too well informed for a man in solitary confinement. Fenton wielded this information against me in his ongoing effort to make me kill myself. He wasn't far off track. Seeing him every week for four straight weeks was already enough to make me hate my own existence. Twenty-two more weeks were certain to take a toll on my mental health.

Finding some clarity in the middle of my rage, I pulled out my phone and called Dr. Ehrenberg.

"Hey, Doc," I said when he answered, "It's James Bryant. Any chance you have an available appointment slot for this coming week?"

I gave him a moment to check his calendar and focused on the road for a little bit. Traffic was light as I traveled north, allowing me to commit less of my attention to the road than normal.

"Wednesday works perfect. Thanks, Doc."

I hung up the phone and set it in the cup holder in the center console.

"I've got a shit load to dump on him this week." I thought to myself.

I opted to sneak downstairs to the department's gym, rather than immediately begin my report. Fenton had provided me almost nothing to document, spending most of the interview bitching about "the system." From what Fenton had described, the case in Joplin should involve nothing more than placing Fenton at the scene. Hopefully the victim had already been identified and family notified. This one was from thirty years ago; hopefully it was nothing more than dusting off a cold case with a new lead.

I changed out of my suit into some workout clothes. I had some pent-up rage to release, and it wasn't going to happen at my desk, typing. I wrapped my hands and worked the heavy punching bag for twenty minutes or so. I imagined each punch breaking Fenton's nose or blackening his eyes. I punched the bag until my rage subsided, and my form went to shit. One bad punch with a partially bent wrist sent a casual shockwave running up my arm. Fortunately, I was too exhausted to put much power into my punches towards the end. It was a good thing too, since I might have saved myself a fractured wrist. I loosened up my wrist for a few minutes, ensuring I hadn't injured it, and cooled down on the treadmill for a little while.

After a cold shower, I settled in at my desk wearing comfy, after-hours clothing. My jeans and T-shirt would have been frowned upon during business hours, but it was the weekend, and nobody gave a shit what you wore.

I spent half an hour on the phone being transferred back and forth between officers and supervisors at the Joplin Police Department. I was finally patched through to someone who confirmed they had an unsolved homicide at the Budget Inn on April 30, 1986. The victim was named Brenda Auckland and she fit the description provided by Fenton. I made arrangements to meet with the Joplin Police Captain the following Monday.

I hung up with Joplin Police, and called Terry to inform him of our next destination.

"Hey! Terry. How do you feel about a trip to Joplin, Missouri?" I asked.

"Not great," he replied. "Like I need to make sure I'm up to date on my tetanus shot before we go."

"Well, it should be a short trip. It's a cold case where they found and identified the body already. We just have to go make sure the pieces fit. We might be able to make it back by Tuesday evening."

"I'm alright with that," he agreed, "I'm up to my ass in this Iowa case anyways. Did Fenton give you anything else on it?"

"Nothing; he stonewalled me on everything Iowa related, and then just kinda tossed me this cold case from Joplin in '86. He likes to draw things out and make us wait. He's a considerate fucker, like that."

"I'm not surprised. There's way more going on in Iowa than he wants to let on," advised Terry.

"He didn't get into a lot of detail, but he described blackmailing and extorting multiple people in Iowa to get information on everyone else. It sounds like he had his hands in everything there." I explained.

"I still can't believe that son of a bitch was in law enforcement. I hope they've updated their hiring practices by now." He exclaimed.

"I don't think they were too worried about the content of character when they were hiring back in the '80's. At least, not in that county," I posited.

"Who knows, we won't be getting much cooperation from them anyways. What time are we headed to Joplin?"

"I'll swing through the Kansas City area late Monday morning and pick you up," I told him.

"Works for me," he replied.

I spent less than an hour compiling my report for my April 1st meeting with Fenton. I checked around to find Shirley, Ross or Lt. Carter, but none of them were in. They didn't often get weekends off between the Joint Task Force and their obligatory call-in schedules. The only positive to come out of my JTF involvement was being off the call-in list. It occurred to me the only reason no one was here was due to the funeral reception being hosted at the community center. I checked the time and saw that it was well after 1800 hours. I sighed, picked up my jacket and headed for the door. I shut off the lights on my way out the door and checked the hallway outside investigations. It was clear; no one was at the department that didn't absolutely have to be.

The parking lot was almost vacant. Patrol was in the middle of shifts, and no one was transitioning off duty for a few hours. My head was busy; full of details I was trying to balance between multiple investigations, and my own psychological issues. For the first time in months I knew I was driving home to an empty house. No one was there to greet me; no one was coming home later. The painful realization brought tightness to my throat. My eyes burned like they were about to start watering.

I shook my head a little as I left the parking lot. Everything was different now. My thoughts were clear, but the memories were painful. All the way home I thought through the denial I had experienced for the past year. I had lost track of months of my life, and had nothing to show for them. The last year had been about keeping my head down in investigations and just doing my job. Looking back, it was hard to believe I hadn't been placed on some kind of extended leave. My head had been clouded and my judgement, certainly in question.

As I thought about it, a lot of things began to make sense. I hadn't been rotated out of investigations as would have been normal after five years behind a desk. I had been relegated to financial crimes and other non-violent offender reports. My department had gone out of their way to keep me involved, but limiting my exposure to the world outside. I was thankful, but also embarrassed. I had been cushioned from active, time sensitive police work and given the long, laborious investigations. These were important, but not urgent; allowing me to take more time than was necessary as I sorted through my emotional baggage.

The drive home was over before I knew it. I was lost in thought and fell into my familiar route home without thinking about it. I opened the garage, preparing myself as I knew Stephanie's maroon SUV wasn't going to be parked inside. I pulled into the garage on the far right side; just out of habit. Someday I might possess the intestinal fortitude to buy another car, or simply park in the middle; until then, it was business as usual.

I took a few moments and walked through the house. I hadn't set foot in the basement in months and had barely made it past the living room most nights. The basement was a cob-web filled disaster area. The basement had been mostly storage, but it seemed to have grown a life of its own. The mildew smell was strong and the southeast corner had clearly started leaking again at some point. I turned on all the lights and set up a few fans, hoping over time I could get the smell to fade and the mold to dissipate.

I left the basement knowing it would be another six months at least until I had the chance to clean it properly. I wandered down the hallway to the office. We had turned the last bedroom on the left into an office, and it served both of us from time to time. I hadn't sat at the desk in at least a year, and the dust reflected it. Piled here and there were pieces of mail, along with other paperwork. It occurred to me that I hadn't checked the mail in a long time. I came in through the garage, and I left through the garage. The mail had a tendency to pile up inside the front door where it was deposited through a slot.

The pile was monstrous. Bills, letters and magazines were scattered across the floor. Exasperated, I started piling them up and taking them to the office an armful at a time.

Most of the magazines were tossed in the trash along with the medical journals, and insurance offers. Coupons for a dozen different fast food restaurants delivered monthly quickly topped off the trash can in the office. I stopped throwing things out, and just started sorting.

I was thankful Stephanie had talked me into making all our bills auto-draft from our checking account. Everything was up to date besides one of my credit cards. I tracked it all the way from "overdue" to "closed due to lack of payment." Fortunately I hadn't been swiping my credit card lately, or I might have been in a bigger mess. The credit card had been my one holdout, allowing me to make purchases when I saw fit, without having to run every purchase by Stephanie. Looking back, I could see she had been right all along. I should have canceled it years ago.

I finally started getting everything in order when I found the insurance checks; one for my wife's SUV and one from her life insurance. They were both posted over four months prior.

I set them all aside and went to the living room. Even though it had been over a year, everything was still too fresh. The very thought of cashing a check as the result of losing my wife seemed to break me down inside. I walked to the fireplace mantle and stared at the framed photo in the center. I took it down and gently brushed the dust off the glass.

I smiled; not all the memories were painful. Some of them, like the one captured in the photo, were beautiful. I remembered the second the photographer snapped that photo. Stephanie and I were on our way back up the aisle, smiling as family and friends stood and cheered. After waiting four long years to get married, until she was done with Medical School, we finally got married. Four years was way longer to be engaged than I had anticipated, but Stephanie had been determined to finish Med School and start her internship before we tied the knot. I had disagreed, but I supported her, even if it meant waiting longer to marry her.

I found a dust rag and cleaned off the photos in the living room, one at a time. Each one held a memory, dear to my heart. I wasn't ready to let her go, but it finally felt like I could survive, if I had to.

I sat back in my recliner, and glanced around at all the memories immortalized on the wall. I felt something for the first time in over a year; peace.

It was a brand new feeling to wake up on a Monday and not only be at home, but make it to work on time.

I had spent my first day off in nearly a month trying to breathe life back into my house. I had slowly transformed it from a home, into a shrine of pain and sorrow. Now, I had to put it back into place. I had unconsciously decided the house was clean simply because I hadn't been in more than four rooms in the house for over a year. The clutter and mess had been carefully hidden away in the office, basement and spare bedroom, giving me the illusion that Stephanie was still there looking after me.

My denial had been over the top, and waking up to that fact on a Sunday morning shocked my system. I skipped church; I hadn't been in nearly sixteen months, what was another week?

I opted instead to make a real breakfast, that didn't involve the microwave, and start cleaning. By the end of the day I was exhausted, with a pile of garbage spilling out of the cans at the end of the driveway. I was done in a reasonable time and in bed early like it was mandatory. I tossed and turned quite a bit; still not use to the idea that I was sleeping alone in a bed my wife and I had spent hours picking out at the store. I finally took a pillow and blanket to the couch and caught a few hours of sleep.

Monday was a completely different kind of drive to work. I still had shit to figure out, but I finally felt like it was possible. For months I had been convinced this investigation was going to be the death of me. I had dreaded every day at work, every scene I went to, and every interview with Fenton. I still dreaded interviewing him each week, but it started to look more like a calendar with days being crossed off. There was an end to all of this; and maybe a new beginning not far beyond.

I picked up bagels and coffee on the way to work and had them set out in the middle of investigations by the time everyone else got there. I munched casually on a blueberry bagel, smeared with honey and hazelnut cream cheese as everyone filed past the table one at a time.

Morning briefing didn't involve me these days. The conversation between supervisors and detectives about ongoing cases and status reports had me on the outside looking in. My only concern was the three bodies at the park still being investigated, and any progress on the bomber. None of those were discussed during briefing with the entire group.

Briefing dismissed and Lt. Carter motioned to me, Shirley and Ross to join him in his office for what had become the standard second briefing of the morning. I topped off my coffee and joined them, closing the door behind me.

"Well, Bryant; thanks for breakfast." Carter said as he smeared cream cheese on his onion bagel.

"You're very welcome, L.T.; I wanted to find the best way to thank the three of you for everything you've done for me over the past year. I had an awakening of sorts and realized I had been living in denial to everything I've been through over the past sixteen months. I wasn't taking care of myself, and I was ignoring the reality that my wife died over a year ago. I didn't realize how many times I had put the three of you in the awkward position of listening to me talk like my wife was still with me. You three looked after me and gave me time to process things until I could get a grip on reality again. I am forever indebted to you for the candor and discretion you possessed when working with me. I took a big step this week; I still have a lot of work to do, but I'm on the right track again. I owe that all to you three and the way the department handled my situation without putting me out on mandatory leave of absence. I like my job, but I love the people I work with every day. Not many people can say that." I admitted.

Det. Ross gave me a pat on the shoulder and said nothing.

I looked around the room at Det. Shirley who gave me a smile. "Welcome back, Bryant."

"I'm glad to hear it, Bryant. You had us worried for a little while. Hopefully now, we can press forward and take care of business," said Lt. Carter.

"That sounds good to me, sir," I replied.

"Ok, down to business," said Lt. Carter, leaning back in his seat. "First, the IT security team has already finished updating all your computers to ensure the highest level of security the Federal Government can provide. All future investigations involving the victims up in Iowa will be handled by Bryant and the FBI, whenever possible. We are going to redouble our efforts locally and try to wrap up the cases of the three bodies at the park. One we have already identified as Spencer Warren, who as we all know, had warrants and ongoing court appearances for a plethora of sex crimes. The other two have not yet been identified. We contacted the families of everyone who has an open missing person case from Kansas, Missouri, Nebraska and Oklahoma. We are requesting DNA samples of all missing persons. We are hoping these last two weren't visiting from too far out of state when they were killed. We have several DNA samples for comparison ready to go to the lab in Kansas City for the coroner to compare to our John Doe's."

I held up my hand and received a nod from the Lieutenant.

"I'm driving through Kansas City to pick up Agent Jones, I can drop off the samples on the way." I offered.

"Works for me, and it saves Ross a trip," replied Carter.

"Yeah, thanks buddy," agreed Det. Ross.

"I take it your meeting with Fenton resulted in a new body out east?" Carter asked.

"That is correct. I am headed to Joplin, Missouri to help them wrap up a cold case from 1986. They already had the body identified and family notified. I'm there to get copies of the case files and collect any evidence they had still for comparison to Fenton." I explained.

"Are we still handling all of that evidence through Dr. Elmore's lab in Lincoln?" asked Carter.

"Yes, sir; as soon as we're done in Joplin I will be delivering anything evidentiary up to Lincoln, hopefully, by Wednesday evening. With the backlog of cases with the KBI, and the amount of evidence and autopsies being handled by the lab Coroner in Kansas City, SSA Wells believes it will be best to utilize Dr. Elmore's team for the foreseeable future."

Lt. Carter smirked a little. "So this one is just a cold case, huh? No stacks of bodies in a shallow grave this time?"

"I'm not making any promises, but it doesn't sound like it." I replied with a brief smile.

"Did anything of substance come up during the interview?" asked Carter.

"Yeah, he knew about the bomb at the park. He not only knew I had just been at Preston's funeral, he knew Preston was a rookie officer at the time of his death. We thought someone was leaking information to Fenton and we were right. It's up to date, accurate, and being wielded to get under my skin." I explained.

"Here's what we're going to do. From now on, every minute of free time is spent researching employees and personnel who have access to maximum security prisoners at El Dorado. Whoever this person is, we're going to smoke them out and lock them up; understood?"

We all nodded in agreement.

———

The road trip to Joplin was much more relaxing than previous trips. I filled Terry in on my recent interview with Fenton and the ongoing interference from our unknown third party. I bought Terry lunch as a thank you for putting up with all my bullshit over the past few weeks. He shrugged it off and tried to downplay it all, but I could tell he was relieved to have me on the right side of sanity again.

I dropped off the DNA samples for comparison at the lab, wishing we weren't hours away from anyone who could help us with advanced evidence processing. The two John Doe's from the park were stored at the coroner's office, waiting for something definitive to help identify them. Their teeth had been partially smashed making a dental match impossible. The delay in those cases was frustrating, but it paled in comparison to waiting for evidence and results to come back from the bomb and the Lane homicides. Someone had a clear motive to kill Tim and Emma Lane, but the case was going nowhere until we had a line of inquiry to follow.

After the first few hours, I realized how much I missed traveling by plane. I hadn't taken an extensive road trip in years. My wife and I had enjoyed many long road trips around the country, but those had all been fun. I was on my way to retrieve a case file full of pictures of a woman with her skull caved in. Not my idea of a fun road trip.

———

The Joplin Police Department was ready us when we arrived. Captain James Sherman gave us the brief tour and took us to the conference room. They had the case files set out on the table and had all the evidence packaged up and ready for transportation. Capt. Sherman handed us each a copy of the file and sat down with us to review it.

"So tell me how you came about this confession? I grew up in Joplin so I'm familiar with this case from when it made the news. It's a hell of a thing to solve a thirty-one year old cold case." He said.

"We had a series of women get abducted and killed in the Manhattan and surrounding area back in the early to two-thousands." I explained. "We managed to catch the killer, who is currently waiting out his last appeal before he gets a lethal injection in December."

"So he's having a Ted Bundy style death bed confession, trying to stave off his execution?" Capt. Sherman asked.

"Not really; he is seeking notoriety as the most prolific serial killer in US history, so he's feeding us confessions on a weekly basis. This case happened to be the one he confessed to this week." I informed him.

"Well you described it to a "T" when you called me last week," admitted Capt. Sherman. "Blunt force trauma, murder weapon was a lamp from the bedside table, body found in the bathtub and a suspect matching Fenton's description who never checked out of the room."

"Fenton is a bit egotistical," explained Terry. "He remembers vivid details of his killings so he can relive them and brag about them to us when the time comes."

"Well the names aren't the same, but the clerk at the time described the man who rented the room as a tall white male in his mid to late twenties. Rented the room for two nights, but is believed to have left after one. Body was found by cleaning staff," read Capt. Sherman.

"He was going by 'Jeffrey Dean' when he checked into the hotel," observed Terry. "Do you have any other records of dealing with someone by that name?"

"I ran all the names through the system again after you called. Everything is digital now, but from what I could see we didn't have anyone named 'Jeffrey Dean' in our records." Captain Sherman advised. "The victim however, had been arrested multiple times for prostitution and drug possession."

"That fits with what Fenton told me." I said.

"And you said the victim's family had been notified already?" asked Terry.

"That's correct; Brenda's mother lived in the area and was notified after the body was identified."

"Did anything else like this happen during that time period?" I asked.

"From what I could tell from our records, this should have been the only unsolved murder from that time period. We had a few other murders around the city back in the late '80's, but nothing that fits this kind of brutality."

"We will be in touch if there are any more confessions to murders in this area." I informed him.

"Do you really think there will be more of them?" He asked, appearing worried.

"There have been a lot of them; we just don't want to miss anything." Terry explained.

"How many?" he asked.

I exchanged a glance with Terry, who I could see was trying to come up with a final count. I started with the eleven he had already been convicted of and tried to count up from there, but got lost around 20, positive I was forgetting someone.

"We have confirmed over twenty different women with the possibility of dozens more." I replied.

"Holy shit," whispered Capt. Sherman. "You said multiple victims from out your way; how many convictions?"

"Eleven," I replied casually, "At least five of which were capital murder charges."

"Now that's a sick bastard right there," marveled the Captain.

"You don't know the half of it." I warned.

We sat in silence for a moment as the Captain contemplated what he had heard and the implications therein. I could tell he had more questions, but was trying not to obsess. The Captain then gestured at the boxes of evidence.

"Well, I won't hold you up much, then. This is everything we have for evidence in the case. It should consist of bed sheets, pillows and pillow cases, the lamp and some of the victim's personal belongings. Let me know when you get something definitive so I can close this case."

"We will be submitting reports to you as soon as we're done as will our lab up in Lincoln, Nebraska. They will have all the evidence analyzed and hopefully be done within a matter of a week or two," I informed him. "They work pretty fast up there."

The Captain signed over custody of the evidence, and helped us tote it out to the car.

We hadn't been there long, but additional time wasn't required. Everything we did from then on was speculation until the lab produced evidence that provided some kind of resolution.

"Thank you, gentlemen, for coming all this way to help us close out this case. I look forward to hearing from you."

We shook the Captain's hand and hit the road. Terry waited until we were around the corner before he commented.

"Don't you wish each of these cold cases would be this cut and dried?"

"If they were, we wouldn't have a task force much longer. This one might be easy, but I promise it is only a matter of time before he serves up another cluster-fuck of a case involving a stack of bodies in a decades old grave. Fenton has either been convicted or admitted to killing women in three graves totaling at least four bodies each. The way they are spread out between Oklahoma, Kansas and Nebraska leads me to believe we have at least one more mass grave to find. Which means; we have him on record as killing more than twenty women and he has to deliver at least twenty-two more victims before he is done. At the pace we are on, his kill count has to be in at least the sixties."

"Shit," he said. "I think you're right. In that case, I'm really going to enjoy the easy ones while we have them. We are going to have our hands full this year."

"I think our hands were full when he dumped the Carroll family case in our laps. Everything beyond that, we're just fucked." I replied.

"Do you ever think the task force is a little light on help, in the grand scheme of things?" asked Terry.

"Two weeks ago I would have told you we were fine, now I agree. We're shorthanded."

"Nothing we can do about it now," said Terry. "The DOJ has already set the budget for this task force. I don't foresee them increasing it any time soon."

"We are on our own."

It was odd to think in those terms after the relative ease of the Joplin case. We hadn't discovered extra bodies from another killer like we did in Manhattan, and we hadn't discovered a pile of bodies where only one or two were alleged to be like in Irvingdale. Each of those had led to subsequent investigations involving more manpower. The case in Iowa was already complicated, and we only had two confirmed victims; if we ever found out who the bone in the casket belonged to. Without a doubt, there were going to be more. I just hoped we were ready for the inevitable shit storm that was about to hit us.

CHAPTER TWENTY

I dropped Terry off at his home in Kansas City and transported the evidence to my department for secure storage. The evidence was placed under lock and key; then the key went home with me.

The implications of my conversation with Terry weighed heavy on my mind. If Fenton truly had a body count exceeding sixty victims, he would get exactly what he wanted; infamy. It would be one of, if not, the highest kill count of any serial killer in American history. We were barely a month into the interview process, and the numbers were truly staggering.

As soon as I got home, I poured a reasonable glass of scotch and stepped out onto my back deck. If the rest of my house had been neglected, my back deck had been completely forgotten. The sliding door almost didn't open, and deck itself was covered in leaves, dirt and debris. I looked for a clean spot on the rail to lean without getting my clothes filthy. Finding no such spot, I opted to stand, just off the railing, and surveil my back yard.

My grass was starting to turn green again, highlighting even more the fact that my yard had become an overgrown thicket over the past year. It was almost all dead now, but it had clearly reached a height of epic proportions.

"I'd hate to be the guy who has to cut that." I thought to myself as I immediately determined I was going to pay someone else to clear my yard.

Losing my taste for the scotch, I tossed the last of the contents over the deck and took the glass inside.

"Not sure if I hate it because it's the cheap shit or if I just don't really want a drink right now." I wondered out loud.

An officer at my department ran a landscaping company on the side, so I called him and got him scheduled to come over and tackle the thicket in my back yard. I was starting to think clearly again and get my priorities in order, but there still wasn't much time for handling all my affairs unassisted. My yard needed work, my house needed cleaning, and my life needed some extreme organization.

I picked up the insurance checks and stared at them for a minute. The thought of my wife's life being boiled down to a dollar amount was disturbing. It wasn't as if it was some kind of surprise; we had applied for the insurance policies ahead of time for this very situation. One of us, left behind without the other, deserved the best future we could provide. Being a cop, I had always assumed I would be the one to die first. My wife made substantially more income than I did. Her insurance policy reflected the same.

In reality, I was set for a long time. The house, the car, the credit cards; they could all be paid off with the two checks I held in my hand. Even after that, I had money to spare. It was both comforting and heartbreaking. My wife had a totally different approach to life insurance. I had always thought of it as burial insurance. I die, cut the checks, pay the mortician, pay the caterer, and buy me a nice hole in the ground; all without having to swipe the credit card.

My wife had spent many a long conversation early in our marriage convincing me otherwise. She didn't want to lose me and then try to hold onto everything we had with only her income. She didn't wish the same on me either. She insisted for weeks that the right thing to do was have enough of an insurance policy to replace the income of whoever died. The math made sense and I would have done anything to keep her happy and feeling secure.

She was right; of course. I just hated to admit it after the fact. I had begrudgingly agreed to the whole thing at the time. Her math was solid, but it wasn't the way I was raised, so I had trouble wrapping my head around the whole thing.

I stared at the life insurance check for a minute, realizing the check was only good for another couple of weeks. I had that much time to cash it; when I was ready. I turned the checks over and signed each of them and put them back on the kitchen table. That was a good step. It was all I could manage at the moment. Maybe next week I'd take them out to the car and eventually go by the bank.

———

I was on the road only minutes after morning briefing. Nothing applied to me in briefing. The DNA samples were at the lab in Kansas City to be tested later today. With luck, we would have results from the samples for comparison to our victims. Everything else was day to day information. The KBI still didn't have information on the bomb from the park. No one seemed to have any answers for us, and it was starting to get old. Everywhere we called had this, "soon, but not yet," response to our inquiries.

Everyone was walking on pins and needles, still feeling somber after the funeral, and trying to determine if it was the appropriate time to move on. There was nothing in the handbook about dealing with the loss of a coworker. There were resources and options available for individuals and groups to get help, but nothing that was positioned to help an entire organization cope and move forward.

I was becoming accustomed to driving in silence, nothing but my thoughts to pass the time as I traveled. I spent a great deal of time dwelling on Preston's family and girlfriend. The rumor around the department was he had been stockpiling money with his eye on an engagement ring. We would never know now.

Wedding's in a police department often become an organizational gathering. Everyone from the officer's squad, both current and past squads, as well as academy friends, and other connections made, would clamor for the same weekend off. Officers would wheel and deal to trade time off to ensure they got to be there for the bachelor party, wedding, or both.

There are precious few reasons to celebrate in the lives of officers. Officers get lost in their career; balancing work and life becomes difficult. Weddings and babies were the best reasons to get together and celebrate the good in life.

A funeral for the right person, at the right time, with the right legacy, could be a truly beautiful and cathartic experience. It's an interesting event when you can attend the funeral of a family member and learn more about them in an hour than you did in your entire life with them. That wasn't the case this time; there was nothing cathartic or beautiful about laying someone to rest in their early twenties. I had seen my fair share of dead bodies, it came with the job. Some of them will stick with you more than others; Preston was at the top of my list. There was just something different about seeing him on the ground, still on fire, and lifeless.

Sometimes we are burdened to carry more weight than others. Law enforcement was one of those professions that came with both expected and unintentional burdens. Either way, we carried them as long as we could. When we couldn't carry them any further, they either broke us enough to seek help or self-destruct. The number of officers who took the latter option was staggering. I had taken the latter option for over a year now; thankful it hadn't gone to the extreme. Hopefully I was ready to make a few changes.

It was a relief to finally make it to the lab in Lincoln. It was a long way to drive evidence on a regular basis, but I liked the destination. Dr. Elmore along with Tommy and Samantha assisted me in bringing in the evidence from my car. Dr. Elmore signed for the evidence so Tommy and Samantha could start sorting through it a little at a time. Dr. Elmore waited for the others to be out of earshot before she turned to me.

"Are you planning to stay long?" She asked.

"There's not much calling me home, right now." I replied. "All our evidence is being analyzed and we don't have anything to actively investigate right now."

"Is that a yes or a no?" She asked with a coy smile.

"Well, I can't stay too long, but I don't have any prior engagements."

"How about a cup of coffee?" she asked.

"I had a long drive; coffee sounds amazing." I replied.

We turned slowly from the lab and walked out into the hallway.

"How have you been?" She asked.

"It's been a rough week." I admitted. "With the funeral and interview with Fenton, I've been struggling to find some peace of mind."

"Would it help to talk about it?"

"I think so…" I trailed off.

"If you'd rather talk to someone else about all this I understand," she said. I held open the door to the lounge as she stepped in ahead of me.

"I want to be able to talk with you." I replied. "I'm just not sure how much of it you'd be comfortable hearing."

"You mean the gory things Fenton put you through?" she inquired.

I shook my head as we reached the counter. We each grabbed a cup and said nothing for a moment as she poured coffee into each of our cups. I stirred a couple packets of sugar into mine, and made a mental note of the two creams and two sugars she stirred into hers.

"I mean," I started, gesturing casually with my cup before trailing off.

She waited patiently as I searched for the right words to say. I found myself wanting to talk to her about everything, while simultaneously wanting to spare her from every detail of my pain.

"I mean, I'm having trouble bringing myself to cash my wife's life insurance check." I finally blurted out.

There was an extended moment of awkward silence. I stared down at my cup wishing there was something I could say to make things less awful. I thought hard, but there didn't seem to be anything I could say, to make the situation any better.

"I understand why you wouldn't want to talk about this with me," she admitted, quietly.

"I do. I do want to talk to you about all of this. I got home this past weekend and realized my house has fallen into complete disarray. I had mail from last year still inside the front door, my lawn hasn't seen a mower in over a year and my basement reeks of mold and mildew. I knew I had been a mess, but I didn't realize how bad I let everything go. It was a bit of a rude awakening for me." I said.

"That's understandable; you've been through a lot," she encouraged.

"I didn't know how far I had fallen. It's going to take me a long time to put all the pieces back together." I confessed.

She nodded her understanding, and gave me a brief smile before she dropped her head.

"I just hope I can help you in some way."

I lowered my head a little to catch her eye so she would look up at me again.

"You've already helped me more than you know."

She gave me a brief smile, blushed, and dropped her head again.

"I'm working through some things right now that I need to talk about to help me make sense of it all," I said. "It's not all stuff I want to burden you with right now. I made an appointment with my therapist for this week. He's the one I want to dump all my heavy burdens on, not you. That's not fair to you. You're not my therapist, and I don't want to treat you like one. I want to get to know you better. To do that properly, I'm going to filter my crazy through someone else so you're not catching it all over dinner."

She seemed relieved I wasn't pushing her away completely. I didn't want to hold her at arms-length, but I had shit to work out so as not to push her away with my issues. For now, I had to bottle up my crazy and only release it when appropriate. We were just becoming friends; I didn't want to ruin that.

"So when is this dinner you speak of?" she asked.

"Soon," I replied casually. I shot her a sly smile over my cup before I took another sip.

"I'm looking forward to it," she stated.

I looked at her for a moment, wondering how it was possible for there to be a second woman in the world who could stand the sight of me. I decided not to pick at that particular scab.

"When the time is right." I said before gesturing at my head. "When I've got all of my issues to at least a 'work in progress' level, I promise you'll get that dinner."

She smiled again, making me hate the very thought of leaving. Each time she smiled at me, it felt like another one of my wounds healed a little more. I had never been a patient man, but I was prepared to learn.

"Can I call you this week?" I asked.

She nodded slowly and glanced up at me, "I'd like that."

———

I sat at my desk the next morning wishing I had the balls to call Dr. Elmore when I got home. She said I could call, now I just had to find enough spine to hold myself upright long enough to do so. I had stared at my phone long enough to memorize every detail of its touch screen face.

After an hour, I knew every scratch, scuff, and blemish; but I still didn't have the courage to make the call.

Maybe I wasn't ready. I was engrossed in a series of investigations revolving around dozens of murders, and all I could think of was the doctor doing all the forensics and evidence testing. I tried convincing myself this was nothing more than a boyish crush, but I couldn't get her out of my head. I was so lost in thought; I didn't hear Detective Ross walk up behind me.

"Bryant," he said, causing me to jump.

"Shit, you startled me." I admitted as I turned my chair around to face him.

"Well, I can only say your name casually so many times before I start making some real noise," he replied. "No shit; we got a DNA match from one of the samples you dropped off Monday."

"You're telling me that worked?" I asked in disbelief.

"One of the missing person's cases got a match. Come on, I'm briefing on it in the LT.'s office," he insisted.

The pull of my headphones reminded me they were still attached to my head as they kept me from standing up from my chair.

"Mother fuckers!" I swore as I ripped them off before I could follow Ross to the Lieutenant's office.

Detective Shirley arrived at the office just before I did and stepped in ahead of me.

Detective Ross stood against the wall as Lt. Carter hung up his phone. Shirley and I each grabbed a chair and sat patiently as Ross opened up his case file.

Ross pulled out a photo and set it on the desk in front of us.

"The lab called me a minute ago and told me the identity of one of the two remaining victims from the memorial garden at the park. Thirty-one year old Tory Holton; black male lived off of Tamarac Court with his boyfriend Harvey Brand. Tory was reported missing when he stopped returning phone calls to his family for over a week. Family was concerned and went to their five bedrooms, two bathroom; twenty-five hundred square foot house to check on them. Tory's sister had done some house sitting for them in the past and had a key. She reported the house appeared to have been burglarized at some point. She reported multiple items missing including a coffee table, a couch, and one of the beds. She reported she never went more than a week without hearing from her brother. She told officers Tory was a notorious home-body who rarely traveled. The house had been cleaned recently, but the reporting party told officers it was common for the house to be spotless. No one has heard from Tory or Harvey since this report was filed. No clothes missing, both of their cars were still in the garage when the sister checked on them. After six months, the banks repossessed the cars and the home. This case was moved from missing person status to possible homicide, but after thorough combing of that house, there was no evidence to demonstrate it was a homicide."

"I remember this case; it was just before I came to investigations in 2012. We never had any trace of either of these guys and no one could explain what had happened at the time. They bought the first house on a cul-de-sac while the others were under construction. They were the only one's living on that block for months before they went missing." I said.

"We contacted both families about this case back then. Harvey's ex-wife didn't even know he was gay, let alone in a long term relationship," continued Ross. "Tory's family stated Harvey had been out of town on the week of March 2nd through 5th on business, and Tory had stayed home. They both worked locally, Harvey traveled often for work, but the two had been living together three months when they went missing. Until now, we've had no trace of them. We didn't even have a DNA sample to collect of Harvey's back then. The house was that spotless."

"Does that seem out of place to anyone else?" asked Shirley.

"Yes it does," replied Lt. Carter. "Some people are clean freaks, but no one is so anal retentive they can scrub every trace of DNA from a house. This was deep cleaned with a purpose."

"Let's divide this up." I insisted.

"Bryant; the original reporting party, Tory's sister Gabriella is coming in later this morning. Go over everything with her; crime scene photos, social media, and timeline; everything. Shirley; the other houses on that cul-de-sac were under construction at the time, find out what company was out there and see if we can get a list of everyone who was working out there at the time. Ross, I want you to see what you can do to find a DNA sample for Harvey. There wasn't anything at the house; call the ex-wife. See if she would have anything we could use."

I returned to my desk and snatched up my phone, checking the file for the number to call.

"Hello, Gabriella. This is Detective Bryant. I understand you are coming in later to discuss your brother's case. Can you bring in any photos of his house you might have? Thank you; I'll explain when you get here."

I spent the next hour looking over the case file for Tory and Harvey. The photos had been snapped in excruciating detail. The house was clean and seemed to be only missing the items Ross had listed. If this had been a burglary, there were several details missing. There was no forced entry, there was no damage inside the house, and there was no evidence. For all anyone knew, the missing items could have been sold online the day before they went missing.

———

Right after lunch, I met with Gabriella in the conference room off the investigations wing. I poured her a cup of coffee and slid the tray of sugar and creamers across the table to her. She began casually pouring a few packets into her coffee and looked at me.

"So, the other detective told me you have some kind of update on my brother? Can you please tell me what's going on? Last week you wanted a sample of Tory's DNA; now you want me to come in and bring pictures of his house with me," she said with concern.

"I apologize for the burden we have put on you. I'm going to try and explain the situation to you the best I can. First of all; does Tory have any additional family beside you?" I asked.

"Why do you need more family? Am I not good enough for you? What else do you want family here for?"

I took a moment to compose myself so I would reply in a way that might be misconstrued as rude.

"In case they wanted to be here when I informed you that we found your brother's remains," I said quietly.

"Remains; you mean to tell me you found my brother?" She asked.

"That's correct," I replied.

"And he's dead?"

"That is correct," I repeated.

"But; the detective the other day said they were trying to get up-to-date DNA samples for ongoing missing person cases; he didn't tell me they had a body," she insisted.

"He told you that, because we didn't have the remains identified. We used the DNA samples from missing person cases and compared them to the remains. That's how we knew we found your brother."

"So is that why you had me come in? You wanted to tell me you found my brother?"

"Not only that; we wanted to tell you your suspicions were correct. We believe your brother was murdered. We believe his house was scrubbed clean to hide evidence of the murder. We also believe it was done so well, everyone was convinced Tory had cleaned just before they disappeared."

"Shit," she whispered as tears started to form in her eyes. "You all had me convinced it was a missing person case."

"We were wrong," I replied softly. "I am so sorry for what you've been through; and I am so sorry for the way the investigation was mishandled. We didn't know. We were as baffled by the house as you were."

She cried for a moment, holding back her sobs, but letting the tears flow for a moment.

"I knew deep down that something was wrong. My brother never missed a phone call from me without calling back. This just wasn't like him." She insisted.

"I know you're going through a lot right now. But this came as an unexpected break in the case while we were working another. I have pictures of the house taken at the time of the original report. Can you look over them and tell me what you see?"

I handed her the photos and she took the folder from me. "Did you happen to bring any photos of the house with you?"

"Yes," she replied, offhandedly, pulling a few photos out of her purse.

I glanced over the photos for a moment. The first one showed Tory and Harvey standing out in front of the house next to a "Sold" sign in the yard. I made a note of the real estate company, but didn't see anything else which caught my eye. The next picture appeared to have been taken at the dinner table. Tory and Harvey leaned in together for the picture which was taken from the opposite side of the table. In the back, just beyond the edge of the couch, I could see a coffee table sitting on a rug in front of the sofa. The angle was bad, but it had been enough to confirm the coffee table was missing back in 2012.

The next picture appeared to be a family picture. Tory and Harvey stood alongside Gabriella and several others in the middle of the living room floor, just in front of the coffee table. I could barely see it between their legs as the stood with their arms around one another. I started growing frustrated as I looked at the pictures. I couldn't place what was wrong with them.

I had Gabriella walk me through the timeline of events and asked her the usual questions about strange phone calls and threatening persons in Tory's past. Her answers fell right in line with the original report she had provided five years prior; nothing new to report.

I fanned the pictures out in front of me and looked them over together.

"Can I make copies of these for our records?" I asked Gabriella.

"Do whatever you need to do, detective." She replied. The dejection in her voice was obvious. Some missing detail; some small (or large) oversight had resulted in this case being filed away with a million unanswered questions.

I strolled to the copier in the office and made digital copies of the photos. I knew Gabriella had to be frustrated. This was an old Band-Aid to rip off, and it was sure to open up all the old wounds.

I gave Gabriella the photos back along with my business card. She nodded at me as I asked her to call if she thought of anything else. She walked out of the building, almost in a trance. She had clearly been expecting this kind of news, but it still hurt to hear someone else finally say it.

I found myself slightly discouraged, even though we'd had more breaks in this case today than any other so far. I returned to my desk and tossed the folder full of photos on my desk, causing some of them to slide out the top. I sighed with frustration and left them there. I needed something to drink and I was tired of coffee. I walked down to the second floor lobby and bought a soda from the vending machine, and sipped it as I returned to my desk. The photos were still scattered when I got back. I looked over each one again as I put them back into the folder, one at a time.

I opted against sitting down and instead walked over to Shirley's desk.

"Have you had success finding the construction company who built those houses?" I asked her.

"Nothing yet," she replied turning in her chair. "Did you get anything from the sister?"

"Nope; I did find out who the real estate company was, who listed the property for sale. They might be able to help," I informed her. I handed her a sticky note with the local realtor information on it.

"Awesome, thank you," she said as she picked up her phone and turned back towards her desk.

The end of the day came and went before I finally gave up on staring at the pictures. No one had checked in with me the rest of the day, so I had no idea what had developed. I had hit a dead end and was growing fatigued. I called it a day around 1800 hours and headed home.

————

I did the same dance again that evening. I tried to focus on cleaning up the house a bit, but wound up pacing back and forth staring at my phone.

It was on me to call; I had asked for permission, after all. I was just really nervous. For yet another evening, it felt like I was back in high school again. All the butterflies were there; all the voices telling me to do it were there; I just couldn't find the nerve.

"Ah; just pick up the phone, you pussy," I goaded myself.

I wimped out; like a little chicken-shit, I went down to the basement and gathered a trash can full of moldy garbage and took it out to the end of the driveway. It didn't solve the issue of locating my spine again, but it did clear some space in the basement. It also managed to burn half an hour of time bringing me closer to going to bed, and further from ideal calling times.

I picked up the phone a couple times and put it back down, bringing myself a little closer to dialing each time I did. I picked up the phone and turned towards the living room. Over the top of my screen, I caught a glimpse of the pictures on the mantle.

That took all my nerve away. I put the phone down on the counter and went back down to the basement.

————

I barely slept that night. I was wrestling with it all over again. It bothered me that I was both struggling to mourn, and struggling to move on. I didn't want the despair to return by taking the time to mourn, but making even the slightest effort to move my life forward turned me right back to my grief.

Dr. Ehrenberg was helpful that next morning. We met for an hour before I went to work.

Perspective; if you see no other reason to go to a counselor, perspective should be the motivator. Someone with an outside view who helps rationalize your fear and helps you develop a recovery plan. Was I cured? Hell no; but I was on my way.

I set a tentative follow up appointment for a few weeks out, and determined I was going to be there. I needed some breakthroughs; this was a way to get there.

I was emotionally drained when I got to work, but I at least I wasn't walking in hung-over.

Ross caught my eye as I walked in and nodded me over towards Lt. Carter's office. I deposited my jacket on the back of my chair and followed him.

"Did you have any luck talking to the sister, yesterday?" Ross asked.

"I got a few pictures of the house taken before they disappeared, but otherwise it was all the same thing she reported back in 2012," I replied.

"Well I got back late yesterday. I met with Harvey's ex-wife and was able to get a DNA sample for comparison."

"She still had something for a usable sample?" I asked.

"The biological kind," Ross replied, "They have a kid together. I dropped some of their son's hair off at the lab in Kansas City; we should have results later today."

"Have we heard anything new from Shirley?" I asked.

"She's interviewing employees of Marten and Flint construction. They were the contractors who built the housing development where our victims lived." Ross explained.

"Marten," I said quietly, "As in Greg Marten?"

"One and the same," he replied as Lt. Carter joined us.

"That name has been popping up all over the place, lately," Carter said. "Did you get anything to compare the scene before and after the victims went missing?"

I tossed the folder with the photos onto the desk. "I have them, but I'm not sure what good they'll do us. There aren't over-all shots of the inside of the house; it's all from family get-togethers." I replied.

Ross and Carter pulled the photos out and started looking them over. I sat back and waited for a moment to see if they came to the same conclusion I had.

They studied the photos longer than I expected, handing them back and forth for several minutes.

"Are you noticing anything different between these pictures?" Carter asked.

"Something looks off, but I can't put my finger on it. I can't tell if it's a lighting issue or camera quality, but the photos look like portions of the living room have been altered. The biggest difference is the lack of coffee table." I pointed out the minor and major differences in the photos as they held them up.

"Why do you think there's a lighting issue?" asked Ross.

"I'm not sure; it's just the way the light reflects on floor." I replied.

"Is it maybe a time of day? There isn't a lot of natural lighting in some of these family pictures." Ross observed.

"It's not just that; there's an area rug missing from where the coffee table was located," said Carter.

"So there was a minor oversight in the initial report, we can add that for old-time's sake, but it doesn't make much of a difference," offered Ross.

"Look at where the coffee table is located here in the family photo. That rug has been there for months. If it is missing in the crime scene photos, why isn't there some kind of discoloration on the hardwood flooring underneath?" Carter asked.

"What do you mean?" I asked.

"Bryant, I've been to your house; it's all carpeted. My house has hardwood flooring. To protect it, we put down area rugs. The irony was, we put down cheap rugs, and over time they wear a patch on the hardwood floors as they shift back and forth."

"You mean where it dulls the wood finish and takes away the gloss?" Ross asked.

"That's exactly what I mean," said Lt. Carter, growing excited. "Look at the crime scene photos. Not only is there not a scuff on that flooring, there isn't even a mark."

Carter circled the desk and pulled a magnifying glass out of his desk.

"Do you seriously have one of those 'Sherlock Holmes' looking things in your desk?" I joked.

"I'm getting old; not so old that I want reading glasses, but old enough that I don't want to strain my eyes to read fine print," he insisted. "Also of course, every good detective has one."

He spent a minute or so staring intently over the detail of the crime scene photos with the glass. Suddenly he switched and grabbed one of the family photos. He examined it for nearly a minute before he casually slid two of the photos across the desk to us and handed Ross the glass.

"Take a close look at the flooring," he urged.

Ross took a minute looking back and forth, but then shook his head and handed them to me. I took as long as I could to examine the pictures before shaking my head as well. Something was off with the flooring; I just couldn't figure it out.

"I've got nothing." I admitted.

"The original floors are hardwood, but the photos in the crime scene file show tongue-in-groove, stained, wood laminate flooring. The color is matched so perfectly, not even the victim's sister could tell the difference." Carter exclaimed.

"Then how the hell can you tell the difference?" I wondered.

"Look at the size of the flooring. The original floor uses stained, perfectly installed four inch wide hard wood. Laminate flooring comes in standard 7.5 inch wide pieces. All the flooring in the crime scene photos is around four feet long. That is standard for boxes of laminate flooring. Look at the pictures from before; some of that wood doesn't even have a noticeable seam. It was built like seamless siding; only put a seam where you don't have a choice. That original flooring was expensive and took skill to install. It would have taken longer to install than standard laminate flooring."

"What does that mean for us?" I asked.

"Someone was in a hurry to cover up what happened in that house. I think either Tory, Harvey, or both were killed in that living room, and I think someone tried to clean it first, and when that failed they put down new flooring. If we're lucky, they cut corners and put the laminate right over the top of the old flooring. If we aren't lucky; all of this is for nothing," said Carter.

"The original report said the place smelled like bleach, like someone had been cleaning it. Even Tory's sister said Tory was notorious for being a clean-freak," I said.

I pulled out the photos from the crime and started reviewing them.

"When this case went cold; they went in and took detailed pictures of everything in the house before the bank foreclosed. They photographed literally everything in that house." I insisted.

"Yeah so?" asked Ross.

"They also photographed all the cleaning supplies in the hall closet."

"Again; so?" Ross asked.

"If you were going to clean up blood from a crime scene, what would you use?" I asked.

"Something ammonia based; it destroys DNA evidence," replied Carter.

"And if you didn't have any ammonia based cleaners?" I asked.

"I'd probably go with bleach," said Ross.

"Can anyone show me in these pictures; a single item that contains bleach or ammonia?" I requested.

"Nothing; this is all hippy, organic shit. It smells nice and it's supposed to be low impact on the environment. Nothing in this house is likely to contain bleach," said Carter.

"Because someone else brought it in to clean," I said. "Tory and Harvey were killed in that house and the place was fucking scrubbed. The coffee table and the couch must have been covered in blood beyond belief. I would also venture a guess that the bed got blood on it too. The only items missing are items normally left behind during a burglary. The rest of the house looked exactly the same. I think there may still be evidence in that house."

"Ross, start working on a search warrant for the house. Bryant, see if you can find the current residents and talk with them about the house; we need to know what they changed when they moved in," instructed Carter.

Ross and I stepped out of the office, on a mission.

"I can't believe old-school in there noticed the different sized flooring." Ross exclaimed.

"Neither can I," I admitted. "I stared at those photos for hours the past two days."

"You managed to notice the discrepancy in the cleaning supplies; that took a keen eye," said Ross.

"I only noticed it because I spent a few minutes yesterday mocking the cleaners for being the organic hippy bullshit, as L.T. called it," I admitted.

"Still, we made some real progress. I'll call Shirley and bring her up to speed, before I start typing the warrant."

CHAPTER TWENTY-ONE

I spent nearly half an hour on the phone talking to Michael Williams, the current owner of the house. We were lucky because Mike was an ardent supporter of the police department. He offered to waive the search warrant, and allow officers to enter the house to look things over first thing that Thursday morning.

Lt. Carter insisted on getting the search warrant in case we had to pull up flooring or search beneath the existing floor for possible DNA evidence. Lt. Carter personally brought the search warrant to the judge and planned to meet us at the scene.

Shirley and I parked in the street a couple houses down from the Williams' residence, and walked the rest of the way. We didn't want a throng of police personnel crowding the house and making a scene. After all, the alleged killer was still out there. We kept it quiet and met Mike at the front door.

"Detective Bryant, I presume," said Mike shaking my hand. "Hi there; Mike Williams." He turned and shook Shirley's hand and gestured with his hand towards the front door.

"Mike," I said, stopping him before he could invite us in. "We need to talk about a few details before we enter your home. First of all; when did you buy this house?"

"That would have been January of 2013. The house was a foreclosure so we got an unbeatable deal on it," he replied.

"What work have you done to the house since you moved in?"

"Nothing; we bought it 'as is' from the bank. We looked it over; no reason to change anything. This place is a piece of modern craftsmanship," he said with a smile.

"The last thing is this; Mike we believe the people who lived here before you were murdered in this house," I informed him.

He paused, deep in thought, before nodding his head slowly.

"I was afraid of that. I don't believe in ghosts or none of that shit; pardon my French. I got that feeling from you when you called me. My wife is at work and my three kids are all at school. I took the day off to be here for this. If something happened here, I want to know, and I want to help. Whatever you need, name it," he insisted.

"Thank you, Mike. For now; we're just going to be looking around," I said.

"Come on in; make yourselves at home," he replied opening the front door for us.

Shirley and I spent the next half hour moving the furniture out of the living room and examining the floor. Lt. Carter had been right; laminate flooring covered the living room, kitchen and dining area. After looking the area over, I called Gabriella for some insight.

"Hey, Gabriella it's Detective Bryant again. Can you tell me about the flooring in the dining room, kitchen and living room?"

"That floor was Tory's pride and joy. He oversaw the installation of that hardwood floor himself. He even helped stain and seal it. We grew up on dirty hard wood floors. Tory said if he ever made it, he was going to have hard wood floors the family could be proud of," she replied.

"So there was no way the flooring in the living room was some kind of laminate?" I asked.

"Not even possible; he would have told you to get the fuck out of his house for even suggesting it. He had the slightest tic marks on the floor where all the furniture went. He was determined to hide the fact that the rugs and chairs were wearing the finish off the flooring already. He told me he was going to re-finish them one of these years; if he ever got around to it," she insisted.

"Thank you, Gabriella," I said, and hung up the phone.

"L.T. was right; the flooring has been replaced or covered with this imitation hardwood." I informed Shirley.

"Hey, this is nice flooring. It was a major selling point for us when we bought the house," insisted Mike.

"You would have loved the original flooring," I said.

I meandered off through the house, and made my way down the hall towards the spare bedroom on the far left side. Each room showed evidence of children and do-it-yourself projects from Mike and his wife. The home was elegantly furnished, but not elaborately. Mike had spoken of the foreclosure sale which had enabled him to buy the house at such a bargain. It was clear Mike and his family would not have otherwise afforded a house of this caliber when they did were it not for the bargain price.

The furniture around the house spoke to their sensible lifestyle in a house they would have otherwise never dreamed of owning. One person's bad luck is another's good. I reached the bedroom on the far left and swung open the door. To my surprise, it swung open swiftly, crashing into the wall behind it.

"Careful with that door; it swings like nothing," warned Mike.

I checked the wall behind the door for damage, but was pleased to find a door stop properly located to prevent such an occurrence. I closed the door behind me and then opened it again. The door indeed, swung as if it was made of air. I opened it gently and stepped out into the hallway.

"I had to install that door stop myself. We kept damaging the sheetrock behind the door. I don't know why they installed one cheap door in the entire house, but this is it," Mike informed me. "See check this one out," he paused and knocked his knuckles against the door to the master bedroom, "Solid as a rock."

I knocked my hand against the other door and found Mike was not exaggerating. The door was solid wood and built to last. I took a moment and walked up and down the halls, gently knocking against each door. I reached the living room and met up with Shirley.

"The second scene is in the back bedroom. It looks like they replaced a door when they replaced the flooring out here," I said. "Fortunately it's all carpet in the bedrooms; should make for low impact investigation."

"I'll call the Lieutenant and have him add that room to the search warrant," said Shirley, pulling out her phone.

It took several hours before the real work began. Carter delivered the search warrant around 1500 hours. There is no low-impact way to lift laminate flooring. We started at the wall near the hallway and started lifting floor from there. Carter had been right again; the flooring underneath was almost identically colored hardwood flooring. The differences between them were so subtle; it required a side by side comparison to tell the difference.

After several hours we gave up for the night. A patrol unit was posted outside the house and the Williams family was put up in a hotel. The carpet in the bedroom had been lifted and replaced with Carter and Ross finding nothing evidentiary in nature. The floor in the living room was half way up. Unfortunately, due to the quality of the installation, the flooring was secured, and did not tear up easy. Most of the pieces were broken along the way, extending the process hours longer than expected.

We were at it again early the next morning; each of us dressed more appropriately for the task at hand. It took several more hours, but the floor underneath was finally revealed. It was exactly as Lt. Carter had predicted. The area where the rug had been was slightly worn, taking from the polished look of the rest of the floor. We went to work with black lights and flashlights, looking for anything that would have indicated what had happened. After slowing the search to examine each inch of floor a little at a time; the black light finally illuminated something. Just to the outside of the worn spot from the carpet was a small dent, with what appeared to be blood.

Shirley did her best to collect a sample from the floor, but had no luck. Lt. Carter finally authorized us to cut the portion of the floor out and take it to the lab. Ross went to retrieve a saw while we sat around and stared at the spot on the floor.

With my hands still perfectly covered in latex gloves, I began meticulously feeling the flooring around the spot. After a while, I found several anomalies. I examined them closely and found them to be oblong indentations in the hard wood near the blood. I checked the spots several times before I realized how I recognized them.

"Did the coroner say what the cause of death was for the two park victims?" I asked.

"Blunt force trauma to the face and head," said Carter.

"Like the kind of blunt force a hammer might deliver?"

"Yeah," he replied, "Exactly like a hammer."

They knelt down next to me and examined the floor.

"Does that look like the kind of mark a framing hammer would make if you missed the nail and hit the wood at a slight angle?" I asked.

"It does," answered Carter as he ran his finger into the divots.

"There are at least half a dozen of these," observed Shirley as she knelt down to get a closer look. "They all appear to have come from the same angle, and landed just off the carpet, denting the floor."

"Take another look at the spot of blood we found," I instructed. They followed my finger as I pointed to the area already marked off to be removed.

"The blood didn't just soak through, it pooled in one of the divots from the hammer," Carter observed.

"That's why they couldn't clean the blood up with the bleach. The hammer damaged the flooring so much that it compromised the seal of the wood. The blood must have sat there for a little while before someone tried to clean." I said.

"So we can confirm this as the crime scene; and the murder weapon is most likely a framing hammer. We need to figure out who was in the area that might have seen something," said Carter. "Shirley, where are we on the construction company? Were you able to interview anyone who worked on this development?"

"Not yet; I checked with the contractor, but they said none of those employees are with the company anymore," she replied. "I'm still trying to track down someone who would have been working here at the time."

"That's priority one from now on; all efforts on this case are to be directed towards finding every employee, sub-contractor, or landscaper that worked around here. Let's just hope someone saw something helpful," instructed Carter.

I spent several minutes taking photos of the damage from every conceivable angle. The detail was hard to pick up with even the slightest blur or less-than-perfect lighting. Everything was photographed once, then photographed with a small scale next to it for reference

———

Half an hour later, Ross returned with the saw. The section to be removed was nearly three feet long by three feet wide. A total of eight divots matching that of a framing hammer were located in the hardwood flooring. They were all facing towards one point where the suspect would have been crouched or kneeling; most likely over one of his victims. A likely scenario seemed to fit that the other victim had died in the bedroom; there was just no way to prove it. The door had been replaced with a cheap, hollow substitute, but there was no way to determine if the carpet had been replaced or not. All the bedrooms had different shades of carpet, and it was impossible to tell if they were the same age. The house had been built less than a year before Tory and Harvey went missing; everything was nearly new, even after six years.

Ross transported the massive section of flooring to Kansas City using one of the department's large, unmarked trucks with a covered bed.

The living room of the Williams home was destroyed. Not only had the laminate been ripped up, the wood floor underneath had a massive hole with large cut marks into the joists underneath.

Carter and I drove back to the department where I immediately downloaded the camera and entered the photos into evidence. I made copies of the photo disk and distributed them to the members of the team. Shirley stayed behind to meet with the first of several home repair experts and contractors to get bids on having the floor fixed for the Williams family.

I spent the rest of that day and all of the next attempting to track down members of a construction crew that had been disbanded for five years now. Construction was a fluid and ever changing business where some kept working for years while other employees spent a summer or gap-year working to save for college.

The only good news I received that day was the positive confirmation from Dr. Elmore via email that Fenton's DNA had been found amongst the evidence from the Joplin homicide. I finished my report for the Joplin Police and forwarded it to Captain Sherman.

I finally reached the end of the work week and made my way home. We still didn't have any witnesses for the Holton-Brand homicides, but we had reached the end of our rope and needed some time to recover.

I still had to prepare for an interview with Fenton the next day. I dreaded it; but then again, I was almost twenty percent done with him; only twenty-two more meetings to go.

I decided not to dwell on it too much, and opted to pick up the phone. I held the receiver to my ear for a moment and listened to the line as it rang. I strolled casually out into the garage and sat down on the step, waiting until I was greeted by a voice at the other end.

"Hey Lydia..."

———

I had no interest in spending additional time at the prison, but there were traitors to flush out. I was there an hour early. After several weeks of trying to get the Warden to meet with me, he had finally agreed. It hadn't been easy getting a meeting to discuss a topic I wouldn't provide him ahead of time over the phone. His curiosity was founded, but the need for secrecy superseded the need for professional courtesy.

The hardest part was getting him to descend from his high tower office and meet me outside the fence. The warden hadn't been wildly fond of my visits to the prison, and had opposed the proposal when he found out the encounters were to be documented for a book. This hadn't been surprising since most decent people involved in the planning process had been opposed to the arrangement. Most people thought, and I agreed, that if Fenton was going to have a last minute confessional about all his victims he should just do it. Everyone thought a "Ted Bundy" like confession at the eleventh hour was the appropriate way to get information on unsolved murders. It took a lot of convincing from the DOJ and testimony from people with knowledge of Fenton's personality to convince everyone to partake in his madness. Fenton would have gone to his grave holding back every detail of his misdeeds as a final "fuck you" to the world. To get what we needed, we had to give him what he wanted. The phrase "Deal with the devil" had never been more appropriately tossed around.

I was parked within sight of the front gate, but as far out of ear shot as possible. No one knew who the leak was, so I wasn't taking any chances. There were a finite number of suspects, but they all had access to Fenton, and anywhere else in the prison they desired.

I had never met the warden before, but we had spent a great deal of time on the phone lately. I was waiting in my car, hoping to see his Alfa Romeo convertible heading towards the front gate. We hadn't talked about many personal topics, but he had effortlessly slid a story about rebuilding his father's car into one of our conversations. He was clearly very proud of it, and I could understand why when I saw it.

The cherry red paint stood out proudly surrounded by the gray walls and fences of the prison gates. The black, soft-top showed no signs of age or wear as it carried on the clean lines the rest of the car displayed. The engine was audible, clean and crisp as he slowly accelerated through the gate. The tiny car had no issue making a casual U-turn for the warden to pull his car in behind me on the side of the road.

A big man shouldn't be able to fit in such a small car, but the warden had folded every bit of his hefty six-three frame into the car and stepped out casually. He buttoned his sharp, gray suit jacket and strode forward to greet me, classic Italian black leather shoes clapping the ground in rhythm as he walked.

"Detective Bryant, I'm Frank De Luca," he introduced as he shook my hand.

"It's a privilege, Frank," I replied. "I'm glad you agreed to meet with me."

"You made a compelling case while simultaneously telling me nothing. I was intrigued and a little impressed."

"I am the unfortunate keeper of a lot of dark secrets these days, it's a burden I don't wish on anyone." I admitted.

"And I take it one of these secrets brings you to me; and I assume it involves a favor," he guessed, accurately.

"It does," I answered.

"Maybe you should start with why this favor couldn't have been posed over the phone," Frank directed.

"Happy to, but first I need you to know; I don't mean any slight to you or your organization here with what I'm about to say." I cautioned.

"Let's see how tactful you are about it," he warned, raising his chin, ever so slightly.

"Three weeks ago, the night after I met with Fenton for the second time, one of my officers was killed with a car bomb. Inside the car was a woman named Emma Lane; we don't know if she was killed by the bomb, or before. Emma, was married to a man named Tim; a reporter for the local newspaper. Tim leaked time sensitive information about a victim we had previously recovered after my first meeting with Fenton. The information was not public yet; but Tim had that information already and leaked it to the victim's family, and to the rest of the local press. Tim agreed to meet with me when I got back to Manhattan, but he missed our meeting. We found Tim's body, hanging from the rafters later that night near the scene where we had just recovered four bodies in our City Park."

"I'm still waiting to see how this applies to me or my prison," Frank interjected.

"I'm getting to the good part," I insisted. "Only a handful of people had the identity of the victim. We've thoroughly vetted all of them; none of them are responsible for the leak."

"So you're suggesting that there is a problem with my vetting process?"

"A coworker of mine received this a few weeks ago by mistake. It was addressed to me," I said as I held up a phone in a plastic bag. "This is Tim Lane's phone. The last five calls tell an interesting story. The first one is an incoming call from your prison. The second is an outgoing call to the victim's father. The third is an outgoing call to his newspaper editor who helped take the story public. The fourth is an incoming call from me, requesting to meet with him when I get back to Manhattan. The fifth is a call to his wife Emma, she never answered. Those five calls cover less than four hours of time that day. The phone was dropped in the mail and post marked the following Monday. It was still on, but now it was unlocked, and unsecure; which is something Tim was adamantly against. He protected his sources, his contacts and his colleagues with the utmost privacy; that's why people trusted him. The last thing he did while he was alive was send me his phone. Why would he do that?"

"There was clearly something on it he wanted you to see," observed Frank.

"Exactly; the only call that isn't from someone he has listed as a contact came from your prison. Someone with access to Fenton, contacted Tim and tipped him off to the story; and then someone killed Tim, his wife, and one of my officers to cover their tracks."

"And you think it was one of my guards?" he asked.

"Maybe not; but someone here at the prison is tipping people off with information known only to Fenton, and the various officers involved in these ongoing investigations. That someone is also feeding Fenton sensitive information about the investigation which he is using to wield against me in my interviews. The only people, who have access to Fenton, work on death row. Do your records still reflect that no one has been in contact with Fenton, by mail or in person?"

"That is correct; he hasn't had a visitor since he received his death sentence," said Frank.

"That's what concerns me, Frank. If no one else is reaching out to him, how is he getting this information?"

"What information did he have that tipped you off?"

I paused for a moment as the sun reappeared from behind a cloud, causing me to squint.

"He knew I had just come from a funeral for our fallen officer, last week. He doesn't get mail, he doesn't get visitors, he doesn't get the news; how did he know that?" I asked.

Frank paused for a moment and looked at the ground. I could tell he was troubled by what he heard and was doing his best to sort out what should be done.

"What do you need from me?" he asked.

"I need a full list of everyone who works on death row with access to Fenton. I need to see their application for employment and anything else you can provide me, such as personnel records. I need to know who I am dealing with so we can take them down. I have to weed out this person and find out if they had anything to do with the death of my officer. If you help me with this, I will see to it that you know every move we make on this person. You should know who is working for you. Someone is undermining the whole system here; we need to find them and put a stop to it." I explained.

"How soon do you need all this information?"

"I'm about to go sit through another three hour interview with Fenton; I need it before I go home this afternoon." I urged.

He paused for a moment, and then reached out and shook my hand.

"Done," he agreed.

"One last detail about the handoff of that information," I insisted.

"What is it?"

CHAPTER TWENTY-TWO

We were back to our old interview room. I had a level head, and plenty of distractions leading into my fifth interview with Fenton on April 8, 2017. Everything was eerily familiar as I walked down the long hall. The walls were lined with cell doors, all with faces pressed against the windows. Everyone wanted to see if it was a new prisoner, or just another guard. No one was expecting to see me, suit jacket, pants and no tie, walking down the corridor. Most just stared at me, trying to figure me out; others could tell I was law enforcement, and made hand gestures accordingly.

I didn't feel as nervous this time. I was more mentally prepared than previous weeks and I could tell the tides were turning in almost every investigation. We were closing in on suspects in five out of six unsolved cases; the progress alone was enough to lift my spirits. Homicide cases so often took months of collecting one witness statement after another, waiting for enough people to come forward, to put a killer behind bars. Half the cases involved were decades old; the other half, so fresh they could have been yesterday.

I was prepared for the electric locks before they popped this time. I was tired of walking into the room after the adrenaline rush of being startled. The door slid open and I stepped inside, brushing right past Fenton to the far side of the table. I sat down and started unceremoniously slapping items on the table. The cigarettes and lighter I tossed at Fenton, catching him off guard as he cupped his hands on his stomach to catch them as they bounced off his chest and slid down.

"Somebody's all ready to play nice." Fenton quipped. "What, no necktie this week?"

"The guards thought it best to limit the number of items in the room I could use to strangle you. Which is too bad, I wore my thickest tie today." I answered as I started the stop watch.

"Oh good, it's going to be one of those therapy sessions where you blame me for all your problems. Haven't we done this already, kid?"

"It seemed to work for me last time I tried it. I thought it might be fun for a second round," I replied.

"I wouldn't have thought a trip to Joplin would have you in such high spirits," Fenton observed.

"It wasn't the destination; it was the trip that mattered. Short and brief is how I like them. You killed a local, known hooker; left her where she would be easily found and easily identified. Your confession last week was the last piece of the puzzle they needed to close the case. When you make my job easy, it's hard to be in a bad mood." I told him.

"There's something changing about you, detective. I feel as if I'm speaking to a brand new man. A couple weeks ago I couldn't smell any booze on you, now it almost looks as if you've turned over a new leaf."

"That's an astute observation coming from someone who has such limited social interaction. Your power of observation has clearly improved during your years of solitary confinement."

"Well," he said with a shrug. "It is hard not to take in the details when all you have is concrete walls to stare at all day long. I enjoy the little bit of the outside world you bring in with you."

"That's why I'm here, to bring your life a little sunshine before the lights go out forever." I joked.

"I'll live on; I have a legacy to leave behind. You get to be the one to write it all down. You may live to see my death, but my accomplishments will live forever." He said pointing at me, "In the book about my life that you're writing."

"I told you before; the story is less about you and more about the investigation. If you want to write it yourself, by all means, feel free. But when all you give me is a location, a name, or an event, you don't give me a lot of detail to write about you," I explained. "You're not much of a story-teller, which is too bad seeing as you've covered so much ground."

"You wanted me to spare you the gruesome details," he responded as he blew smoke in my face. "It's hard to tell a great story when you're boxing me in like that. If you'd like me to paint you a more graphic word picture, just say so."

"I'm ok with the amount of detail you're providing now. I have a soul, so it's good to limit the bad shit I have to store in my brain each day. You wanted me to write it, you're stuck with whatever I write," I said.

"I'll have to see the first volume and decide for myself. I do like the idea of telling my stories in more vivid detail. I feel like you'll 'church' it up a little more than I want."

"That's most definitely the case," I replied. "With what you've given me, people will already have to show an I.D. to buy a copy."

"Real life is unrated; people should get used to the idea."

"It's not like you gave anyone a choice," I observed.

"That's quite the common theme with you. You seem to forget; I have a longer list of people I didn't use than people I did. For every college age bimbo and high school slut I took back to my place, there were a dozen I never had the chance to have. For every window I opened in the middle of the night, there were a hundred locked ones. People choose whether or not they are going to be a victim. It's not so much they looked at both options and opted to be a victim; it's that some people choose not to be a victim. Did you know you can tell if a girl owns a gun by the bumper stickers on their car? Did you know it only takes a few hours watching a girl to know if she owns a dog or has any roommates? There are so many women who took the time to make things difficult for me. Those women are still alive. Those women never woke up to me standing over them in the middle of the night. Life is about the choices we make. Those who choose not to be a victim, even if I had managed to get into their homes or take them in a dimly lit parking lot, they would have fought me tooth and nail. Had I managed to take them, I might have been hurt. There were a few like that in the early days; A few girls who had to be subdued violently instead of quietly. Once I learned to tell them apart; it was almost too easy."

"You have the ability to grossly over-generalize people. People have the right to live peaceful lives without having to fear monsters like you," I said.

"Children have irrational fears of monsters under their beds. What they don't realize is that most monsters are people they know and trust. The idea of stranger danger being the biggest concern for children makes no sense. We tell kids that monsters aren't real; but you and I know differently. I may be a monster for some, but I was just Richard to others. Monsters exist; they take the form of whatever we fear the most. Some people have irrational fears like speaking in public. That makes no sense. If you care about what people think of you, you will never have true control over your life. Some people face their fears, or at least prepare for them. Once you face them, they have less control over you. If you face them over and over again, they have no power over you."

"I seem to remember a story you told me weeks ago where you seemed to care an awful lot about what a girl thought of you. Are you telling me you are afraid of women?" I asked; "Or just what they think of you?"

"What teenage boy doesn't suffer from a little insecurity around the fairer sex?" He asked. "I did what strong people do; I faced my fear, I overcame my insecurities and I conquered them both. Can you blame me for having a little fun along the way?"

"Blame you? Yes; we can also convict you for your, fun," I said throwing up air quotes, "In five different states. That's my favorite part of the story."

He leaned forward and leered at me, speaking past the cigarette in his mouth.

"The fact that you barely landed double digit convictions against me is what entertains me the most. I've already given you more dead bodies in the past month than you had in convictions for the past three decades of my work. I'm an accomplished man; especially since your conviction rate against me is lower than the national average."

"You went to trial eleven times. You were convicted eleven times. I'm batting a thousand against you. You received the death penalty in two states and life sentences in two others. If you somehow lived past all that, you'd still have to serve thirty years in Nebraska. Conviction rate is about what you take to trial, not about what else that person has done in their criminal career," I explained.

"Well, shouldn't it be?" He asked.

"There is no way to hold everyone accountable for everything they do. It would take a system of surveillance and oversight that no logical human would ever agree to. You of all people should agree with that. People have the right to freedom and privacy. Part of that freedom is the freedom to choose between right and wrong."

"Government is either absolute or obsolete. What's the point of having limitations? If the government isn't going to intervene on behalf of victims, why would they be involved with anything at all? Government is mostly useless; like God. What's the point of having faith in something to be there for you when it's never around when you need it?"

"If it's the government's job to take care of everyone, then everyone would stop taking care of themselves. You just sat there advocating that people ensure their own safety and prevent themselves from being victims. You can't have it both ways," I insisted.

"That's why I said it should be all or nothing. If the government won't do it all, they should just stay out of the way," he sneered.

"That only works for people like you. No government, there's no one to hold you accountable for your actions; all powerful government, the bad things you say happen to you are somehow wished away. It's ignorant at best and childish at the least."

"No one seems to have any solutions to the problems as they are; maybe it's time to do away with the whole system," he suggested.

"Maybe we should stop trying to fix everything at the same time and break it down, problem by problem," I suggested.

He flashed a condescending smile and shook his head. "It will never happen," he promised.

I stared at him for a moment. I knew this was the extent of his inter-personal contact for the week, so he had to pose his crazy ideas, insane theories and conspiracies to someone. He wasted my time on useless conversations so that he could fill the three hour void which would ulti-mately end with a half-assed confession. He would try to brag about it, but he felt the need to force me to do as much work as possible on each case. The fact that he had tossed me a simple case last week indicated he only had enough elaborate schemes to fill better than half of our meetings. The others, I could tell he planned to waste my time and then throw me a confession to a murder he had done little or nothing to cover. I was relieved, knowing that not every case would involve organized crime fami-lies and mass graves. That was most likely going to be the only positive revelation from our fifth meeting.

"So you claim people are only victims if they choose to be; tell me why Brenda from the motel in Joplin wanted to be a victim?" I requested.

"Any idiot with access to any statistics knows prostitutes are at risk of being killed higher than almost any other profession. It's partly because of the locations they frequent and the company they keep. It could also be the rampant drug use. Either way, they opted to sacrifice their bodies to make a few dollars. They should really be more careful with what they're willing to sacrifice."

"Some people might say they're simply trying to make a living," I suggested. "Some people even support legalizing it."

"Some people support legalizing drugs and suicide too. People think for some reason, changing the laws will somehow give them more control over their lives; but they're wrong." He insisted. "Lots of people think legalizing things would somehow make them safer and free. They like to ignore the fact that as soon as those things are legalized, the government will simply charge a fee to make it happen. Wanna sell some drugs? Go right ahead; we're going to tax the business and the customers to make it worth our while. Here's something to keep in mind; if a politician is in support of changing a law that has been in effect for decades or more, they are making a profit from the change. They legalized gay marriage just so they could charge a fee when they apply for the marriage license. They legalize pot so they can tax the business, product and customers. The government doesn't care about anyone but themselves. You're part of the problem; you're the military arm of the government that steps in to ensure the government gets its money. You're an armed tax collector, detective; that's it."

"I prefer to think of my job as one half of the most elaborate game of hide and seek ever." I joked. "People like you leave bread crumbs around for years and years and eventually we catch you and haul you off to jail. The funny thing is; if people like you stopped leaving a trail of destruction behind them, my job would be obsolete."

"There's always going to be people like me, though. So this big government you support is always going to be there, breathing down the necks of the people. What's the difference if it's me, or the government imposing our wills on the people?" he asked.

"People deserve the chance to make a life, making good choices for themselves, their families, and their future. It isn't the job of the government to make sure people stay in line; it's their job to hold accountable, those who don't," I explained, pointing at him. "The government shouldn't exist to oppress the people, but neither should we."

"Pretty shitty system, if you ask me," he said.

"You advocate for an all or nothing system. The best form of government lies somewhere between the extremes. It's up to society to determine where the balance lies, and how best to maintain it." I said.

"You expect a lot of people who expect nothing from themselves."

"And you expect a lot out of people while simultaneously taking advantage of those weaker than yourself." I growled at him.

"They system favors the 'have's' while punishing the 'have-not's;' can you blame me for finding an alternative way to be among the 'haves?'"

I was starting to get annoyed with the 'round and round' nature of the conversation.

"You still didn't tell me why you killed the woman at the motel in Joplin," I observed.

"I thought you already cracked that code with your privileged, educated conclusion that I'm," he pause and shook his head and hands sarcastically side to side, mocking me in a sing-song voice, "Afraid of women."

"I don't think you're afraid of women; I think you hate women," I said.

He said nothing for a moment. He took a long drag on his cigarette and held it in for a moment.

"And if I do?" He asked slowly exhaling the smoke.

"It would make sense, given what you've told me about your mother." I explained.

"My mother was a fat, lazy, bitch," he said.

"Exactly," I replied.

"My father was an angry drunk who beat me. Care to explain why I haven't killed men spanning six states?"

"There are a few schools of thought on this subject. One could be; you see your father as a victim in his marriage. You hated your mom; you told me you believe she manipulated your dad into marrying her for financial security. You could see the toll taken on the marriage and decided whose side you're going to take. You saw your dad get manipulated, used, and mistreated so you determined you wouldn't follow in his footsteps. But rather than simply make different decisions than he did, you made it your life's work to punish women who were never at fault in your shitty childhood, and never did anything to hurt you. You told me about the first girl you killed when you were a teenager. You believed she was mistreating you so you determined to make her pay because you believed if you didn't, you were going to turn out just like your father." I paused for a minute to let it all sink in. "Does any of that sound about right?"

"It must be nice to have all the answers. It's easy to sit on that side of the table and make excuses for why someone else is the way they are. But can you actually propose some kind of alternative response for a person going through what I went through, before they start down my path?"

"That would be the difficult part. You would have to have someone who you could talk to about anything and trust completely. The person in your position would have to confide in someone and ask for help. You didn't. You locked it all away inside and then found an outlet for your emotions that suited you. There are a lot of ways to deal with childhood trauma or parenting issues; none of them involve killing the girl down the street for calling you a retard. You complain about how soft everyone is, but you're the one who let someone else's words lead you to extreme violence. I guess I never realized how delicate you are." I said, half sincere.

"Go fuck yourself, kid," he snapped at me.

"Now I'm starting to see it. You're sensitive and vulnerable. To hide that from people, you kill random women. Can I ask you a serious question about your process? How many of the women you killed, actually did or said something to you that could be interpreted as rude, insensitive, or mocking?"

He was glaring at me in a way he had not done before. Fenton had become so use to the idea that he had answers to all the problems and that his superior intellect was what had allowed him to operate without repercussions for so long. He hated the idea that anyone might poke a hole in his flawed logic of misogyny and vile behavior. I was slightly proud of myself for putting him on the defensive. He had spent weeks antagonizing me, so it was nice to be the one on the offensive for a change.

He flicked his cigarette into the corner and casually slipped another out of the pack. I couldn't tell if he was at a loss for words or if he was simply trying to come up with something to say to regain the upper hand. He had spent years justifying what he had done by blaming others for mistreating him. The logic was flawed, but he had held to his dogma with fierce loyalty no one had questioned; until now. Fenton prided himself on being the smartest person in the room. He hated, even for a moment, thinking that it might not be true.

I thought for a moment, as he smoked in silence, about the number of people who used childhood traumas, inadequacies, and upheaval as justification for the things they did. The pattern of the abused child going on to abuse his own family was seen far too often. But for every wife beating son of a bitch that I met, I met another who spoke of their childhood suffering as the determining factor in how they would live their own life differently. It was a matter of choice; a matter of facing your fears, problems, and emotional wounds, and seeking out the healthiest means of coping. There were thousands of articles, papers, books and stories on the subject. People across the world were fascinated by the complexities of childhood anguish, and how it manifested in adults.

Not everyone was going to deal with their pain as Fenton had. Many of them would stop short of killing people, opting for violence instead. Others still, would take it upon themselves to break the cycle, and choose a different way of living. You couldn't always tell which way someone was going to go, because the results could land anywhere on a spectrum. This was one of the conundrums facing society, and everyone had a different prescription.

I snapped back to the present as Fenton cleared his throat.

"You believe in a free society, don't you, detective?" He asked.

"Yes I do," I replied.

"You believe people should be left alone to make their own choices and live their lives the way they see fit?"

"Yes I do," I replied again.

"Then you can't really stand against someone like me for doing whatever I want to."

"That's where you're wrong," I insisted.

"Then enlighten me," he said, goading me to explain myself.

"When this country was first getting its foundation; it declared its independence from Great Britain. In the Declaration of Independence, they listed what they called 'certain unalienable rights.' They listed them in this order; life, liberty and the pursuit of happiness. I believe they did that for a very specific reason. In policing, we have what is called the safety priority list. At the top, innocent, uninvolved third parties, the second on the priority list is hostages; third is officers, and last is the suspect. The goal for any policing situation is to ensure that at no time do we create a situation by either action or inaction that changes the order of that list. I believe the founding fathers listed the order in the Declaration of Independence in the same way. People have the right to life, liberty and the pursuit of happiness. However, people do not have the right to infringe on someone's life in the pursuit of happiness or as a means of exercising their liberty. The next step down, your pursuit of happiness can't infringe on someone's liberty. When it does, you are out of order and the government we have should be designed around ensuring that no one is allowed to change the order of that priority list for their own personal gain or interests. You claim that you should have the right to do what you want, but you can't when your actions take the life of another person. The system doesn't always reflect that perfectly, but I believe the intentions of our society and our government should be to honor the order set forth in the Declaration of Independence. That's why I have a job, to keep things in order. That's why you were put away for the rest of your life. You repeatedly took the liberty or taking away someone's life; in doing so, you're liberty was taken away."

"And soon my life," said Fenton. "By your own admission, isn't the death penalty taking my life as a liberty of the government?"

"Like I said; the system isn't always perfect. If you'd like, we can debate the validity of the death penalty."

He stared at me for several minutes, contemplating my offer.

"Maybe another time, kid. I have another conquest to tell you about," he said.

"Works for me." I said, "That's why I'm here anyways."

"The year was 1991 and I found myself in Council Bluffs, Iowa. I was on my way out of the state after making my way through the Carroll family business and gathering as much dirt on them as I could. I was traveling light, and living comfortably off of all the cash I had made as a valued member of the family. I had new identities, which you already knew about, so I was living as someone brand new," he detailed.

"Which name were you living under at the time?" I asked.

"Does that really matter? I mean in the grand scheme of things, the name I used to sign into the hotel that night is completely irrelevant. I signed a paper contract with a recently assumed name; I guarantee that record is long gone now. The only thing that remains of that night is the fact that I offed yet another prostitute."

"I'm starting to see a trend." I observed.

"Not really a trend as it is a way to pass the time until someone tastier comes along. I prefer girls in the sixteen to twenty, range; but they don't make up a large portion of the hooker population; at least not back in my day."

He sat back and smiled, clearly picturing something heinous he had done.

"Hookers do a lot more than walk the streets waiting for "Johns" to drive by and take them to a dark alley for a blowjob. A lot of them will frequent upscale bars and hotels, waiting for a traveling businessman with handfuls of cash to pay for their company. In almost every way, I prefer this type of whore to the "lot-lizards" knocking on trucker's doors for some easy meth money. These girls are classier, well dressed, bathed, groomed, and most importantly, have all their teeth."

He shuddered as he talked about their teeth as if the thought of someone without all their teeth was the most awful thing he had ever seen.

"Classy hookers are the ones who know how to get you there. Now I know I'm preaching to the choir here, even though you refuse to admit you've picked up a whore from time to time, but some hookers just know how to please a man. This girl in Council Bluffs was one of those gals."

He paused to take a long drag of his cigarette and stare at the naked lady on his lighter for a second.

"This girl was maybe in her early to mid-twenties. Long brown hair with perfect hazel eyes; absolutely gorgeous. If there was one slut I think back and wish I had spent more time with, it would have been her. She wore this black dress that went down just barely to her knees. It was the perfect balance between classy and nasty. When a bitch's skirt is too short, you can tell they're use to hiking it up in an alleyway and bending at the waist. When the skirt is long, you know she'll take you to bed and ride your dick until it's raw. This girl said her name was Candy, but you know she was fucking lying. No respectful adult ever names their baby, Candy. If it was her real name, she was destined for that line of work all along. It's amazing to realize that a name can determine how far someone can go in life. Candy was destined to wind up face down in a pillow taking it like a champ. She was also destined to go diving off a bridge into the Missouri River. Well it was less of a dive, and more of a belly flop. Dead bodies just don't fly right; they do kind of a short summersault and land awkwardly. It would be more entertaining if I didn't have to leave immediately."

"So you tossed this one in the river? That's a little out of the ordinary for you." I observed.

"It is a little different than my usual tell-tale signs of conquest, but hookers aren't really a conquest. They're more of a convenient spot to dump a load when you're tired of beating your dick six days a week."

"So you didn't leave your signature behind when it was a prostitute?"

"There's no real accomplishment in fucking a hooker, or even killing one for that matter. It's like signing your name to a "paint by number's" canvass; it just doesn't make sense to take credit for it."

"But you're taking credit for it now," I observed.

"Well yeah, now; I have to give you something. Each week I have to give you the location or identity of a body. I wouldn't be able to hold up my end of the bargain if I wasn't throwing you a few easy ones, now and again. Just like the hookers were for me; these will be your easiest cases. Except this one cause I have no idea what her real name was or how far down-river she floated before someone fished her out of the drink. She could have made it all the way to the gulf for all I know. Then she's pretty much shark bait."

"Do you remember which bridge you threw her off?" I asked.

"I rarely forget a dump-site for a body. That's one of my favorite things about killing bitches; hiding the body. In this case, I went south to a small suburb called Bellevue. There is a bridge just east of Bellevue along Highway 370. Back in 1991 it wasn't as heavily traveled so it was a decent place to stop and toss a body. Fortunately for me, the women I pick up are always on the slender side. Do you have any idea how big a hole you have to dig to hide a fat chick? It's just not worth the trouble. That's why I always went after younger, slender women who haven't had the chance to get fat. As soon as they have a few fat years at college or have a couple kids, they're basically un-fuck-able," he declared.

"I think you're just afraid to get your ass kicked by a woman with a little muscle. A guy in your position can hardly be expected to pick a fair fight." I observed.

"I don't pick fights I can't win," he replied. "That's why I'm playing these little mind games with you. Intellectually, you're no match for me."

"I like to let you think that." I said with a smile. "Only an idiot shows his entire hand this early in a game. I'm holding cards back, just as I'm sure you're holding some back."

"Of course I am; I like to be one step ahead at all times. It's what makes me an unbeatable opponent."

"That's entertaining; coming from the guy chained to the table." I said, giving him a sarcastic smile.

"That's because you think locking me away is the end of the game."

"Well, in a way it is." I said.

"You should know better by now," he interjected. "I am more than just an accomplished man, I'm a legend. Legends never die. Out there in this crazy world, there are other people just like me living in the shadows, outside the control of government and popular opinion. Some of them I inspired; others, like me, found their own way to turn their way of life into a legacy. Those people will carry my banner for years to come. You like to think you're winning this game, detective; but I'm only a single piece on the board."

He leaned forward as he spoke, attempting to menace me with information I already had. I gave him a blank stare and tried not to reveal anything in my expression. I knew he wasn't the only player in the game. I knew he was playing puppet-master to someone else; pulling strings from behind bars.

Everything I did over the coming months was a matter of timing. If it was all done on the right timeline, the other pieces would be revealed, and fall, one by one.

Still trying to maintain the upper hand, I redirected him back to the topic at hand.

"So you said this girl, Candy, was already dead when you threw her off the bridge. How did she die?"

"You mean, how did I kill her? You can ask me a direct question without sounding so politically correct. Leading questions only affect your case if you're attempting to get a conviction from the confession you're coercing," he said, arrogantly.

"It's not coercion," I insisted.

"Of course it is," he snapped. "Every time a cop sits down to interview someone, its coercion. You don't know any other way."

"Ok, then; I'll be direct, how did you kill her?" I asked.

"It's a funny thing with hookers; they never like to look a man in the eye when they're sucking his dick. They're all about taking care of business and moving on to the next customer. In the same way, they like to fuck facing away from you. In her case, she preferred the face-down position; which is really ideal for wrapping a bedsheet around her neck and strangling her while I dump a load in her back door."

I tried my best to hide the cringe that crawled up my spine. Just like that, I wanted to kill him again. I managed to hide my anger just enough to check the stopwatch and see that we were almost out of time again. I showed it to him and then tapped it three times on the table.

"Anything else you'd like to share with me before I leave?" I asked.

He slipped the last cigarette out of the pack and casually lit it before sliding the lighter across the table to me.

"I think that about does it. Have fun scouring all the cities along the Missouri river looking for my hooker. I'm sure you'll find it a bit more challenging than your trip to Joplin," he teased.

"I'm sure it will. I'll be sure to take in all the sights and sounds of freedom while I'm driving up and down the highway. I might even rent a convertible for the occasion. I'll think of you and how moldy it smells down here on death row, while I'm cruising with the top down, enjoying freedom."

He plastered on a smile to hide, what I'm sure was annoyance, and flipped me off.

I spent a few minutes gathering the last of the items from the table, and stowing them in my bag again.

The locks on the door popped. I was expecting it, he wasn't.

"Leaving a few minutes early, detective?"

He stopped there as he heard the footsteps approaching from behind him. He turned to look, and managed to keep a blank expression on his face.

"Fenton, I'm sure you know the Warden, Frank De Luca." I said.

Frank handed me a sealed, white, business-size envelope, then turned around and immediately left the room.

"Just what I've been waiting for," I said stowing the envelope in my interior jacket pocket, and standing up to leave. "I'll see you next time, Dick."

CHAPTER TWENTY-THREE

It was unfortunate to find out how many bodies were recovered from the Missouri River over the past few decades. Between bodies dumped by various serial killers and murderers, I also had to sort through the accidental drownings and unidentified remains or partially dismembered corpses.

Fenton hadn't said anything about dismembering the bodies, but it was hardly a stretch to think he wasn't capable of doing so, and then simply omitting that fact during our interviews. He was determined to have his story told his way, but struggled to find balance between telling his stories and playing a game with investigators.

The Missouri River was an evidence destroyer all on its own. The river was thick and muddy and allowed bodies to be submerged for extended periods of time, degrading any evidence left behind. It was often said the Missouri River was too thick to drink, and too thin to plow. The affect it had on corpses after extended exposure was extensive. The longer the body was underwater, the more degraded it became. To complicate matters, there was well-known history of a serial killer partially dismembering bodies, and throwing them into the Missouri River. The victims spanned wider than Fenton's preferred age range, but that didn't mean he wasn't capable of branching out.

Four different dismembered bodies had been pulled from the river between 1986 and 1991. Unfortunately that fit perfectly into Fenton's time-line, at least the most recent one did. It was unfortunate that so many bodies had been recovered south of the dump site Fenton had described. This meant coordinating with multiple jurisdictions to gain access to case-files and evidence.

Fenton had not exaggerated when he said this case wouldn't be as easy as the last.

I spent several hours at my desk, researching various jurisdictions along the Missouri River from Iowa, Nebraska, Missouri, and Kansas. I checked local news articles for stories about recovered bodies, and compiled a list of departments to contact. Fortunately there hadn't been a large quantity of recovered victims from 1991, so hopefully the search could be narrowed down a bit.

After compiling the list of jurisdictions, I spent an hour on the phone calling around, requesting case-files on all the recovered bodies. Surely one of them had to be Fenton's victim. I put in a call to the Council Bluffs Police Department and requested a list of their missing cases from 1991 and 1992. Hopefully the combination of the two lists would result in the identification or confirmation of Fenton's latest victim.

After hours online and on the phone researching possible victims, I finally managed to leave for the day. I opted to work on my report Monday since there was no time sensitive information involved.

———

That Sunday was the first day off I truly appreciated. I did a little cleaning around the house, changed the oil in my car and spent some time of the phone with Dr. Elmore. We were still getting to know one another, so the conversations weren't that long. We would catch up a little bit before ending the conversation as soon as we hit a lull. I wasn't fond of spending time on the phone in silence, just for the sake of being on the phone together.

I managed to get a few hours of sleep in my bed before returning to the living room. It was still weird to sleep in the bed by myself. This was a new development for me after spending years on the midnight shift; I slept alone four to five days a week. This was different somehow. I knew it wasn't a temporary thing until I reached the weekend; now, I was truly sleeping alone.

I didn't sleep well; but that was far from out of the ordinary. I was so used to alcohol induced slumber, that trying to sleep without supplementing it with booze seemed a difficult task. I added a second cup of coffee to my breakfast and hoped it would be enough to get me through another day, pouring over articles and case-files about missing women from Iowa.

I had another task to oversee. Frank De Luca had done just as I asked. He brought me the list of people who had contact with Fenton and handed it to me in front of Fenton. Leaving Fenton to wonder what was in the envelope seemed like little more than harmless fun. I wanted him to worry, and I wanted him to dwell on it. Every secret I could wield against Fenton could be the one to give me the upper hand. So far he had been the master of hidden information; now it was my turn.

I made hard copies of the list provided by Frank De Luca and passed them on to the other three members of the team. I had my hands full with Fenton's latest victim; I needed as much help as I could get.

I was thankful to have the team helping me. They were taking primary role in the triple-homicide at the park allowing me to stay focused on the bevy of unpredictable bullshit Fenton was shoveling my way. For all his habits and predictable flaws, Fenton still possessed the ability to remain an enigma.

The case files poured in one at a time throughout the day that Monday. Ranging everywhere from Council Bluffs to St. Louis, there was a lot of ground to cover. I was able to sort out the odd drowning cases and anything involving men. Unsurprisingly, this only narrowed the cases down by half. The longest part of the process was waiting for the next case to roll in. As the day progressed, the number of cases being faxed in had ground to a halt. I had a pile of cases fifteen high, and none of them matched the information provided by Fenton.

The team concluded the day with a short briefing in which none of us had anything to report. It was all, "In Progress," meaning no one had anything interesting or conclusive to share. We all went home on time that day; possibly, for the first time in a month. The volume of work didn't require the overtime investment so we hit the road a few minutes before five.

I came home that night to a freshly cut back yard. It occurred to me that I had no idea who had been tending to my front yard for the past year. It was likely a thoughtful neighbor, but I realized I had no clue, who. The back yard was a disaster. The grass from the previous year had been so overgrown, that cutting it to an appropriate height had all but destroyed the lawn. What was left was dead and wilted. I found a bill and a note from the lawn company detailing what had been done, and more importantly, what needed to be done. I texted Darren, the officer who ran the lawn company on the side and told him he was clear to start seed or sod, whichever he believed was the best approach to fixing the lawn.

"That is not going to be cheap." I mumbled to myself.

I took that opportunity to move the two insurance checks from the house, out to my car. I wasn't sure if I was ready to cash them, but I was getting a little closer.

———

Tuesday was just like Monday. I reviewed case files from half a dozen jurisdictions before lunch and still didn't have a good fit for my victim. Right after lunch, I finally received a stack of missing person reports from Council Bluffs.

Of the many demographics represented in the various cases, there were surprisingly few that matched the description I had. This either meant there were few possible victims, or a hooker had managed to disappear without being noticed. This wasn't uncommon; but it made it difficult to be sure I had the victim report I needed.

I compared the cases I had to the missing person cases from Council Bluffs and found absolutely no overlap. I was still waiting for half a dozen jurisdictions along the Kansas-Missouri border to respond with their recovered body cases. These seemed the most likely locations a body would be found if dumped in Iowa. The odds of a corpse making its way south to Kansas City and then east towards St. Louis seemed fairly slim, though not impossible. I was stuck again, so I did a little writing and polished my report from the past week.

———

That afternoon we held our first brief on the employee list provided by Frank De Luca. I was happy to finally have something to do after my investigation into Fenton's latest victim had stalled. I finished the morning on the phone with the jurisdictions that hadn't responded to me. A friendly chat with several of them resulted in them finally issuing promises to have the files over by the end of the day.

I met Ross and Shirley in the investigations briefing room. They had small information packets assembled for the employees being reviewed. I leafed through the packet for a moment as we waited for Lt. Carter to join us.

"Did anyone jump out to you as an obvious suspect?" I asked.

"Yeah, that's why we assembled information on all of them," Ross replied, rolling his eyes.

I looked at him and smiled for a second. "Sorry I asked."

"We like to make it look like our job is difficult, when it's really a walk in the park," offered Shirley.

"Again, I'm sorry I asked. It's been a dull day of case file review and I'm just looking for something that might provide us a little momentum to keep pushing forward." I said.

"Same here," replied Shirley. "We're hoping to begin narrowing this list down. Unfortunately, more than half of what we have to do is background checks and those take a while. We have everyone's employee file from the prison, but there isn't much in them that would indicate psychotic behavior, general lack of concern for human life, violent history; nothing. It's a long process and we have fifteen names on this list."

"This is going to take while," advised Ross. "At the end, all we're going to have is background information. That information has to have something indicative of this type of behavior. We need more than that. We have to find a way to narrow down who has been having the most interaction with Fenton. The best way to do that would be to interview the staff members. The problem with that approach is we have no idea where to start and would ultimately be tipping off the suspect in the process."

"We need someone to come forward." I said, "But I have no idea how to incentivize someone to do so."

"You're right," Shirley agreed. "We need a way to separate the employees from each other. We may be able to sort out whose behind this if we can narrow down who might be Fenton's connection to the outside world."

"I could talk to the Warden, Frank, and see if there's anything he could do to help us." I offered.

"We could also see if there is anyone who recently transferred off of the death row assignment in the past year," Ross proposed. "Maybe we should start there. Find out how long each of these men has been on this assignment and see whoever isn't there anymore so we can talk to them about behavior or the other corrections officers on that assignment."

"I'll call Frank as soon as we're done here." I said, making a note at the top of my packet.

"Any luck on your latest Fenton victim?" Shirley asked.

"I've been sent more than a dozen case files from a dozen different jurisdictions. So far, none of them match the description of the female Fenton described to me. I might have a match on a missing person case filed a month after Fenton allegedly killed her, but unless someone found that body in the river then I'm shit out of luck." I replied.

"Well, you got off easy last week," said Ross, "It's about time to challenge yourself again. You were starting to get lazy."

"Yeah, that sounds like me." I laughed.

We all sat up in our chairs a little as Lt. Carter entered the room and sat down at the head of the table. He picked up his packet and flipped through it briefly before he turned to the group.

"Bring me up to date," he instructed. "Bryant, you go first."

"I still have case files from all along the Kansas-Missouri border pouring in on the fax machine. So far I've had no luck pairing any of them to the missing person files from Council Bluffs for 1991. I have a possible match on a missing person case, but I won't know for sure until the corresponding case comes in detailing where they found the body," I informed them.

"And Council Bluffs didn't have a hit at any time on this missing person case?" Carter asked.

"In 1991 it would have been impossible to know for sure where a body came from if it went down stream more than a few counties. Unless they suspected the body was dumped in the river when they filed the missing person report, they would have had no reason to believe that's where the body would be located." I replied. "The missing person report is still listed as 'open."

"That would be a pretty good example of outside the box thinking for that time period," said Carter. "Since they didn't have reason to believe it was homicide related, they may not have been digging into anything, especially if the body made it out of the Iowa-Nebraska area of the Missouri River. Bryant, keep me posted as soon as we have something concrete. We will all pitch in and do our best to resolve your case as quickly as possible so we can focus as a group on our suspect at the prison."

"You got it, L.T.," I replied.

"Ross, fill us in on the first person on the El Dorado employee list," he instructed.

"Right now I'm just going to give you an overview because we don't have anything on any of them that would make someone stand out as an obvious suspect. In your packet you have a list of fifteen men who work on death row at this time. Bryant has been tasked with contacting the warden and getting a list of possible people who use to work on death row. If there is anyone no longer on the assignment, they might be able to give information on who spent the most time with Fenton," said Ross.

"I'm on board with that. One thing; we wait until we have something concrete on someone before we start talking with other employees. We can't risk the suspect catching wind of what we're doing. Ross, please continue," Lt. Carter instructed.

"Of the fifteen employees, three of them have worked for the prison since they were old enough to apply. Those three have no previous work history other than the odd jobs during and right after high school. All three of them have been there over a decade and were at the prison just before Fenton was arrested. Eight of the employees have prior military experience and the other four came from smaller, local jails before taking jobs with the prison."

"Did any of these employees start right after Fenton was transferred to El Dorado?" I asked.

"Five of them," replied Shirley. "They were doing a big hiring push back in 2011 and hired over twenty new corrections officers. The five who were hired right after Fenton arrived all put in to be on the death row assignment at the same time. Death row has a pay incentive because of the heightened security measures. Lots of employees put in for it as soon as they can."

"Tell me about those five employees," said Carter.

"Ok, flip through your packet and circle them as I read them off," instructed Shirley, "DeMarcus, Dieter, Foster, O'Hara, and Patterson."

"Let's start with DeMarcus," said Carter, flipping back to the front of his packet.

"Sean DeMarcus is a 28 year old from Iola, Kansas. He first worked for the Allen County Jail back in 2010 through 2011 before applying for and accepting a position at El Dorado. He played college football at Fort Scott where he got an Associate's Degree in communications in 2009. He is listed as an employee in good standing by El Dorado and transferred to maximum security in 2016 where he was assigned to death row the same October. His employee file shows good report with coworkers and inmates. He has only one complaint for use of excessive force which was determined to be unfounded. He has a nearly perfect attendance record with only minimal use of sick time. They keep a regular log of who works which position in maximum security. He is typically the internal tower guard and control operator. His interaction with the populous is fairly minimal," advised Ross as he read from his packet and notes.

"Dieter is a 35 year old from Albany, New York. He joined the army in 2003 where he was stationed at Ft. Bragg, Ft. Meade, and later Ft. Riley where he received an honorable discharge in 2010. He served two tours in Afghanistan where he received several meritorious awards for his service and one Purple Heart. He worked as a correctional officer for Shawnee County in 2010 and 2011 before applying for and receiving a position at El Dorado. His employee record shows four complaints for excessive use of force against inmates. Three were found to be acceptable while he received a one week suspension for the other. Dieter applied for maximum security in 2015 and hasn't had a complaint against him since. Dieter has shown no issues with abuse of sick time and appears to have been in good standing since his reckoning period from the suspension ended in 2014. Dieter was promoted to Sergeant in 2016 and is one of the shift supervisors for the overnight watch. This watch is listed as having minimal contact with the populous," advised Shirley.

"Foster is a 36 year old from Minneapolis, Minnesota. He joined the army in 2002 and was stationed at Ft. Benning. He served one tour in

Afghanistan before he was charged with derelict of duty and transferred to Ft. Riley. He finished his four year commitment on desk duty working for various Army Officers. Although charges were filed, he was never convicted and received an honorable discharge in 2006. He moved around a lot working numerous jobs from Texas to Colorado before moving to the El Dorado area in 2011 where he started working for the prison. Foster put in for maximum security three times before finally being selected for the job in January 2016. Zero complaints from coworkers or inmates during his six years with the prison. His main duty involves screening visitors prior to visitation, serving meals and overseeing inmates during their solo time in the yard. He is listed as having extensive contact with max security inmates, but is listed as an employee in good standing. According to his record, he has taken less than five sick days since he started the job."

Lt. Carter held up a hand to Ross before he had the chance to continue.

"Bryant, any chance you know any of them so far?" asked Carter.

"Maybe the last guy," I replied. "I've met most of them, but I'm not really familiar with any of them."

"Do what you can over the next few visits to keep your eyes open and see what you can learn about them," Carter instructed.

"You got it."

"Sorry for the interruption, Ross. Please, continue," Carter beckoned.

"Next is Patterson. Patterson is a 28 year old from Lawrence, Kansas. He dropped out of the University of Kansas after one semester and worked construction for a while in the Greenwood County area. He is listed as married with three kids. Started working for El Dorado in 2011 and was promoted to maximum security in 2013. He has been there ever since and is the day shift Sergeant for the weekend squad. He has only one complaint against him during his six years which was dismissed after the investigation concluded the use of force was acceptable within policy based on the situation. He has used an extensive amount of sick time during his six years and had a thirty day reckoning period back in 2015 as a result."

"The dude's got three kids. Of course took a lot of sick time." Carter said, dismissively.

"He is currently listed as an employee in good standing with glowing reviews by subordinates and supervisors for his handling of interpersonal conflicts. He is listed as having extensive contact with inmates due to all complaints or issues they experience being directed to him for documentation and investigation." Ross finished.

"Last of these five we have O'Hara. O'Hara is a 27 year old who was born and raised in the area around El Dorado. His father was a Major working in the jail administration before he retired in 2015, and had a great deal of influence in getting his son the position; both on staff and in the maximum security detail. O'Hara is listed as a "loose cannon" with four complaints for excessive force against inmates. The first two appear to have been swept under the rug by his father while the second two resulted in a three year reckoning period and a 14 day suspension without pay back in 2016. Since then, he appears to have gotten his shit in line and hasn't had any recent complaints. He works in the control room during the day shift and is listed as having minimal contact with the inmates. O'Hara takes an above average amount of sick time, but has not reached the realm of disciplinary intervention as a result. He is currently listed as an employee under review due to the reckoning period he is still in," concluded Shirley.

A reckoning period, in law enforcement, was a period of additional scrutiny and limitations used as a disciplinary measure. Employees in a disciplinary reckoning period were usually ineligible for promotion or advancement, and were subject to further discipline or termination if they violated certain elements of policy or procedure.

"There you go, L.T. That's the five you asked about. Do you want us to brief you on the other ten?" asked Ross.

"Let's break it down a few at a time. First, Ross; get ahold of the supervisors with any of these fifteen employees who had military records. I want their service records if we can get them. If not the records, then find someone from their particular branch who can fill us in on their time in service. Shirley; contact De Luca and get me reports on these disciplinary incidents. Bryant, start reviewing the packet and get familiar with everyone starting with the five we just discussed. I want you to know these people on sight if you encounter them at the prison from now on. You're our only inside man for the time being. Find us something we can use," Carter commanded.

"Yes, sir," I replied.

Ross and Shirley stood up and left to complete their assigned tasks while I stayed behind to begin the familiarization process with the corrections officers in the packet. I recognized a few faces, but was having trouble placing any of them during my past visits.

The similarity to the corrections officers I worked with every day in our own jail made it difficult to be objective. I hated the idea of thinking one of these people was capable of colluding with a serial killer and feeding him information. Half of them were former military which made it even harder to believe one of them was selling us out. I knew I had to find a way to put aside my personal bias if I was going to rationally review these files and try to uncover the identity of the traitor.

As I thought about it, I realized there wasn't much that could be done with this person beyond having them fired for unprofessional contact and interaction with an inmate. Talking with an inmate wasn't a fire-able offense, and neither was tipping off the media about the identity of a murder victim. If a reporter had done it, they would have called it cutting edge journalism. But it wasn't a reporter, and it wasn't journalism. It was sabotage.

CHAPTER TWENTY-FOUR

"Did you have any luck yesterday?" Ross asked as I walked into the investigations wing.

I asked, "With the Fenton case?" As I joinied him at the coffee pot and grabbing a cup.

"Yeah," he nodded. He poured coffee into my cup and the returned the pot to it the burner.

"It took all day to get additional reports on possible victims. They arrived so late I didn't have the chance to go over them before I left," I replied. "How's the employee review going?"

"The same as yesterday," he replied. "We have a pile of names with basic biographical information and nothing more."

"Sounds enthralling." I said, sarcastically. I took a sip of coffee and decided it needed a little sugar.

"The good news is that Shirley is on her way back from storage with all the evidence from Holton and Brand's missing case files," said Ross as we strolled towards our desks.

"I didn't know there was any," I said. I blew on my coffee for a moment and took another sip.

"Apparently they frequented the bars on Moro Street. Shirley say's there is footage they collected of Holton out at the bars by himself the weekend before the report was filed. On top of all that, she found a former employee of Greg Marten's that worked in that housing development by Holton and Brand's house. He's coming in tomorrow for an interview," advised Ross.

"She did all that and has been working on the employee list from El Dorado too? It makes you wonder; what the fuck have we been doing?" I joked as we reached my desk.

"Exactly," Ross agreed, "Now get to work kid. You're making us all look bad."

I laughed a bit as Ross continued over towards his desk in the back corner.

Some days were just like that. One person can't catch a break while another is out running down leads and making progress on a case. I had learned in my first year in investigations that this was going to happen. Sometimes you struggle to fit pieces together, other times you're writing affidavits and taking quality cases to court every week. The key is to stay focused on the work you're doing without letting the distractions around you prevent you from making progress.

I grabbed the top file off the pile of cases I had been faxed the day before, and started reading. It took a while, but I finally managed to get through all but a few. I was still without a match, which was unfortunate, since I wasn't expecting any more reports to be faxed over. I was burnt out, and out of coffee.

I left my desk and took a walk around outside the building. I was having trouble focusing, and used the walk to clear my head and get the blood flowing again. A cool breeze kicked up which seemed to calm and relax me. After another minute or so the breeze started to chill me, making me wish I'd thought to bring my suit jacket. Having satisfied my need to move, I entered the building through the main entrance and used my key card to access the investigations division.

As I walked down the hallway towards my desk, Shirley stepped out of the in front of me.

"Hey, my first witness is coming in over his lunch hour. We might have something helpful to add to the afternoon briefing," she said.

"Sound's good," I replied. "Hopefully I have something to add by then."

"Looking forward to it," she said as we walked to our desks.

I struggled through another file, finding nothing useful to the investigation.

———

Even leaving for lunch didn't help me feel motivated. I read far enough into the next file to know it wasn't the one I was looking for and put it aside. The mountain of useless reports on my desk had become precariously perched over the past few days. I took a moment to rearrange it to avoid a catastrophe and grabbed the next report off the pile. As I was beginning to open it, my computer beeped at me to indicate the receipt of an instant message. I clicked on it.

Jeanine is starting her interview; you need to tune in-Ross

I opened up the link to our internal camera system, and started scanning through the options. I found Detective Shirley's profile, and accessed her active recordings. Shirley had shared the link to Ross, Lt. Carter, and I so we could view the interview while it was in progress. The system allowed interviews to take place in more comfortable rooms without the obvious one-way mirrored glass. I didn't recognize the man she was speaking to. I checked the interview information to see if Shirley had filled it out ahead of time.

Interviewer: Det. Shirley

Interviewee: LaDarius Fournier

I still didn't recognize him, and the name wasn't familiar either. I turned the volume up all the way until I realized my headphones were plugged into the computer. I lowered the volume and slipped the headphones on over my ears. LaDarius was a big guy. Shirley was almost six feet tall, but even seated; LaDarius seemed to fill the room. LaDarius was clearly in some kind of construction business, based on the clothes he was wearing. The tan boots he wore were covered with white paint or putty, as were his jeans and t-shirt. LaDarius was at least six feet four inches tall with dark black skin. He sported a clean shaven head and face, and looked like he had stepped off the field at the Superdome to start a painting business.

"How long did you work for Greg?" Shirley asked.

"I worked for Greg for nearly a decade. I did most of the sheetrock and painting work in his new housing developments. We were just starting on that massive development in the northwest when he said he was going to start contracting with another sheetrock group."

"Did he say why he was using someone else?"

"No, he didn't."

"Can you tell me what had been going on in the weeks leading up to him letting you go?" she asked.

"Not much. We had finished the first house months beforehand. This gay dude had already bought the first house and the bank had agreed to extend the load to Greg for another twenty-five units. We had a lot of work ahead of us."

"Can you tell me about this," Shirley paused for a minute, trying to remain professional, "Gay guy?"

"Well, there's not much to say. That was the first house on the cul-de-sac completed. The initial loan for building in that area had been for four houses. The bank wanted to know how fast the first one would sell so Greg threw everything into that house. He even put in this gorgeous hardwood flooring for the guy. After the first house sold, Greg started finishing the next three on that cul-de-sac at the same time. Six months later, we were trying to sheetrock three houses in the span of about four weeks. It was a tall order. I didn't have a big crew so we put in some serious overtime trying to stay on schedule. Have you been to those houses? They're huge."

"Tell me about the guy," Shirley encouraged again.

"It caught me off guard is all; I wasn't expecting to see a gay couple moving into the house. I was a little surprised to see the dude out there with his arm around some short white guy taking a picture in front of the "sold" sign."

"Why were you surprised?"

"Because the dude had bought the house like three months before that," LaDarius stated. "He had moved in and been in and out of that house for a while. He came over the first day we were installing sheetrock in the next house. He brought over cookies and lemonade and started chatting up my guys while they were on lunch. It made me feel uncomfortable."

"Why is that?" she asked.

"Because he was hitting on my guys," he replied. "He was touching on their arms and complimenting their physique. He was distracting them and making everyone nervous. I had to ask him to stop dropping by."

"So he was harassing your employees?"

"Not so much harassing them as he was flirting. To the best of my knowledge, none of my employees were gay. They didn't know how to respond. He brought food and drink and was being super nice about it all. I asked him if he could give us some space to do our work and take lunch in peace."

"And how did he react?" she asked.

"He was unbelievably cool about it. That's part of why I felt so bad. He didn't really seem phased by it. The next week he put a sold sign in the yard and moved the other guy in with him. They were staples in the neighborhood for the next week because they were the only ones that lived there. We knew which cars were there's and we'd give them a friendly wave whenever they drove by."

"How were they acting after they were both moved in?"

"Normal at first," LaDarius replied. "The white dude either was taking his time moving in or he traveled a lot. He was gone for days at a time. That's when we started noticing the other guys."

"What other guys?" Shirley inquired.

"Every time the white guy was out of town, the black dude was bringing other guys around."

"So he had friends coming over while his boyfriend was out of town?"

"I don't think they were friends," he replied shaking his head a little.

"What do you mean?" she asked.

"He was always bringing them home late. The only reason I knew they were there is because they were taking taxi's to get home the next morning as we were starting work."

"So when was the last time you saw them?"

"I honestly couldn't tell you that," he replied. "It's been years since then."

"Did you notice anything out of place at the house while you were working in the other houses?"

"Not really. I guess you could say the remodel was kind of oddly timed," he said.

"Remodel?" she asked.

"Greg and his kid spent a couple days out at the house doing a remodel. I saw his truck out there one morning and went over to say hi to him. I must have caught him at a bad time 'cause he told me to leave him alone. That was the last time I talked to him before he fired me."

"You said you saw his son with him?" Shirley inquired.

"Yeah; I guess he was in town helping his dad. That wasn't uncommon with as long as I knew Greg. I don't know if you were here for it, but his daughter went missing several years before that. Greg had his son with him all the time after that; At least during the summer months. It seemed out of place because it was March. His kid was usually away at college during the week."

"Did he say what they were remodeling?"

"No, he kinda snapped at me and said something about the queers," LaDarius through up air quotes, "Not being satisfied with some of the work. He never said what it was they were fixing. They weren't there more than a couple of days. The whole thing seemed odd because the home-owner and his boyfriend never left the house during the whole remodel. I saw their cars in the garage, but I never saw them leave. That was weird as hell 'because they were some active dudes. They were always leaving for an hour or so and then coming back."

"But Greg was there working?"

"Yeah," he replied.

"And so was his son?"

"Yeah, I saw him. They were unloading the back of Greg's truck. I couldn't tell what they were unloading. They had the truck backed up to the open garage and they were packing stuff back and forth inside the garage one morning."

I took off my headphones and sat back. The connections to Greg and Conner were beginning to stack up. It was very possible they were the last ones to see Tory Holton and Harvey Brand, alive.

I started reviewing my case files again. Every now and again I would distract myself by putting on my headphones and catching another bit of the interview process. Shirley was digging for specifics and ways to tie the timeline together to determine what else could be gleaned from LaDarius' statement.

The second to last file finally held some good news.

The Leavenworth Sheriff's Office had recovered a body matching the description of Fenton's prostitute after it had washed up along the west bank of the Missouri River. Recovered November 7, 1991, the victim was a woman in her early twenties wearing a black dress with evidence of recent sexual activity. The coroner's report indicated signs of anal penetration, and ligature marks on the neck consistent with being strangled. Petechial hemorrhaging to the face and neck indicated extensive interruption of blood supply to the victims head. The lack of water in the lungs was consistent with the finding that the victim had been strangled to death, and then tossed into the water. There was no identification on the body and the fingerprints had been badly deteriorated by scavengers and long term exposure in the water. Leavenworth County had understandably been unable to identify the body.

I compared the body located in Leavenworth County to the missing person report I had set aside from Council Bluffs, Iowa. The body was partially deteriorated, but the pictures matched the missing person's report. Her name was Michelle Wright; a prostitute with several minor arrests for drug possession and one documented contact in which she had been listed as a possible prostitute. She had been a witness to some kind of vehicle burglary in 1990. During the interview with responding officers, she neither confirmed nor denied her location on the street was due to working that particular corner.

Clearly over the year and a half in between, Michelle had taken her business to a higher class and started working the hotel bars in town.

I checked the unattended death report and found that Michelle had been cremated after she had gone unidentified for several months.

I took the two reports and faxed them to Terry and SSA Wells.

I sat at my desk for a moment staring at the picture of Michelle, provided by her family for the missing person report. I wondered for a moment what had brought her into the profession of being an escort. It was difficult to place myself into the shoes of someone else, especially someone so very different than me. It was hard to relate to someone whose life had taken such extreme turns.

It made me realize how incredibly lucky I had been. I was doing better than a lot of people in the world. My problems weren't anything so unique that no one else was experiencing something similar. Other than my weekly heart to heart with Satan, I didn't have much to bitch about. I had lost people; so had everyone. I had experienced emotional trauma; I needed to take my place in line.

My phone vibrated from its spot on the desk. It was a text from Terry

Road Trip to Leavenworth tomorrow?

I texted back:

For starters, then we are headed to Council Bluffs, IA for the family notifications.

I spent the rest of the day on the phone with Council Bluffs ironing out the details of our trip the next day. The supervisor on duty assured me they would track down the next of kin and get back to me.

I finally had what I wanted all day; something to bring to briefing.

It was an uneasy feeling to think that my good news was someone else's worst. I had this thought every time I had to make a next-of-kin notification; this time was no different.

CHAPTER TWENTY-FIVE

I was back in familiar territory; on the road back to Kansas City to pick up Terry before we started north towards Leavenworth. Neither of us was looking forward to making another next-of-kin notification, but it was part of our role in the task force.

It was the first time since my heart to heart with Dr. Elmore and my visit with Dr. Ehrenberg that I had time to talk with Terry.

I waited until we were on the highway before I broached the subject.

"I got something for you." I said as I reached behind his seat and retrieved a gift wrapped package.

"Why did you get me this?" He asked, holding the package up in confusion.

"I took your advice and talked to my therapist. We had a good session last week." I told him.

"Well that's good to hear," he said. "So why did you get me a gift?"

"Last time we were in Lincoln, I had a major revelation."

I paused for a moment, searching for the words to say without sounding too pathetic.

"I had a late night talk with Dr. Elmore." I informed him. "I had been wrestling with a lot of guilt and inner turmoil. I hadn't realized how extensive my denial had become. I talked with Dr. Elmore, and had a moment of actual clarity for the first time in almost a year and a half. I just needed to find a way to thank you for the delicate way you've been handling my fractured psyche the past month."

He looked warry and slightly concerned. I could tell he wanted to guess what I was alluding to, but was hesitant to mention it if he was wrong.

"I realized how deep I had buried my guilt over losing my wife." I said.

He breathed a sigh of relief.

"Shit man, you had me scared." He admitted.

"I'm sorry to keep you in such suspense. It's not easy to talk about for the third time in three weeks." I confessed.

"I am so sorry you've been going through all this," he offered. "I had no idea how to handle it. When Dr. Elmore asked me about it when you first met her, I didn't know what to tell her. After a little while it became super awkward around you two so it made it even harder to approach you about all that. I just wanted you to get some help. I didn't know you'd go to her about it before me."

"Yeah, neither did I." I agreed.

"So what did you get me?"

"Yeah," I scoffed, "Because that's how it works."

"Scotch; nice," he exclaimed after he tore off the paper. "Thanks buddy."

"You're the one who needed to be thanked. You were looking out for me when I needed it the most." I replied.

We sat there in awkward silence for a moment. I was being sincere, but it still felt weird to be that open with a friend. I was having a lot of honest moments lately, and it was a new feeling for me. I glanced at Terry, who looked back at me for a moment.

"So are we gonna make out now, or something?" he said, with feigned sincerity.

"Shut the fuck up and give me that bottle back. You lost your scotch privileges," I replied, shaking my head at him.

"I'm just so proud of you," he said, faking a sniffle.

"Fuck you!" I said, "Now you know why I didn't talk to you first."

"Oh yeah, 'cause that's the reason," he replied with a scoffing laugh.

"What's that supposed to mean?"

"Don't bullshit me; you've had the hots for the pretty doctor from the moment you met her."

"That's not why I talked to her first." I insisted.

"I'm busting your balls man. I'm happy for you. It wasn't easy talking to you while you were stuck in the past. I can hardly encourage you to think about moving on with your life when you aren't even aware of what you need to move on from," he informed me.

"I know it. I've been a pain in the ass. Sorry that my life's pain has brought you so much stress," I said with a laugh.

"Apology accepted," he said, chuckling.

I shook my head and let the smile slowly fade from my face. Everyone was having a different reaction to my recent mental and emotional breakthroughs. Terry's was by far the most ridiculous response, but it was nice to have someone not treating me with little kid gloves.

We drove in silence for a little while. The tension was finally broken, and we could finally act like ourselves.

"You're an asshole," I told him.

He laughed hard then, and slapped his thigh.

When he finally stopped laughing, he took a deep breath.

"So are you going to ask her out?"

I ignored him for a moment as we reached the city limits of Leavenworth. I merged casually into the early lunchtime traffic traveling north along Highway 7. I spent a few minutes navigating until I was pulling into a parking spot in the 600 Block of South 3rd Street.

I shut the car off and turned to Terry.

"Eventually," I told him.

Samuel Everett, the Leavenworth County Sheriff, dispensed with the formalities and got down to business. A local politician who had recently been elected Sheriff, Sam was not the traditional County Sheriff. He was cooperative, but his shortcoming in law enforcement experience was telling.

Fortunately, his undersheriff was there to assist him. Aaron Talley, the Undersheriff, had over a decade as a county deputy under his belt, and it helped the process.

Sam spoke very little about the business we had come to discuss. He seemed more focused on local politics and operating his county under his own version of political correctness, than he was on assisting us with our investigation.

We let him talk our ear off for a moment before we caught Aaron's eye. He gave us a brief nod and then turned to the Sheriff.

"Sam, if it's okay with you; I'm going to take these gentlemen to retrieve the evidence for this case. They have a next-of-kin notification to complete. I'm sure these two are very busy and would appreciate getting this process started," he said.

"Absolutely," agreed the Sheriff. "It was good to meet you boys."

We shook his hand his hand and exited the office as quickly as we could.

"How is it working for a politician?" I asked.

"Ask me again in a year," Aaron replied. "It's too soon to tell. He means well, but he keeps trying to apply all the latest political talking points to police work. He's struggling to maintain rapport with the deputies. His only good decision so far has been making me his second in command. I act as his go-between with the deputies, and head off his really bad ideas before they make their way down to the rank and file. He wants to change a lot of policy, and its making him really unpopular."

Aaron answered our questions as he walked us down the hallway to a locked door. He opened the door and led us down a set of stairs towards their evidence department.

"He has family money. He ran on a policing reform platform which was really popular after a few public embarrassments for the Sheriff's Office. We had a really public use of force situation in 2015 that really turned public opinion against us for a while. He used it to get elected by promising to turn the department around."

"That's tough," I said.

"Morale is at an all-time low," he said. "Wages have been stagnant in this county for nearly five years. Officers max out early and can't get anywhere in their career unless they promote. Unfortunately we don't have a very big department, so those opportunities are pretty limited."

Every now and again I would have the realization that I was better off than even I understood. The struggles in the law enforcement profession were felt some places more than others. I was one of the lucky ones; my struggles were minimal.

Aaron signed over the evidence to us and helped us cart it back upstairs. I felt bad for him, knowing the difficult position he was in. Unfortunately, there was nothing I could do to help him. We didn't say anything after that. We shook hands and then he walked back into the building. There was something almost dejected about the way he walked. Gone were any signs of enthusiasm, passion or purpose; it was just a job to him now.

I had seen it several times in my decade of service. An officer loses the passion they started with and starts to fizzle. If this happened early in their career, they changed paths and left law enforcement. If this happened anywhere past the seven to nine year mark, we often saw a dejected, unenthusiastic officer do their best to ride out the next five or six years until they could collect their pension.

That wasn't what law enforcement was meant to be, but it happened. Not everyone was cut out for it. Some people just took longer than others to determine if they were fully invested, or just collecting a check.

We loaded the evidence boxes in the car and hit the road, still trying to shake the depressing feeling that seemed to follow us as we drove north out of town. A few times through my career I had asked the same question's Aaron had.

Am I really cut out for this? Do I want to do this for another ten years? Do I have what it takes to still pour as much of myself into this job as possible? Have I already invested too much?

Those were just the questions that came up after a few years on night shift. That didn't take into account the shitty calls; the uncooperative drunks, the people who just want to fight, the bloody crime scenes, the rape victims, the abused children, or the dead bodies, dismembered from violent car crashes.

Those experiences were often enough to collapse the intentions of even the best officers.

"Do you think that will happen to us?" asked Terry.

"You mean the depression and self-loathing, or the political red tape making it impossible to do our jobs?"

"Both," he replied.

I paused for a moment and thought about it. Three weeks ago, I was already planning on getting out as soon as this was over. Now I was hoping to use it to round out my last few years until I had enough time in service to retire early.

"Sometimes, I think it's just a matter of time before something comes along and motivates me to get out early. I've certainly seen enough dead bodies lately. They're all motivating me to get the fuck out and do something else. I don't even know what else I would do." I said.

"I've thought about doing private security a few times," admitted Terry.

"It's a pretty good gig if you can get it." I said. "That's something I could see myself going into when I decide to hang up the badge."

"Well you're closer to getting out than I am," offered Terry.

"It still feels like it's an eternity away."

I was feeling down in a way I hadn't been in a while. I had my share of depression and bitterness as a result of losing my wife and being forced to meet with Fenton. This was something new; hopelessness.

"That place kind of fucked us up, didn't it?"

"No shit," I agreed. "How is it possible for a place to do that after less than half an hour?"

"I think that speaks to the environment they've created there. They have to be struggling to hire and keep good candidates," said Terry.

"All I can say is, let's change the subject. This whole conversation makes me wanna kill myself."

"Well that's fucking dark," exclaimed Terry.

"Seriously though; let's talk about anything else." I begged.

"Okay," he replied.

We drove in silence, still trying to shake the feeling we had picked up. I turned the radio on just to have some background noise, and tried to get lost in the music enough to forget my troubles.

"So; are you gonna ask out, Dr. Elmore?"

I shook my head in exasperation, "Just give it a rest; buddy."

———

Council Bluffs had done a good job tracking down Michelle Wright's next-of-kin. Over twenty-five years had passed since Michelle had been killed; which meant her family could be anywhere.

I wasn't prepared for what was waiting for us in the Wright's home.

Michelle's father, Peter Wright, had died several years prior. Michelle's mother Pamela had moved four times in the past three decades and was living in a small area of Section 8 housing on the east side of Council Bluffs near the Iowa Western Community College. Staying with Pamela was Michelle's twenty-six year old son, Tanner.

"Can I get you anything to drink?" Pamela offered, struggling to stand from her reclining chair.

"No, thank you," I replied. Pamela sat back down as Terry echoed my response.

"The officer yesterday said they were checking for possible witnesses to an armed robbery in the area. Is that why you're here as well? We told the young man yesterday that we hadn't seen anything," Pamela advised.

"No ma'am, that's not why we're here," I said pausing briefly as I searched for the appropriate words to say. "We're actually here about your daughter, Michelle."

"Michelle? We haven't seen her in twenty-five years. She disappeared a few months before Tanner's first birthday."

Pamela reached from her chair and patted Tanner on the arm as she spoke. I caught Tanner's eye, and could tell he was wary about what we were there to accomplish.

"Yes, ma'am, I know that. The reason we stopped by today is because we found Michelle. She was killed back in 1991. I am so sorry to have to tell you this," I said.

Pamela nodded quietly as she listened, grasping Tanner by the hand.

"I was afraid of that," she admitted.

"I apologize for the length of time you had to go before you received this news. I can't imagine what you went through these past years," I consoled.

"Honey, you don't look much older than my grandson. I find it hard to believe any of this is your fault, but I appreciate your compassion." She said.

I was a little surprised to hear her say that. After the last victim notification in Irvingdale, I had been prepared for the worst.

"The Council Bluff's Police Department is standing by with their Police Chaplain; is that someone you'd like to speak with today?" I asked.

"Thank you, young man. I would greatly appreciate someone sitting down to pray with us."

"Are there any questions you have for us?" Terry inquired.

"Do you know who killed my mom?" Tanner asked.

"Yes we do," I replied. "He's been behind bars for nearly a decade."

Tanner nodded his head as he hung it slightly.

"I was afraid we were going to get this news someday." Tanner admitted.

"It wasn't an easy conversation, but I told Tanner years ago what his mother did to put food on the table. We long suspected something like this happened to her. I knew, all those years, that she loved her son too much to have left him behind," said Pamela.

"My grandma told me she was going to do everything she could to provide a better future for me than my mother had. That's why we live here. I'm working and taking classes in the evening to support us both. It hasn't been easy, but I understand that my mom, and my grandma each sacrificed everything they could to make sure I had a chance at a better life," said Tanner.

"This is my card," I said setting one on the table. "If you have any questions about your mother's death, please call me. I'll do everything I can to answer your questions."

Tanner picked up the card and glanced over it.

"You're from Kansas?" He asked. I nodded. "Why are you involved in my mother's case? Did she end up in Kansas somehow?"

"Yes she did," I replied. "The reason I am involved in your mother's case, along with Special Agent Jones," I said gesturing at Terry, "Is because the man who killed your mother killed other people too. We're part of a task force helping solve old cases in which this man was involved. That man is currently awaiting a death sentence in Kansas. I know that doesn't answer all the questions you have; but I promise you, your mother's killer is being put to justice."

The room was quiet for about a minute. I had said my piece and was currently waiting to see if they had any further requests for information. I nodded at Terry to indicate it was time for us to leave.

"Ms. Wright, Tanner; I'm sorry we met under these conditions. If you don't have any further questions for us, we are going to get back on the road." I advised.

Pamela began attempting to get up again until I approached her chair and shook the hand she offered. Tanner gave me a firm handshake and nodded at me sharply. His eyelids held the tears at bay, but his pain was starting to show. Terry and I made a smooth exit and informed the Chaplain he could meet with Pamela and Tanner.

"Wait, just a minute." I called after the Chaplain.

I opened the trunk and removed the urn containing Michelle's ashes.

"Would you please return her to her family?" I asked.

"Absolutely," the Chaplain agreed, taking the urn from me and cradling it carefully in his arms.

We watched the Chaplain walk to the front door along with one of the police officers who had been standing by with us. When they disappeared from sight, we climbed in the car and drove away as quietly as possible.

We transported the rest of the evidence up to Lincoln, taking turns driving so the other could get some sleep. I wanted to spend some time with Dr. Elmore, but she was out of the lab at a staff meeting. I didn't really have time to see her anyway, so this worked out for the best. We exchanged brief pleasantries with Tommy and Sam as they signed for the evidence from Michelle Wright's case.

Before we could discuss anything in-depth, Terry's phone beeped. He read the text message silently and then turned back to me.

"Wells has an update for us. He's going to call in a couple minutes," he advised.

"It was good seeing you both again," I said to Tommy and Sam, giving them a brief wave as we left the lab.

Terry's phone rang as we reached the car.

"This is Agent Jones," he said as he answered it.

He pulled the phone away from his ear and placed it on speaker as he climbed into the passenger seat.

"Jones, Bryant; our first affidavit for Simon Carroll got kicked back. They need something more concrete before they issue a warrant. Did you get an update on the Jessica Childress case while you were at the lab?"

"No sir," Terry replied. "Dr. Elmore is out of the lab at the moment and isn't expected back for at least an hour. We were going to get an update after we get back at least to Kansas City."

"That works for me." Wells agreed. "We need that evidence locked down as soon as possible."

Terry hung up the phone and stowed it inside his jacket pocket.

"We were reaching a little with that first affidavit," admitted Terry.

"I can't blame you," I admitted. "We're all hoping to make a little headway on that case before we go back to Cass County again."

After an hour, Terry switched seats with me to drive the last of the leg back to Kansas City. I was exhausted. Spending this much time in the car was wearing me down, making it difficult to stay awake as I drove.

Just as I was about to fall asleep, my phone rang.

I cleared my throat for a second before answering, "This is Bryant."

"Hey Bryant, it's Ross; I've got an update for you in the Holton-Brand case."

"What is it?" I asked.

"Shirley found a connection in the case. We can tie Conner and Greg to Holton and Brand."

"No shit?" I exclaimed.

"No shit," he replied. "I just wrapped up an interview with Greg Marten. He tried to stonewall me, but he can't explain why he and Conner were remodeling at Holton's house. Along with that, do you remember where Holton and Brand were recovered?"

"Hayley Marten's Memorial Garden," I answered.

"Greg and Conner built that memorial garden themselves, that's the connection. He told me as much during the interview. Lt. Carter wants us in at 0700 hours tomorrow. I'm working on warrants for Conner and Greg as we speak. We're about to start splitting shifts monitoring the house as soon as the warrant is signed."

"I will see you at 0700, then," I agreed. I hung up the phone and leaned my seat back.

"Good news?" asked Terry.

"We're making progress on our City Park victims. We finally have suspects," I informed him.

"That's good to hear. You've certainly got your hands full," Terry observed.

"You're not kidding," I agreed.

CHAPTER TWENTY-SIX

That Friday was a flurry of activity. Search warrants were drafted and held on standby. The likelihood of evidence existing years later in Greg's house was highly unlikely. Conner lived miles away in Lawrence, making it a difficult task to monitor him. A request was put in to the Lawrence Police Department requesting information on Conner. At this point we didn't have enough to hold either of them, but any assistance we could get would be helpful. Search warrants often had a time sensitive nature about the, but arrest warrants for years-old cases were not as urgent in the eyes of the judge. The arrest warrants were written as close to completion as possible and held until the evidence collected at Holton's house could be processed and added to the warrant. The key detail was connecting the crime scene, the suspects, and the burial site. We needed the evidence to seal the deal.

For weeks it had seemed unlikely we would make much progress on these various cases. Now we seemed to be moving forward on all fronts, and it was very overwhelming.

It was difficult to go from Fenton's latest victim, to City Park victims, then to reviewing employees from El Dorado. I shook off the need to check in with Ross about the Holton-Brand cases for the fourth time that morning, and started reaching out for information from Ft. Riley. The dynamics of the investigation had changed. The task of attaining military records on the El Dorado employees had fallen to me.

Two of the employees had former military service and had each been discharged from Ft. Riley. I spent the morning being passed back and forth between the FROC and various division leaders, trying to determine who could help me.

I finally made contact with Colonel Jason Moore, who agreed to meet with me and discuss the military history of the two employees in question. Colonel Moore agreed to meet with me that afternoon after he retrieved the records for Dieter and Foster. I made note of my meeting with Col. Moore on my calendar and went to give Lt. Carter an update.

Lt. Carter saw me approaching and waved me into his office.

"I set up a meeting with a Colonel Moore from Ft. Riley Division Command. He's coming in at four this afternoon with service records for Dieter and Foster." I informed him.

"Glad to hear it," Carter replied. "That gives you a little free time this afternoon ahead of that meeting."

"Yes, I suppose it does." I agreed.

"We're starting surveillance on Greg Marten today. Take a piss, grab a bite to eat and head over to his house off Colorado. You're taking the first watch on the house. We currently have no information on his whereabouts or what vehicles he might be driving. We're going to start watching the house, and then add someone to watch his business. As soon as we have eyes on him, we don't lose him," he instructed.

"Yes sir," I replied and made a swift about-face.

I did exactly as Lt. Carter instructed. I had several hours ahead of me of sitting in a car doing nothing, but watching a house. This task required a totally empty bladder, a burger, and a caffeinated beverage. I slipped my vest on and threw a light jacket over the top. I grabbed a set of keys to an investigations vehicle and used the restroom before I left.

"1262-dispatch; I'm 10-8 in an unmarked vehicle on special assignment." I said into the radio.

"10-4, 1262, 10-8 in unmarked on special at 11:46:37 hours," dispatch replied.

I accelerated hard out of the parking lot and hit the highway for a minute before reaching the nearest burger joint. I grabbed my lunch to-go and headed to the 600 block of Colorado. I sat a block away from Greg Marten's house and had my lunch. Surveillance was a monotonous task unless something exciting happened. This wasn't likely, as I had no reason to contact Greg if I saw him.

We were in hands off mode. This time period, while frustrating for patrol, meant very little work in the meantime for me. Hands-off mode usually didn't involve surveillance; in fact it usually forbids such activity. This was a homicide investigation though, meaning the stakes were higher and the rules were a little different than a drug investigation.

The next few hours were completely uneventful. I monitored the house from a distance while nothing moved. I hadn't quite mastered the art of lying in wait in situations like this. As a result, I had to pee after the first two hours. I squirmed for a little while and debated chugging the rest of my soda in order to free up a cup to piss in. While occasionally necessary on surveillance, it was highly frowned upon to take care of business in this manner; especially in broad daylight. Overnight, you could get away with it a little more. On the upside, a full bladder made it really easy to stay awake and alert.

1500 hours passed as my misery reached an all-time high. Just as I was beginning to reconsider whipping it out to pee in the cup, my phone rang.

"Go for Bryant," I answered.

"Hey it's Ross. I'm headed your way now; any movement?"

"Nothing so far," I answered. "I haven't approached yet to see which of his vehicles are in the driveway."

"10-4, as soon as I get close, you drive past the house and call out any tags you see," advised Ross.

"Can do," I replied. "How far away are you?"

Radio: "1233-dispatch, 10-8 in unmarked vehicle on special assignment."

Radio: "10-4, 1233; 10-8 in unmarked on special."

"I'll be there in five minutes," Ross advised me.

"Thank you God; I have to piss," I told him.

"Alright; well put a clothes pin on it and hang in there," he replied.

I hung up the phone and went back to shaking one leg or another in an effort to distract myself from the impending, piss-soaked pants in my near future.

Five minutes can fly by without a thought when there's nothing creating a sense of urgency. Five minutes when you have to pee, is an eternity.

Finally; mercifully, my phone rang again.

"I'm two blocks out and headed to your position. Go swing by the house and let me know what you see," Ross instructed.

I put my phone on speaker and pulled the car away from the curb. I tried to keep it slow and casual, while finding the balance between lurking and speeding.

"Nothing; there's nobody in the driveway or parked around on the side," I said.

"I'll let Shirley know to start her surveillance shift over at his workplace off 177," he replied.

"Sounds good," I replied, "Gotta go."

I hung up the phone and hauled ass to the nearest gas station. I tried to look subtle as I awkwardly walked in and made a bee-line straight for the bathroom.

———

True to his word, Col. Moore was at the front desk at four O'clock that afternoon. I was glad to be back at the department instead of sitting on surveillance duty. I met Col. Moore in the conference room and set us both up with cups of coffee. Col. Moore was six feet of old school Army. He was clean shaven; square jawed, and dressed in a standard camouflage uniform weighed down by numerous ribbons.

"Thank you for coming in so quickly, Colonel." I said, shaking his hand.

"I'm happy to help with whatever I can," he replied.

"I'll try not to take up any more of your time than necessary," I insisted.

"Well then fill me in," he instructed. "You didn't provide me a lot of information over the phone."

"Well, I see you brought the personnel files I requested so I'll cut to the chase," I replied. "We are in the process of investigating a series of murders that happened here in town. They are all tied to an investigation I am completing with a convicted serial killer who is currently sitting on death row. Someone working in the prison where he is housed is feeding him information about our ongoing investigations. This person is believed to have contributed to the killing of three people in City Park last month.

We are researching each of the employees of this prison to find out if there is any way to indicate which one of them might be involved. Unfortunately, several of our persons of interest have former military service meaning there's a portion of their lives that are not public record. We need an insight into these people at every moment of their lives. The only way to get that is from accessing their service records. That's why I called you."

"I'll see what I can do to help," Col. Moore replied.

Col. Moore handed me two files from his stack and set one out in front of him as well.

"Quick disclaimer," he mentioned. "These are for official use and review. When I leave, these files leave with me. If you find any of this information pertinent, I recommend you make some notes."

"Understood," I agreed. I pulled out a notebook and set it down next to the files.

"First on the list is Corporal E-4 Dieter, Phillip. Dieter served from 2003 to 2010 where he was a member of the 1st Combat Aviation Brigade here at Ft. Riley. He served two tours in Afghanistan where he flew Apache helicopters. He saw limited action and was mostly there as local air support for ground troops. He received an award for backing a medical evacuation in which he landed under fire so that three wounded infantryman could be medevacked to base. All three of them survived, two of which would not have survived the Humvee trip back to base. Dieter was credited with saving their lives and received the Silver Star when he cycled back to Ft. Meade in 2005. Dieter was transferred to Ft. Riley and assigned to the 1st C.A.B. in 2006 before deploying to Afghanistan a second time. He flew more than thirty missions as an Apache pilot on that deployment. On his last mission, his Apache was hit by enemy rocket-fire and shot down. Despite having a broken arm and severe burns to his back and legs, Dieter defended the rest of his crew with nothing more than his side arm against dozens of insurgents. He had fourteen confirmed kills before they were rescued. He was one of only two from that mission to make it back home. He was awarded the Distinguished Service Cross and a Purple Heart for that mission. He spent most of 2007 and 2008 in recovery from his wounds and began studying to be a mechanic. After he passed his physical fitness tests to become active duty again, Dieter enlisted for three more years in 2008 as a flight mechanic. He received an honorable discharge in 2010. Dieter shows no record of disciplinary action for any reason, on or off duty. Do you have any questions about Dieter?" asked Col. Moore.

I spent a few seconds looking over the very short list of notes I had made while listening.

"No, sir," I replied.

"If you're ready then; I'll continue with the next filed," he posited.

"Please, continue," I said opening the next file.

I spent a few minutes looking over my file as Col. Moore took a sip of coffee and opened his. I could see he had highlighted several portions of the second file, making me wonder if he had done so in the first file and I had just missed it.

"The second file you requested me to bring you was that of Private Foster, Amos. Unlike Dieter, there is quite a bit more to go over with Foster," advised Col. Moore.

"What do you mean?" I asked.

"Flip to page four of your file, we'll just start with the disciplinary record," he instructed.

I flipped a few pages and started looking over the list as Col. Moore read them out loud.

"Starting in 2002, Foster received a written reprimand for disobeying orders. Here in town, they had a local bar that was creating issues for soldiers. Soldiers were forbidden from going there. Foster not only went there, he was arrested for disorderly conduct and battery on a law enforcement officer. Later in 2002, an official complaint was filed against Foster for harassing a female soldier in his unit. The other soldier transferred to another unit and Foster received a written reprimand for his actions. In 2003, while deployed in Afghanistan, Foster received three written reprimands for failure to follow orders. Foster was documented several times harassing local women and using vernacular harmful to the mission."

"What do you mean harmful vernacular?" I asked.

"He was being an asshole to the local's calling them, and I quote, "towel-heads, sand-Negros;" I cleaned that one up for obvious reasons, "camel jockey," and "raghead." Foster saw limited combat while in Afghanistan. During one mission, he was at the center of a war crimes investigation resulting from the death and alleged rape of one of the local women. They never found anything concrete and the investigation is still open. He lost the support of his brigade and commanding officers, and was rotated back to the states four months before the rest of his unit."

"Does that happen often?" I inquired.

"Not unless you get injured," he replied. "Foster gave the Army a bad name. He contributed to disrupting efforts to reach out to and help the locals on his deployment. When he saw action, he deliberately disobeyed orders which resulted in two different missions failing before they even reached the front lines. That's how you get sent back to the states. The fact that he wasn't in shackles on the plane is the interesting part. He was put on desk duty and spent the next two years essentially locked in an office pushing paper. He might be one of the only soldiers I've ever reviewed who never received so much as a pay raise during his time in-service. That's pretty difficult to do, I might add. Everywhere you go, every bit of training you take, provides opportunity for advancement. He never took any training beyond basics in demolition in early 2003 before he deployed. He was listed as 'enthusiastic and gifted' in his demolitions training, but was dropped from the program early after they found him trying to smuggle materials out of the building. He was documented several times making comments about using explosives to resolve the conflict in the middle east; permanently. Unfortunately these comments weren't added to his official file before he deployed. If they had, he would have never left the country. They compiled these comments along with his other insubordination and harassment complaints. They were working on a possible court-martial before he filed his paperwork to be discharged. He eventually received an honorable discharge instead of prison time and a dishonorable discharge, which is what he really deserved. I tried calling around to find out why the paperwork wasn't processed faster for his court-martial. Unfortunately, that was over a decade ago and most of the people involved in that process are either discharged or retired by now. I couldn't get any answers about him. In reality, when he was cycled back stateside early, he should have been processed for immediate dishonorable discharge. His documented actions alone were enough for that. If any of the allegations in that war crimes case were founded, he should still be in a prison cell in Leavenworth."

"Holy shit," I exclaimed.

"Holy shit is the official stance my office took upon reviewing his files," he said.

"Wow!" I said as I continued scribbling down notes as fast as my pen could write.

"Do you have any other questions for me?" asked the Colonel.

"Hang on," I mumbled as I tried to write even faster. My hand was starting to cramp from all the writing but there was so much to record.

Finally; mercifully after another minute, I had written down everything I could think of pertaining to Foster's service records. I shook my hand a moment in an effort to regain proper circulation.

"I do have a couple questions." I said. "First, can you put me into contact with anyone in his bomb making class? Second; can you find out who was in his unit in Afghanistan and see if they can provide some clarity on what happened over there?"

"I will pull the records as soon as I can and get you the most up to date contact list we have," he replied.

"Thank you, I appreciate everything you've done to help us," I told him.

We stood up from the table and stacked the files together before he set his briefcase on the table. He loaded the files into the briefcase and closed the lid.

"Please let me know if there is anything else I can do to assist you investigation," he said, shaking my hand.

"We have a long list of employees we haven't covered yet. Several of them are former military, so we may be sending you another list to check out."

"Just let me know," he replied. "I'll compile the list of contacts you requested and send it over as soon as possible."

"Thank you for coming in today," I said.

I walked the Colonel back to the front lobby and then did a swift turn-around to my desk. A thought had occurred to me as I thought through the situation we were trying to resolve.

I took a few minutes and looked through a stack of old reports. I finally found the one detailing how Tim Lane's phone had been received in the mail. There had been a search warrant and detailed printouts of all the activity on the phone. I needed something specific. I breathed a sigh of relief, when after several minutes of searching, I finally located the report.

I picked up my desk phone and then sorted through my cell phone for a number. I dialed it and waited, hoping I wasn't calling too late.

"Frank; it's Detective Bryant. How far back does your security system maintain footage?"

I waited for a minute as Frank De Luca consulted with his assistant before replying to me.

"That is awesome Frank. I need you to do something for me in regards to the investigation we're conducting with your employees. I'm going to give you a time and date. I need you to get me footage of anyone making a phone call from one of the prison land-lines at that exact time."

I paused for a minute as he jotted down a few notes.

"March 18, 2017 at approximately 1330 hours," I said. "Give me a five minute time span on either side of that. If someone makes a call on one of your phones in that window of time and it's on camera, I want the footage."

I hung up the phone a bit too enthusiastically, hoping I hadn't deafened the warden in the process.

I stood up from my desk to look around over the top of my cubicle walls. Shirley and Ross were both out on surveillance details. Knowing the level of commitment required for surveillance, I knew they wouldn't be back any time soon.

I finally spotted Lt. Carter in his office, and headed that way.

I knocked and then let myself in.

"Heads up; I might have a person of interest, and a way to confirm if they made the call from the prison to Tim Lane." I informed him.

"Excellent."

CHAPTER TWENTY-SEVEN

The conference room was crowded the next day. There were two investigations to continue, and we had reached the capacity of the four person team to handle them both. Joining our team of four was an assortment of people. The KBI had sent two agents to assist with the City Park case. SSA Wells and Agent Jones were in attendance from the FBI's office in Kansas City. My buddy, Sgt. Jason Ellis was in attendance along with two officers from his squad. Lt. Carter had opened up the surveillance duties to uniformed personnel who wanted to pick up some overtime with plain clothes surveillance. Lt. Carter was taking charge of surveillance of Greg Marten. SSA Wells assumed the supervisory role of the investigation into Amos Foster.

I was exhausted. Col. Moore hadn't bothered to wait for the following day to begin following up with members of Foster's unit. He passed my phone number to each person he talked to and had them call me that night to provide their testimony to Foster's character. Four members of Foster's squad called me to fill me in on Foster's behavior during his four years in the Army. The more I heard, the more concerned I became. Finally, by 2100 hours that night, I called Lt. Carter and filled him in. He immediately put things in motion to more than double the size of our team.

So there we were; two o'clock the next afternoon, crowded into the conference room. Eleven of us sat in a circle around the table as Detective Ross gave a presentation on Greg and Conner Marten. He detailed the double homicide of Holton and Brand and what the team was waiting on to get the arrest warrants issued.

"The evidence we have so far is very damning of them, but we are waiting for the lab in Kansas City to come back with definitive evidence that one or both of the victims was killed on the living room floor of that house. As soon as we have it, we are greenlighting the warrants and making our move," he explained. "The KBI has sent two agents to assist here in Manhattan; two more have been dispatched to Lawrence to surveille Conner Marten along with a small team of LPD officers. We will be emailing the warrant to Lawrence for Conner as soon as it is signed. These warrants will be full extradition, just in case either of them makes a move to leave the state or the country."

"What are our responsibilities while we're keeping them under surveillance?" asked Sgt. Ellis.

"Until we have warrants in-hand; everything is to be kept at a distance. Do not make contact; do not identify yourselves as officers. If confronted by anyone, Greg included, make an excuse for why you are there and promptly leave. If you are made, contact your backup and immediately move to switch to another unmarked vehicle. The neighborhood around Greg Marten's house is notoriously unfriendly to police. The KBI has provided several vehicles complete with tinted windows. They are not standard issue unmarked units. They will allow a certain level of privacy for surveillance. These vehicles are not the primary units being used for this task. They are primarily back-up and will be stationed in the area in case Greg starts moving. Keep your distance and report all movement to Lt. Carter; any other questions?"

Everyone in the room turned to look around. Seeing no hands raised or people speaking up, Det. Ross continued.

"The team surveilling Greg Marten will include Lt. Carter, Sgt. Ellis, our two patrol volunteers, our two KBI agents and I. Together we will rotate shifts as often as permissible. Everyone on the team is subject to a call-in at any time over the next few weeks. We will not call in patrol officers while they are on duty; nor within the seven hours after they get off duty. Keep in mind, we may be running a lot of shifts, so get sleep as often as you can. I'll turn it over to SSA Wells of the FBI who will be detailing the team surveilling Foster," concluded Ross.

"Thank you Detective. Unfortunately, this case is on a need to know basis and some of you, don't need to know. Patrol, KBI; if you could please excuse yourselves from the room," requested Wells.

We spent a few minutes shifting our chairs around while the five others left the room. Once the door was closed behind them, the rest of us settled back into our places as SSA Wells picked up the remote and began clicking to the first slide of his presentation.

"There are a lot of unknown's with Foster. I worked with Detective Bryant this morning to compile this presentation with what we do know. Foster is former military; took some bomb training and was also listed as an expert rifle marksman. Foster's military career was tainted by numerous complaints of misconduct, harassment of female soldiers, extremist and homicidal comments. Foster never got the chance to pull the trigger overseas. He was cycled back to the states amid allegations of insubordination, and an open war crimes case. Members of his unit firmly believed he was responsible for the alleged rape and murder of a local teenage girl. He was never convicted, but the word on the street is he was not only capable, but willing to commit such atrocities. Keep in mind; at this point we have no hard evidence tying him to Fenton in any way. We have a pattern of behavior established over a decade ago with nothing to demonstrate it has continued. The one thing we do have is the connection to your local case. With that; I will turn it over to Detective Bryant momentarily for our most recent update on the case," said Wells, gesturing to me.

I stood up and cleared my throat.

"Yesterday, I made contact with Frank De Luca, the prison warden, and requested anything he might have to show who made the phone call from the prison to Tim Lane the day that he died. Frank emailed me a fifty second video showing our boy, Foster here," I said gesturing to the photo Wells put up on the screen, "Making a phone call at the same time Tim received the phone call from the prison. This was the only phone call made during a fifteen minute window spanning on either side of Foster's call. The prison records all incoming and outgoing calls for security purposes. The warden advised he would be sending me an audio recording of the phone call as soon as he could unearth it," I said. "We believe Foster is our inside man at the prison who has been keeping Fenton informed during his incarceration."

"From all employment records from the prison, Foster is a model employee. He has zero complaints or disciplinary actions against him during his nearly six years at the prison," continued SSA Wells as I sat back down. "We are surveilling Foster in an attempt to greater understand what his motive might be. According to Detective Bryant's reports; Fenton has a tendency to find like-minded individuals and providing them guidance in the ways of a serial killer. This is a lot of reading between the lines. Nothing Fenton has said so far has pointed to anyone in particular, but we know Fenton has a man on the inside of the prison with access to the outside world. The cause for concern is based around the idea that this person is like-minded enough to have done some killing of their own. If they have, we need to establish the pattern of behavior and put a stop to it. While we are watching Foster, the rest of the team will be researching his past to see if we can put him in the same vicinity as previous murders, missing persons, or possibly even rapes. We will gather all evidence available to us and compile the most comprehensive case we can. As soon as we can, we will make a move on Foster to severe his ties to Fenton and the other investigations still ongoing. Any questions?" he asked, finally.

"I think we're all clear about our responsibilities," I said after no one spoke up for a moment.

"Excellent; Jones, Bryant, Shirley and I will be the rotating surveillance on Foster as long as we can manage it. This is a priority; but if we have other cases provided by Fenton, we will not abandon them in the process of chasing Foster," instructed Wells.

"As of now, Foster is still listed as a person of interest. We have nothing besides video of him making a phone call to, who we believe, was Tim Lane. The purpose of this surveillance is to gather intelligence on Foster's patterns, habits and lifestyle. We need something concrete to put on a warrant. Remember, everything we do here can affect the outcome of this case. Respect court precedent on curtilage and surveillance. Since we are investigating this as a bombing investigation, we have gained a little leeway on our surveillance since a lot of it can fall under the patriot act and national security concerns. That is why the FBI is overseeing this portion of the surveillance," I advised. "We can't take any risks by over-stepping our boundaries. Remember, we're investigating the death of one of our own officers; don't do anything that might result in new court precedent that might jeopardize this entire investigation."

"Building on what Detective Bryant said; if you have any questions about what might fall under the Patriot Act or national security concerns, ask me. This is not cut and dried. Any leeway we have under the Patriot Act will be slim to none due to the severity of the incident we are investigating and the person we are investigating. This does not qualify as terrorism due to the definition of terrorism involving someone trying to attack in the effort to drive, change or influence policy in some way. This is a murder investigation, first and foremost. We should all act in accordance with that. Everything we do will most likely be charged at a state level. The FBI has not officially taken up this case to charge it federally. If we develop strong evidence against Foster at any time, I will appeal this up my chain of command and try to charge this federally where the punitive measures taken are more severe and the prosecution better funded. Again; any questions?" asked Wells.

I scanned the room to see everyone's reaction. Everyone exchanged a glance between making notes for themselves.

"Butler County Sheriff's Office is aware of our presence in their area. If you are approached by a deputy, tell them you are a part of 'Operation Over-Watch' and refer them to the Sheriff for questions," instructed Lt. Carter. "Use everything at our disposal for this investigation. We are still in search of solid probable cause. No enforcement action should be taken on Foster at any time while we're in this phase. Get Tags on any of his vehicles and pass them along to the sheriff. We are compiling a list of anything he drives so they know to keep their distance from him. Remember; we believe Foster is a misguided disciple of Fenton's. If we are right about that, he will be heavily coached in avoiding detection from Law Enforcement. Do not underestimate his intelligence or his determination to survive. He will absolutely not go down quietly, so we have to be prepared to think through every angle. This portion of the investigation is the most crucial aspect; don't fuck it up."

"Yes sir," we echoed together.

"Dismissed," said Lt. Carter.

Everyone scattered to their desks while Lt. Carter stayed behind to speak with SSA Wells and Agent Jones.

I finished packing up the necessities from my desk into my gear bag. I was scheduled to cover the evening shift watching Foster's house. While I was in proximity to El Dorado, I was going to stay the night in a nearby hotel. I had to be there the next day for my next interview with Fenton anyways.

I reviewed my notes from the meeting and started thinking through what we would need to properly conduct the investigation. I had a pair of binoculars in my bag already next to my expensive Canon digital camera. The camera was equipped with a high power lens capable of capturing detailed photos from a ridiculous distance. The camera was mine; an investment I had made several years ago to aid in my investigation responsibilities.

I made a few additions to my notes and then checked my email.

"Shit, is that what I think it is?" I mumbled to myself.

I clicked on the top email and opened it.

Detective Bryant,

This is the audio recording from the phone call made to the number you provided me. It isn't paired to the video, but it should be the phone call you're looking for. I have spoken with people familiar with the subject, and can confirm it is the individual we spoke about earlier. The individual on the security footage is the individual speaking in this recording.

I hope this helps with your investigation.

Sincerely,

Frank De Luca

I double-clicked on the attachment and waited as the audio player loaded. I slipped on my headphones and made sure they were plugged in to my computer. I listened for a few seconds before I ripped off the headphones and returned to the conference room as fast as I could walk.

"Lieutenant, I have something you need to hear," I said. "Follow me."

Lt. Carter followed me back to my desk as Det. Shirley and Det. Ross got up from their desks and came to join us.

"I got a reply from the warden. He sent me the audio recording of the phone call we were looking for," I told the group.

I clicked play on the audio player and unplugged my headphones. I reached over to my speakers and turned the volume up as the file began to play.

Tim Lane: Hello

Foster: I have information on the body recovered from City Park this past week. I thought you might be interested.

Tim Lane: And who is this?

Foster: Let's just say I'm a concerned citizen who believes the people should know the truth.

Tim Lane: Well, that's what I do for a living; keep the people informed. What do you know?

Foster: I know the identity of the body they recovered.

Tim Lane: Really? Are you involved in the investigation somehow? I could really use someone close to this who could keep me a step ahead of the competition.

Foster: Like I said, I'm just a concerned citizen. Do you remember a girl who went missing in 2003 named Hayley Marten?

Tim Lane: Of course I remember her; I covered that story for weeks. What else can you tell me?

Foster: What else do you need?

Tim Lane: How can I verify this information? None of that information is public knowledge yet.

Foster: Lt. Carter is going to be your point of contact with the police department. I guarantee if you drop Hayley's name, he will immediately confirm it was her.

Tim Lane: He will?

Foster: His reaction will. The family is in the loop, keeping the information quiet at the bidding of the police.

Tim Lane: But why would the family keep it quiet?

Foster: You should ask them. Her father can be reached at 785-XXX-XXXX. You might catch him at work, but I'm sure he would be happy to have someone to talk to about this.

Tim Lane: I still don't understand why they would be keeping this quiet. How do you know all this information?

Foster: I'm close to someone in the investigation.

Tim Lane: Can I contact you if I have more questions about this story? Is 316-XXX-XXXX the best number to reach you during the day?

Foster: Shit

Tim Lane: What is it? Is there a problem?

Foster: Don't EVER fucking call this number. Do you hear me? I WILL FUCKING KILL YOU, if you call this number.

CLICK!!!

"Holy shit," Ross whispered.

"It is official; ladies and gentlemen, Foster just went from person of interest to suspect number one," announced Lt. Carter.

"I'll get this onto a disk and down to evidence," I said as I started shuffling through my desk.

"Bryant, Shirley; as soon as that audio is placed into evidence, get your asses to El Dorado. We have shit to do," Carter instructed.

———

Foster's home was nestled perfectly out of sight of the roadway. Although the plot of land wasn't massive, it encompassed enough acreage to keep the house secluded in a thick patch of woodlands. Everything about the location of the house threw up red flags. Using available online aerial photographs of the land, it showed thick woodlands surrounding the property with at least a fifty yard open area around three quarters of the house. The open area was confined to the front and sides facing the roadway. The open area was longest where the driveway led up to the house. To the unsuspecting observer, it looked like a well-manicured lawn. To me, it looked like a firing range. Everything was incredibly linear in nature. The driveway made two hard turns through a thin area of the woods which resulted in approaching vehicles having to slow way down to navigate the turns prior to approaching the house.

The gravel driveway was lined with a decorative fence-line. Nestled atop several of the fence-posts were small flags. The flags changed colors from darkest to lightest as they got further from the house. Again, to the casual observer, these might have appeared decorative, but they weren't. The flags became easier to see the further they were from the house. They were set to specific distances from the house and allowed an expert marksman to judge wind-speed at every distance. The driveway emerged from the roadway, what I estimated to be approximately three hundred yards from the house. As I sat in the passenger seat of the unmarked unit, I concluded it was a safe bet there were bullet holes in the fence-line and tree line. Nobody marked off a range in this much detail without practicing extensively.

The entrance to the driveway was isolated from the aerial

photographs. The trees hung over into the roadway and completely obscured the entrance. The mailbox wasn't even at the end of the drive-way. It was located nearly half-way up the block from the driveway.

Behind the house, nestled amongst the trees was an outbuilding of some sort, the aerial photos didn't provide much detail. According to public records, the house was a three bedroom, two bathroom home with a two car garage. All told, the house was approximately 1600 square feet.

There weren't a lot of good places to watch. The house was secluded, the driveway was obscured, and the gravel roadway outside of El Dorado was sparsely populated. Det. Shirley and I found a spot near a utility access point and did our best to reduce the vehicle's visibility from the roadway. This didn't leave us with much of a vantage point, but it was as good as we were going to do.

I was in the middle of shifting my legs, trying to get comfortable when my phone rang.

"Hello? Hey Dr. Elmore," I said, trying to hide my enthusiasm to speak with her.

"Hello, Detective Bryant; are we in professional mode at the moment?" she asked.

I could hear the smile in her voice and did my best to suppress one of my own.

"As a matter of fact, yes we are. What can I do for you?"

"I just wanted to call you and bring you up to date on the most recent victim evidence you brought me," she said.

"Absolutely," I replied. "I'm sorry I wasn't able to brief you on it in person while I was there."

"That's okay, Detective, my team brought me up to speed. I analyzed the clothing and rape kit they collected. I can confirm, Fenton's DNA was found on the body," she reported.

"That is good news. Will you be forwarding your report directly to Leavenworth County or sending it to me first?" I asked.

"I will be sending copies to you and Leavenworth County. It should be in your inbox now," she replied.

"Thank you, Dr. Elmore. I look forward to reading your report."

I hung up the phone, wishing I had the chance to speak with Dr. Elmore in private. Once again, my time was not my own. I glanced around, checking the area surrounding the vehicle. Detective Shirley, a consummate professional, was sitting quietly, sipping from a tall to-go cup of coffee.

We sat there for a while with the windows down, letting the breeze keep us cool. Even though we weren't that far outside the city of El Dorado, there was almost no traffic. The traffic that did go by didn't seem to notice us parked twenty feet or so off the roadway. The grass around us was getting tall enough to hide our sedan, whose silver paint wasn't doing much to help us blend in with the trees behind us.

We were parked in silence for nearly half an hour before the quiet buzzing of Det. Shirley's phone broke the silence.

"Hello?" She paused for a moment as she listed to the other end of the call. "Text a screen shot, if you can. Have we confirmed what he's driving?"

She stopped and pulled out her notepad from a jacket pocket, made a few quick notes, and then set the notepad between her legs in the driver's seat.

"Okay; thanks L.T." She hung up the phone and set it on the dashboard in front of the speedometer display.

"Anything new?" I asked.

"L.T. is texting me Foster's work schedule for the next week. He's driving a dark blue 1995 Ford F-150 with Kansas Tag XXXXXX."

Just then, her phone vibrated again.

"He works the 0700 to 1700 hours shift. He should have been off half an hour ago," she reported.

"Let's see if Agent Jones has eyes on him," I said, pulling out my phone.

"Hey Terry; are you still watching Foster?"

"Yeah, he left work right at 1700 hours and he stopped at a hardware store after that. He's been inside for a little while now. I'll keep you posted if he moves again," said Terry.

"Sounds good," I said, and hung up the phone.

"They have eyes on his vehicle at a hardware store at the moment," I told Det. Shirley.

"Did they say which one?" she asked.

"Terry didn't specify," I replied.

"Ok; if he had we could verify how far away they are. I'd love to get the drone in the air and get some up to date video of his land. We have a lot of unknowns at the moment," she said.

"Does he work tomorrow?"

She glanced down at her phone for a second and flipped to her text messages.

"Yeah, he does. Same shift," she replied.

"If I see him before I go into my meeting with Fenton, I'll call or shoot you a text. That should give you plenty of time to get here and get some new footage. We're going to need as many descriptors as possible when we go for our search warrant." I said.

"That works for me. I'll drop you off at the prison after lunch and double back here. If I get word from you on Foster's location, I'll get the drone airborne as soon as possible," she advised.

We sat there for hours, watching as nothing happened. The small talk burnt out after the first hour leaving us to take turns napping and watching.

The sun started to dip down below the trees as the nothingness stretched on for another hour. The sun went down, and still we waited; until 2200 hours rolled around.

"Something's off," said Detective Shirley.

"What do you mean?" I asked.

"I mean; who spends five hours at a hardware store on a Friday evening?"

"Maybe he works there," I suggested. "That doesn't sound right, though. I reviewed his personnel file; he wasn't listed as having secondary employment anywhere."

"Like I said, something's off," she said.

"I'll call Terry; maybe he forgot to let us know when Foster left," I said.

Terry picked up on the first ring.

"Terry, are you guys still at the hardware store?"

"Yeah, I'm staring right at Foster's truck. I don't know where the fuck he went. The hardware store has been closed since 2100 hours. His is the only vehicle in the parking lot. He doesn't work a night shift stocking shelves by any chance, does he?"

"Not according to his personnel file. Is there any chance he made you guys?"

"It's not likely. We followed at a distance and parked at the Wal-Mart across the street from the hardware store. We're surrounded by other cars, even now," advised Terry.

"What do you want to do? We haven't seen anything move out here in the past hour."

"Wells says we're going to sit and watch until the parking lot clears out enough that we lose our cover. Take another hour and then head to the hotel. We will try again in the morning," said Terry.

"10-4," I replied, and hung up the phone. "Terry says the truck hasn't moved yet. I'm beginning to agree with you; something if off."

"I wish this spot had a better view of the roadway. We've been sitting here watching for Foster's truck that we haven't been paying attention to any of the others as they go by. I'd say we try to figure a way to get tags as vehicles go by. We can start matching tags to local addresses and figure out who goes where. Anything is better than just sitting here waiting for one truck to go by."

"And we're certain that Foster only has the one vehicle?" I asked.

"According to the State of Kansas, he only has one vehicle registered in his name," she replied.

"Hmm," I mumbled.

"What are you thinking?" she asked.

"Does it fit the stereotype of someone attracted to Fenton's way of thinking to only have one vehicle?"

"Fenton lived for years outside of the normal conventions of the law. He never had a vehicle in his name and never got stopped for driving a car that wasn't his. Not only that, he had an impeccable driving record. What are the odds of someone living that squeaky clean while killing twenty plus people across five states?" She asked.

"I would venture to say it's highly improbable." I replied.

"How does someone live off the grid like that while working a seven to five job for the national prison system?" She wondered, out loud.

"Shit; you're right. We're missing something." I admitted.

CHAPTER TWENTY-EIGHT

I slept poorly that night. I was constantly harassed by hypotheticals, detailing what I might have missed the night before.

To top off all the unanswered questions, Terry reported that the truck was gone when he returned to the hardware store at 0600 hours. All the way past 2300 hours, we didn't see Foster come home. Terry and SSA Wells stayed in place watching the truck until after 0200 hours before they called it a night. I felt bad for Terry, making the fast turnaround to check on the vehicle so early in the morning. The whole situation spoke to the intricacy of the suspect we were watching. What we were seeing was extreme paranoia, extreme caution, or a heavy combination of the two.

To make the scenario even stranger, the warden confirmed Foster was at work; and that he had arrived in his blue truck. This saved me the awkward task of trying to text Det. Shirley as soon as I saw Foster that afternoon. Shirley and I went out to our spot from the day before so she could get the drone footage she wanted.

While Shirley had the drone in the air, I drove to every conceivable spot along the roadway and took photographs of everything I could around Foster's house. The view was still limited, but the massive zoom capabilities of my lens enabled me to get through some of the wooded area and get some pictures of the house. It was not the most effective use of our time, but it beat sitting around watching cars go by.

Shirley surprised me by having a battery powered camera with motion capture technology. She set it up on one of the utility poles along the roadway allowing it to capture footage of any vehicles going by. We were out on public property making it perfectly legal to have recording equipment set up. Our combined efforts along with the footage and photos collected made it seem like we had made a little progress that morning. We had a limited amount of time to do surveillance on Foster before the next Fenton case inevitably diverted most or all of our resources elsewhere.

————

It was hard to act as if nothing had changed as I went through security that afternoon. I had changed out of my dusty clothes from the morning surveillance, and was back in my standard slacks and button up shirt. I hadn't realized how often I had seen Foster as I was going through security over the past two months. He was always there, checking in my items and locking them in a locker. I was relieved when he handed me the key to the locker after I stepped through the metal detector. I hadn't brought anything with me dealing with our investigation of Foster, but I was suddenly more paranoid about this part of the process than I had ever been before.

It was a new feeling to be relieved when I reached the room where I met with Fenton. Typically my anxiety started as I reached the room, now it was slowly relieved as I passed through each door, leaving Foster behind at the security checkpoint.

I was in the room before I even realized it. My mind was so consumed with everything going on outside these walls that I was too distracted to even speak. I absentmindedly placed each of the required items on the table, sliding the pack of cigarettes over to Fenton last. I started the recorder and timer, and then sat back in my chair.

"Ah," he sighed, as be exhaled his first cloud of smoke, "My little piece of heaven."

I ignored him, and flipped open my notebook to the first blank page. Reaching into my jacket pocket, I took out a picture and slid it across the table until it was in front of Fenton.

"Do you recognize her?" I asked.

He studied the photo for a second. Holding it up with one hand, he took a long draw from his cigarette and removed it from his mouth with the other.

"There is something vaguely familiar about her," he replied.

"Her name is Michelle Wright. She is the prostitute from Council Bluffs, Iowa you told me about last week. The Leavenworth County Sheriff's Deputies located her body in the Missouri River the same month you said you put her there." I informed him.

He tilted his head out of apparent curiosity, "Leavenworth County; really? That's not very far. I was hoping she would float at least as far as Kansas City. You see, I'm still having trouble placing her. Do you have any pictures of the back of her head? I'm sure I'd remember her from that angle."

"Sorry," I replied, taking the photo back from him. "This headshot is the best I can do for you."

"It's amazing, you know? I can't remember what she looked like face to face, but I can still remember the way she felt, wrapped around my dick. Like I said, she was one of my favorites."

"Do you think it is possible, that the reason she was one of your favorites was that it was a consensual encounter? Granted, it was a solicited encounter, but consensual nonetheless," I said.

"Why do you think I mixed in a hooker from time to time? Not having to work for it was a nice change of pace. Sometimes a hunter gets tired of waiting in his tree stand, so he decides to go to the store and buy some hamburgers. You can take them back to your place and enjoy them at your leisure. You don't have to catch them, you don't have to clean them; it's just good old fashion American fun," he jested.

"So that's why you picked up a hooker; laziness?"

"I call it taking a day off. Sometimes you just want something with a big rack to show up at your hotel room, and volunteer to be mounted and stuffed. It's not laziness, its leisure." He insisted.

"So explain to me why you kill the hookers? There's a certain amount of self-preservation involved with killing your other victims after you kidnap and rape them, but why kill the hookers?" I asked.

"They are the face of the problem I intend to exterminate. Women are leeches. They suck a man dry, first in the backseat of the car, then in their marriage, then in their finances. When it's all said and done, women take everything a man has and then leave him for another man she claims has more time than the first. Over time, they work their way to a guy rich enough to give them the lifestyle they want. If not, they simply bleed a man dry, and then they discard him." He said, flicking his cigarette to emphasize his point.

"Did you ever consider the fact that not every woman is just like your mother?" I inquired.

"Of course I considered it; I've just never seen any evidence to the contrary." He replied.

"Maybe you haven't been looking in the right places," I suggested. "You're never going to meet a nice woman as long as you're paying for their time or abducting them in the middle of the night."

"Says you," he snapped back.

I was picking at a part of his personality I knew to be delicate and fragile. Fenton had long justified the shitty things he had done by blaming his mother or women in general. Pointing out that his approach had been doomed from the start, and destined to fall short of having any real meaning was, I hoped, a great way to get under his skin.

"So if you're trying to exterminate women then why would you ever pass one up? You said yourself last week that you could tell if a woman had a dog or a gun before you made an attempt to take them. Why didn't you devise a way to kill women everywhere you went?"

"That's easy," he replied. "If you are determined to kill all of them, you can't move on from one to the next until the last one is dead. If I can't pass a woman on the street without killing her, I would have been caught thirty years ago. I like to have my fun. What I did for all those years, bordered on simplicity. I pick off the easy ones and get my rocks off along the way. You don't put up my kind of hall-of-fame numbers by killing women willy-nilly."

"Can you speak about why you killed the ones you did? Was it body type? Did they remind you of someone? Or were they just the easiest targets you could find that couldn't fight back?" I asked.

"Yes; yes, yes; and of fucking course," he replied arrogantly. "My first taste of pussy was a tight little number from my home town, remember? It was both amazing and exhilarating. Just like a meth head, I was chasing that original high. I branched out a little as far as age range and hair color, but I was hoping to replicate that first pair of tits. My victims were all about the same height, weight; and within five or so years of age of that first girl I killed. That first girl didn't give a shit about me until I was choking the life out of her. In the final moment of a person's life, they care most about the person who holds the power over them. Terminal patients long to see the doctor or nurse deliver the drugs that might bring them relief. That doctor is the most important person in the world to that patient. On the opposite end of the spectrum, when you're killing someone, they care very much about you. They will say anything they can to get you to stop what you're doing. With every one of these girls, I held their attention at the end of their lives. I held the power; I had all the answers to all their questions. When they needed food, or water, or a good dicking, they told me so."

"You can't really expect me to believe any of these women asked for a, 'good dicking' as you put it in such douche-like fashion." I interjected, glaring at him.

"Well; not the ones I abducted. Those were more or less the ones asking me for water, food, freedom, bandages for their bleeding, to be let down from where they were hanging upside-down," he said. "It's amazing what can change someone's perspective. Being hung upside down by their hands and feet gave these women time to think about their pathetic lives. The world looks a lot different upside-down. These women were gifted the chance to see the world differently before they die. In a way, I did them a favor."

"I doubt that," I snapped.

"Of course I did," he replied, shaking his head at me. "People are so one-dimensional. They always have been. Perspective is really the only thing that separates people from one another. If the rich had the same perspective as the poor, don't you think they would do more to end poverty? If the government had the same perspective as the people, do you think things would be different? Of course they would be. This American experiment had reached the end of its time. People don't elect representatives; they elect puppets that will do the bidding of whoever has invested the most money into them. Puppets are the public persona of the puppet master hiding behind the curtain; nothing more. Sometimes the puppets speak for themselves, and the puppet masters have to silence those puppets. The days of America electing politicians that do the bidding of the people has been over for decades. The system is broken.

When a system is broken it must be torn down and rebuilt by those of us willing to do what is necessary. Anarchy is a truly beautiful thing to those of us who know how to live within its freedoms."

"So you're blaming a broken political system for your actions? Why didn't you try to start a cult or some kind of alternate civilization within the rules you think should exist?"

"I'll admit I have a way with people, but I'm no Charles Manson. Besides, I have no interest in turning one race against another. The government does that well enough already. Every now and again I came across a young mind capable of being molded to see the world through my eyes. I did the best I could with those people, but it's never enough. I have met people along my journey who believe what I believe, but there are never enough people willing to do what is necessary to change society. They say if you want to change the world, you must first change yourself. That's a crock of shit. I didn't change who I was, but the world changed anyways. If I had changed, it would have had no effect on the world."

"Thirty-plus women would still be alive if you had." I pointed out.

"But does anyone really miss those women?" He dismissed.

"I met a young man in his twenties this past week that missed his mother." I insisted. "He would have greatly appreciated you being different than you are."

"That's the thing though; no he wouldn't. He is the way he is because of me. If his whore of a mother was still around, he would have been a pariah, living on the outer fringes of society where his mother kept him. His mother died and as a result, he has a chance to be something in this world."

"So you're saying if your mother had died early in your life, you would be a different person?" I asked.

"Absolutely," he replied. "Women are only good for breeding purposes. Let's face it, without them the human race wouldn't exist. However, to your question, if my mother had died, say, when I was two or three years old, I would be a better man for it today."

"How do you figure?"

"Simple," he said with a shrug. "Women like my mother exist for only two purposes past childbirth; to soften their children, rendering them incapable of surviving in this cruel world, or tainting their son's image of what women should be. My father was a pathetic man, but he was her masterpiece. She twisted him into the cynical, angry, resentful son of a bitch he was. Take her out of the question, and what happens? My father works to raise his kid. He bears the responsibility alone and is forced to thrive in order to provide for his child. My mother stole that opportunity from him."

"So in your twisted version of logic, you can blame your mother for all of her choices, and all of your fathers?" I asked.

"Of course not, my father made his choices, but my mother never even gave him a chance," he insisted.

I sat back and shook my head at him. "It seems like you're making all the excuses for your father and none for your mother. Would it not be a simpler perspective to say that they were two imperfect people who could have and should have done better in life? Think about it; if they don't settle for each other, you never exist. It sounds like everybody wins in that scenario."

"But when someone twists your world and manipulates your emotions making you think you need them, that person is the problem," he said.

I could feel the conversation beginning to turn back on itself. Fenton was never going to admit his way of thinking was flawed, even slightly. His logic spat in the face of personal responsibility, and freedom will. Every choice had consequences. Fenton didn't believe in consequences, so it was impossible for him to see the flaw in his logic, or the error of his father's ways.

The world was full of people who made the wrong decisions in one way or another. It was also full of people who were making the best of their circumstances in spite of their poor choices. A shotgun wedding could end in divorce just as it could result in a long, happy marriage. People could make any situation better if they truly made an effort. Fenton thought everyone had the responsibility not to be a victim of someone else, but also believed he was a victim of his upbringing who could not escape the mistakes of his parents. Again; totally illogical, but then again, so was everything else he had done in life.

"Well I feel like we're not making any progress in this conversation, so why don't we switch and talk about your next confession." I suggested.

"I don't really see any of what I say here as a confession. If it was, I would be begging for something in return or hoping for leniency in my other cases," he replied.

"You are literally begging to have your stories told in book format so that your miserable existence can be twisted into some level of infamy." I replied. "Once again, you are doing the exact opposite of what you claim."

"There's a big difference between begging and bargaining. Begging means I have given up, and hope to find some measure of mercy in the twisted system that has already sentenced me to death, three times. I have bargained to hold you captive for three hours a week, I have bargained to have my stories told so that the world will know how much I have accomplished. Nothing I do will ever amount to begging; and fuck you for suggesting it has," he said.

"It's funny," I said with a slight smile. "It still sounds like begging to me."

"Why don't you go kill yourself, detective? Become another statistic. You certainly aren't bringing anything to the table today," he snarled.

"Why don't we bargain for another one of your stories?" I asked.

"Why don't you lose your fucking tone?"

"Why don't I go home and print off a copy of your story, just so I can burn it? You aren't satisfied with your life; that's why you gave us a list of demands. Your life never held the meaning you wanted, so you had to turn to the very system you hate so much in order to find an ounce of self-worth. You went to death row for less than a third of the people you were convicted of killing; which was less than a third of the people you actually killed. Now you bargain with us as if having a story about yourself will somehow give you meaning; it won't. People will still make their own judgement about you. Sick people will find another kindred spirit to credit for all the sick shit they do. They don't need you, no one ever has. The one redeeming quality these meetings of ours have is that you're giving people closure. It may be the only good thing you've ever done in your life, but it means something to a lot of people. I know that's not why you are doing this; but it is entirely why I am doing this. Your story lives on so that the families of your victims know the end of each of their stories as well."

"Don't try to make this into something it isn't. I do this for me; my infamy is my only motivator in this agreement," he insisted.

"And closure for the families is the only reason I do this," I replied. "It's time to realize that though our motivations are different, our end result is the same."

"I just realized; you're an asshole."

"It took you ten years to figure that out?" I asked. "Maybe you're not the smartest person in the room today."

"No; I just like making sure you're aware, that I am always the smartest person in the room."

"So why don't you tell me where I'm going next?"

"As if it is ever going to be that easy," he insisted.

He sat back and lit a cigarette, blowing big, white, clouds of smoke in my face. I checked the time on the stopwatch, regretting my decision as soon as I saw how much time was left.

"You should really start caring less about how much time you have left, and more on the weight of what you're being given. There are hundreds of real writers out there who would turn my life into a bestseller. People like you don't appreciate what you have until it's gone. I assume you have quite a bit of experience in that area," he asked?

"I have enough," I replied.

"I've met a lot of people like you in my time," he said, letting the smoke roll slowly out his nostrils. "My time in Cass County was spent largely organizing and participating in search parties for women I had already buried. You have no idea how it feels to know you're wasting your time until you're searching for a person you know for sure is already dead. It's difficult to be professional; it's difficult to be personable. Everyone is looking to you for answers that you are intentionally withholding. I did this, not once, but three times. The area surrounding Atlantic, Iowa was a target rich environment. There was a small population, but they all congregated into the towns for school, church or community events. I could mark multiple women for attention without so much as following them home. I had community and criminal records at my disposal while I was a deputy. Think of all the fun you could have with the advances in technology. Someone like me would have an absolute fucking field day in your position. All the runaway juveniles and all the drug addicts before they get the meth mouth and the heroin track marks all over their body; they would be like fish in a barrel."

"That's precisely why people like you shouldn't be in my position," I insisted. "Not only are you there to abuse the system, but you're there to victimize people already in difficult positions."

"That's why it would be so much fun." He replied, with a short laugh.

I exhaled in frustration and shifted in my seat.

"As it so happened," he continued. "When I was in your position, I had plenty of opportunity to do what I do best. It was the most relaxed hunting I've ever done. Women would show up on my radar by their own fruition, and then I'd have a full set of contact information at my disposal. Then they would go missing; and no one would be surprised. The search for those girls would be over in a matter of days. Some of them I held for weeks at a time. I found it to be an amazing accomplishment to hold a woman for as long as possible. I couldn't tell you what my record is, but I'm positive I've held women for as much a year before. When no one is looking, and no one knows where to look, it gets pretty easy to just have them locked away for your own personal use."

"Was that a frequent technique you would use?"

"As often as I could," he replied. "Every now and again there's too much heat to keep someone; the other times it was all a matter of location. If you know where to go and you know where to stay, you can make a killing."

"Do you care to elaborate?" I asked.

"I can expound on that a little bit," he said. "The longer I'm in an area, the more prepared I become. I can find the most isolated locations to keep a girl until I've taken all I can from her, and then find the perfect spot to leave her. It was the second biggest rush I could find in my endeavors. The biggest is obviously the moment I take a woman from her home or neighborhood and steal her away to a second location. It's like driving around with the world's biggest secret tied up in the back of your vehicle. It's a thrill to move a girl around town, driving past the police station or through a sobriety checkpoint. Over time I started to really challenge myself to find the toughest route to drive. It's a rush similar to blowing a load without having to change your pants."

"So you were starting to get bored with your exploits? When did that occur?"

"It would come and go over time," he replied. "If holding a woman for months at a time wasn't doing it for me anymore, I would challenge myself to return to the location of another body and try to leave a another one. That's why I love piling bodies into a shallow grave, to see how many I can collect in one spot."

"Well I've seen two different gravesites with four bodies in them and one with five; is that the most you ever did?" I asked.

"Unfortunately," he answered with an evil grin. "That question transitions us perfectly into your next destination."

"I'm all ears," I said, encouraging him to speak further.

"I hid at least four bodies on at least six or seven different occasions," he explained. "If you're trying to do that math, you're still a mass grave or two short."

I couldn't help shaking my head as I made a note of this statement. Fenton had been convicted for eleven murders, eight of which had been found, in just two graves. Irvingdale had consisted of a pile of five bodies in total. Knowing there were this many more mass graves was disheartening. It meant the numbers I had estimated Fenton having where still short of the grand total.

"I can tell you're impressed with this latest revelation," he sneered. "I can promise you, the next place you're going will be quite effective at clearing a list of missing person cases. This time, there will be five of them. One of them," he paused for emphasis, "has already given you a leg up in your investigation."

I thought for a moment. He was clearly trying to drop a vague hint he thought to be clever. A thought occurred to me, making me both hopeful, and hesitant.

"Are you speaking of the bone we found in Jessica's casket?" I asked.

"Very good detective," he said, pausing to awkwardly clap his restrained hands a few times. "Keep earning that government paycheck. That is the very leg I speak of. That one was unique because I had already achieved a rare accomplishment. I had five bodies in one grave; I was excited to add another. Unfortunately the sixth body was Jessica Childress and I had special plans for her. To top it all off, I had to dispose of the seventh body I wanted by burning the good doctor in Jessica's place. Unfortunately, that was not the day I would reach six bodies in one grave. It had taken me years to reach five bodies; imagine my disgust at having to discard the next two in such a manner and then leave town. My dream was to have a grave so full, that instead of digging everyone up, they just decided to build a fence around them and start a graveyard. Alas; it was not to be."

"What can you tell me about the five women in the graves?" I asked. I was hoping to redirect him back to the subject matter at hand to reduce the amount of time he spent relaying his sick fantasies.

"Well; like I was telling you before. This was all a part of my exploits during my stint as a Cass County deputy. Some of the girls were the runaways and troubled youth I described earlier. Others were just tight pieces of ass I saw around town. Like I said; it was a target rich environment," he said.

"So where can I find these women?" I asked.

"That's my favorite part," he replied. "You're headed back to Cass County. There are five women buried side by side on the west side of Lake Anita in Lake Anita State Park. They are about a hundred paces from the edge of the lake. This grave is almost perfectly centered from north to south on the west side of the lake. I am giving you very specific directions this time for one reason, and one reason only; you will have a short window of time to retrieve these bodies. There are not enough Park Rangers in this particular State Park to handle a major homicide investigation. They will immediately refer this case to the Cass County Sheriff for investigation. You know who the sheriff is, and you know of his family connections. The park rangers won't step on their toes, and I already told you about the Carroll family's connections with the local FBI. One of the women in that grave ties Jessica Childress to me, and then to the Carroll family. One grave might have been located on accident, but having both graves connected to me ensured the connection to the Carroll family, through me, cannot be disputed. You can tie the baby Jessica is carrying to Simon Carroll, and you can tie all the bodies in the second grave to me. It reinforces the assertion that I am the deputy seen on the little home video I left in Jessica's casket, and that I acted at the bidding of the Carroll family. I can't do much to help you beyond that."

"Why did you take so much time to frame the Carroll family? I thought out of everyone, you would find a way to appreciate the corruption," I said.

"Normally I would," he admitted. "The problem with the Carroll family is that they didn't allow outsiders to prosper beyond what they deemed necessary. If I'm going to be involved in something that organized, I want to be the one holding the wheel. They had the whole organization locked up already. They had plenty of need for errand boys, but not much for people with my level of ambition. They kept me out of the inner circle, so I stashed their dirty laundry all around the county in order to burn down their little playhouse when they least expect it."

"So you don't have a problem with that level of corruption as long as you're the one in charge?"

"That sounds about right," he replied. "It's more than that, however. I believe the whole system is corrupt. I believe the system is broken and twisted to favor the powerful and rich, over everyone else. The Carroll family became powerful and rich and they had the privilege of becoming untouchable over time. I hate the system, but its people who use the system like them that make the system a total fucking shit-show. If it's broken, fix it or fuck it; don't play around in it. Again, I'd have done it if I were in their position; but I'm not."

"So once again you're speaking against something you would gladly do until it doesn't benefit you, so then it's the enemy?"

"Precisely," he replied.

"The irony is that you would fit comfortably into the political environment that's popular today," I said. "Everyone wants to tell others what to do, as long as no one is telling them what to do. Everyone wants the benefits of canceling everyone else as long as they can proceed uninterrupted. Believe it or not, you're almost qualified to be a politician."

"There's just one problem," he said.

"What's that?"

"I'm open and honest about my sexual predilections and interests; politicians like to hide their pedophilia."

CHAPTER TWENTY-NINE

I had grown accustomed to the solitary drive home after meeting with Fenton. After six weeks, this was the first time I wasn't making the trip alone. Det. Shirley was waiting for me as I stepped outside into the sunlight. After all this time, it was still a struggle to ascend from the dark depths of solitary confinement and step back out into the daylight.

Det. Shirley was leaned against the grill of the car, waiting for me as if I was getting out of prison myself. She was rocking a gray power suit that was tailored to perfection for her tall, slender frame. She gave me a head nod after taking a sip from her go-cup of coffee.

"Did you remember to say hi to Satan for me?" She asked with a smirk.

"I do everything I can to avoid talking about women he hasn't killed. He has a tendency to get really graphic without it being within the context of a friend and/or coworker; I'd hate to give him another person to objectify," I replied as I circled the car.

"That's awfully chivalrous of you," she said, strolling to the driver's door.

"I don't do it out of chivalry; believe me. I do it to protect my ears. Some of the shit that comes out of that guy's mouth is enough to give me nightmares." I told her as I stood next to my open door. "Do you remember my trip to Iowa a couple weeks ago?"

"Yep," she replied climbing into the car and closing the door, "Teenager in the casket, right?"

"That's the one. He left a video of him raping her for our viewing torture." I said.

"That's fucked up; even for him," she admitted.

"I know it," I replied as she turned the car towards the gate. "He's made several comments about writing portions of the books so he can ensure they're about him more than they are about our investigations. I hope to God he doesn't follow up on that. I really don't want to have to proofread his rape stories for grammatical errors."

"Won't the publisher be the one to do that?" She asked, watching as the gate opened slowly.

"The structure of these stories is largely up to me," I replied. "If he demands to have his own input, there's going to be serious issues making this available to the public. I don't even want this to be public information; if he adds his two cents, I wouldn't even want it published as research for law enforcement purposes."

"I hear you there," she replied.

"Are there any new developments on the Foster investigation?" I asked.

"That's what we're about to find out," she replied. "Wells and Jones want to meet us. They said they had some kind of development."

"Any idea what it is?"

"If I did, we could do this over the phone," she replied. "What I do know is that Wells called me an hour ago and asked for every detail I had from the aerial footage we got from the drone yesterday. I even emailed him some of the photos you took this morning. He didn't give me any details."

The drive was longer than I expected. We were on the road for over twenty minutes until we reached a small town called Bel Aire, Kansas. Det. Shirley maneuvered the car in next to Wells' Town car and parked in front of the City of Bel Aire building on North Cambridge St.

Wells and Jones were waiting for us, standing on the sidewalk in front of their car. They were each holding file folders, and were deep in conversation.

"Bryant, Shirley; thank you for meeting us here," said Wells. "We have a lot to go over and very little time. Wichita Police is in the process of getting a search warrant signed for Foster's residence."

"How? We don't even have probable cause enough to take action." I wondered.

"But they do," Wells replied. "We stumbled into the middle of something without even trying. Last night, a nine year old girl was kidnapped from her front yard on the south side of Wichita."

Wells handed me a file and indicated for me to share it with Det. Shirley.

"This is D'Arriana Quincey. She was playing in the front yard of her house with her three older siblings. At approximately 2000 hours last night, an unidentified white male approached the house on foot. The male asked for help locating a lost dog and asked the kids to help. The kids split up to help find the dog, D'Arriana went with the suspect to knock on some of the neighbors houses. They knocked on two doors until they were a few houses down the street. D'Arriana's oldest brother reported when he had finished checking in the alley behind the houses, he circled the block in time to see the suspect forcing D'Arriana into an SUV. He chased after the car for nearly four blocks before he lost sight of it. He managed to get a partial tag on the vehicle. Detectives just got done confirming with one of the gas stations nearby and they got the complete tag to the vehicle. The 10-27 is in your file folder," advised Wells.

"This is coming back to an LLC," observed Det. Shirley, examining the State Tag printout.

"Registered right here in the city of Bel Aire. We just confirmed with Wichita Detectives; the LLC has one person on the record," said Agent Jones.

"Foster?" I asked.

"Correct," Wells responded. "Foster is the sole proprietor of the LLC listed for that tag. We caught up with the hardware store where we lost Foster yesterday. He wasn't dodging us, he was switching vehicles. They have him on video buying a shirt and pants matching the suspect descriptors from the kidnapping. Then he exits the store through a side entrance and gets into the vehicle the suspect used to kidnap D'Arriana."

"So it's been less than 24 hours since she was taken?" asked Det. Shirley.

"Correct," Wells replied.

"Any reason to believe he knows we're onto him?" I inquired.

"Darius Quincey, D'Arriana's older brother said the vehicle appeared to be traveling the speed limit and was stopping carefully at every stop sign and light. Either Foster was playing it safe, or he didn't know he was being followed. It was near dusk at the time, so it's very possible he didn't see a sixteen year old kid chasing him from half a block away," Jones advised.

"What's our time frame?" I asked.

"They're assembling their TAC Team and bomb squad for a team entry. They were grateful for our help. The timing is beyond coincidental. We advised them what we were investigating and gave them all our suspicions, especially the part about his bomb training and marksmanship," said Wells.

"How did you even hear about this?" asked Shirley. "And how was he not picked up before he left work?"

"We were at the Wichita FBI office and heard all about it. The connections started adding up so we met with Wichita PD and have been advising ever since. We didn't know anything definitive until about an hour ago. There was no way to know it was Foster before he left work. No one has seen him since, and they have local ATL's and BOLO's out for him already. It's been a busy afternoon," said Jones.

"This is an unexpected opportunity for us," stated Wells. "Wichita PD and the Wichita FBI office have graciously allowed us to tag along."

"What's our part in this?" I asked.

"We are the last ones to hit the scene. TAC and bomb team are breaching and securing the scene. Once they've got it secured and they have what they need for this investigation, we can enter the scene and look around. The parameters for the search aren't ideal for us. The warrant dictates we can search anywhere a nine year old girl could be hidden. That doesn't give us much to work with, but it's better than what we had," said Wells.

"When do we start?" asked Shirley.

"Gear up," instructed Wells. "They have people in route to Foster's residence to begin surveillance as we speak. They're dropping a sniper team to ingress and start surveillance on the house. They have their drone team in route as well."

"Let's, fucking do this," I said.

We looked out of place gearing up in front of the Bel Aire City Hall. Det. Shirley popped the trunk to allow us access to our plate carriers and gear. We opted to leave the rifles in the trunk, locked into place. We weren't going in first, rifles weren't necessary. I tightened the Velcro strap on my vest into place and slid two extra magazines into place in the front pockets. We packed fairly light given our limited involvement. Wells and Jones, on the other hand, looked like they were getting ready to breach a terrorist compound.

The FBI patches on their vests stood out from a great distance, removing any doubt in people's minds if we were law enforcement. They packed their vests to the max complete with Tasers, handcuffs, OC spray, and extra rifle magazines.

"Hey fella's; you know we're not the ones breaching the door, right?" I asked, casually.

Terry looked at us for a second before looking down at his loadout. He sheepishly unslung the rifle from its location, hanging from his neck.

"We don't get to do much in the way of tactical shit," he admitted. "Sometimes we get a little excited."

I smiled and shook my head. Terry's enthusiasm was contagious. It was a lot easier to be optimistic when the people around you have a positive outlook on the situation.

We piled back into the vehicles, and headed back towards El Dorado. The trip was much less comfortable this time. The gear was designed for a lot of purposes, but comfort was usually the lowest priority.

———

We met the Wichita TAC team a few miles from Foster's house. For as much as we had geared up, they had gone to the extreme. Unfortunately, this was a necessity for them. The team was facing a myriad of unknowns as they prepared to serve the search warrant. The biggest problem was resolving the issue of safely breaching the house without putting the child, believed to be inside, at risk.

The TAC team had been briefed on the explosion at City Park which had claimed Officer Preston's life. Unfortunately again, there were few details available to us regarding the makeup of the bomb used in that incident. The TAC team discussed at length the issues of proceeding with caution, maintaining the element of surprise, and saving the nine year old girl being held.

There were no records of Foster's house on file with anyone who could help us. He had built the house himself, leaving everything about its interior in question.

I hated being on the outside looking in at times like this. The TAC teams, along with Butler County Deputies, were the only ones going in with the first wave. Butler County held jurisdiction, and was involved to ensure the warrant was being properly executed in their county. Even still, they were at the end of the line of people standing by to serve the warrant.

The TAC team piled into an armored personnel carrier, utilized for situations like this one, and started down the roadway. Everyone not involved in the initial contact held back for several minutes.

This was the most difficult part about working in someone else's jurisdiction. Everything we did was on their timeline, and our involvement was already set to be the bare minimum.

The team was using a closed circuit communication system to organize. Knowing Foster's level of preparation and paranoia, it was safe to assume he would have a police scanner. In a far worse scenario, radio traffic could trigger a bomb if it was wired to a radio transmitted detonator. The system in use utilized cell phone towers and communicated like a huge conference call. Members of the team had the comm. system for communicating; the rest of us had a receiver on the hood of one of the Butler County Sheriff's Deputy's patrol units. We gathered around the patrol unit and strained to hear everything as it was broadcast.

"TAC team is one minute out, sniper one; report."

"Sniper one; no movement; going on 73 minutes; covering front entry and west side including out-building."

"Sniper two: report."

"Sniper two: No movement; front entry and east side covered. No open space on the north side of the house."

"TAC team is thirty seconds out. All units lock and load. Bomb team personnel take point to breach the front door, TAC team fan out and find cover."

"TAC team is on scene, headed up the driveway."

"Squad one, break out in 10, 9, 8, 7, 6, 5, 4, 3, 2, 1, GO! GO! GO!"

"Squad two, GO!"

"Squad one, camera deployed, breaching the front door."

"Squad two, camera deployed; front window, west side."

"Squad one, has clear visual inside the residence. Front door breached."

"POLICE DEPARTMENT!"

"Kitchen and dining room are clear."

"Squad two has eyes through a window on the west side of the house."

"Bedroom, southeast corner; clear."

"Bedroom; northeast corner is clear."

"POLICE DEPARTMENT! SHOW ME YOUR HANDS."

"Squad one has eyes on the girl. Dispatch EMS as close as we can get them to the house. We're bringing her out. Dispatch, let EMS know she needs to be treated for asphyxiation. She had a plastic bag over her head."

"DISPATCH WE HAVE A PULSE. SEND IN ANOTHER UNIT THAT CAN TRANSPORT HER TO AN AMBULANCE."

Behind us, we could hear another patrol unit disappearing around the corner. The unit had thrown gravel as soon as they heard the request for EMS.

"Thank you, Jesus," whispered SSA Wells.

"Does something seem off to anyone?" I asked.

"They found her with a pulse, but there's been no sign of Foster," answered Shirley.

"Which means he can't have been gone for long," I said. "That house has been under surveillance for over an hour."

"We'll know more when we get inside," said Wells. We all turned back to the hood of the car, listening intently as the search continued.

We all ducked our heads a little as an ambulance drove by, kicking up dust as it went past us, and down the road.

"Preliminary search is complete. Squad 2, fan out and check the surrounding area. Two by two everyone; nobody goes anywhere alone."

"Squad one, start secondary search of the house."

Everything went silent for several minutes. The silence carried on for so long the dispatcher started checking everyone's status.

"Squad one leader, are you 10-4?"

"We're 10-4 dispatch."

"Squad two leader, are you 10-4?"

"10-4 dispatch, we're checking the outbuilding right now."

"10-4, Squad leaders."

"Squad two to squad one, can you send us a bomb technician?"

"10-4 squad two, what do you have out there?"

"This outbuilding is full of guns and ammunition, and it's wired to blow on a timer."

"Squad two, withdraw immediately. Respond to the main house and assist in the final search."

"Squad one bomb techs, give me a status update on that bomb as soon as you can."

"Bomb team is direct, in route to the outbuilding."

"Squad leaders; the Captain has instructed all unnecessary personnel to evacuate the area."

"Terry do you have a decent camera?" I asked.

Terry looked up at me from his spot opposite me across the hood of the patrol unit.

"Yeah I do," he replied.

"Wells, I think we're going to have a limited window of time to check for evidence in the house and outbuilding. I'm requesting permission for Terry, and I to get in position at the end of the driveway so we can get in there, photograph anything we can and collect evidence if we find it," I requested.

"Take your car and get into position. I'll call you in a minute as soon as I know if we're going to be able to get in there," said Wells.

"Let's go, Terry; we only have one shot at this."

Terry ran to his vehicle to retrieve his camera. Det. Shirley tossed me the keys to our car.

"Good luck," she said.

I ran to our vehicle and pulled out my camera from the trunk. I tossed the sling around my neck and climbed into the driver's seat. Terry joined me seconds later, and together we tore off down the road towards Foster's house.

Terry's phone rang just as we were reaching the end of Foster's driveway.

"Hello? Understood," he said, and hung up the phone.

"Wells says the bomb is set to go off in eleven minutes, we have six minutes to get to the house, do our best, and get out," he said.

"Hell yeah," I replied.

We tore up the driveway and navigated the hard ninety degree turns in the tree line before we hit the straight-away headed towards the house. We parked near the armored vehicle in a way that no one would be blocked in, and jumped out.

A man approached us in what appeared to be a massive space suit. The bomb suit consisted of heavy gray material with a massive video game-like helmet to go with it. The man inside was clearly sweating profusely, pulling out a handkerchief; he lifted his helmet to sponge off his face as he reached us.

"You must be Agent Jones and Detective Bryant. I'm Lieutenant Snyder with Wichita Police. One of you will go with me to the outbuilding; the other will go meet Sgt. Sims at the front door. We have five minutes and fifteen seconds; after that, we will haul you out of here."

"I'll go with the L.T.," I said.

"Done, let's do this gentleman."

I jogged after the Lieutenant around the side of the house.

The outbuilding was an all metal structure with tan metal siding and a green metal roof. A single garage door was centered perfectly on the face of the building with an entry door on the far right side of the building. Both doors were open as members of the bomb team, dressed identically to Lt. Snyder, slipped out of building and congregated to our right as we approached. I paused briefly to get one good, overall photo of the building, before chasing after the Lieutenant again.

"Detective Bryant, start here at the open garage door and take some photos while I brief you on the situation," Snyder instructed.

I immediately started snapping photos, starting on my left and panning slowly around to my right.

"Every crate, every table, every pile of ammunition in this building is located on top of a pressure plate switch. If anything is lifted, shifted or moved from its location, the bombs will detonate prematurely. Do not touch anything without my say-so. The floor is concrete and we haven't found any other forms of booby traps or trip wires during our search. If I tell you to run, you fucking boogaloo, do you understand? If you have a question, I am here. If you have evidence you deem necessary for the purpose of your investigation, tell me, I will ensure it is safe to collect, and collect if for you. If you don't have any questions, you can enter the building," he instructed.

I stepped in and continued snapping photos as fast as I could. Most of the building was just as Snyder had described. Ammo was stacked on pallets and shelves, and guns lined the walls. All the guns had what appeared to be anti-theft devices on them. The guns were wired to the anti-theft devices which had cables running into the walls at centric points in the middle of each group of guns. None of the guns could be touch without potentially triggering an explosion.

I circled inside the building until I reached the back wall.

"Four minutes, Bryant," called Snyder from his place five feet behind me.

The back wall was lined with a large wooden desk, complete with a set of tools on the wall over the top. The desk area appeared to be the only spot in the building not plastered in miscellaneous guns and ammunition. I kept the camera snapping photos as I slowly approached the desk.

"Lieutenant, can we collect the diagrams and blueprints on the back wall?"

"Stand aside and let me check."

I stepped to my right to allow Snyder access to the desk and all it contained. I looked up as I kept the camera going, the flash illuminating the dimly lit area around the desk. Snyder pulled out a small, square mirror on an extendable handle and began checking around, behind and underneath everything on the desk.

"Can you look over my shoulder, Detective?"

I approached Snyder from his right side before answering.

"Yes I can," I replied.

"Turn the flash off on your camera. If you can see my mirror, I have it tucked slightly behind one of the diagrams on the board. Do you see the small round black object sticking out of the pegboard behind the paper? It's a small light sensitive photo-eye. It's designed to trigger outdoor lighting when the sun goes down."

"I can see it," I answered, "Why would he have that behind paper on his board?"

"If he knows how to reverse the setting on those sensors, he can switch it to send a signal when it sees light, rather than when it doesn't. I can't know for sure, but I believe he has these set up to ensure nothing he has on the board here can be taken without triggering something. All the wiring for this is behind the board so there's no way to trace it. If we could find the switch, we could collect all these documents, but we don't have the time."

I looked down for a moment as I changed the setting on my camera.

"The lighting in here is shit," I observed.

"He did that for a reason. A bright flash of light could have set off one of these sensors. He knew if the lighting sucked we'd come in with flashlights. He would have killed an entire squad if we had waited until after dark to serve this warrant. Photograph everything you can on the board without the flash. From what I can see, they appear to be wiring and design schematics for explosive devices."

"If you find anything detailing car bombs with triggers on the doors, let me know. That's the kind we suspect was used to kill my officer." I instructed.

"You got it," he replied, "Three minutes left."

The lighting was truly shit. I got as close as I dared to the desk and zoomed in on each piece of paper to take the best photo I could manage. There were too many of them. I had to stop taking photos of each one and start taking photos of three or four of them with an over-all shot.

The desk was neatly organized with containers of miscellaneous hardware, parts and pieces. I photographed them the best that I could, but once again, there were too many to document.

"Two minutes," called Snyder.

I did my best to quicken my pace. The need to be thorough was quickly being replaced with my need to get as much documented as I could. I made my way down the desk, which was nearly thirty feet long, spanning the length of the back wall. Snyder was several feet ahead of me checking everything he could to ensure I wasn't walking into an explosion.

"Bryant, I think I found what you are looking for," he called out to me.

I increased my pace yet again and kept snapping photos as I approached him.

"That looks a bit like what you described. Did the car bomb you experienced involve an aerosol dispersant with a trigger wired to the door?" he asked.

"That sounds about right. I know it used an aerosol dispersant which had been somehow contained in the vehicle. It went off as soon as one of the doors was opened," I replied, listening to the shutter of the camera as it captured a blurry picture of the diagram Snyder was indicating.

The diagram was one of several detailing how an explosion of that nature could be replicated.

My understanding of bomb making was extremely limited, but I could understand enough to confirm my belief that Foster had been the one to plant the bomb in Tim Lane's car in City Park. I photographed the diagrams repeatedly, doing my best not to block the small amount of light available in the building.

"We're out of time, Detective," advised Snyder.

"Fuck," I muttered under my breath. I had barely been through half of the building in the time I had allotted to me. I followed Snyder towards the door, snapping pictures as I went.

Lt. Snyder picked up his pace as soon as we reached the door. I jogged to keep up with him as he proved to be more agile in the space suit than I would have guessed.

Right on time, Terry stepped out of the front door and jogged to keep up with his member of the bomb team. Terry and I were quickly escorted to our car before Snyder and his Sergeant broke off and jumped into the armored vehicle.

I had left the ignition on allowing me to throw the car into drive as soon as the doors closed. We retreated down the driveway like we were being shot at, and turned up the road towards the rest of the team.

The armored vehicle was right on our bumper as we cruised down the gravel road away from Foster's residence.

"Was there anything interesting in the house?" I asked.

"Fuck yeah," he answered. "That dude puts preppers to shame. He had stockpiles of emergency rations, guns and ammunition all over that house. He could have holed up in any room of that house for weeks as a time if he wanted to, but that isn't the best part. They found a tunnel. It leads from the crawl space under the house to a shed back in the woods. The whole reason he has three quarters of the area around his house wide open is so he can sneak out through the woods behind the house. If the woods weren't an option, he had a tunnel. Apparently they found tire tracks leaving through the woods in the back. We didn't have enough people on the team to surround the entire block to prevent his escape."

"So he had another car hidden in the woods and didn't even have to use his driveway to get to his house? No wonder we didn't see him go by with a nine year old girl in the car. He didn't even pass us." I said as we reached the rest of the team.

We jumped out and joined the rest of the team as they gathered in front of the armored vehicle.

"We have less than sixty seconds until that ammo dump goes up in flames. Have we cleared all the neighbors out?" asked Lt. Snyder.

"Yes sir," replied one of the other officers. "The last team just cleared the final house on the next block. All affected persons in the area have been evacuated."

"County Fire is already in route to this location. To a certain extent, we're going to have to let that building burn until we can be sure the ammo has all gone off. We will not be risking emergency personnel trying to preserve a crime scene. As long as the fire is contained to the suspect's property, we won't be approaching any time soon. Do we have any updates on the girl?" asked Snyder.

"Yes sir," answered another officer from the back of the group. "EMS is treating her and monitoring her for lingering effects of asphyxiation. We found her with a plastic bag zip-tied over her head. She managed to chew a small hole in the plastic. It doesn't look like he took the time to do the job properly. We believe we just barely missed him."

"Make sure the bag, ties and restraints we found on her are entered into evidence as soon as possible. I want results as fast as we can get them," instructed Snyder. "Everyone get their body worn cameras docked and get their photos into evidence as quickly as you can. Investigations' wants to review every bit of potential evidence against this guy as soon as it's in the system. Bryant and Agent Jones, send me those photos as soon as you can. We will do the same for you; whatever we can do to aid in your investigation, let us know; any questions?"

"Dismissed," hollered Sgt. Sims.

SSA Wells waived us over as the crowd began to disperse. "Let's head back to Manhattan. We're going to do a full debrief before we all go our separate ways." In the distance, the sound of the explosion made everyone jump, and duck their heads a little. My ears rang slightly as I got back in the car, thankful I had been nowhere close when it went off.

CHAPTER THIRTY

The best part about conducting a meeting on a Sunday evening is the peace and quiet. The department was void of usual personnel working a standard eight to five. I had spent the rest of the day there, typing up my report from my recent meeting with Fenton, and reviewing the photos from Foster's house.

Terry and SSA Wells had occupied the conference room, using it as an extra office for the day. I reviewed reports on everything related to Foster, and the triple homicide at the park. We had evidence to suggest that Foster had been responsible for the bomb, but we were still working to gather enough to write up an affidavit for an arrest warrant.

Wichita Police had everything they needed to issue an arrest warrant for Foster. If we were lucky, someone would pick him up on the kidnapping charges from Wichita, allowing us the additional time to finish getting evidence back which might support our own charges against him. Lt. Carter advised the team that the chief of police would be requesting a "no bond" warrant for Foster when the time came.

It was hard to change gears from the Foster investigation to the looming investigation into Fenton's latest confession. It took all day Sunday to complete paperwork and evidence for the Foster investigation. Det. Ross made the rounds to everyone working to let them know that Lt.

Carter wanted to meet in the conference room at 1800 hours to discuss the latest case developments.

After hours at my desk typing, the walk to the conference room was a welcome excuse to get my blood flowing again. I stopped by the coffee machine to pour myself a cup and lace it with the required amounts of sugar and creamer. The additives cooled it down slightly allowing me to sip it faster and attain its caffeinated benefits. I turned towards the conference room as Shirley, Ross, and Lt. Carter rounded the corner. I knocked, and then opened the door to admit the four of us into the conference room.

"We have a lot to cover," said SSA Wells as we seated ourselves across from him.

"Let's start with the Foster investigation," said Carter. "How are we doing on it, Bryant?"

"I have the affidavit typed as far as I can get it," I answered. "We're still missing irrefutable evidence to guarantee the warrant gets signed. We have to find a way to place Foster in Manhattan at the time of the bombing. All we have is the phone call, the threatening remarks made to Tim Lane, and the diagram of the bomb used in the park. While that is a lot of evidence, it's not enough in my opinion. I spoke with Lt. Snyder from Wichita Police Department about the diagram today. He said it's a series of printouts of plans that can be found online. We have nothing to tie Foster to the bombing at this time."

"Keep us updated," instructed Lt. Carter. "Shirley, Ross; where are we on the Holton-Brand investigation?"

"I have unearthed every bit of available evidence from past incidents involving Conner Marten. I'm hoping to find something else applicable to these investigations. I also located the evidence from the original Holton-Brand missing person's case. I have hours of video footage to review, but hopefully I will know more when I get done," Shirley reported.

"Lawrence Police reported Greg made a trip to see Conner in Lawrence over the weekend. Greg then returned to Manhattan and hasn't left his house all weekend," advised Ross. "We still have our team watching Greg. We're still waiting on evidence to be analyzed with the KBI. We'll know more whenever they get done with it."

"Has anyone heard how the little girl from Wichita is doing?" asked Shirley.

"I spoke with detectives from Wichita Police this afternoon," answered SSA Wells. "They believe she is going to make a full recovery. The team got there just in time yesterday. Another minute or two and she might have suffered serious brain damage."

"That's good to hear," I said.

"That might be the only good news from Foster's place. The fire wiped out the outbuilding and the house. Any evidence inside was totally destroyed," said Wells. "The fire burned into the night before it was contained and extinguished. Early this morning, they believe they found a shallow grave. I haven't heard an update yet, but it seems this was most likely not the first person Foster has abducted."

"Did they recover the body yet?" asked Shirley.

"Not as of this afternoon. The last I spoke with them, they had secured the entire block and were checking it from end to end in case they find any more graves. Once they heard of his potential connection with Fenton, they expanded their search to make sure they don't miss anything," reported Wells.

"I know we're all thinking it already; but if they do find other bodies on Foster's property, that cements his connection with Fenton as far as I'm concerned," said Lt. Carter.

"I agree," said Terry.

"Alright then; that concludes our previous investigations. Bryant, why don't you tell us where we're going next?" requested Wells.

"We are going back to Iowa," I replied. "Fenton detailed, very specifically, the location of a grave site where five women are buried. Fenton also informed me that one of these women is the owner of the mystery bone we found in Jessica Childress' casket. The burial site is on the west side of Anita State Lake in Cass County, Iowa. The last body we found involving the Carroll family, was located outside of Cass County, making recovery a fairly simple task. This one has four additional bodies which I can assume are not going to be preserved in a casket like the last time we were up there. We are going to be facing a hostile jurisdiction with corrupt money at play. Fenton is certain they will do everything they can to take over the investigation and keep it local, to ensure none of the victims have any connection to the Carroll family."

"How the hell are you supposed to exhume five sets of remains and ensure they are properly identified and processed for evidence when you're in a jurisdiction that is determined to undermine the investigation?" asked Terry.

"Smoke and mirrors," I replied.

"What are you talking about?" asked Lt. Carter.

"We are going to need the full team for this one. Wells, if we can contact the FBI's K-9 victim recovery team, we are going to need them. We need Dr. Elmore and her team as well. Everything we do has to be 'need to know' with information only dispersed as necessary," I advised. "Another thing; have we confirmed the identity of Agent Sanders?"

"Yes we have," replied Wells. "He is assigned to the area around and including Cass County. He's been there a while and is listed as a close personal friend of Simon Carroll."

"Good; it's time we found out what side he's on. Terry, I'm going to need you to make a victim notification," I said.

"To whom?" he asked.

"It's time the Childress family was notified that we found their daughter. It's been almost three weeks, they need to know," I admitted.

"What else?" Terry asked.

"Now; we get some sleep. We're headed to Lincoln in the morning. Wells, if you can, have the K9 team meet us there.

"What can we do to help?" asked Shirley.

"Find us some probable cause to arrest the Martens or Amos Foster. We might be busy this week up in Iowa; whatever progress you can make is going to take a substantial amount of burden off us when we get back," I replied.

———

I did my best to hide my excitement on the way to Lincoln. I hadn't seen Dr. Elmore for several weeks, and I was looking forward to it. I didn't expect to get more than a minute with her amidst all the ensuing chaos, but I was excited none the less. My excitement was heavily curbed by the dilemma I was facing. I had a pile of details to sort through in order to pull off a real life slight-of-hand. I was ironing the details out in my head and checking on the availability of resources as I sat in the back seat of the car.

Terry was driving while SSA Wells did his best to assist me in lining up our necessary resources before we got to Cass County. I couldn't tell if I was explaining the plan poorly, or if Wells was just struggling to understand its complexity. I was certain I was explaining it poorly, but continued to try my best as the trip carried on.

By the time we reached Dr. Elmore's lab, Terry and Wells were on board with the plan, and almost as excited as I was. SSA Wells had confirmed with the K-9 team, and they agreed to meet us in Iowa on Wednesday. Wells and I filled them in on the plan via a conference call in the break room at the lab.

"Gentlemen, I hope I'm not interrupting anything."

I turned in my seat to see Dr. Elmore entering the room. I did my best to hide the smile that threatened to stretch from ear to ear. It wasn't easy, but I managed to keep a professional persona as Wells and I shook her hand.

"Good to see you again, Dr. Elmore," said Wells. "How is your team doing?"

"They are doing well, thank you, Agent Wells. They've just wrapped up the project they were completing. Would you like to have them meet us in here or do you want to have this briefing in the lab?" she asked.

"In here will be fine," he replied. "We might as well be comfortable."

"I'll get my team," she replied. "It's good to see you again, Detective Bryant."

"Likewise," I said, nodding at her.

Terry entered the room from the opposite side as Dr. Elmore exited. He had his hands outstretched to the side and was sporting a big smile.

"Tell me you've got good news," I told him.

"We've got a boat," he replied.

"Is it going to be big enough?" I asked.

"It's the biggest one they had," he replied.

"Perfect; is it pontoon or speed?"

"I asked for a boat with the biggest amount of deck space. They said this one should hold twelve people comfortably," he answered.

"We won't have that many people," I stated. "I think we should be good to go."

Behind us, the doors opened, and Dr. Elmore entered the room leading her team.

The group took a moment to exchange quick pleasantries before everyone found a seat

"I know everyone enjoyed our last trip, so I decided, along with help from Fenton, to take everyone to the same area again," I said.

"Oh good; I can't get enough Iowa," joked Tommy.

"I was thinking of you when all these plans were made," I quipped. "The best part about this trip is that there will be a lot to do, and very few people to do it all. The worst part is also the best part. The biggest issue we will face is potential interference from local politicians and law enforcement. Everything we do will be guarded closely to ensure no one knows we are working in the area until the time is right."

"How will we know the time is right?" Tamara asked.

"You won't, we will. There are certain aspects of this recovery that will come down to timing. The variables include the following: early interference by locals, amount of time it takes to dig out five bodies and the difficulty of getting them out of the county before the locals can stop us. We don't have local support this time. We were all there in Montgomery County three weeks ago when the locals gave us everything we needed. This time, they will actively try to stop, interrupt or obstruct our recovery efforts. Everyone will have a team, and every team will be reachable at all times once the clock has started. The clock starts when the K-9 team locates the bodies. Team one is SSA Wells and I; team two is the K-9 recovery team; team three is Dr. Elmore and her four interns; team four is going to be Agent Jones and another FBI Agent to be named later. Is everyone clear on their teams?"

I looked around as everyone exchanged nods and glances. I cleared my throat and continued.

"Armed with the specific details of my report from Fenton, we are sending in Agent's Martinez and Davidson with the K-9 unit posing as simple hikers out at Anita State Lake, on Wednesday evening. The K-9 team will have a GPS beacon to allow us to find them fast. We will have a second team consisting of Dr. Elmore, Tamara and Samantha. They will arrive in one vehicle and immediately hike to the grave site to meet with Agent Martinez. You will need comfortable clothes, none of which can be labeled with anything associated with your school or Dr. Elmore's lab. You will walk in empty handed, other than small backpacks with collapsible shovels inside. There is no way to carry all of your equipment through the thick brush on the south side of the burial site."

"How are we going to get our equipment on scene if we can't carry it in?" asked Samantha.

"Hang on, I'm getting to it," I insisted. "Michael and Tommy, you will arrive with Dr. Elmore and the others, but not proceed into the woods at that time. When SSA Wells and I arrive, the two of you will take our vehicle, and Dr. Elmore's, and drive it around to the dock to meet with Agent Jones and Agent Davidson. Davidson will deliver the three of you, along with the equipment, across the lake to the grave site. He will then take the boat back across the lake and drop off Agent Martinez, who has other commitments. Once everyone is on scene, we will work in shifts to exhume the remains. Now, to answer Samantha's question; we have acquired a boat which will launch from a public dock on the east side of the lake. The boat will have all of your equipment on board and be docked just off shore with a raft to take all the supplies ashore. Once we get to the detail work, Dr. Elmore's team will be tasked to complete the dig and recover the bodies as fast as possible. One of the bodies is going to be missing a femur when you find it. That's the bone we found in the casket last time. Wells, Jones, and I will return in the boat to the dock where we will be dropped off before the sun comes up. Our duties at the burial site are concluded at that time. We will be making every effort to run interference with the locals from that point forward. We will buy you as much time as possible, but everyone has to work fast. Are there any questions?"

"How are we going to get the bodies out?" asked Michael.

"That's why you won't have space to carry equipment in. You will have to haul the remains out and carry them to the public parking area. We are enlisting the help of several local funeral homes to transport the remains. We just have to get the remains to them. Everything depends on the local Sheriff, Ryan Carroll, not finding out what we are up to. If he does, we are royally fucked. He will seize the remains and we will never see them again. Secrecy is everything, once our cover is blown, we will have little to no time to get the remains out of the county, onto the plane that will be standing by, and back here to the lab. With that, we will dismiss for now," I said, wrapping up my instructions.

The interns looked confused and slightly disoriented. Three of them raised their hands, indicating they still had questions.

"Dr. Elmore will answer all your questions when we get reach the burial site." I said, waving them off.

The confusion continued on the interns faces as I strolled casually out of the room.

"Excuse me, Detective Bryant," said a stern voice behind me.

I turned to see Dr. Elmore striding confidently through the door and into the hallway.

"Care to explain yourself a little better? How am I supposed to answer questions for my interns if you haven't given me all the information I need to answer them?"

She sounded frustrated, and slightly annoyed. I had been expecting this, so I kept walking down the hall and into the lab.

"We have two days before this whole operation goes underway," I advised. "There is plenty of time to provide you and your team with all the necessary information."

"Then what was the point of having a briefing tonight? Why can't you just tell me what's going on?" she asked.

I casually opened and held the door to her office to allow her to walk in ahead of me.

"Do you trust me?"

"What are you talking about?"

"Lydia; do you trust me?" I asked again. I looked her in the eye, waiting for her response.

"James, what are you talking about?"

"Do you trust me?"

"I want to say yes, James, but I feel like a barely know you. That's a loaded question for anyone to ask," she replied, still avoiding the question.

"Will you have dinner with me?"

That time I caught her off guard. She started to respond before realizing what I had said.

"We're here a day early. We could have arranged to meet tomorrow, but we didn't. You just said your team was done with their current project and was ready for the next trip to Iowa; which means you don't have any work to do tonight. I'm hoping that means you don't have any plans. Will you have dinner with me?" I asked again.

She smiled at me, with a mixture of frustration and surprise on her face.

"Yes, I would love to have dinner with you," she replied.

"Good," I said with a smile.

I reached into my back pants pocket and pulled out an envelope. The envelope was sealed, with nothing more than Dr. Elmore's name on the front.

"I want you to be able to trust me," I said. "Everything you need to know that I haven't told you is detailed in this letter. This letter is for your eyes only. I am giving this to you now, but I want you to wait to read it until you reach the burial site. I want to be able to trust you too."

"James, why couldn't you just tell me everything over dinner tonight?" she asked with a curious smile.

"I didn't ask you to dinner so we could talk about work. I asked you to dinner so we could talk about us; I hope that's okay with you."

Her smile told me everything I needed to know.

CHAPTER THIRTY-ONE

I spent the next thirty hours or so after my dinner with Dr. Elmore, trying to focus on my work. It wasn't easy; but I found a way to concentrate on the long list of tasks at hand.

On Tuesday the team drove three vehicles to Des Moines and hit the sack early. We had a long forty-eight hours ahead of us which may or may not provide the opportunity to get any sleep. The vehicles were completely out of the ordinary. Terry and I made the trip in a rented Ford Mustang. The sleek blue, molded body was perfectly accented by the black stripes on the hood. SSA Wells drove part of Dr. Elmore's team in a gray mini-van you might expect to see a college debate team travel in to a competition. Dr. Elmore opted for a full size pickup truck and piled the rest of her team and equipment into it.

Not only did we abandon anything slightly official, we didn't even travel together. Terry and I packed two sets of golf clubs into the cramped back seat of the Mustang and left five hours before the rest of the team. We diverted south and played eighteen holes of golf at the Crestwood Hills Golf Course located at the north end of Lake Anita State Park. We took this route so we could drive through the area and quickly scope out the area around Anita State Park. It gave us the chance to unwind a bit, while giving us the chance to familiarize ourselves with the area.

Dr. Elmore, along with Samantha, left second and headed straight to a hotel in Des Moines. The bed of the truck included a cover which locked, allowing them to leave all the equipment in the back. Dressed like two girlfriends having a weekend away, they hit a bar near the hotel for drinks prior to calling it a night.

SSA Wells had really embraced the idea that he was a professor on a scholastic competition trip. Although they didn't list a school, they kept up the façade of being a group of college students along with a professor. Michael, Tommy and Tamara didn't enjoy being a part of the only group that didn't have any fun, but they were team players, and acted the part.

The wild card of the task force was the K-9 team. They were not completely at our disposal due to the constant demand for victim recovery, nationwide. They flew into Des Moines along with their dog, Major, late Wednesday afternoon and met us in a small town just off I-80 called Stuart. They were briefed at around 1800 hours, and went straight to work.

I was nervous as we got closer and closer to the point of no return. The K-9 team was almost to the public parking area at Lake Anita. The trickiest part of the operation was the shuffling of vehicles. I joined Terry in the truck and followed SSA Wells in the Mustang to the dock. The boat was a rental, just like everything else that week. We had paid dearly to have the boat overnight, which was not normal procedures, according to the clerk at the rental desk. We loaded up all the equipment into the boat, and then moved the boat as far away as possible along the dock. We were trying to reduce our public exposure, as we didn't know who might be working against us.

"The K-9 team is on the ground," said Wells, checking his phone.

"Everything is in motion." I said.

"No turning back now, gentlemen. We have parts to play. Let's make them Oscar-worthy." Wells encouraged.

Terry waited with the boat while SSA Wells and I took the Mustang to another location in the State Park. Hindsight indicated the level of idiocy we had possessed when we rented such a flashy vehicle, but it was already done. We tried to find a spot within easy driving distance of the parking area, but the park wasn't big enough to allow us to do so while also appearing detached from the location ahead of time.

It took nearly an hour to get the confirmation from Agent Martinez. They had found the burial site, and they were ready for the next step.

SSA Wells drove us to the public parking area. The van was already there, with Tommy and Michael standing behind it, indicating the rest of Dr. Elmore's team had already set off on foot. We pulled up to the edge of the roadway and spotted Agent Davidson walking Major out of the wooded area. We took a quick turn around the lot, ensuring no one else was there, before parking the Mustang on the backside of the van, blocking it from being seen from the road. Agent Davidson loaded Major into his SUV and immediately left the scene without saying a word to us. SSA Wells handed Tommy the keys to the Mustang as he stepped out, and stretched his legs.

The smoke and mirrors was mostly for show at this point in the game. The important detail was ensuring no one could tell something was going on in the wooded area north of us.

SSA Wells and I were decked out in the best hiking gear our wardrobes allowed. We completed the ensemble with backpacks and walking sticks. We set off, Wells leading the way, into the forest. Behind us, we heard the Mustang start, and then exit the parking lot. Neither of us looked back, knowing the van, driven by Michael, was leaving the parking lot as well.

Wells checked his phone, which displayed the GPS location where Agent Martinez was waiting for us.

The timing of the rotation was perfect as Dr. Elmore, Tamara and Samantha had already broken ground and stood ready for a reprieve by the time we arrived on scene. Wells and I immediately took our turns digging as the sun dipped down below the horizon. The area had been heavy on small shrubs, but didn't have a lot of trees to contend with us. The location was perfect for our purposes. The waist high brush cascaded down a small hill to the edge of the lake which lapped gently against the shoreline to accompany the breeze.

Our only indication that the boat had arrived was Dr. Elmore, Agent Martinez and Samantha heading down the hill towards the lake. Fifteen minutes later, they returned along with Terry, Tommy and Michael. Tommy and Michael took a turn digging, giving us the chance to catch our breath. We took five minute rotations, ensuring everyone was getting plenty of rest in between. We cycled like this for several hours until the hole was nearly two feet deep and nearly four feet wide. The ground was more mud than dirt as we dug. We switched things up to include a team of two with pick-axes to break up the ground when it got too tough to dig.

When the sun disappeared completely, we set up small lights, placed on the ground, pointed away from the lake. The lights weren't very bright, but we couldn't afford for anyone to look across the lake and see a team of people digging, silhouetted by flood lights. Agent Martinez left in the boat with Agent Davidson. Agent Martinez had played her part, and was already being requested to help with a recovery in the Appalachian Mountains. We were thankful Agent Martinez had the agility to work solo. The only way this operation would work the way I had designed it, was if Agent Davidson was able to stay behind to operate the boat from time to time.

Each team took time to grab a bite to eat in between shifts in the ever-growing hole. To Fenton's credit, he rarely dug a shallow grave. This worked against us, but it was an anticipated obstruction.

Terry and I teamed up with Dr. Elmore and Tamara to form a four person rotation. Terry and I would swing pick axes for a few minutes before the ladies would shovel the dirt out of the hole. Finally, after half an hour, the other team took over, allowing us the chance to sit down by the edge of the lake. Terry sought higher ground in an effort to find a spot to relieve his self, leaving Dr. Elmore and I down by the water by ourselves. Tamara stayed with the dig site and stretched her back a little.

"Do we need to adjust our pace to make sure we don't shatter any bones?" I asked.

"It all depends on how much time we have," she replied.

I checked my watch before replying. "It's a little after one O'clock."

"The way Agent Martinez had the area cordoned off, the bodies were all placed side by side," she said. "As I see it, we have a little ways further down to go; but were going to have to expand the hole sooner than later."

"How about we go for depth now until we reach one of the bodies, then while your team is working to uncover the body we have, the rest of us work to expand the hole." I suggested.

"I like that plan," she replied. "That way we have the extra muscle while we still have bulk digging to do."

I watched for a moment as a breeze kicked up, blowing her hair around her neck. The moonlight reflected perfectly off the water, illuminating her face. I made a conscious effort not to stare, but found it hard not to examine every detail of her face with the help of the moonlight.

"Are you warm enough?" I asked. I realized she was shivering against the cool night air, and that I didn't have a jacket to offer her.

"I forgot to pack a jacket. It's was so warm yesterday, I forgot how chilly it was going to get overnight."

I scooted close to her until my side was right next to her.

"It's unprofessional to put my arm around you, but if you wanted to lean up against me and share a little heat, I'd like to help however I can."

She turned to look at me, before smiling, and ducking her head a little. We sat that way for a few seconds while she made up her mind. Finally, ever so slowly; she leaned her shoulder up against mine. She tucked her arm underneath mine, and slowly traced her fingers down my arm until she reached my wrist. She slowly ran a finger around my wrist and palm area, sending a shiver up my arm, and then down my spine. After another few seconds, she slowly laced her fingers in between mine and gently gripped my hand.

"Dr. Elmore," I said, quietly admonishing her. "That's not very professional."

She laughed quietly as her right hand reached across her chest to grasp my bicep. Her hands were cold, but not for long. Slowly, our body heat began pushing back against the crisp, cool, April night air, until we were almost to a comfortable temperature. I smiled as she leaned her head over and laid it against my shoulder. Despite all we were trying to do, in the face of everything that was working against us, I found myself experiencing a level of happiness I hadn't had for an eternity. I heard her take a deep breath, and let it out as a soft sigh.

"Listen," she said softly, "I would love to sit here like this for another hour, but we have a lot of work to do."

"That's too bad," I whispered back to her, "I was just beginning to enjoy myself."

"Also," she said casually, pausing to take another short breath, "You smell like a gravedigger's asshole."

She caught me off guard with that comment. I didn't doubt I was packing a stench on me, but I had hoped she wouldn't notice.

"Oh thank God," I whispered back to her. "I thought that was you."

"You dick," she said playfully as she pushed herself away from me before crossing her arms, and leaning back against me.

"I'm serious," I said. "I just didn't know how to broach the subject."

We shared a laugh, enjoying a moment of levity while we could. I sighed a little, knowing we didn't have much time left.

"Bryant, breaks over," called Terry."

"Of course it is," I said, sighing again.

"We should find another view like this some time," she said as I stood up in front of her.

"I agree," I replied as I offered her a hand up. She took my hand and allowed me to help her back up off the ground. "You just name the time and the place, and I'll be there."

"Deal," she agreed.

The digging progressed slowly the rest of the night. The deeper we got, the slower we had to proceed. It took until nearly five in the morning to reach the first body. Fortunately, we had been digging the entire area out, so the second body was unearthed right after the first one.

The team was exhausted. Terry and I did our best to handle the bulk digging whenever possible, but there was so much to do, it was nearly impossible. We had three of the bodies uncovered by the time the sun was starting to light up the morning sky.

I felt bad for Dr. Elmore's team as SSA Wells, Terry and I began one at a time taking a bar of soap down to the edge of the lake to wash up. We were about to transition from digging mode to professional mode, and we had to at least look the part. Agent Davidson arrived around 0600 hours and transported the three of us back across the lake. I waded out to the boat, which was beached just off shore on a shallow sand bar, and climbed up the ladder on the back. I walked to the bow of the boat and sat down, gazing back at the burial site where the team was completely hidden, clearing off the bones at the bottom of the hole. The only person in sight was Dr. Elmore. She walked down the hill a little ways and pulled something out of her back pocket. The light was dim, but I could make out the shape of the white envelope I had given her two days before.

I smiled at her, and gave her a big nod. She tore the envelope open and walked back up the hill. She read the letter for a moment before she summoned the rest of her team out of the hole.

It meant a lot to me that she had trusted me enough to wait for the right time to open the letter. It was nice to trust someone again.

The trip across the lake wasn't nearly long enough. Just as I was beginning to enjoy the wind whipping through my hair, the trip was over. We unloaded our gear from the boat, and left it in the care of Agent Davidson again. We took turns hiding behind the van, changing into more appropriate clothing.

Terry and I took a turn through the town of Anita, checking to see if there was any flurry of activity. Finding none, we took another lap before calling SSA Wells.

"Anita seems to be right on the edge of sleepy this time of morning. How's Atlantic?" asked Terry. Terry listened for a moment before he hung up the phone.

"So far, it seems like we're pulling this off." He told me while I turned the Mustang back around at I-80.

"That's good," I said, "What is your timeline for the Childress family?"

"1500 hours; I have to pick up Sanders at 1430 over in Atlantic."

"Everything depends on timing. I'll keep you up to date on the developments on this end," I told him.

"How long did Dr. Elmore think it was going to take to recover all five bodies?" he asked.

"She told me they had around eight hours of work left. We took almost half the team when we left this morning, I wish there was a way we could have stayed to help longer," I admitted.

"I know it," he replied. "But we have a lot to do, and we can't do any of it if someone sees us walking out of the woods, covered in dirt."

"I agree. We're still on track with the plan, I just hate to think of what could go wrong over the next few hours," I said.

"Let's worry about us for now," he advised. "Dr. Elmore is no slouch. She's gonna make that deadline, we just have to be ready ourselves."

————

At 1400 hours, Terry dropped me off at the public parking area. SSA Wells was already there, in full suit and tie, as if he'd just steered out of a funeral procession.

"Good luck buddy," I told Terry, before I closed the door.

He waved at us and then turned quickly out of the parking lot.

"Get that tie and jacket on, Bryant. We won't have much time once the ball gets rolling," Wells instructed.

I adorned the required attire and then pulled out my phone. I retrieved a list of phone numbers from my pocket and reviewed them. They were meticulously placed in a certain order, ready for when the time was right.

"Dr. Elmore just uncovered number five. She said she needs thirty minutes to get them all ready for transportation." SSA Wells stowed his phone away in his jacket pocket.

"Perfect," I said, breathing a sigh of relief.

"Wait another ten minutes and then start calling. We need all of them here, lined up and waiting when Dr. Elmore's team gets done.

Ten minutes seems like an eternity when you're just watching your phone for a possible update, or worse, bad news.

Finally, the time had passed, allowing me to start the next step of the process.

"Start calling, I'm going to set up the tape."

"You got it boss," I replied.

I paced back and forth, waiting for someone to pick up the phone. Finally, after listening to the ringing at the other end of the line, someone answered.

"Hello, my name is James Bryant; I'm working with an FBI task force out at Lake Anita State Park. We have recovered a body and are in need of transportation. How soon can you have someone here? Fantastic, I will meet you at the entrance to let you through the barrier. Thank you very much."

"One down, four to go," said Wells.

The next ten to fifteen minutes were spent of the phone. Wells coordinated with Terry and Dr. Elmore while I finished calling funeral homes. It wasn't normal to call funeral homes to transport remains that weren't fresh, and the result of natural cause, but this wasn't a normal situation.

"Terry and Sanders are making the notification now. We should know before too long if we were right," advised Wells.

"This is one of those situations where I would love to be wrong; but I don't think so," I replied.

"Let's see if we can't get a little attention," he said.

I smiled at that. We had spent the past twenty hours trying to avoid attention; now we were about to invite the entire county to know.

SSA Wells hung his jacket up in the back of the van and put on his ballistic vest, complete with FBI printed in oversized letters on the front and back. I pulled out several magnets from the back of the van and attached them to the doors of the van. The magnets read, "FBI" in black letters with a white background. The nine inch tall letters could be read at quite a distance, ensuring we would get the attention we were seeking.

Wells pulled out an old fashioned "cherry" and attached it to the top of the van, turning it on. The red light rotated inside the fixture, creating a slow, flashing red light to anyone who saw it. We moved the van next to the entrance and parked it at an angle. We then assembled a plastic road barrier and placed it, blocking the rest of the entrance to the parking lot.

Over the next twenty minutes, three of the hearses arrived, and were instructed to wait at the north end of the parking area. The personnel accompanying the hearses were confused at our request to wait, and our announcement that we would be bringing the remains to them. They wanted to know why a hearse was requested, but were not satisfied with the answers provided. To top it off, they were all very confused each time another hearse arrived on scene.

Finally, all five hearses were lined up along the edge of the parking lot, waiting for their precious cargo. Not only was this unorthodox, it was unheard of to have five separate competitors in the funeral game on the same scene at the same time. They all stayed in the vehicles, uncertain as to what was going on.

"Do you hear that?" asked Wells.

I listened for a moment, unsure if I was mistaken for a moment.

"That sounds like sirens to me," I replied.

"It looks like our secret it out," he said.

"It was going to happen sooner or later." I admitted.

The sirens got louder and louder until we spotted the flashing lights in the distance, getting closer.

One at a time, identical white Ford Explorer patrol units came screaming up the roadway towards the public parking lot. I counted six in total, which was surprising. The first unit in the line turned into the parking lot, stopping just short of knocking over our barrier before it came to a complete stop, and turning off its sirens.

A tall, white male in his fifties stepped out of the driver's seat. He sported a tan Stetson hat which matched his uniform perfectly. He had a dark brown tie covering a smartly buttoned shirt with a star badge over his left shirt pocket. He slipped on a pair of sunglasses to complete his "old school sheriff" appearance, and strolled towards us as if he hadn't just been driving eighty miles per hour to get here.

"Well boys, what have we got here?" he asked.

"I am Supervisory Special Agent William Wells of the FBI. To whom am I speaking?"

"I'm Ryan Carroll, Sheriff of Cass County where you happen to be standing. Is there a particular reason you are conducting an investigation in my county without doing the courteous thing and notifying me first?"

"Well, Sheriff, we didn't want to bother you. We were working on a series of cold cases from 1987 and 1988. We were acting on a lead from someone who lived in the area back then. We weren't sure if we would find anything, so we didn't want to bother you until we knew for sure," explained Wells.

"That's highly irregular, especially for the FBI. Besides, we have our own local FBI office, is there a reason they didn't know anything about this until this afternoon?" asked the Sheriff.

"Same reason, we didn't know the quality of our intelligence."

"Well did your intelligence pan out?" he asked.

"Not sure yet," replied Wells, shrugging.

"Then why do you have barriers up and hearses standing by? In my experience you don't call a funeral home until you have a dead body." Sheriff Carroll was clearly beginning to get agitated.

Wells continued to stall, working hard to prevent the Sheriff from taking over the investigation.

"We are just trying to be prepared," said Wells.

"Then why are there five of them?" he asked. "That's awfully specific."

"We were told there was more than one victim. We just like to be ready."

"Look, Fed; I've been awfully professional with you while you are clearly feeding me the words worst line of bullshit. You don't have the right to come in and take over, what was obviously a local case, without permission. So if you don't get real specific real quick, my boys and I will throw you, and your little partner here, the fuck out of my jurisdiction."

The Sheriff was past the point of being agitated, and quickly reaching a point of open anger.

"Look, Sheriff; your local Bureau office called you, why don't you give them a call back and have them work this out with us?" suggested Wells.

"I'll give my guy a call, but that's just so he has it on record that I'm pissed that he ignored procedure, just like you did," he snarled.

I looked around a bit while the Sheriff paced back and forth with his phone to his ear. I was concerned that Dr. Elmore and her team would be wrapped up at the burial site soon and heading back this way. We had officially run out of time, and we were in danger of losing everything from the recovery effort.

"That's odd," said the Sheriff, staring at his phone for a second. "My man at the Bureau appears to be unavailable."

"Then maybe we can come to an agreement," Wells offered.

"Tell me what case you are working on," the Sheriff ordered.

"We were given some information on several cold, homicide cases here in your county. We already have a suspect in custody for other crimes; he is working out a deal to get a comfier jail cell down in Atlanta. He said he had been a deputy here in the late eighties, and had a hand in some young women disappearing. We are just trying to confirm what he told us," explained Wells.

"Maybe I'm familiar with these cases. That was right around the time I became Sheriff here. Did this man tell you who was buried here?"

"He did, I can't remember the names off the top of my head; can you James?"

"I think Mr. Dean mentioned the last name Childress," I said.

There was no way to tell which of the two names dropped was having the biggest shock effect on the Sheriff. The shadow on his face cast by his wide brim prevented us from seeing if he had changed a shade. He stood there, with a blank face, clearly trying to control his breathing. He turned to me as if noticing me for the first time.

"Childress you say? Is that why my contact at the FBI was making a victim notification to them here in Atlantic?"

"That would be why, yes," I replied.

"And you have positively identified her then?" he asked.

"Yes we have," said Wells.

The conversation trailed off into an awkward moment of silence. I could see the wheels turning as the Sheriff did his best to remain calm, and think of a way out without arousing suspicion at the same time.

"Sheriff; on your left," called one of the deputies standing behind him.

Everyone turned to look towards the wooded area to the north.

My heart sank. Dr. Elmore and her team were navigating a small cart with body bags on top, out of the woods towards the parking lot. Behind Dr. Elmore, Tommy and Michael appeared with two more body bags laying on a make-shift gurney.

"Just playing it safe, Agent Wells? It looks to me like you've been here for a while already," snarled the Sheriff. "Boys, go help bring up the bodies."

"That's really quite alright, Sheriff. My team can handle it," insisted Wells.

"Nonsense," he replied, waving a hand casually. "It wouldn't be right for your team to do all the lifting on a local case. We'd be happy to help since we will be taking this case off your hands."

"No you can't do that," I insisted, taking a step forward.

"Know your fucking place, son." The Sheriff was spitting as he spoke now, pointing a gnarly finger in my direction. His anger was beginning to return as he became more determined. "Go to it boys."

"Sheriff, this is highly unprofessional. We've already recovered the bodies; just let us finish our investigation," begged Wells.

"All you had to do was call me first," spat the Sheriff, pointing a finger in Wells' face. "If you had gone through the proper channels, all of this could have been avoided. I could have saved you the trip. You tried to circumvent me and my office. This is a local case, with local victims, as you've already confirmed. It did not cross state lines and therefore you have no jurisdiction over this case. I will want everything you've done so far, and I want access to your suspect."

"All of that would be easier if you just work with us," Wells insisted.

"That's not going to happen now. We will take the bodies with us to be processed. I expect you to sign them over to us immediately."

"There's a proper way to do this," I interjected.

"Shut the fuck up," he ordered. "The next time you open your mouth, you'll learn better at the butt end of my 1911."

I held up my hands, and backed up a little.

"Stay out of my business. Had you called me, I could have told you all this over the phone," he insisted.

I turned to watch as the deputies reached Dr. Elmore's team. They unceremoniously took the cart and gurney from the team, and pushed Michael and Tommy out of the way as they began to protest.

"Tell your guys to take it easy," demanded Wells. "My team is just following orders."

"Your team should be thankful I don't have my deputies tune them up a little bit before we leave."

Wells and I stood by, dejected, watching as the deputies took each of the five body bags to their patrol units and loaded them in the back hatch area.

"James; what the hell is going on?" asked Dr. Elmore.

"The locals are taking over the investigation." I replied.

"They can't do that though," she insisted.

"Oh, but I can," called the Sheriff. He pulled his sunglasses down a little ways and gave Dr. Elmore a once over before turning back to his patrol unit. "Boys, check their van. Make sure they aren't hiding anything from us."

We were pushed aside as five eager deputies opened up the van and pulled its contents out, and threw them on the ground.

"Is this seriously happening?" she asked.

"There's nothing we can do about it now," said Wells. "Everyone stand down."

We watched in anguish as the deputies tore through the van and then left everything outside on the ground.

"Thanks for doing business," one of them sneered as they pushed through the group again, back towards their units.

"I will be filing a complaint with your department," Wells threatened.

"I'd be happy to hear your complaint," the Sheriff said with a smile. He leaned out of his open window and called out. "I'll be sure to read it first thing in the morning. We take complaints very seriously around here. Now if your team needs something to do, have them secure the burial site. My deputies will be back shortly to relieve them."

The team stood by, helpless as the Sheriff led the parade of patrol units as they turned around and started back towards I-80.

"What an asshole," said Tommy, shaking his head.

"You said it," agreed Tamara. "What are we supposed to do now?"

"We're all in one vehicle now. Let's clean up this mess and then head down to the department so I can file the complaint," Wells instructed.

I sighed with frustration, and bent down to pick things up off the ground and load them back into the van.

"Do you wanna tell the funeral homes their services are no longer needed, or should I?"

"I'll tell them," Wells replied. "I feel badly for making them come out here and waste their time."

We packed the vehicle and climbed inside. I sat in the passenger seat while Dr. Elmore and her team filled in the back seats. Everyone was exhausted, with nothing to show for it.

I looked over at SSA Wells as he went from one hearse to the next giving them the bad news. One at a time, the hearses drove past us out of the parking lot. Wells reached the last hearse and stood by to watch it leave. He turned his back on the van, and watched a single boat circle the far side of the lake.

CHAPTER THIRTY-TWO

I was in a staring contest. Fenton was holding out, trying not to be the first one to speak. I was waiting to see if his curiosity would get the better of him. Foster had been on the run for a week, which meant Fenton would be aware of his absence. I had no way of knowing how often they communicated, but it only made sense they would do so before I met with Fenton each Saturday. Between Foster's absence and the intricacies of the Anita Lake recovery effort, Fenton was sure to have questions.

Another minute passed in silence. The quiet was unsettling, but it was a nice change of pace from listening to the ravings of a lunatic for three solid hours. Any reprieve I could get from his insanity was a welcome break.

He smoked in silence, finishing one cigarette and then lighting another without dropping his gaze. I scooted my chair back a little and slouched, lacing my fingers together behind my head. I stared up at the dingy, concrete ceiling over Fenton's head; examining the discoloration from moisture trapped in the room, two floors underground. The humidity had nowhere to go, leading to a sticky, uncomfortable environment. Fortunately the temperature was low enough to make the humidity tolerable. I spaced out for a moment. I had done this for the last six weeks, so I knew Fenton was secured to the table, and to the ground.

My thoughts wandered back to my dinner with Dr. Elmore, which evidently brought a smile to my face.

"Something's different about you today, detective." Fenton observed.

I dropped my eyes from the ceiling to match his gaze. My smile turned into a smirk as I stretched my legs out in front of me, and then sat up in my chair.

"It's always possible." I agreed, casually.

"I was already starting to miss the slurring, boozehound that used to sit across from me with his head down." Fenton said with a sneer. "Now you sit there, looking up at the light as if you haven't a care in the world."

"Life's pretty good when you're not chained to the table." I observed. "Too bad you'll never know."

"I've made my mark on this world already. Now I can sit back, enjoy my three hot's and a cot, and watch you try to make meaning out of your pointless life as a government stooge."

"At least this stooge can leave today." I replied.

"You sit there and act as if you know something I don't," he said. "I'm not fond of the idea."

"It's almost as if I sorted out your system, and now I'm one step ahead of you." I replied, with a careless shrug. "That's how it's supposed to be anyways."

"It is a little odd. I seem to be without a friend in this world," he said casually.

"You never had any friends, just lackeys. People to do your bidding without any creative thought of their own," I added.

"Oh they're creative," he insisted. "I don't mentor anyone without an imagination."

"Is that all it takes to be in your inner circle?" I asked.

"You're implying that I've had enough people around me to make a circle. You would be wrong," he advised. "I only mentor one at a time. I prefer a master and apprentice style of tutoring. Chaos begins when too many people try to do the same thing. That's why the government doesn't work; too many people. A truly great movement has only one or two people at the helm; anything beyond that creates too much opportunity for collapse."

"So you never opened a school for psychos?" I quipped.

"There are more than enough people like me in this world to fill a classroom. The problem is the volume of people involved in a classroom. People learn better with one on one attention. My lifestyle is a solitary existence. The best work I have ever done was in the joy of walking alone. People like me thrive when we are left to use our imagination. Do you think I would have come up with the idea of stuffing a cum-covered red rag into my victim's mouths as they bleed out, without having the opportunity to concoct such an idea in solitude? I've been in solitary confinement for most of the last seven years. If I left this prison for even a week, the level of fucked up shit I could accomplish would only be mentioned in well-lit rooms with the doors locked. You'll see," he said.

"Are you expecting to take a little vacation soon?" I inquired.

"As long as I have a protégé on the outside, my genius will live on," he insisted.

"Why don't you tell me about your protégé?" I asked.

"You'll have to be more specific; which one?"

I hesitated. I didn't want to tip my hand to what was going on with Foster, but I also wanted to see what he would be willing to discuss.

"Why don't you tell me about the one you have now?"

"Let's just say he's a true visionary," replied Fenton. "He has an approach that makes even more sense than mine; and he took the time to develop a few extra skillsets to aid in his techniques. He knows how to fly under the radar, almost as well as I do."

"How did you find him?"

"I didn't; he found me. Very ambitious, this one; something else I admire."

"He found you? How did he do that?" I wondered.

"Stop pretending like you don't know. We both know you already know who he is. However, I know you haven't caught him yet. I don't expect you will either."

"Everybody makes mistakes," I said.

"Not him, you think you have something on him, but you don't." Fenton drawled, slowly. "He will always be one step ahead of you. If you got close, it's because he let you. He is a master of deception, and he knows how to lead people on. He learned in his early years, that there are consequences for doing things the wrong way. He's a fast learner, and he doesn't repeat his mistakes."

"So what is it about his approach that makes him so much better than you?" I asked.

"I didn't say he was better than me, I said he had a better approach," he growled. I had clearly touched a nerve, but that had been my objective.

"What is his approach?"

"He took my life as a lesson. He saw the mistakes I made, and the oversights I made, and he fashioned an approach that helps solve my problem before it becomes a problem."

"I don't understand," I admitted.

"I'm trying to solve the problem of women in this world. The problem is women aren't as vulnerable as they get older. You have to stamp out the disease when it's young, and impressionable."

"Is that's why he kidnaps children instead of adults and teens?" I inquired, tipping my hand.

"It makes sense, doesn't it? Rather than let the problem grow, he solves it before it can even become a problem. Revolutionary, isn't it?" He beamed with pride, making me hate him all-the-more.

"It sounds more like a pedophile justifying their actions by killing children when he's done with them." I said, struggling to contain my growing anger.

"Why should he be demonized for appreciating the human form at its purest stage of life? Is his way of life so terrible? Isn't it judgmental of you to look down on him for living his life, true to his self?"

"Nope; he's a shit person for taking advantage of the most innocent people available." I replied.

"How can you live with yourself?" He asked, catching me off guard a little.

"I do just fine." I insisted.

"Do you, really? I think you fall in line with a long established list of social morays, and pass it off as piety. Anyone can enforce a law made by someone else; it takes all the responsibility off of you. I'd say it's almost lazy," he taunted.

"There are plenty of things I disagree with how the government operates. That doesn't mean I ignore our differences, it just means there is enough good to be done with what I do, that it's still worth doing." I insisted. "No system is perfect, but it's useless to oppose an entire system just because it is flawed. As long as people are involved in government,

government will be flawed. It doesn't matter which form of government, and it doesn't matter how many people are involved, it's going to be flawed. Everyone has a different idea of how the system should work, that doesn't mean their method will be any more perfect than the one already in use."

"That sounds like a great excuse to follow the rules and not challenge the status quo. Me; I'm a one man revolution. I'm one of a kind. Nobody governs me, I'm totally free."

"Well," I smirked. "You used to be."

"I'm leaving behind a legacy. What about you, detective? What are you leaving behind; certainly not any children?"

My blood ran cold.

"You must have known by now that I know everything about you." Fenton taunted. My grip tightened around my pencil as I braced for his follow-up. "Do you really think something like your wife dying would escape my thorough scrutiny?"

"Watch yourself," I warned, "I'd hate for you to have an accident the same week you lose your little fucking protégé."

"Empty threats," shrugged Fenton, waving a hand dismissively at me, rattling the chains a bit.

"Care to find out?"

"I'd love to see you bring your pathetic existence to a pitiful end, just as you were about to have everything you wanted. So go ahead and kill me, detective. My legacy lives on; yours dies with me," he warned.

I slowly inhaled, realizing how close I had come to passing out. The tension in my forehead began to diminish, and my hand unclenched. I had to find a way to regain control of the conversation. If I allowed him to derail the conversation into the painful portions of my past, I would never recover.

"Well," I started, "I'd hate to make you the world's shittiest martyr, so why don't we redirect our discussion to something more productive?"

"That's what I'm trying to do, Detective. You should really do better at having a conversation without making idle threats. It's a waste of your time. I," He paused, "Never make idle threats."

"I suppose it makes no sense to threaten to kill a man who's walking slowly towards his own death," I suggested. "Sometimes I just get a little impatient to see the expression on your face when the needle goes in."

"All in due time," said Fenton with an unexpected smile. "You'll get to see me die, but not before I see your entire world collapse around you. Everything you hold dear, everything you love, will slowly be taken from you, and I will be here every Saturday to watch you fall to pieces. Remember, I never make empty threats."

I smiled at him, dismissively.

"It's kind of difficult to take you seriously while you're chained to the table; maybe if you were a free man I would take to heart what you're telling me," I said.

He leaned forward, slowly, as far as his chains would allow him.

"I can tear down your world without stepping foot out of this prison. Believe me; your world will come crashing down. Eventually, I will be the only one who will have anything to do with you; and then I'm going to die. Every connection you have with this world will be severed, and then just as you are about to have everything you wanted in life, you will discover this world has nothing to offer you anymore. You will be completely alone, and your despair will fill you until it consumes you, and drags you to hell to reunite with me."

Fenton's voice lowered beyond anything I had ever experienced before. There was something earie about his foreshadowing. Fenton had already managed to pull more strings from behind bars than I had thought possible. We had severed his tie with the outside world though, rendering him empty-handed in his war to beat the system.

"Now who's making empty threat?" I asked.

"I never make empty threats," he repeated.

"I know; all you do is murder helpless women."

"Once again you underestimate me," he said. "I am so much more than a high body count."

"And yet, the only reason I'm here each week is to document the people you've killed."

"What we're doing here is far beyond a few useless bimbos discarded to the sands of time. It's going to be infamous," he promised.

"That's funny, because it seems like every week ends with you telling me where to find another body. If that's what you call infamy, you're more delusional than everyone thinks," I said.

"So let's end things a little differently this week," he offered, retrieving a cigarette from the pack and tapping it on the table.

"How would you like to do things differently?"

"I'll tell you where you are going next now, and then you tell me about your adventures at Lake Anita. How does that sound?"

"I'm not opposed to mixing things up; keeping it from getting boring here," I said, shrugging.

"GAME ON," he declared, slapping the table with both hands. "Now I can tell you about my first threesome."

I shook my head and fought the urge to roll my eyes for the hundredth time. Listening to Fenton often times felt like listening to a college guy relaying their sexual exploits. They mischaracterized everything they did as an awesome accomplishment, regardless of how trivial or pointless it might have been. The only twist with Fenton, every story of an exploited woman ended with their inevitable demise.

"Kansas City in the '80's was a great place to meet whores. Downtown, north of the river; almost anywhere you went, you could find a decent pair of meat flaps to wet your dick. If you had a little money, you could own that town. The key was finding that first slut willing to do whatever you wanted for a price. They always knew someone else to work with, so it made the hunt a walk in the park," he said, with a big smile. He paused, and took a long draw on his cigarette, his dead eyes smirking at me over the top of his hand.

"Go on," I said.

"Just a heads up, since you're a single man; if you find a lady named Janet, she has a friend who will let you do some fucked up shit to her body. In fact, both of them will. It was the first time I ever had women who wanted me to choke them, it was awesome. Unfortunately, I was a big fan of choking them for my grand finale. They inadvertently took all the fun out of it," he explained.

He paused for emphasis, making me fight the urge to roll my eyes again. His twisted perspective on things was a lot to be forced to absorb. This was the job now, unfortunately; so I tried to keep the ball rolling so it would be over, sooner than later.

"So where did you meet these women?"

"They were out walking the streets," he explained. "I found Janet after a few stops, asking around to see if any of the girls were down for some group play. It didn't take long, but after I had Janet in the truck, she quickly took me to her friend Becky, and the fun began."

He paused to light another cigarette and sat back, smiling a little, as he relived yet another memory from his fucked up past.

"There was a time back in the day that the riverfront area wasn't developed the way it is now. Back in 1986 it was just a great place to corn-hole a couple prostitutes. It wasn't as easy to access, but once you were in, you had a decent amount of privacy; even for an open air kind of setting. To their credit, this wasn't their first rodeo. They knew how to keep it quiet, which ended up being to their detriment. Had they made a little noise, someone might have been around when I started going to work with my tire iron."

He paused and shrugged a little, taking the cigarette from his mouth.

"I know how it sounds, but I wasn't as refined a killing machine in my twenties. Something like that only comes with age, but like I said, they ruined all the fun of choking the life out of them. However, in hindsight, it's hard to strangle one woman when there's another watching you. The second one never seems to understand what you're doing, so they get really bent out of shape and start screaming. Fortunately for me, we were in the bed of the truck with a tire iron handy. I just hit Janet as soon as she started screaming. She was a tough one though, she took that hit and managed to jump out and start running away. That was the longest I ever had to chase a girl. She nearly got away, but I managed to catch her and finish her off. Then I carried her back to the truck where the other one was starting to recover. I already had the tire iron in my hand, I just went to work. Have you ever seen a piece of solid metal bounce off a woman's head? It's both unsettling, and rewarding; take my word for it. I will say it's not as entertaining as strangling a woman or watching them bleed out while you have your way with them, but it has its moments of fun. The only drawback is the mess. Head wounds bleed and spurt unpredictably, which means you end up getting messy. That was when I learned that I needed to refine my technique. I had already started leaving my signature, as you know, but it became more obvious that beating bitches to death needed to be reserved for special occasions or extreme circumstances. What can I say; I'm always learning?"

"So what did you do with these two after you had killed them?"

"They were friends, so it only seemed right to leave them together. I propped them up side by side against a tree facing the river. They would have been on the Missouri side of Kansas City. I didn't make my way into

Kansas for nearly a decade after that. I thought it might make a good place to retire, and here I am," he bragged.

"I suppose you're right," I said. "You picked a state that hasn't had someone put to death for over a decade, and managed to land yourself on death row; hell of a retirement plan."

"I could do worse," he admitted. "But I get my own room, I never have to worry about where my next meal is going to come from, and no one bothers me. Sounds like retirement to me; this is the dream. If everyone had what I have, people could be happy."

"You've got a funny version of the American dream," I said. "In fact, yours is quite depressing."

"But mine is a reality everyone can achieve," he insisted. "The fantasy dream of building a fortune in this country is dead. No one can ever really get ahead with corporate and government systems like we are subjected to in America."

"People are doing it every day," I informed him. "Just because you didn't make a living out of killing women, doesn't mean there aren't other careers that actually work."

"They never worked for me, so I assume they aren't universal," he replied.

"Nothing ever is," I told him. "Universal is a fantasy. Nothing is guaranteed in life, and as soon as you try to make it that way, you will lose it."

"Have it your way detective, it will never work for people like me."

"You mean the lazy and exploitative? No system will ever benefit people like you forever, which is why you find yourself having it so easy here; you don't have to make any effort. This isn't a reality for people to live on a daily basis. This level of provision and attention is only available to those who have given up all their rights. It's going to end," I promised.

"You have a lot of responses, but not a lot of answers. Typical government man; lots to say, not much to offer," Fenton drawled.

"I have a lot to offer you," I answered. "Legacy, infamy, all that bullshit; don't you remember?"

"Well then let's see what you have to offer the rest of the world. Tell me about Lake Anita. Did you find my little treasure trove of Iowa's finest delinquent women?" He asked.

"Yes we did," I replied. "They were right were you said they would be."

"I have an impeccable memory for location. It's one of my many gifts. Did you have any complications during your recovery efforts?"

"Just the one you predicted." I said.

"Ryan Carroll, the baby brother to the Congressman; he never could step outside his brother's shadow. How was the sheriff? Did he start out professional and end with threats of violence? Typical law-man," said Fenton, dismissively.

"There's nothing typical about Ryan Carroll. He embodies the corruption you so greatly decry. People like him are why it's so difficult to make advancements in police-community relations. Corrupt leaders hold up progress, and exist only to serve themselves, not their community," I said. "It's a credit to your description of him, however; he did just that."

"Thirty years later, and he still uses the same move on everyone. I can't believe that still works on anyone."

"It only works on people too scared to oppose him." I advised.

"And you're not on that list?" Fenton asked, as if he found it hard to believe.

"Absolutely not," I replied. "He doesn't even know who I am. He has no power in my corner of the country, and his time is running out on the power he has in his own jurisdiction."

"So I take it he tried to strong-arm you to take the bodies?"

"That was definitely his play."

"Did he even know who you were there to recover, or did he just try to muscle you out on some bullshit jurisdictional excuse?"

"He believed we were there for someone specific; someone who would inevitably force him to take over the investigation out of self-preservation," I hinted.

"I'm curious now; who did you tell him you were there for?"

"I told him we found where you buried Jessica Childress," I replied.

Fenton was clearly surprised. He tilted his head to the right, and took the cigarette out of his mouth.

"Now that's a ballsy move, detective." He shook his head, but in an approving manner. "I'm impressed. How did he react?"

"Like someone walked across his grave. He was pretty shocked to hear Jessica's name, or maybe it was your name that shook him. It took him a few seconds to process the news; but then he became very adamant about handling the investigation locally," I explained.

"Now that is something I would have paid to see," he said, nodding his head. "Like I said, detective, I'm impressed. Did his reaction tell you anything?"

"It told me he knew all about her disappearance, and would do anything in his power to hide what he had done. Unfortunately for him, he still doesn't know we have him on film, helping you carry Jessica's unconscious body into a barn for the purpose of her murder and disposal."

"I would love to make a new deal with you," said Fenton. "I would give you all the information for the next nineteen weeks, all the victims, all the locations, in one sitting, if you let me watch you play the video for the sheriff. I would give you all of that just to see his reaction when he found out he was going to prison for the rest of his life."

"As tempting of a deal as that is, I don't see a way to make it happen," I replied.

"I assumed it would be a long shot, I just really hated that son of a bitch; almost as much as his entitled brother, Simon."

"If Simon is anything like Ryan, I understand your sentiment," I admitted.

"They are carbon copies of one another. The only difference between the two is the level of ambition they hold. Ryan wants to run the family business; Simon wants to run the world. Either way, they are both powerful people who will stop at nothing to control everything within their reach. It's the reason I both despise, and admire them."

"No wonder you found yourself in such familiar company while you were there," I said.

"It's the reason I knew you were in for such a challenge last week. The Carroll cartel is never going to make it easy for anyone to wield leverage against them. Those that do don't last very long."

"I'll take that under advisement," I replied.

Fenton shook the pack of cigarettes, finally freeing the last one. He lit it casually, and then looked over at me again.

"You still haven't told me how you faired at Anita Lake," he said, gesturing to me with his palm up, indicating I should continue with the story.

"There wasn't much to tell. We found the grave using a K-9 victim recovery team from the FBI. We walked in a team to dig out the body, and used a boat to deliver the equipment to the gravesite. We dug up the bodies, five of them; just like you told me there would be. Then the Sheriff arrived just as the team was carrying the body bags out of the forest. The Sheriff had his minions take the body bags; end of story," I said casually.

He looked displeased with the succinct nature of my story. "I certainly hope you're writing my tales of conquest better than you just told that half-assed anecdote. There was no suspense, no creative descriptors; just flat statements that sound like little more than bullet points. I have to say; I'm disappointed in you, detective. Did I select the wrong person to write my story?"

"Without a doubt, you picked the wrong person. However, my job is not to entertain you while I'm here. I'm here to plant my ass in a seat for three hours and collect the name and/or location of the next body on your list," I explained. "The three hours is simply a part of the deal. We are not friends; we don't like each other. You hate me, and I hate you; let's keep it that way. You have already told me what I needed to know; now I'm just here to complete my allotted time requirement."

"Well pardon me for being curious, detective. I gave you a lot more than I needed to in the grand scheme of things today. I could have given you a location and a brief description, but I went beyond that. I told you how they died, what their last few minutes of life were like; why can't you do as much for me?"

I checked the stopwatch, "Because we're out of time."

"Nice job running out the clock." He commended, slowly as I packed up everything on the table.

I stood to leave, stretching my legs a little, before walking to the door.

"Detective," he called after me. "How did you keep the sheriff from taking the bodies?"

I paused at the door, waiting for it to open as I pondered whether or not to answer him. The door lock popped, but I hesitated to step outside the room. I swiveled back to look at him with his head turned to the side, waiting for me to respond.

"The remains weren't in the bags, they were on the boat." I said, and then stepped out the door.

CHAPTER THIRTY-THREE

The rest of the weekend had been mine to enjoy. I finally finished getting my house in order, and managed not to get called in for anything. Ross and Shirley hadn't been so lucky, as they were taking point on the City Park victims. They were working long hours to bring home the last few details to get arrest warrants signed for Conner and Greg Marten. Det. Shirley was reviewing hours of old, grainy security footage from the bar district collected after Holton and Brand had been reported missing. Det. Ross was interviewing as many former and current employees, subcontractors, acquaintances, suppliers, and contacts of Greg and Conner Marten as he could find. Their workload had increased dramatically as they continued to develop the case to build probable cause for the warrants.

The manhunt for Amos Foster was being led by the FBI and Wichita Police Department. They had a no-bond warrant for kidnapping along with several federal warrants through the ATF for violations committed when he rigged his outbuilding to explode. The Wichita FBI field office was leading the investigation after another victim was found on Foster's property. None of the details were being released publicly about the second victim, but it appeared Foster would be facing possible murder charges on top of everything else already on the list.

I spent the first hour Monday morning, meeting with the bomb team from the KBI who had been investigating the car bomb which had claimed Officer Preston's life. I presented all the photographs I had from the warrant at Foster's, and emphasized the photos which contained the diagrams for the car bomb. The KBI was tight-lipped about the investigation, and refused to confirm or deny if the bomb in the diagram matched the one from the park. I stepped out of the meeting with more questions than answers, wondering why they hadn't at least provided some kind of update or confirmation on what I had collected.

Fortunately, I didn't have much time to rage about the lack of inter-department communication. As soon as I returned to my desk, I had a message from the Kansas City Missouri Police Department. After I had returned from El Dorado on Saturday, I had reached out to KCPD to request information on Fenton's latest confession. To my surprise, they responded early Monday, and indicated they had found the case in question.

Lt. Carter immediately green-lit my trip to Kansas City, hoping I would wrap up the investigation there in short time so I could return to aid in the increasingly complicated Marten investigation.

I hit the road by 1000 hours, on my way to meet Terry at the Kansas City Police Department East Patrol Campus in the 2600 Block of Prospect Avenue. The long drives to Iowa by way of Lincoln, Nebraska made a trip to Kansas City seem, almost routine.

Terry met me outside the Kansas City Police Department East Patrol Campus about fifteen minutes before our scheduled meeting. After a big win in Cass County the week before, we were still feeling motivated.

"Terry, it's good to see you again." I said, smiling and shaking his hand as he walked up.

"Sorry we didn't get a chance to catch up after everything went down in front of the Cass County Sheriff's Office building. The drive-by with Sanders in the front seat of the car was a stroke of brilliance," he said.

"I appreciate the compliment; the sheriff's reaction was everything I was hoping to see."

"No kidding; did you see his face when I had Sanders wave at him while still wearing the handcuffs? It was priceless; I just wish I had a camera," laughed Terry.

"That was my second favorite part of the trip." I said, laughing with him. "My favorite, by far; was his reaction when he opened the first body bag full of sticks, rocks, and leaves. He nearly shit himself."

"I'm so pissed I couldn't see his face then, I was already on my way to Kansas City with Sanders by then. Describe it to me; what color did he turn when he realized he had been handed some of Iowa's finest tree limbs instead of five homicide victims?"

"It was a deep red, almost a purple," I replied.

We were laughing, almost to the point of crying. Sheriff Carroll had been handed nothing from the Lake Anita investigation, and it had been almost more than I could handle, even when pretending to protest his acquisition of the body bags on scene.

"He has to hate us; we not only made him look like an asshole in front of all his deputies, we managed to skip town without him ever knowing how we did it," Terry said, wiping tears from his eyes.

"I'm sure he will get to read about it from behind bars. Please tell me we're getting close on warrants for them." I begged, hoping for some good news on that front.

"We're close; the video was enough for Ryan's warrant, we're just waiting for official confirmation from your girl that the baby Jessica was carrying belongs to Simon." Terry advised, finally finding his composure. "Wells wants to hand down federal indictments all at once; he doesn't want to tip anyone off by picking them up, one at a time."

"I can hardly call her "my girl" after having dinner together once, but I'm sure we're only days away from having everything we need to round up half the Carroll family." I said.

"How did she handle everything on scene?" Terry asked.

"Brilliantly," I replied. "She was a good sport about not knowing until the last minute and acted like she didn't have a clue. She arranged everything from her end, and even mixed up the body bags so her own team wouldn't know about the switch until they met Agent Davidson at the dock. We dropped her and the interns off to ride with Davidson so the rest of us could go file a complaint with the sheriff's office. After he figured out we had tricked him, he was pissed, so we decided we didn't really need to file a complaint."

"I'm surprised he didn't retaliate with you and Wells standing in front of him." Terry admitted.

"I'm sure he would have if we were still out at the lake. He didn't really have a choice since the Sheriff's Office parking lot is so public. I'm sure most of those deputies have no idea what he was trying to hide from the world. They were all too young to have been deputies back when Ryan and Simon were making all the strong-arm moves to take over the county. How did the Childress family react to the news?" I asked.

"Surprisingly well; well that's not true. They both cried, but I could tell they were just relieved to finally have some answers."

"Are they going to cooperate with the federal investigation against the Carroll family?"

"That's where the conversation took a positive turn," Terry answered. "I told the Childress' that we were recovering Jessica along with four other bodies out at Lake Anita State Lake. That's when Sanders excused himself from the room. I had the Childress' wait for me while I stepped outside far enough to overhear Sanders tell the sheriff we were recovering bodies from Lake Anita, then I took him into custody."

"How did he take the news?"

"He wasn't happy, but he knew if I used a Taser on him at his age, he was going to drop dead from a heart attack. He cuffed himself; I disarmed him and then sat him down in front of the Childress' while I informed them of the federal investigation, starting with the arrest of Sanders, who had been proven to be a corrupt FBI agent. As soon as they saw I was on the level, and that I wasn't part of the local organization, they agreed to help us out. They said as soon as Ryan is in custody, they're prepared to go on the record against the Carroll family." Terry explained.

"Did they ask for immunity for their own underhanded dealings?" I wondered.

"They mentioned it. They explained their hands hadn't been squeaky clean during the process of the Carroll family coming to power. They knew what they were up against, so they had kept it quiet all these years until they had confirmation on what the Carroll family did to their daughter," said Terry. "Apparently Fenton tipped them off years ago?"

"Yeah, he did. He handed them some leverage, but didn't answer all their questions or explain his involvement in it all. Did you spare them the gruesome details?"

"I only told them enough to make sure they were on our side. I didn't tell them about the pregnancy, or how Jessica died. They don't need to know any of that; at least not yet. They were happy to hear the killer was behind bars, and the rest of the guilty parties would be facing justice soon." Terry concluded.

"That was a good fucking trip, wasn't it?" I asked. I was struggling to hide my enthusiasm as we entered the building, and made our way to the front desk.

"We accomplished a lot; I don't know how we could have that level of success again," admitted Terry.

"I agree, that trip was one in a million," I said as we reached the desk. The attendant at the front desk stood up and approached the glass. She pressed the button on the desk in front of her and spoke through a speaker in the glass.

"Can I help you?"

"Detective Bryant and Agent Jones, FBI task force; we're here to see Detective Salvador," I replied.

"I'll page the detective and let him know you're here," she replied. "Have a seat behind you, he should be out shortly."

"What do you have going on the rest of the day?" Terry asked, as we found a couple seats in the lobby area.

The chairs had light gray cushions on black metal frames. Surrounding the chairs was an opaque room with light blue carpet, illuminated by huge bay windows and a small skylight in the middle. We grabbed a couple chairs across from each other over a lightly stained, wooden coffee table, and waited.

"The usual," I replied, casually. "I'll take the evidence up to Dr. Elmore's team, and then circle back home."

"You two going out again?" he inquired.

"I certainly hope so." I said with a quick smile. "It's hard to have that conversation when we're meeting at her lab each time. There were too many eyes and ears around when I dropped her off last week. Hopefully I'll get to talk to her about it today."

"Good to hear," he said, casually.

We relaxed for a moment, enjoying the small portions of the job when we weren't being pulled every which way by various investigations.

"Detective Bryant?" a voice asked behind me.

I stood up and turned around and spotted a short, Latino man, wearing a long sleeve white button up shirt, black slacks and black tie, walking towards us, out of the secure doors on the north end of the lobby.

"Detective Salvador, I presume," I said, addressing him as he approached.

"You must be Detective Bryant," he said, shaking my hand.

"Pleased to meet you; let me introduce my FBI compatriot, Agent Terrance Jones."

"Call me Terry, please."

"It's great to meet you both, call me Sal, everybody does. Follow me gentlemen, I have everything you need back in the conference room."

We fell in line behind Sal and followed him back through the security doors. We entered immediately into a small room with a second door, which Sal scanned an ID card to allow us entry. Beyond the second door was a wide open room, stacked from end to end with cubicles. The room was lined with offices, complete with windows looking out into the open area. We followed Sal as he circled the large room along two walls before reaching a conference room, located on the far corner of the office area.

"This place is massive," I commented when we finally reached the conference room.

"This is just one of several locations utilized by the KCPD. We have several other buildings and facilities around the city. There's just too much to contain to a single location," Sal replied.

"It dwarfs the department I'm from. Our one building isn't even as big as this one," I observed.

"You get used to it after a while," Sal assured me. "Right here in the boxes is everything for case number 86-10482H. I have complete files on the two victims, crime scene photos, murder weapon, victim clothing, lab results; the works."

"Thanks, Sal; I really appreciate the speed of your response," I said, shaking his hand again.

"It's my job. We have so many cases each year, eventually they start devolving into a cold-case status. When they do, they become my problem. When I got your message, I was relieved. We don't often get thirty year old homicide cases solved, so it's a good day for us when we do."

"How many detectives investigate cold cases?" asked Terry.

"There are just two of us at the moment," Sal replied, "And it's less investigation and more management. Every now and again we get a breakthrough, but it's rare. Typically we push to investigate the cases that still have support and oversight from the families of the victims. So many of them, there's nothing we can do. There's never any new security footage to collect, and anything that has a DNA sample available, got tested. We don't update the DNA profiles every year to see if there's suddenly a match in the nationwide database; that would take up most of our time every year. Your case was last run through the database back in 2006. It didn't have a match then, so it got put on a shelf in storage where it's been sitting ever since."

"Well, we should have a match for it now," I offered.

"I read up on your guy, Fenton. He sounds like a good match for this case. Sitting on multiple life sentences isn't he?"

"And three capital convictions," I advised. "He's set for execution, Christmas day."

"Good riddance to shitty people, I say," offered Sal before he threw up his hands, looking defensive. "Just don't tell my wife I'm pro-capital punishment; she thinks I agree with her, 'cause I like to pick my battles."

"I'll change your name for the official record," I said.

"Thank you; my marriage thanks you," said Sal, with a laugh. "Is there anything I can do to help you with case review before I sign all this over to you?"

"I have to read through it all anyways," I replied. "I'll call you with my questions in a week or two if I have any, and I'll send over the confirmation as soon as we have it."

"Do you investigate all these back at your department?" he asked.

"Actually, he does, but I review them since I'm the one signing for them," Terry informed him.

"Either way, it clears a spot on my shelf in storage. I'm sure it won't be empty for long."

"If you ever need anything or have any questions, give us a call," instructed Terry, handing Sal a business card.

"Thank you gentlemen, I look forward to hearing from you."

Sal escorted us back out through the security doors and shook our hands again before leaving us to be on our way. Terry and I carried the two boxes of files and evidence to my car, and parted ways.

———

The way to Dr. Elmore's lab had become all too familiar after the past six weeks or so. I was excited to get there, and pushed the speed limit just a little bit.

I was greeted casually by the team as they raised their heads from their work to wave or give me a nod. I set the box containing the evidence down outside Dr. Elmore's office, before knocking on the door.

"It's open," I heard her call out from inside.

I turned the handle slightly, rendering the door slightly ajar, before I picked up the box again and backed into the office, pushing the door open with my shoulders.

"Detective Bryant, it's good to see you again," she said when she saw me.

"Good to see you too, Dr. Elmore," I replied, closing the door behind me with my foot.

"Hi, James," she said again, smiling this time.

My heart did a weird flip in my chest, making it difficult to respond immediately. I tried to mask my uncertainty by setting the box down on the table next to her printer.

"Hey," I said when I finally found the courage to speak.

"Should we start with pleasantries first, or get right down to business?" She asked, her smile growing more mischievous.

"That depends on what you mean by business." I said, trying to match her flirtatious tone, "And by pleasantries."

Her face changed instantly, as did her tone.

"I meant small talk, and updates on the case," she replied, stepping out from behind her desk. "What did you mean detective?"

"Um," I stumbled to find the words to say that would salvage the awkward situation. I froze a moment longer until she was standing in front of me, hands on her hips, looking stern.

I was speechless for an apparent eternity, before her face cracked into a smile.

"You are so gullible." She said, her smile turning into a laugh.

"Wow, that's really unprofessional," I said, feigning a stern face.

"You can't turn this back at me, I own this game," she advised.

She slipped her left hand into my right, and moved in close, pressing her body slightly against mine. She looked up into my eyes for a second, and appeared to be holding her breath.

"Is there something I can do for you, Lydia?"

"I don't know, is there?"

I held back as long as I could before finally leaning forward, and kissing her gently on the lips.

I lifted my head, and opened my eyes sooner than I wanted. If I kissed her much longer, I'd be throwing everything off her desk in another second. We weren't quite ready for that, so I did my best to keep things as calm and casual as possible.

I exhaled slowly, and met her gaze again as her eyes opened again.

"Was that business or pleasantries?"

"Both," she replied with a roguish smile.

"That's what I was afraid of," I replied, with a quiet chuckle.

"You should visit more often," she said, still staring into my eyes.

"You should visit; period," I responded.

"I'll have to check my schedule," she offered.

We separated, and I dropped her hand. There was still official business to attend to, and plenty of it.

"What have you learned about our five victims?"

"They're all Fenton's victims, late teens to early twenties. We matched our bone from the Childress casket to one of the five victims we recovered, but we have no idea who is who. Unless Cass County releases the files on the missing women in their area, we are going to struggle to find out who is who." She advised.

"Has your team had any luck using other avenues to figure out who they might be?"

"Not yet," she replied. "We're checking in surrounding counties in that area to see if any of them has records of missing women around that time-period; so far, no luck."

"We're going to need an act of God to get the sheriff to hand over those files to us. There are rumors of a fire years ago that destroyed a bunch of police records, but no one knows if it was set intentionally or even what was lost. I just know we aren't going to get any cooperation from them, especially after the stunt we pulled." I admitted.

"Yeah, that didn't make us any friends," she agreed. "Did the other part of your plan work out?"

"It did; we flushed out the crooked agent and Terry took him into custody. He's in federal custody now facing a plethora of charges, the least of which include identity fraud and criminal conspiracy. Hopefully he sings for us; because he has to be loaded down with several decades' worth of dirt on the Carroll family." I said.

"How about your investigation down in Wichita; how did it go?" She asked.

"The team recovered a nine year old girl, and got her out before she could suffer any more torment. I'm not sure what happened to her, but I'm glad they got to her in time." I replied.

"Was she in danger?"

"She had a plastic bag zip tied over her head. If the team got there any later, she would have suffered permanent brain damage. I don't know much more beyond that," I told her.

"But the guy got away?"

"Unfortunately," I replied. "He's a smart one, but they have federal warrants out for him; he can only hide for so long."

"Let's hope so," she said, sitting back on the edge of her desk. "Sorry I don't have anything concrete to give you. We're working with a lot of unknowns here."

"Don't worry about it," I told her. "In time, we will figure all this out. In the meantime, I brought you another Fenton case. This time, the bodies were found after a day or two, back in 1986, so there's no body to examine."

"But that's the interesting part of the job," she answered.

"This one is just like the ones a couple weeks ago. They have a DNA sample from the tire iron used in the murder. They just need it compared to Fenton to make sure we have the right case and the right suspect in custody."

"These are always a slam dunk." She replied, taking a look in the box, "So this won't take me long. Are you going to be in town long?"

"How long did you have in mind?" I asked.

"Long enough to grab dinner," she replied, taking a step towards me.

She moved in close again, leaning her body against me as she placed her hands on my chest.

"James, is that your phone? Or are you just happy to see me?"

"Shit," I said, taking a step back. I pulled my phone out of my pocket to see who was calling. I looked at her apologetically, "I have to take this."

"Don't apologize for doing your job," she instructed, stepping back towards the box.

"Hey Shirley," I said as I answered my phone.

"I'm on my way to the courthouse with the warrants right now. We have enough for Conner and Greg Marten. Lt. Carter wants you back this evening," she advised.

"I'll be there." I advised, and hung up the phone.

I stared at my phone for a minute, wishing I hadn't answered it.

"Go." I turned to look at her as she stared at me, leaned up against the desk again. "Go do cop stuff, and let me do my science stuff." She said, "But you owe me a dinner date."

"Deal," I said, and kissed her goodbye.

CHAPTER THIRTY-FOUR

"Ok, bring me up to speed," I requested.

The team was gathered in the conference room again. Ross and Shirley had paperwork in their hands, and were prepared to give their final remarks on the Holton-Brand homicides.

"I reviewed every bit of available security footage from the weekend Holton and Brand were believed to have disappeared," started Shirley. "I found footage of Holton at the Golden Bar and Grill. It's been out of business now for a few years, you probably know it as Baron's Nightclub now. The Golden was known as the best, gay friendly bar back in 2012, and Holton was a frequent customer there. Holton was known to frequently attend events there, and had a reputation for one night stands."

"Det. Shirley found this footage of Holton the Friday night before he was reported missing," said Ross, turning his laptop around for everyone to see. "He is seen here for over an hour with an, until now, unknown male subject in a corner booth. The two ordered several rounds of drinks, before leaving together. They appear to be quite close, and appeared to be acting romantic with one another, according to bar staff that was working at the time."

"We followed up with every staff member from the Golden Bar who worked on the weekend in question. Most of them had already been interviewed previously, and had to be tracked down again. We didn't have any specific person of interest during the investigation five years ago. With the addition of Conner Marten as a possible suspect, we made it through a second round of interviews, complete with a suspect photo lineup. Four of the employees named Conner as the person seen with Holton that night; three others recognized him because he frequented The Golden Bar back then. They all agree they didn't see him at The Golden Bar after this weekend. Most of them don't believe they've even seen him around the bar district past that weekend." Shirley continued.

"We followed up with Spencer Warren's mother as well. We had already notified her about finding Spencer's body; this time, with the help of one of the patrol officers, we did a double blind photo lineup with Conner's picture included to see if she recognized anyone. She picked Conner out of the lineup, and informed us he had been seen with Spencer several days before she reported him missing. She apparently thought nothing of him at the time because she said he appeared to be a friend of Spencer's," said Ross.

"We researched the playground construction timeline. It turns out, after Greg Marten had successfully had the entire city government voted out and new blood in power, he started doing contract work for the city again. Greg Marten was in charge of pouring all the concrete foundations and slabs for the playground back in 2008. The week Spencer Warren went missing, they were pouring the foundation for the playground equipment where we later found Spencer, thanks to the information provided by Fenton through Det. Bryant," said Shirley.

"We later found Holton and Brand underneath the flowerbed in the Hayley Marten memorial garden. It was completed in 2012, less than two weeks after Conner was seen leaving the bar with Tory Holton. That's two different coincidences in which Greg Marten was responsible for construction which was used to conceal the location of homicide victims. Detective Shirley and I don't believe in coincidences and neither does Judge Hollinbrook. He signed the arrest warrants for Greg and Conner Marten last night. As soon as we have eyes on them, we will take them into custody," declared Ross.

"Sgt. Ellis and one of our plain-clothes patrol officers have eyes on Greg Marten's house. They will notify us as soon as they have eyes on either of them," said Lt. Carter. "The task force will respond to the house and make the arrest."

"Does anyone have any questions?" asked Det. Shirley.

The group shook their heads and looked back and forth for a few second.

"This is where we earn our paychecks," said Lt. Carter. "Let's do it right."

The team dismissed from the conference room, going their separate ways.

I returned to my desk, and spent the next half hour reviewing the case from KCMO. There wasn't much to build on, and not much to go on. The case had gone cold decades prior due to insufficient leads and lack of tangible evidence. The hopes of solving a case of this type were slim to none back in 1986 with an isolated location, victims with high-risk lifestyles, and a suspect from out of town who kept on moving. Shy of a confession, this case had no hope of being solved. It was one of many cases across the country that would have been relegated to the cold case vault, and never seen again. The biggest challenge facing Detective Salvador was going to be tracking down the families of the two women to let them know their loved-one's killer had been caught.

"Mount up, team; Sgt. Ellis has eyes on Greg and Conner. They're at Greg's house, and they may have made the surveillance team. Everyone, get to the conference room for warrant assignments," ordered Lt. Carter as he walked through the cubicles.

I slung my outer carrier vest over my shirt, and snapped it into place on the sides as I made my way back to the conference room.

The team did their best to get into their gear while simultaneously listening to their assignments.

"We are not forcing this," started Lt. Carter. "We know they are in there, and they are by themselves. We have no exigent circumstances forcing us to make entry. We are going to get them on the phone and get them to come outside one at a time. Ross, you will set up as over-watch sniper. You will take a position across the street and ensure we have a marksman watching the process. We have no indication they are violent or intend to resist, but we aren't taking any chances. Shirley and Bryant; you will be on contact and control. I will talk with them on the phone, and P.A. system if need be. As soon as we have them where we want them, the two of you will handcuff and detain. As soon as the first one is detained, we will secure them behind a unit, and then bring out the second one. Sgt.

Ellis has orders to cover the back door in the alley to ensure they don't escape that way. Is everyone clear on their assignments? Let's go."

Shirley and I climbed into one of the unmarked investigations units, and Ross and Lt. Carter in the other.

"Warrant team, 10-8, in route for warrant service," Lt. Carter called over the radio.

Lt. Carter called out badge numbers for all four members of the team, and received a confirmation from dispatch.

From my spot in the driver's seat, I did my best to slow my heartrate and breathing. I had a tendency to get too excited before a serious call, an emergency run, or a big warrant service. The key was to stay calm; otherwise you risked increasing stress hormones and making poor decisions. I heard Shirley doing the same in the passenger seat. I slowed my breathing, taking deep breaths to stay calm as we hit the main drag towards our destination. We weren't in any kind of hurry, but we weren't in the habit of dragging our asses either. We had to get there safely, handle business, and get the fuck out.

I was still doing my breathing exercises as we turned off onto the side streets, and started navigating between cars parked on either side of the road.

A block out from our destination, Ross climbed out of the car in front of us, and retrieved his rifle from the back seat of the car. He put the sling over his neck, hung the rifle down by his side, to reduce the amount of attention he would get as he walked to the alley on the other side of the street. We parked our units behind several other cars on the side of the road and gave him several minutes to find his spot, and give the signal to advance.

Over the radio, I heard Sgt. Ellis and the other officer check in, announcing they were in position in the south alley with eyes on the target house. Finally Ross announced he was in position, giving us the go-ahead to move in.

Lt. Carter lit up his unit, the limited amount of lights on the unmarked unit flashing off the houses on either side of the street as Det. Shirley hit the lights on our unit.

Lt. Carter pulled his unit in, parallel with the street, and just out from in front of Greg Marten's house. His angle allowed him to see the front and west side of the house for optimum visibility. Det. Ross' position was covering the front of the house and the east side, ensuring the team could see the entire house since Sgt. Ellis had eyes on the back of the house. I let Shirley out of the car while she was positioned behind the Lieutenants vehicle before I pulled slightly further forward, just barely positioning my unit further east along the roadway. This allowed me to see both sides of the house, while having the best position to move forward to handcuff them as they came outside.

Radio Traffic

"Dispatch, give the subjects a call, see if they will step outside."

"10-4, in process now"

I held my breath a little, still waiting to see how this was going to play out. I climbed out of my unit and shut the door behind me. The window was rolled down, and I had the receiver to the radio hanging from the steering wheel, within easy reach. Det. Shirley positioned herself with the trunk of our unit, and the hood of Lt. Carter's as cover, and took a knee where she had a good view of the house.

"Dispatch to units on Colorado, we made contact with Greg, He hung up on us, we can no longer get him to answer the phone"

"10-4, dispatch, we will make contact via the P.A. system, clear channel one"

"10-4, dispatch to all units, move all traffic to channel two until notified otherwise, clear channel one for felony warrant service"

P.A. SYSTEM TRAFFIC

"GREG MARTEN; THIS IS LT. CARTER WITH THE POLICE DEPARTMENT. WE HAVE A WARRANT FOR YOU ARREST, AND FOR CONNER AS WELL. FLASH YOUR PORCH LIGHT IF YOU CAN HEAR ME."

Nothing happened. We waited, breathing deeply, as we all watched with anticipation, for the light on the porch to flash. The longer we waited, the more concerned we became.

Suddenly, it flashed.

"GREG, I SAW THE LIGHT FLASH, THANK YOU FOR RESPONDING. I NEED YOU TO DO EVERYTHING I SAY, EXACTLY AS I SAY IT. DO YOU UNDERSTAND? FLASH THE PORCH LIGHT TWO TIMES IF YOU UNDERSTAND."

This time there was a shorter pause, followed by two brief flickers of the porch light.

"THANK YOU GREG. I APPRECIATE YOUR COOPERATION. WHAT I WANT YOU TO DO NEXT IS OPEN THE DOOR, BUT STAY OUT OF SIGHT. FLASH YOUR LIGHT TWICE IF YOU UNDERSTAND MY DIRECTIONS."

Two more flashes emitted from the porch, indicating the occupants understanding.

"OPEN THE FRONT DOOR ON MY COMMAND...OPEN THE FRONT DOOR, DO IT NOW."

The door opened, revealing the lights were off inside the house.

"GREG, I WANT CONNER TO STEP OUT INTO THE DOOR WAY WITH HIS HANDS UP ON MY COMMAND... STEP OUT... DO IT NOW."

A figure stepped into the doorway, his white long sleeve T-shirt standing out against the darkness inside the house.

"L.T., I've got a visual," I called out.

"CONNER, I WANT YOU TO REACH BACK SLOWLY AND OPEN THE GLASS DOOR WITH YOUR RIGHT HAND WHILE KEEPING YOUR LEFT HAND ELEVATED ABOVE YOUR HEAD, THEN PUT YOUR RIGHT HAND BACK OVER YOUR HEAD...DO IT NOW."

Conner reached back slowly, tripped the latch on the glass door and left it slightly ajar, and then raising his right hand over his head again.

"CONNER, WHEN I TELL YOU TO; TAKE TWO STEPS BACKWARDS, MOVING YOU OUT ONTO THE FRONT PORCH...DO IT NOW."

Conner stepped backwards, once...then twice; pausing as the glass door closed slowly in front of him, finally latching.

"CONNER; YOU HAVE THREE STEPS LEADING UP TO THE PORCH. WHEN I TELL YOU TO, STEP BACKWARDS DOWN EACH STEP, ONE AT A TIME, UNTIL YOU REACH THE SIDE-WALK; DO IT NOW...ONE STEP...NOW TWO STEPS...THAT'S THE THIRD STEP; NOW STEP BACKWARDS ONTO THE SIDE-WALK. YOU'RE DOING GREAT CONNER, THANK YOU FOR YOU COOPERATION. WHAT I WANT YOU TO DO NEXT IS TAKE BIG STEPS BACKWARDS, AS BIG AS YOU CAN TAKE. I WANT YOU TO TAKE ONE STEP AT A TIME, AND THEN PAUSE BEFORE YOU TAKE THE NEXT STEP. I WILL ALERT YOU

WHEN YOU ARE APPROACHING THE CURB. DO NOT TURN YOUR HEAD TO LOOK AT US; JUST TAKE BIG, SLOW STEPS UNTIL I TELL YOU TO STOP. DO IT NOW, NICE AND SLOW."

We watched from our places behind the cars as Conner took large steps backwards, keeping his head turned away from us and his hands in the air over his head. Conner continued this way, slowly approaching the street to my left; one step at a time.

"ONE MORE STEP CONNER AND YOU WILL BE AT THE CURB. STOP WHERE YOU ARE...NOW. CONNER; USING YOUR LEFT FOOT, REACH BACKWARDS WITH YOUR TOE AND SEE IF YOU CAN FEEL THE EDGE OF THE CURB; DO IT NOW. STEP DOWN SLOWLY OFF THE CURB; DO IT NOW. NOW TURN SLIGHTLY TO YOUR LEFT, CONTINUING TO LOOK AWAY FROM US. NOW TAKE TWO BIG STEPS BACKWARDS."

"Bryant, can you handle verbal commands from here?"

"10-4, L.T.," I replied. "Conner, can you hear my voice? Tell me if you can."

I watched as he nodded his head before replying, "I can hear you."

"Conner, I want you to listen to me as I give you instructions, do you understand me?"

"I understand," he replied.

"Take two steps backwards towards the sound of my voice." I instructed, "Do it now."

Conner did as I instructed, stepping backward until he was even with the front driver's side bumper of my unit.

"Conner, take two more steps backwards towards my voice; do it now," I commanded.

Conner did as he was instructed, taking two steps backwards, placing him behind my vehicle where I could handcuff him.

"Conner, what I want you to do next is go down on your left knee, and then on your right knee until you are kneeling, do you understand?"

"I understand," he replied.

"Do it now," I told him.

Conner slowly knelt down, one knee at a time as he had been instructed.

"Conner, now I want you to cross your feet behind you as you kneel. Do it now."

Conner crossed his feet behind him; a position which more difficult to stand up quickly.

"Conner, keeping your feet crossed, I want you to sit backwards onto your feet until you can feel your weight pushing down on your feet; do it now." I paused as he followed instructions and then continued. "Now I want you to lean your head forward and remain in that position until I finish handcuffing you, understand?"

"I understand," he answered.

"Holstering," I declared.

"Holster," replied Shirley.

I stowed my sidearm in its holster and pulled out a pair of handcuffs. Keeping my eyes on Conner, I held the handcuffs up in front of my face, adjusting them to the proper position. I stepped to the right and slowly approached Conner, as Shirley adjusted her position to cover me as I did so.

I grabbed Conner's right arm first, clasping the handcuff onto it part of the way before directing his hand behind his back. I reached up and grabbed his left arm, pulled it down behind his back, and placed the other handcuff on his left wrist. I clicked the handcuffs into place and checked to ensure they weren't too tight, before double locking them.

"Uncross your legs," I instructed him, "When I lift you up, get a foot underneath yourself and stand up slowly."

"I want my lawyer," he said.

"Noted," I replied.

I tucked my left arm under his right shoulder and hoisted him up from his kneeling position with my left hand on the top of his shoulder. Keeping my left hand in place, I leaned Conner over with one arm, keeping his head down below the top of the car until I walked him over to the Lieutenants unit. I opened the door with my right hand, still controlling his movement with my left. I slipped my arm out from under his and moved around to his left side, helping him sit down in the back of the unit. Lt. Carter used the button on his driver's door to lock the car doors, ensuring Conner could not get out. I resumed my position at the front of my car, waiting for the second round. I took a knee, keeping the engine compartment in between me and the house, and waited for the next step.

"GREG; IT'S YOUR TURN. STEP INTO THE DOORWAY

WITH YOUR BACK TO THE DOOR AND YOU HANDS UP. DO IT NOW."

Greg stepped out the front door, hands at his sides, descending the front steps, ignoring Lt. Carter's instructions as he did so.

"GREG; LISTEN TO ME. STOP WHERE YOU ARE AND WAIT FOR INSTRUCTIONS."

Greg didn't appear to be in any hurry, but he was ignoring directions, which made us all nervous. Over the radio, Det. Ross made an announcement in a level tone.

"L.T., he has a handgun in his waistband."

I looked closer. Ross was right; I could see the handle of a black handgun protruding from his waistband, in the appendix carry position.

"GREG; I NEED YOU TO STOP WALKING TOWARDS US AND PUT YOUR HANDS IN THE AIR. GREG! PUT YOUR HANDS IN THE AIR."

I could feel the tension building in my body as I displayed my sidearm over the top of the hood. I resisted the urge to start yelling instructions at Greg as he continued to slowly approach, walking straight towards me. Greg wasn't making any threatening movements, but each step he took increased the likelihood that he would. This approach had been used before; someone moves slowly, approaching law enforcement until the distance is minimal, before reaching for their gun. I was unfortunately running out of distance. Greg was almost to the curb, which meant he was less than fifteen yards from me.

"Greg listen to me," I called out. "Please don't do this Greg. It doesn't have to end like this. We can work this out. No one needs to get hurt."

He stopped in his tracks, locking eyes with me, recognizing me from our previous encounter.

"I already lost my little girl; please don't take my son away from me," he pleaded.

"I don't want to take anything away from you, Greg. I want to stop all of this before it gets any worse," I told him.

"I didn't have a choice; that monster robbed me of my only daughter. I would have done anything to protect my son," he cried. I could see the tears running down his face.

We were mixing a dangerous cocktail now. Desperation, combined with the loss of a loved one and impending criminal charges had been more than enough to drive someone to madness in the past. This had all the volatile ingredients of a suicide by cop, and we were running out of time.

"Greg; I know you feel like you've lost everything and everyone you care about, but you haven't. Your son is still alive. You've been there for him through everything; don't abandon him now when he needs you the most." I begged.

"Just kill me," he sobbed.

"I'm not going to do that, Greg. You're not a bad person, okay? Everybody makes mistakes, but yours don't have to be a death sentence." I said, trying to change his perspective. "You've done exactly what good parents do; they protect their kids. You were just protecting your son, I get that. He is lucky to have you as his father. But if you do this, Greg, if you force us to do the one thing we don't want to do here, you're depriving Conner of his father. Don't do that; don't do that to Conner, he needs you."

The Taser went off at the opportune time. Sgt. Ellis had seized the opportunity to sneak up from behind Greg, approaching at a ninety degree angle from my right until he was within range to make the shot with his Taser.

Greg locked up, hands to his sides, he fell on his face in the grass, two feet shy of the curb.

"Greg, stay down," I called out. "Put your hands out to your sides or you're going to get Tased again."

The clicking of the Taser stopped, allowing Greg to relax and catch his breath as the pain ceased coursing through him.

"Greg, put your hands out the side. Don't make us Tase you again." I instructed.

Greg was done after that. He reached his hands out to either side, allowing Lt. Carter to leave cover, circle behind his unit and approach Greg from behind. Greg continued to cooperate, even as the handcuffs clicked into place.

It was finally over. Both of them were in custody, ending the standoff, only minutes after it had started.

I let out a huge sigh, holstered my weapon, and sat down with my back against the front bumper of the car.

"We're clear," called Lt. Carter.

"Thank God," I said, sighing again.

"Not bad kid," said Det. Shirley, offering me a hand up.

"Any day I don't have to shoot someone is a great day." I said, wiping the sweat from my face with my sleeve.

"You did good work," she said, "Let's get these two booked."

I took her outstretched arm, and pushed myself up from the ground. To my surprise, I was a little too heavy for her to lift. Just shy of being able to hold myself up, she started falling on top of me.

That's when I heard the shot.

It was a ways off, but it was clear, crisp, and distinct.

I got my feet under me, and stood up pushing Jeanine up onto her feet as I did so. I caught her as she started falling backwards, holding tight onto her hand as she leaned away from me, just far enough to display the blood running down her chest.

"SHOTS FIRED! GET DOWN," I screamed.

Jeanine crumbled in front of me, unable to stand. Her shock was evident as she looked me in the eyes, a single, painful, tear escaping, and running down her face. I quickly circled around behind her, tucked my arms under her armpits, and started dragging her in a tight circle to get her out of the street and behind our unit.

I whipped my head back and forth, trying to figure out where the shot had come from. I couldn't see anything; no cloud of smoke, no retreating vehicles; nothing. My left arm failed me, causing me to pause as I nearly dropped Jeanine. At that moment, I became aware of the bullet hole in my shoulder.

I adjusted my grip, trying to find the best way to get Jeanine out of the street with only one working arm. As I struggled, I heard a high pitched whine. It was getting louder, approaching from down the street. I turned to see what it was. A remote controlled car, less than ten inches tall, was hauling ass towards us from the east. But it wasn't just a car, it was a bomb; or so I'm told. I don't remember it going off.

CHAPTER THIRTY-FIVE

The following chapter was written based on events, as witnessed by Special Agent Terrance Jones April 25-April 29, 2017

No amount of training can prepare you on how to respond when your friend nearly gets killed in the line of duty. My wife and I were in the middle of dinner when I got the news, and I didn't see her again for nearly a week after that.

My boss, Supervisory Special Agent Wells, responded to my house and honked the horn from the driveway. I had a bag already prepared, and kissed my wife goodbye as I sprinted out the door.

"How is he doing?" I asked as soon as I whipped the door open to Wells' car.

"I haven't heard. The last thing I heard was he was on a life-flight to Kansas City."

"Are we headed to the hospital, or to the scene?"

"Neither," Wells replied sharply.

"Then where are we going?"

I was frustrated. There was nothing I could do for James as long as he was in need of emergency medical care. There was nothing I could do to figure any of this shit out until I could get to the scene or join in on the manhunt. Not knowing where we were going was frustrating, but I soon figured it out.

We were hauling a different kind of ass, headed northbound; and there was only one place I could guess we were going.

"We're going to Lincoln aren't we?"

"That young man has no family, whatsoever. All he has is his work, his coworkers, and the team. Most importantly, he has her. If he's going to bounce back from this any time soon, he needs everyone who cares about him, right there, making sure he has all the support he can manage," he explained.

"I didn't even know you knew about them."

"They're not as subtle as they think," said Wells.

Dr. Elmore was doing her best to hold it together when we picked her up. She was standing in the parking lot outside her lab when we arrived, suitcase in hand. I had no idea how long she had been waiting in the dark, but her apprehension was obvious. She wasn't the calm, cool-headed professional I had come to know over the past two months.

"Tell me what's going on." She demanded, closing her door behind her.

"Bryant and his team had warrants to arrest two individuals in connection to three bodies they found at City Park, in Manhattan. They had successfully served the warrants and had both suspects in custody when the team was ambushed. They think it was two people, but they're working with almost no information right now. Bryant and one other detective were shot before a bomb was detonated at the scene. Bryant and the other detective were the only ones in the blast radius. Bryant was put on a life-flight to Kansas City, to the med center there; I haven't heard about the other Detective," explained Wells.

"Do we know the status of the other detective?" she asked.

"I promise, I just gave you everything I know," he replied. "We're on our way to Kansas City to drop you off with Bryant. Once we know his status, Terry and I will be responding to meet with Bryant's Lieutenant to see what we can do to help."

From the back seat I heard Dr. Elmore choke back a sob.

I hated leaving Dr. Elmore by herself to wait at the hospital, but there was too much to do. Bryant had just gone into surgery when we left, and they had no updates for us.

I had made the trip from Kansas City to Manhattan on multiple occasions, but it's a long trip when you're driving in silence. What do you even say at a time like this?

The chaos and confusion we were feeling was infinitely insignificant next to the level of chaos we experience upon our arrival. The flag was at half mast, and no one would tell us who it was for. We were sent to the investigations conference room to wait, as everyone who had any information to offer was receiving an after-action debrief.

It took an hour of impatient pacing in the conference room before we saw a familiar face.

Lt. Carter looked as if he'd aged a decade since the last time we had seen him, even though it hadn't been two weeks. His face was drawn and gaunt, masked with a combination of anger and grief. He cleared his throat, sat down at the table, and struggled to find something to say.

"How's our boy doing?" He asked, sounding as if he was in shock.

"He's was in surgery when we left. Carter, the flag is at half mast, who's it for?" I inquired, fearing he knew something about Bryant before we did.

I wish I hadn't asked. It seemed like a selfish question since he had just asked about Bryant. The pause was agonizing as Lt. Carter ran a hand over his head, struggling to speak.

"We lost Jeanine, um Detective Shirley, as you probably knew her. She never even made it to the ambulance." He replied. His eyes welled with tears, his grief becoming infectious.

"Tell us what we can do to help," instructed Wells. "That's why we're here."

Lt. Carter stood with his hands on his hips, looking up at the ceiling, attempting to regain his composure. Finally he looked down, and shook his head.

"I don't even know where to begin," he admitted. "My ears just stopped ringing from the blast. I'm not running point on the investigation, so I don't know what to have you do."

"Who is handling the investigation?" asked Wells.

"Uh, it's... probably Capt. Hamell, my investigations Captain," he replied.

"Is there anything we can do to help you, specifically?" Wells persisted.

"I have a ride home already, but you can help us catch these motherfuckers. Don't let any of this be for nothing. Make sure Bryant's work in El Dorado doesn't get interrupted. I have no idea how he's going to recover from all of this, but we can't break this deal. Find a way to ensure this taskforce can complete the mission."

Everything Bryant ever told me about Fenton echoed through my mind. After two and a half days of assisting with the active investigation, I had been given a particularly sinister task. I had to convince Fenton to adapt the agreement to adjust for Bryant, who was in a medically induced coma.

I stared through the glass at the empty room on the other side, nervous, but not sure how to hide it. I had done countless interviews with suspects who were varying degrees of monsters, but this particular visit had me stressed.

After several minutes of waiting, the door on the other side opened.

I had always known Fenton was a larger man, but I wasn't ready for the bulky, bearded behemoth which sat down in front of me. Fenton's hands were still chained and restrained by belly chains in the front, meaning he had to reach up with both hands to take the phone off the hook.

I tried to hide the deep, anxious sigh I let out, and picked up the phone on my side.

"You're new," Fenton observed, as if to dismiss my presence completely.

"I know; I'm Special Agent Terrance Jones with the FBI. I've been assigned to the task force investigating all the victims you have been revealing to us each week with Detective Bryant," I informed him.

"Ok," he replied, indifferently.

I watched him for a second, waiting for him to continue, but he didn't.

"I have been sent here by the task force to make a special request of you. I need to meet with you this week instead of Det. Bryant."

"No."

"There isn't another option."

"No."

"Why not?" I asked.

"Because I didn't make this deal to sit down with you every week, fed; so go fuck yourself."

"Is there any way you would reconsider?"

"No."

"Anything I can do to make your stay more comfortable?"

"No."

I was getting pissed and fighting to keep it from going on full display. I took a deep breath and did my best to stay calm.

"Why the sudden change, big brother?" He asked, with a sinister hint of arrogance.

"Detective Bryant can't make it to your scheduled appointment tomorrow. Would you consider putting the deal on hold for a few weeks until he can make it here in person?"

"No. If he fails to show tomorrow, the deal is off."

"He can't make it tomorrow."

"Then the deal is off. I'll leave it to you to tell all the families of my victims why they aren't getting any answers."

"We don't even know who the families are until you tell us who the victims are. No one is lining up demanding answers from us. Your secrets die with you Christmas Day, and no one is the wiser," I explained, trying to make sense of the situation.

"Do you really think I only have one way of releasing my list of accomplishments to the world? Do you really think I wouldn't have a fail safe? I'm doing this to illuminate the incompetence of law enforcement agencies across the country, not just to have my story told. If you don't play my game, I will do this another way; and I've already made those previsions."

"What can I do to convince you to alter the deal?"

"Nothing," he replied. "Have Detective Bryant here tomorrow afternoon at 1:00pm as the deal dictates; otherwise everything I haven't given him will be released through another source."

"HE'S IN A COMA." I blurted out, before I could control my response.

He paused, appearing inquisitive and pompous at the same time.

"How did that happen?"

"He was executing arrest warrants for two suspects in connection with the other victims from City Park that you helped reveal in his first meeting with you. Someone ambushed the team, shot Bryant and one of the other detectives and detonated a bomb. Sound like anyone you know?"

For the first time, Fenton looked frustrated. He had been perfectly content to push me away and be unreasonable until he heard about the bomb.

"So not only did you figure out who was working for me, you let him get away? You're all FUCKING INCOMPETENT!" He yelled into the phone. I flinched a little and pulled the phone away from my ear.

"That sums it up pretty good," I replied.

"The problem with mentoring creative young minds is when they decide they no longer need you, no longer need to follow the plan, and have to make a name for their selves. When the student tries to become the master too soon, they FUCK EVERYTHING UP. I told him exactly what to do, when to do it, and how to get away with it. Instead, he calls the reporter from a landline here at the prison. He then has to kill the reporter, his wife and a FUCKING COP to hide what he did, which in the process, led you straight to him. Everyone around me is FUCKING INCOMPETENT!" he yelled again.

"So Foster was working for you the whole time?" I asked.

"Not the whole time, weren't you listening?" He jabbed his finger against the glass and screamed again. "FUCKING INCOMPETENT; just like the others, I mean I thought I had met my intellectual match with the detective, but he clearly surrounds himself with people who are inferior to his own intellect. But so is the life of a brilliant man; everyone else is retarded in comparison."

"Foster went off script several times; and he's doing it again. Anything you'd like to tell us that might help?"

"Good luck to you, Agent Jones. That's what I have to offer you; positive vibes. Because I'm not going to help you catch him, because it goes against everything I trained him to do. I could tell you that I taught him to live off the grid as much as possible, but you already know that; and he was doing that long before he came into my employ. All I will say to you, Agent Jones, is that I hope you catch him before he does anything else to fuck up my plans. Now; HAVE THE DETECTIVE HERE TOMORROW OR THE FUCKING DEAL IS OFF; DO YOU HEAR ME? I DON'T CARE IF YOU HAVE TO WHEEL HIM IN HERE ON A HOSPITAL BED WITH TUBES RUNNING ALL OVER THE FUCKING PLACE; TOMORROW; ONE OCLOCK."

He smashed the phone down so hard on the other side of the glass that he almost deafened me again. He stood up, flipped me off with both hands, and turned towards the door.

––––––––––––

"Absolutely not," said Dr. Elmore.

"We don't have a choice," I explained. "Without Bryant in the room, the deal is off. The longer we keep Fenton talking, the more likely he is to tell us something that might lead us to Foster."

"How can you even be entertaining this? You're supposed to be the sensible ones," she said, indicating Wells and I as she did.

"We wouldn't be considering this, even for a moment, if we had any other option," Wells disclosed.

"This is so incredibly fucked up," she said, in disbelief.

"We are working with the doctors here to see what can be done to transport him safely. They think there is a way to do it. He's shown positive progress over the past twenty-four hours and they think they can get him to an ambulance, down to El Dorado, and then set up a make-shift room for him while he's down there," I told her.

"If something happens to him; I don't think I could ever forgive you two."

"I know," said Wells. "And I don't blame you. The hospital is sending two nurses and a doctor with him in the ambulance. They're coordinating with a hospital out of Wichita to ensure he has all the equipment necessary to stay alive."

"I'm going with him in the ambulance," she demanded.

"Done," Wells agreed.

"If we're doing this, we need to get him started," I advised. "I don't know how long it will take to prep him for transport or get him set up at the prison."

The trip to El Dorado was made more harrowing with Dr. Elmore hovering over Bryant, worrying about every slight variation in his breathing or heartbeat. The hospital staff in the ambulance was at their wits end when we finally pulled into the gates at El Dorado.

True to their word, the prison had a room prepped for this incredibly random visitation. With the help of the hospital from Wichita, they had a room set up with the necessary machines and supplies to keep Bryant alive.

The worst part was the visual access to the room via the one way mirror. The medical staff was moved out of the neighboring room, preventing them from being within earshot of Fenton. No matter how hard I plead with her, Dr. Elmore refused to join the medical staff. Arguing with her was proving to be pointless, so Wells consented, with the condition she remain silent; so we could hear what was happening. An extra microphone was set up in the middle of the room to ensure we could hear everything loud and clear.

At five minutes to one O'clock, Fenton was led into the room and directed towards a chair several feet from Bryant's bed.

"No, huh uh," he said, standing still, resisting the guards as they tried to direct him. "Move me closer to the bed. I'd hate for him not to hear me."

He turned and looked at the glass, appearing to stare straight through it, and into my soul.

"Fed, I know you're in there. Tell the guards to move me towards the bed, or the deal is off."

Wells shook his head with desperation, reached for the talk button on the intercom, and hesitated.

"Are you seriously considering this?" asked Dr. Elmore, crossing the room swiftly to stand next to Wells, staring him down.

"Dr. Elmore, please have a seat and remember our agreement." He pushed the intercom button and spoke to the guards in the room. "Handcuff his hands together in front of him, and then cuff him to the chair and the rail on the bed. Make sure he can't reach any of the equipment on Detective Bryant. Fenton; I am starting the timer now."

Fenton sat down in the chair and allowed the intricate level of restraints to be applied to his wrists, keeping his hands suspended between his torso and the bed. Fenton could lean against the bed slightly, but he couldn't reach Bryant, or any of the tubes or wires attached to his body.

Dr. Elmore moved her chair closer to the glass and sat down, chewing nervously on a nail. I gathered two more chairs and set them down next to her. I sat myself between Wells and Dr. Elmore, hoping to keep them from arguing with each other again.

The guards exited the room, leaving Fenton tied to the floor, the chair and the hospital bed rail. Fenton leaned forward, and appeared to be talking to Bryant.

"Turn up the volume, I can't hear anything," ordered Dr. Elmore.

Wells checked the equipment as fast as possible before he turned to us. "It's all the way up, he hasn't said anything yet."

The bed was set up facing the glass which meant we could see Fenton's hands as they rested casually on the bedrail. He stared at Bryant, displaying his contempt.

We waited apprehensively as Fenton sat in silence. Time dragged on, eclipsing the twenty minute mark before Fenton said anything.

"What should I even say to you, detective; you can't hear me? Is all of this just for the benefit of the worried bystanders in the next room? How did I let them talk me into doing this? As much as I enjoy seeing you here, at deaths door, I enjoy so much more saying things you can hear; just for the benefit of watching you squirm uncomfortably as I say the most fucked up thing I can think up. How big is my audience in the next room? One, maybe two people at most, I assume. You don't really have a group of people in your corner, do you? You're a solitary creature, just like me; aren't you?"

He sat back as far as his chains would allow, which wasn't that far.

"I wonder if they're as sensitive as you are detective. Do they want to hear a long, detailed story about all the underage pussy I've crushed? Or do they want to hear me detail how long it takes a sixteen year old girl to bleed out when you hang them upside down by their ankles? I have so many options; it's hard to know where to start." He laughed, maliciously. "I'm having so much fun; I almost forgot they haven't given me my pack of cigarettes yet."

"Next to his right hand," said Wells, into the intercom.

"Ah, the voice of God calls me to redemption," he said, moving Bryant's hand to uncover the pack of Marlboro's located underneath.

"That's a hell of a baritone," he said, looking up at the ceiling. He looked back down at Bryant, "I wouldn't mind having him read me a bedtime story. Such a soothing baritone is enough to make, even me, a little sleepy. Unfortunately, this is between you and me; so if the man behind the curtain opens his mouth again during my allotted time, I'm going to void the deal. If you understand over there; say nothing."

Wells sat back in his chair, his frustration growing with every passing minute.

"How the hell does Bryant put up with this arrogant asshole every week?" asked Wells.

"He had an alcohol problem for a reason." I advised.

Dr. Elmore shushed us as Fenton, content with getting no response, continued.

"It's funny to see you here like this, detective. You always talk about what it will be like to see me in a hospital bed, tubes running out of my arms as I'm about to die. Now I get to see you in the same position. If you die, that will be the world's greatest irony, yet. If only you could see things from my perspective, detective. I think you would appreciate the irony. The only thing I'm going to miss is the look on your face as you take your last breath. That's my favorite part of killing people, you know? I enjoy being there at the last second of their lives. They go full circle, from total panic, to total relief. It's like I'm the doctor, curing them of their afflictions."

Beside me, Dr. Elmore scoffed in disgust, but otherwise maintained her silence.

"Women, these days, think they can do anything they want to without a man," Fenton continued, "But they can't. They can't make a baby without us. They can't do anything that isn't secretly for the approval of men. They live to please us, but they do such a shitty job at it. Look at you; you had a wife; you thought you were happy; but what did she do to you? She left you alone; checked out before you were ready to let her go; didn't she? I bet you secretly hate her; don't you? I would. I would resent her for leaving you alone on Christmas day, just so she could go see her shitty, fucking family. To top it all off, she became an entertaining statistic. Everyone knows women are shitty drivers, but no one ever tries to stop them from doing it. You're the lawman; shouldn't there be some kind of law against it? Women let you down every time. I never met a woman who didn't let me down. I'm sure all the women in your life are letting you down in one way or another. If you look for it, you can see their short-comings. They try to hide them; with makeup, careers, children, book clubs, garden parties, bitch friends who they think will make you thankful for the woman you're stuck with. It's all a huge game to them, and we're their little pawns. That's why I stopped playing their little games, and started a game of my own. They aren't very good at my game, but then again, we aren't very good at theirs; are we?"

Fenton blew a cloud of smoke into Bryant's face, making Dr. Elmore cringe again. I could tell she was struggling to keep her cool, but she was determined to hold on throughout the entire ordeal.

Fenton flicked his cigarette butt towards the wall on the other side of the bed, and casually lit another.

"He is going to set off James' oxygen, please make him stop," Dr. Elmore pleaded.

"The oxygen tank isn't in the room. The fire hazard is absolutely minimal. Stop talking, please," replied Wells, clearly becoming agitated with the interruptions.

"Nothing's going to happen to him, I promise," I said, trying to reassure her.

She crossed her arms and said nothing. She was struggling to hold back tears, and clearly hating the situation.

"Now, detective; if you recall, I seem to remember telling you something like this was going to happen. I can assure you, this wasn't part of my plan, but I told you there were going to be consequences to your actions. You disrespected me, just like all those women did. Those women died for the way they lived; maybe it's your turn. I told you this was going to happen. I told you to watch your fucking mouth with the way you talked to me. I didn't plan THIS, but I knew it was going to happen eventually. I inspire a different kind of loyalty that you could never understand. Do you really think there is only one person out there trying to kill you? Everywhere you go, one of my disciples will be there. Every step you take will be dogged by those who seek to carry out my legacy. But the war they're waging isn't just on women; it's on cops, and politicians, and anyone who twists the system to make a billion dollars. Your little friends in the next room should be aware; they're all on my shit list. I won't rest until I see each and every one of them pays for their part in this. People like them live their cushy, government funded lives while the rest of the country foots the bill. They are part of the sickness, and I am the cure. I only wish I was going to be there when they meet their untimely demise."

He turned casually, leaning against the bedrail, smoking casually until he finished his cigarette.

"I wish they hadn't opted for such an incredibly uncomfortable position to leave me," said Fenton, staring at the glass. "It doesn't seem anyone cares that I'm still a human being. Some things never change. To be noticed, I had to slaughter bitches from here to Little Rock, and they still don't see me as anything but an outcast; just like my parents. The times change; technology changes, but people don't change. They're still just as selfish as they've always been."

Fenton casually lit another cigarette, and leaned against the rail again. He smoked in silence; as if he was lost in deep thought. His face was expressionless, which was unnerving. Fenton had an uncanny ability to get your hackles up, just by looking at you. His mouth moved as if he was whispering something. Nothing was coming through the speaker, leading to our increased level of apprehension.

"What's he doing?" asked Dr. Elmore.

"I think he's plotting. Foster threw a wrench into his operation, so he has to adapt his plan, and his expectations." I replied.

"How can he even have a plan? He's been behind bars for ten years; when has he had the chance to concoct his original scheme?"

"He's had ten years to work on it," said Wells. "But six years ago someone found him here, and helped turn his scheme into a game plan. They've been slowly setting the pieces in motion for years now, waiting for their time to come."

I held up my hand, as Fenton began speaking again.

"You survived," he said casually. He almost sounded disappointed. "I never really intended for you to die until the very end. That's what I get for working with loose cannons. People are so predictable, and yet, not predictable at all. I easily predicted my own protégé would go off the rails, and I easily predicted how you would react to almost everything I said. Foster wasn't always able to be in the next room to listen to us talk. He had his cover to protect. I assume you tied him to some of the mishaps in your investigations, but I also think it's safe to say, his predilection for children caused him to stray from the end goal. I can relate you see; you caught me when I was picking up yet another college girl from your city. You just came out of nowhere, almost like you knew where I was going to be, and when I was going to be there. But how could you? How could you know in advance when I had only started watching that girl the day before? I used three different vehicles to watch her, but somehow you knew where I was going to be? Maybe I should have known better. After all, I had already done a great deal of work in your neighborhood. I don't often circle back to a familiar hunting ground. I mean; I had only ever done it once before. Ah, but the '80's were a simpler time; you could get away with almost anything."

Fenton paused for a moment, smoking casually, this time with a smile on his face.

"Well, I'm getting bored of this," he declared loudly. "What's the fun of holding you here for three hours when you can't even hear me tell you what a fucking piece of shit you are, detective? Your friends at the bureau managed to get you here, which is a task I didn't think they were going to pull off. I thought I was going to get to keep a few of my secrets, after all, but I was wrong. I guess I'll just have to carry on with my plan how I originally intended. Spoiler alert," he leaned in as close as possible, "It ends with you watching everyone who means anything to you, die a slow and painful death. That might be a short list, but I will have my vindication either way. I still own you, detective. Every week, I own you for three hours; but I can't hold a man captive who doesn't even know he is here. You've successfully taken all the fun out of putting you in prison once a week. I'd be mad at you, if you hadn't nearly died in the process; which let's be honest, that's a bold move, even for you. The next time you find yourself with a bullet hole or a concussion, it will be the last one you ever have. One by one; everyone around you will drop dead, until it's just you, your issues, and a handgun. When it's all over, you will deep throat a pistol, just to end your misery. I will destroy you, a little at a time. And when it's all over, I'll know what happened to you, because you won't be able to make it to my going away party. I'll have the distinct pleasure of looking out over a crowd of people I don't know, and telling them all to kiss my ass, because I won."

He turned towards the door, where the guards had disappeared, nearly two hours before.

"Guards, I'm ready to go back to my cell," he called out, before turning back towards Bryant. "I took a couple years off starting back in 1995. But when I came back, I was like a new man. Here, I wrote down everything about my glorious return to the stage. I told you I was going to have a heavier hand in volume two; this is your first sample. In it, I will tell you, and the world, about how I actually do, what I do best. I can only assume you've been writing about yourself instead of me. I can see why you would do it that way. You're trying to protect the world from reality, but you can't. I am a legend in my own time, and I'm going to see to it, that my story is told the proper way. You can't censor the real world, detective. You above all others, should know that."

Fenton pulled a few loose pieces of paper from his waistband, and awkwardly tossed them onto the bed as close as he could get them to Bryant's face.

"Enjoy my story; it will be the first of many." He warned.

The guards entered the room, and began unlocking Fenton from the bedrail.

"Don't worry, casual observers," he called out. "You have kept your end of the bargain. I will be back next week to captivate you with my wit and charm; and regale you with another story of my sexual exploits. There was a nineteen year old girl from Grand Island, Nebraska who got to learn firsthand at the end of my love stick. Read all about it in my little memoir there. I'm sure you'll find it to be a good read."

The guards started to escort him towards the door, but he resisted, making sure he remained in the room long enough to say his piece.

"You should definitely read it sooner than later, you might not get the chance to read it later."

I wish there was a proper way to describe the cackling laugh he emitted. Somewhere between a roar and scream, the laughter echoed down the hallway for nearly a minute as they dragged him slowly, and finally, out of earshot.

We sat there in silence.

I got it then. I understood how Bryant lost himself in a bottle of whiskey after an encounter like this. Fenton was evil, pure evil. Whatever good had been a part of him had been abandoned decades ago. There was nothing left but treachery, vile intentions and wicked imagination.

I didn't want to know the details of his exploits, but I had already signed on to the task force. There was no way to escape it.

I stood up, leaving Wells and Dr. Elmore behind, still stunned in their seats. The locks leading to Bryant's room clicked loudly, allowing me to enter the room.

The cloud of smoke filling the air had a smell I wasn't familiar with; evil. It was the only explanation. I listened intently for a second, rewarded by the sound of Bryant's heart monitor.

I breathed a sigh of relief when I saw his chest slowly heaving with each breath. I waved my hands over the bed, trying to clear out some of the smoke, but to no avail.

I eyed the papers on the bed, wishing more than anything else in the world that I could just take them outside and burn them. I wanted to be sure no one could ever read them; that no one could ever be emotionally tortured, or psychologically tormented by the words Fenton had written. It wasn't my call to make, and before I asked, I knew what the answer would be.

I picked up the papers, forgetting for a moment they had been stuffed down the front of Fenton's pants. The papers were folded in half, and heavily wrinkled. I carefully grasped the paper by the edges, and unfolded them to see what was there.

Written in bold, all capital letters, and heavily pressed pencil at the top of the page:

MEMOIRS OF A DEATH ROW INMATE

ABOUT THE AUTHOR

Daniel Donovan was born in Missouri and raised in Kansas for most of his life. He always had a passion for creative writing, but it wasn't until he spent four years in law enforcement that the spark for crime thrillers was really ignited. Donovan aims to bring his readers into the novel by incorporating real-life details into his works of fiction while giving readers the thrills and chills they seek.

For more information, visit www.danieldonovanauthor.com.

9 798218 226886